The Last

Toltec King

A novel by

Julie Black

OBSIDIAN WRITERS' GUILD
AUSTIN

Obsidian Writers' Guild
7801 Shoal Creek #124
Austin, Texas, 78757 USA
www.obsidianwritersguild.com

Cover design by Julie Black
(Aztec warrior image; Jesus Helguera)

Ollin Symbol by Juan Jaramillo

Map of Tula by Julie Black

LCCN 2014916704

ISBN-13: 978-0-692-26724-0
ISBN-10: 0692267247

Map of Tula

Map of Tula~Tollan~Xicocotitlan

Palace of Previous Kings
Pyramid of the Sun
Pyramid of Tlahuizcalpantehcuhtli
Palace of Quetzalcoatl
Tianguis Market

For a larger version of this map visit
www.thelasttoltecking.com.

Acknowledgements

I would like to thank my son, Adrian Torres, for his endless listening, tireless support, and creative input over the span of his lifetime, without whose enthusiasm and powerful confidence the elaboration of this work would never have become what it is today.

I greatly appreciate the late Ignacio Torres Manzo and his wife Sol for their inspiring conversations on pulque production –old style. A heartfelt appreciation goes out to Adriana Mondragon, friend and colleague from U.N.A.M., for sharing her research on dwarfism in pre-Hispanic Mexico. Christie Kremers' medical explanations were of paramount importance in dealing with childbirth, battles and snake venom. A special mention goes to Shawn Jonas, professional snake handler of Central Texas, for his expertise in all things snake related. I offer prayers of gratitude to Paul Kruse for his conversations regarding penance and states of higher consciousness.

I am forever grateful to Deanna Couras Goodson and Jean Shaw for reading, commenting on, and editing the manuscripts. Forget sugar and spice and everything nice. Reading a manuscript is what true friends are made of.

Countless hours of imagination were spent with the music of Ennio Moricone (soundtrack from The Mission) and the late Jorge Reyes. The art of the grand master Jesus Helguera was so inspiring that a scene from the chapter Blood Moon was written around it.

My sincere thanks to Jill Stimson, Raul Sanchez, and Rey Garcia, and all the other many friends and relatives who have had to listen to me talk about, over and over again, the same ol' same ol' thing. Your positive encouragement means more to me than I can describe.

I have made every attempt to honor the historical dignity of the ancient Mexicans, and have only been able to bring this story to light because of the intellectual and cultural works of master historians, philosophers and great thinkers. Therefore, even though sources are not typically mentioned in historical fiction novels, I have decided to include them at the end so that those who wish, may satiate their interest in further reading.

Author's Note

It is often customary in works of this genre, time period and setting, for English writing authors to Anglicize Nahuatl names and terminology, as they can be exceedingly difficult to pronounce and interfere with the continuity of the narrative. My purpose in writing this work of historical fiction is to teach, not only the mythology of the ancient Mexicans and their culture, but also to present this past with as much dignity and historical integrity as possible. It is for this reason that I have chosen to use the original Nahuatl names and terms throughout this work. A Nahuatl glossary is provided at the end.

Table of Contents

Book 1

A Prophecy Begins

Snake Woman

"You there, Citlali!" She always called people by their birth name instead of their day name. "My, my, my. Come here, child. Come here." A long, bony finger beckoned me forward.

In deference to Snake Woman's age, and keeping down cast eyes, I complied.

"You disobedient scoundrel," she pushed my shoulder; "you've been roaming about the fields again, haven't you?"

It was true. I hadn't been working, doing my part for the survival of our clan. Nature distracted me. The wind carried the soft smell of desert flowers and whistled as it blew over Mother Earth and through the fields. Tall, strong stalks of corn glistened in the sun, while their golden beads peeked out from behind soft, green husks. I treasured the sound made when they danced together, the wind and the corn.

In the fields, among the tall, reaching stalks, under the bright blue sky and among the chatter-chatter and buzzing of insects, I felt completely at peace. Weaving to and fro through the jungle of stalks, I would immerse myself in childish fantasies, pretending that I, Corn Woman, was Mother of the Universe, and the very essence of corn. As a goddess, I decided when the corn would sprout out of the earth, when its buds would emerge, and when it would bulge, full of life, ready for harvest. For, I, Corn Woman, gave the corn permission to grow, and it was only because of my ability to seduce Tlaloc, God of Rain, that the corn would grow at all. I could stay in the fields forever, thinking of ways to seduce Tlaloc.

I'd finally headed for home toward the *calpulli*, my village, skipping and running over the soft dry earth, my dark brown body sweating in the golden sun. The *calpulli* lay over the next hill. I ran past craggy mesquite trees, fields of cactus plants, giant magueys and brilliant but delicate flowers budding out of desert shrub.

Each time I entered the *calpulli* it was always the same. I had to pass the hut of the old hag Snake Woman, and each time Snake

Woman would peer out her door and leer at me. Sometimes I would make a smart comment about how the old woman should replace the cane leaves on the roof of her hut, or some other insolent remark. Other times I would just run by. The truth was that the thought of Snake Woman chilled me to my bones.

Craggy Snake Woman would come out her doorway with her sweeping broom and grumble indignant things to any child passing by. Her long, white hair, unkempt as it was, fell out of a dusty shawl that she was always flinging back over her shoulder in an effort to keep it on. Over a lifetime, this flinging motion had become a habit, so that the old crone was always bobbing up and down. Her face had all but dried up like a lizard, with two flashing eyes and a shriveled little mouth puckered around her now-and-then rotting teeth. The boys in the village rumored that at night when she was alone in the pitch dark, if you got close to her hut, you could hear a hissing sound, just like a snake. She was really a snake, they said, that in the daytime made herself look like an old hag.

However decrepit she seemed, it was Snake Woman who arranged marriages in the village. Because of her privileged position, she was excused from her indecencies.

Wrenching me from my silence, the crone scolded, "If your father were not on the High Council of the *altépetl,* your disgraceful behavior would not be forgiven! You defy the gods!" She let out a long hissing sound. I was certain that then and there the old hag was going to turn into her other snake self and suck the life juice out of me. I stood motionless, which gave the hag time to come closer.

"Well now," breathed Snake Woman, bobbing up and down. "Let's have a closer look at you. Ah, yes. You are getting to be quite a beauty. Look at me, you wretched little thing!"

Obediently I raised my eyes, and realized that never before had I been this close to Snake Woman. The crone made a gurgling noise, and with a knotted, veiny, old hand, she pinched my cheek, inspecting it for firmness like a piece of fruit at the market.

With that touch, Snake Woman saw my future and she knew.

"Take this," she hissed. Reaching into her layered clothing, she pulled out a small jadestone and shoved it into my trembling hand. "You would have fetched me a fine trade when it came your time," she said, throwing her shawl over her shoulder. "You have twelve years by the sun, do you not?"

"Hmmm?"

"Answer me!" but before she could say any more, I spun on my heels and fled. Tucking the jadestone into my belt, I ran as fast as I could toward home.

Our People Came from

Teotihuacan

Home should be the place of tranquility, comfort, and well-being. With a father like mine, and an ancient, bed-ridden medicine man for a grandfather, home was tempestuous. It didn't help that my mother had died during my birth, and that my father was never able to overcome the pain from his loss.

My father, Quiahuitl, was a boisterous man, caught up in his small-time political affairs. His name, which means rain, told of his personality. He was an explosive man, passionate, and demanding with himself as well as others.

My father could have been more in tune with the divine movement of the gods, but he was a practical man of the Here and Now. He wore the cloak of ambition. Ambition was frowned upon. It meant that a person was putting their own interests before those of the gods. In his own defense he often challenged us, "Who are we to judge the will of the gods? Is it not the gods themselves who have made me thus?"

He became fairly prosperous, that is, for a peasant. Most of the time, he was able to control his explosive character and constructively channel his energy toward the greater good. Even though he was just a mere *macehuatl*, a man among the peasant class, he derived his pride from constantly reminding everyone around him that he was Toltec. "We are *macehuatl*," he would tell me, "but we are Toltecs. Among our people we are but lowly peasants, tillers of the soil, workers of the land. We, who live in the desert fields, they call us the Dirt People, but never forget, Citlali, we are Toltecs! We are superior to the wandering rogues of the seven caves, those North People, who live like *itzcuintlis*, dogs that scavenge off the remains of dead animals. We are the children of the Earth. We are Toltecs!"

Arriving at my two-room *chantli*, the only adobe house in our *calpulli*, I noticed something different from what I usually encountered when I got home from my cornfield. Where was my father, who just the day before had returned from a hunting party?

"He went to gather the council of Father Elders," said little, old Tomatl, my father's houseman. He cooked for us and tended the chores, and in exchange my father looked after him. One thing I admired about my father was that he ignored the gossip about the effeminate, wrinkled old man doing woman's work at our home.

"He wants you to stay home now, and take care of The Ancient One. I prepared the meal so that you should eat."

"Yes. Thank you, Tomatl." I was courteous to Tomatl. He was an excellent cook. In addition to always serving my favorite stew of beans, squash, chilli, and corn, he had the knack of combining all the right flavors in the special dishes that he would conjure up; chayote in fermented cactus juice with mint and cashews. Oh, it was delicious! Sometimes he made stewed corn in tomato mash with epazote and green fire pods. The most delectable flavors came out when he added everyone's favorite, the *iztatl* salt that my father always insisted on having. (It came from as far away as the ethereal waters of the land of the setting sun. Father traded for it at the *tianguis*). So, as long as Tomatl continued to create these tasteful pleasures, nobody wanted to risk making him mad. He might add too many fire peppers the next time, or throw a temper tantrum and not cook at all!

I went into the *chantli*, leaving Tomatl to stir his earthen cooking pot. The smells of fresh vegetables rose into the air, combined with the dry smoke of the cooking fire. The flavors and smoke twined together past the thatched roof and beyond. I should have appreciated my home more, and the people who looked after me. While I was always courteous to Tomatl, I never took the time to listen to him, get to know him for who he really was.

Not wanting to wake my ancient grandfather, I walked silently over the dirt packed floor and sat down on the mat at the table stone.

I thought about my friend Miyáhuatl, who lived in a stick and mud hut. Miyáhuatl didn't have any of this, I knew. Her family didn't have an obsidian effigy of Quetzalcoatl. Theirs was made of clay. They didn't have a houseman, they didn't have a table stone, nor did they have corn shuck beds. They slept on mats and that was that, but Miyáhuatl had brothers and sisters and I didn't. It seemed she was always laughing and happy, and even though her brothers would pull her braids and make her mad, they always ended up laughing again.

As I ate my meal alone I wondered where my father could be.

✂

"Grandfather, Grandfather. Wake up."

"Uuuh..." grumbled the elder, still half asleep.

"Grandfather, I'm here to sit with you. It's me, Citlali."

Anticipating his wishes, I handed him the long pipe that I'd prepared with a blend of calming damiana, fragrant deer tongue and tobacco. I offered him a tiny flame from the burning oil pot. His favorite ingredient was the tobacco. Quite a luxury it was, too. It came from another land in the One World, from the Hot Lands where they said it grew as high as the mountains. My father Quiahuitl was always able to trade for the dried, brown smoking plant from some merchant he knew at the *tianguis* market that took place every fifth day. All the villages in the *altépetl* came together at the *tianguis* to barter and exchange their goods.

The smoke from the tobacco made swirling rings in the mid-afternoon light that passed through the one window.

"Grandfather?" I whispered.

He raised his soft, old hand.

I sat at the foot of his sleeping mat with my legs properly folded under me. Like I did every afternoon, I silently waited while the Ancient One smoked. I enjoyed the time I spent learning from my grandfather, Ollin Ehécatl.

His little, brown, shriveled body was consumed by a mass of long, white hair. I would often untangle it with a wooden comb as I listened to his wisdom, his many stories, and his life experiences.

[23]

My medicine man grandfather was old and tired, and hardly left the comfort of his bed. When the people of the *altepetl* wanted to speak with him, they came to him for council and sat before him in his dark room while he indulged himself in his smoking plant.

He never revealed the secrets of knowledge to them, nor to anyone, except to me. I knew not to tell, for I was sworn to secrecy, an oath I had made before the gods Quetzalcoatl and Tezcatlipoca, the Smoking Mirror. If ever I were to divulge the sacred knowledge, I would die the bloody death for sure.

During our times together, Ollin Ehécatl, his name meaning Changing Wind, told me about the seasons, about the wind and the rain, and about how the wind carries the rain and makes the corn grow. He told me that the stars dancing in the World Above change with the cycles of time. It was from my grandfather that I learned about the cycles of time: when to expect the rains, when to plant, when the rains would end, when to reap the harvest. He taught me about the cycles of the Lady Moon Meztli and the sun god Tonatiuh, and when these two 52-year cycles would come together, joining their beginning and their end. That is how I learned the difference between the calendar of the sun and the calendar of the moon. The knowledge he shared with me was to be jealously guarded: a privilege only among the Knowers. Only Knowers were permitted to have knowledge. Any breach of oath, any telling of the secrets, was a defiant and vile act against the gods.

One time, twenty months before this day, my grandfather told me how our people first got to our land. "Long ago," - He would always begin with *Long ago* - "before there were fields, our people came to this valley from the East, over there." He pointed in the direction of the rising sun. "They came from Teotihuacan, the City of the Gods. There they lived among the gods, where the greatest of their warriors, just a chosen few, sang and danced among all the natural beings, the deer, the rabbits, even the jaguar. They swam in natural springs that came up out of Mother Earth, and for nourishment they feasted on butterflies and flowers. There, in the City of the Gods, they lived together in harmony with the gods."

"Why did they leave, Grandfather?"

"After many generations, outsiders came to Teotihuacan, people who didn't fear our god Quetzalcoatl. They spoiled the harmony of the city by speaking their own languages and following their own gods. They took whatever they wanted from the good people that lived there, but that wasn't why the city died.

"The outsiders started using the trees around the city to build their houses and burn their fires. When they cut down the trees, they didn't tell the trees for what purpose they were being cut down and sacrificed. Then the trees, because they didn't know their purpose in the world, refused to grow."

"Do trees need to know their purpose in the world, Grandfather?"

"Oh, yes my child! Just as anything. As I've always told you, everything has a spirit, and therefore, everything that exists has a purpose in our world. The spirit of the tree is not the tree itself, Citlali. The essence of the tree is that which makes it a tree. It's this very *tree-ness* that is its god-spirit."

"So, when the people of the City of the Gods cut down the trees, why didn't they tell the trees their purpose in the world?"

"They tried, but they failed. Their invocation was tainted with the violence and chaos that they were living. The true invocation goes thus..." His eyes closed as he remembered the prayer. "*Tla xihuallauh chiucnauh tlatetzotzonalli, cítlal cueye ytlachihual, Mictlán mati, topan mati,*" which means, "*Oh tree, son of the kingdom of stars, you know both the heavens and the underworld. What are you thinking now? Be glad that I have finally come, I the priest, prince of sorcerers. I am the Plumed Serpent, and I bring with me a demon, this bright red axe. Do not despise me. The time has come that I shall cut you down to the ground.*"

During his lengthy stories, my elder grandfather would often take leisurely puffs of his smoking pipe, contemplating the intricacies of his tales.

"In time there were no more trees," he'd said. "The people didn't have enough wood to build their fires to cook upon. Quetzalcoatl became angry and began to war with the gods of the foreign peoples. Soon, many terrible things came to pass. Tlaloc didn't bring his rains to feed the earth. The land became sick and dry, and in the drought, no harvests grew. The people began to hunger, for they didn't have anything to eat. They became ill and impoverished, and plague and illness followed. The sacred city fell into ruin."

The old man sighed in compassion.

"Because of all the disorder, the rulers could no longer defend the city against invasions from even more people. Warriors came from the North. They attacked and burned the precious city of Teotihuacan, raped and pillaged, and imposed themselves anywhere they could.

"Many people fled.

"With their women and children, the good warriors of Quetzalcoatl followed the direction of the Setting Sun. They came to this valley where we now live. With them they brought their knowledge of planting and how to dance and pray to the gods for rain. They worked, and with their hands they created all that you see here.

"This was in the time of our ancestors, those who brought us to this life in the Here and Now."

I remembered with great fondness the stories my grandfather told me. But I have to admit, if I'd known then what I know now, I would have heeded the lessons in his tales of death and destruction. They always seemed so long ago and far away - events that happened to other people, not to me.

Ollin Ehécatl's Vision

I sat there and looked at him with adoring eyes as he finished smoking his long pipe.

"Grandfather," I whispered.

"Yes, child?"

"Grandfather, does Snake Woman really turn into a snake at night?"

He became very serious. "That is what they say, is it not?" His eyes, clouded over with age, searched for me. "Why do you speak of Snake Woman, child?"

"Snake Woman called me to her when I came back from my cornfield." I dared not tell him about pretending to be Corn Woman, Protectress of the One World, and my passionate affair with Tlaloc.

"She touched my face, Grandfather, and her black eyes turned white. Then she gave me this."

I took out the jadestone and held it up for Ollin Ehécatl to see. It was shiny and smooth, the size of a quail egg. He took the gem, a piece of the Heart of the Earth, and wrapped his bony fingers around it. His eyes filled with emotion. I looked at him with wonder. The flame from the oil pot began to sputter. An evening breeze blew through the window.

"Grandfather?" I whispered.

"Ah, Citlali. This stone. This stone reminds me of... This stone has a story."

I looked at him, my deep, brown eyes full of anticipation, but my lips said nothing.

"Long ago," began Ehécatl, "when the fields were still being claimed, when our people were still coming into this valley, a city was built, a city which you have never seen, and which you will never know."

I looked at him bewildered.

"A city is where many people live together in one place. They build stone houses stacked high on giant slabs, and they have great walkways between their houses called *caltzalantli*. The city I tell you about is many days walk beyond those hills." He indicated with a glance.

"It is Tollan."

I looked at the jadestone that he clutched in his shaking hand. Wisps of his long, white hair danced in the breeze that came through the one window. "But why..."

"There came a time," he continued, ignoring my interruption, "when the North People began to attack the lands of our people, the way they had attacked Teotihuacan. I was still a young man. The nobles and their fierce king Huetzin consulted many sources to find the weakness of the North People so that they could defeat them. They held council with their priests and Knowers, but only in vain. Then one day, several men came to me. They were *pipiltzin*. They were nobles. They had heard that I was a Knower, and even though I was *macehuatl*, they came to ask me to seek the weakness of the North People. They brought me gifts, among them some brilliant green tail feathers of the gentle *quetzal*, and elegant cotton cloth for my woman, your grandmother.

"Cotton is the finest and softest of fibers, like the dancing clouds in the sky," he said, answering the expression on my face.

"The *pipiltzin* asked me to consult the seeing cactus *peyotl*. You remember *peyotl*, the green buttons we use when we make the tea for my visions." I nodded. "So I began a journey into the mountains to search for the answer to their question. I had to find the weakness of the North People.

"For ten days I fasted, drinking only water from the river. Every day I made a sacrifice of my own blood to our beloved god Quetzalcoatl by drawing a cactus thorn through my thigh. I caught the sacred Fluid of Life on *amatl* paper as it dripped out of my body, and I burned the paper together with the precious Fluid, allowing Quetzalcoatl to nourish himself upon the Fluid's altered state. Then, on the tenth day, and with all certainty that the god would hear and answer my prayers, I ate the pungent cactus buttons." His fingers tightened around the jadestone.

"In my vision I became an egg. I was in a clear pool of water nestled between the smooth stones on the bottom. Then I hatched into a short bodied larva with gills and a tail. I began to swim and I could feel the water swish around me and through me. As I grew, I absorbed my own tail, and my gills disappeared. I began to form the legs and body of a frog. Finally I emerged from the water and hopped onto the land. I had gone through a complete change, from a slimy egg to a fully developed frog. In my excitement at being fully mature I began hopping wildly about, so much so that I attracted the attention of a great snake, far stronger than I.

"The snake attacked me and swallowed me whole, a process so painful that my screams could be heard throughout all the One World of Anahuac. But then I became the serpent's eye, and as it moved about the earth, writhing and slithering, I saw. I saw the birth of a woman child. She was a healer, who grew to become a great woman among men. She witnessed the destruction of the great City of Tollan. Then I saw the face of a *tlatoani*, a king, dressed as the god Quetzalcoatl!

"When I awoke I lay among a slimy mass of hatched snake eggs, as though I were in some kind of nest. Looking down I saw that one of the eggs was not an egg, but a jadestone. I took the stone and returned to the village where the *pipiltzin* had stayed, awaiting my return. We then arranged a council, and I explained my vision to the men.

"'The battles that you now face to protect your city and your lands are small compared to the suffering and destruction yet to come.' I told them. 'I saw a woman child who will grow to become a great priestess among men.' But as I began to relate my vision, the men became angry. 'What does a woman child have to do with the weaknesses of the Chichimeca to the North? This in no way solves our dilemma with the invaders! This is not what we asked you. You young fool!' One of the nobles turned in front of me, his high hand falling across my face with an indescribable sting. Another forced him to stop. The *pipiltzin* then left the village, storming off, taking their hostility with them. They also took the jadestone.

"Later I learned that as they left the village they encountered a beautiful maiden near a stream who was singing and bathing her feet. In a hideous defiance to the gods and the Order of Things, they forced themselves upon her, one after another, violently breaking her open. During their furious aggression, the jadestone

[29]

that I'd found among the nest of eggs made its way out of their hands and rolled down into the stream.

"After they had emptied themselves into her they laughed. Then the evil *pipiltzin* left her there, disgraced and broken. When the young maid finally gathered herself up, she caught sight of the precious stone and took it away with her.

"Despite her shame she later confided in me, seeking to heal her spirit. She asked me about the stone. I told her what I tell you now. Keep the stone. Jade is the Heart of the Earth. It is a healing stone, and has the ability to protect you in times of need."

The nest of eggs... the jadestone... Snake Woman.

I suspected that the stone had bewitched Snake Woman, changing her into the decrepit old hag that she was.

"You should be very careful with this stone, my child," said the ancient Ehécatl, once again reading my thoughts. "Ah," he sighed, "night befalls us." He looked out the one window to see that the crimson-orange sky had turned to a deep purple-blue. "Go now, Citlali. You have permission to go."

"Thank you, Grandfather. My heart guards the knowledge you have shared and I respectfully leave." The words flowed out of me automatically, for this act of reverence was a requirement when leaving the presence of an elder.

Circle of Stones

"Tomatl!" bellowed my father, Quiahuitl. The old men made an unusual skirmish as they came through the foliage.

"Tomatl!" he bellowed again. "Raise the fire and prepare *atolli* for the men!"

Adjacent to our adobe house there was a thatched-roof where Tomatl's earthen cooking pot bubbled over a fire. This is where he carried out the daily drudgery of cooking. My father's take-home from yesterday's hunt hung upside-down from the rafters – a couple of fat turkey hens and a few hares.

"Yes, my sir. It is already done," said Tomatl, adding small pieces of wood to the fire. The flames began to glow in the twilight.

Peeking through the loosely woven maguey fiber door, I could see the father elders arranging themselves on the giant mats in the clearing out front. In the middle of the mats, there was a circle of stones where each elder placed his own sacred talisman, combining his personal magic with that of all the others.

I secretly looked on as the Important Ones sat on the ground, each in his own dignified way; one properly accommodating his waist skirt, another arranging his long white braids, another still proudly adjusting the feathers in his hair.

They were the Elders of the High Council of the *altépetl*. Each man came from his own *calpulli*, a village bound by lineage and family ties. In our world, the *altépetl* was the entire community of village *calpullis* that were bound together by custom and tradition. The men had spent the entire afternoon going from one *calpulli* to another, calling upon all the Elders for a council meeting of the *altépetl*.

I dared not make a sound, for if they'd known I was listening to them, my explosive father would be furious. I was sure to be beaten and sent to bed with no *atolli*.

Searching their wrinkled faces in the dusk I could just make out who each man was. The same father elders always came: Two

Feather, yes, and Tecoyotl, who always came first and ate and drank the most. Itzcuintli Coyotl and Cuetzpalincóatl were there, too. So was Corn Woman, the wise old man who had been named after my precious goddess. Having a goddess' name was a special honor the council had bestowed upon him for his wisdom.

Then, just beyond Elder Tecoyotl, I saw Cuauhtli Océlotl! He was there! He had come with his grandfather Tecoyotl! Oh, I was just about to die! My heart nearly leapt out of my body. When I looked at the way his long, black hair fell down his tawny, muscular body, I could feel my heart beat throughout my entire body. It was as though my whole body became a great, beating heart.

I listened as hard as I could, concentrating on what the men were about to say. I could hear the sound of crickets and the fire crackling.

Tomatl served the hot *atolli* beverage in small, dried gourds. Wisps of vapor rose out of each cup, twining up into the moon lit sky. I longed for a serving of the honey-sweetened corn beverage, but I knew that Tomatl would bring me some in time.

As always, my father began the council of stones with much pomp and ceremony.

"We gather here as brothers, husbands and fathers," he said, "with the responsibility to guide and protect our own." (My father always started with this same declaration. Sometimes I would imitate him in my own mind, in a deep, low voice - *We gather here as sisters, wives and mothers, with the responsibility to guide and protect our own*).

Then his focus took a serious turn.

"What we must do now is look at a new danger, think upon it, consider the views of each man here, and decide how we are going to respond."

He glanced around before he continued.

"As you all know by now, The Noble Lord Cozcacuautli Miquiztli, whose very name means Vulture Death, has claimed rights to some of the *altépetl* lands that we hold in common. The lands that he claims to be *his* are the long corn fields beyond the maguey," he indicated with a glance.

"As if anyone could *own* the earth or the air," someone interjected.

[32]

Several of the elders nodded their heads in agreement.

"The fields involved," continued Quiahuitl, "belong to the *altépetl*, and are held in common by the patriarchs and matriarchs of all the *calpullis*. These fields give us almost half the annual tribute that we pay to our *Tlatoani*, King Naxac in the city of Tollan, tribute that is required by law."

There was a skirmish among the men and grumbles about the excessive tribute that they had to pay each year. They all rattled their wristbands and bracelets.

"Settle down, brothers, settle down." He began again, "if the *altépetl* does not submit to Lord Miquiztli, surely he will bring destruction to the people of our village, perhaps even burn our fields and homes. If, on the other hand, we surrender the lands to Miquiztli, and not pay the annual tribute to our king, Naxac, the noble *pipiltzin* will send warriors from Tollan to punish us. Our houses will be burned, our women ravaged, and our children will be taken from us to become their slaves."

"Either way we face the wrath of man," someone flatly said.

There was an outbreak of commentary, everyone speaking at the same time. Bracelets rattled and tongues flew in defiance. Quiahuitl raised his hand in a motion of silence, and the comments settled to a murmur. "We must listen to what each man has to say."

"Perhaps we could fight off Miquiztli," said Itzcuintli Coyotl, "but how could we ever defend ourselves against the warriors of the *Tlatoani* Naxac?"

"We shall go to the *Tlatoani* Naxac and tell him! Surely he will protect us," demanded Two Feather.

"Yes, I agree." added Cuetzpalin. "By protecting us, The Tlatoani protects his own tribute."

"There is just one thing."

Everyone looked at Cuauhtli Océlotl in silence. As a younger, he was not allowed to speak.

"Continue, my son," said one of the elders.

"Lord Miquiztli is a vicious and cruel man. If we betray him by going to our king, we could become victims of his vengeance. Not only might kill us all, but worse, he could sell us as slaves! I would rather die than be forced into slavery and disgrace our ancestors who, as free men, laid these lands with their bleeding hands."

[33]

"I must agree with my grandson, Quiahuitl." said Elder Tecoyotl. "But truthfully, I don't know what we can do about it."

"We should consult the Knower Ollin Ehécatl." suggested Two Feather.

There was a commotion of general agreement.

"Agreed." said Quiahuitl. "This evening I shall tell him the whole of it, and tomorrow I will inform you of his answer."

"But we have no time. Tomorrow may be too late," urged Tecoyotl. "We must make a decision while the Lady Moon Meztli is still upon us." A few of the others openly agreed.

"Brothers, brothers!" My father raised his bellowing voice over the rest. "Silence, please."

The racket settled down. "Elder Tecoyotl. You are the best of our Rememberers. So that we may be clear about our situation, would you please recite to us the amount of tribute that we pay each year?"

"Yes, brother." They all looked at Elder Tecoyotl with reverence.

"Each year of the sun we are required to pay our *Tlatoani* Naxac twenty times twenty urns of *elotl* corn, completely full so that not one more piece can be packed in. We must render fifty *petlacalli* baskets of peanuts, forty hand-polished gourds of different sizes, twenty *petlacallis* of seeds from the giant yellow flowers that follow the sun," Tecoyotl hesitated, tapping his middle finger to his thumb, "and twenty *petlacallis* of yucca root soap. We also pay them the goods we make from the agave cactus; thirty braided mats made from the leaves, twenty earthen containers of the mucous pulp, and fifteen cloth pieces woven from the giant, fibrous leaves."

The Elders were now beginning to wear tired and strained looks on their faces, as Tecoyotl continued down the lengthy list of tribute.

"Finally," Tecoyotl concluded, "we give them various *petlacallis* of fruits that come from the mesquite tree and the prickly pear cactus, fresh dahlias, hydrangeas, and zinnias, and last of all, at times the most difficult of all, one live eagle."

"Is that all?" asked Cuetzpalin bitterly.

"Yes."

"The fields that Miquiztli threatens to take from us provide us with the annual tribute of *elotl* corn. Twenty times twenty urns," another elder emphasized.

[34]

The discontent began again among the old men.

"Brother Tecoyotl," said Quiahuitl, "you may pass to consult the Knower Ehécatl. I will stay here and wait for you with my brothers, that you shall tell us of the Knower's wisdom."

As Elder Tecoyotl got up, I bolted from my crouching position at the door.

Tecoyotl stepped right past me after he flung aside the maguey fiber door. I tucked myself into the corner, made myself busy picking bugs out of a gourd full of seeds. He directly entered the small, dark room of my grandfather and didn't even notice me. Thank you, Mother Goddess, for making me invisible!

"Wise Knower, Ollin Ehécatl Changing Wind," I saw Tecoyotl sit down and fold his legs under him. "I come to seek council."

Outside, the father elders waited restlessly, but respectfully kept their comments to themselves. They fed the fire, while Tomatl served them more of the steaming hot atolli. The sound of crickets rose, owls hooted gentle songs, and in the distant mountains an occasional coyote released his soul to the elegant Lady Stars above.

After what seemed an eternity, Tecoyotl finished his counsel with my grandfather. "Thank you, Grandfather Elder. My heart guards the knowledge you have shared, and I respectfully leave," I heard him say.

Elder Tecoyotl whisked outside. The decision had been made. He strode calmly over to the circle of Elders to take his place next to Quiahuitl and then sat down. While the men waited patiently, he leaned over and whispered something for only my father to hear.

Quiahuitl raised his arms out to the elders and said, "We shall surrender the lands to Miquiztli." There was absolute silence. "It is the council of Ollin Ehécatl that we give up our fields, but that we arrange with the noble Lord Miquiztli to continue to work them, raising the crops. In exchange he will allow us a portion of the harvest for our labor. This way we will still be able to pay our tribute of maize each year." There were some stern faces, but no one dared make a sound. "When Tlaloc brings the rains once again, we are to seed new corn fields... at the base of those mountains over there. Tomorrow when Miquiztli comes I am to beg him to accept our labor."

The elders looked at Quiahuitl to see if he might say anything else, but he did not. Realizing there was nothing else to hear, they quietly got up, and looked for thick branches to serve as torches on their return home.

Walking alone at night was a dangerous risk, but armed with fire a man could defend himself against the night god Tlaltecuhtli, Lord of the Earth. After dark Tlaltecuhtli became the terrible Night Creature, took the form of horrific beasts, and preyed upon the flesh of the weak and defenseless.

The Elders walked away, some shaking their heads, each man returning to his own *calpulli*. Tecoyotl was one of the last to leave.

From where I sat, I could see Tecoyotl and my father still speaking. Tomatl came in with a gourd of steaming hot atolli, the sweet smells filling the dark, little room, and he placed the drink on the table stone.

"Now, now, child. That's enough for one day." At times Tomatl was maternal. "Drink your atolli and on to bed with you, lest the Night Creature finds you awake and eats you up."

"Oh, Tomatl. There' s no Night Creature. That's just something that mothers invented so that children will go to sleep." I felt bold and a bit defiant with my new realization. Then I thought of Snake Woman and realized that I wasn't completely sure. "Anyway," I added just in case, "if the Night Creature comes I'll already be asleep."

Just then, my father Quiahuitl stormed through the doorway, brazing past us. Our startled faces followed him, our eyes wide and our mouths slightly open. He stopped right in his tracks and confronted us for staring at him.

"You there!" he barked at Tomatl. "Get out! You've spent enough time with my daughter. If I even suspect you've touched her I swear to Xipe Totec I'll lash you till your bones show!"

Tomatl quietly and calmly got up from where he'd been sitting at the table stone. We knew that Quiahuitl would never consider carrying out any of his violent threats. Tomatl was far too valuable and too dear to all of us.

I still sat crouched in the corner with the seed gourd in my hands. My father glared at Tomatl as the bony little man huffed out.

"Hmmmph!" snarled Quiahuitl, and he turned around again and entered my grandfather's room.

I drank my *atolli*, enjoying it all the more because Tomatl had made it.

Quiahuitl was carrying on with The Ancient One, screaming as though he were spitting fire. He didn't even sit down and fold his legs under him! "That twisted Miquiztli! I curse the day he was born!"

"He who scorns others the most is the most deserving of scorn," my grandfather calmly stated. At least my father had the self-control to stop speaking. "All your life you have valued *things*. You have looked to acquire status and possessions. Look at this house you live in, the fields you control, the manservant you have. You never thought to seek the path of knowledge as your elders did before you. Knowledge can never be taken away from you, Quiahuitl. All of this, all that you see here, it can all be taken away from you. And now you are angry because a man more powerful than you is taking away something that you control, the corn fields of the *altépetl*."

By this time, I was slipping under my rabbit skin blanket, sleepily watching the dancing shadows that the fire outside was casting on the door curtain.

"And another thing!" my father went on, barely hearing The Ancient One's words, "Tecoyotl wants to pay Snake Woman to arrange a marriage between my virtuous daughter and that sniveling grandson of his! Imagine, *my* daughter, the model of womanhood, hardworking, serious and stern. She's... she's... well..." he sputtered. "She has so much self control you can see the femininity in her face! (This was the highest compliment a person could pay to a woman in all the One World), and to pair her up with that snot-nosed boy... I won't allow it!"

On hearing this, my sleepy eyes opened wide. My heart raced with excitement as I thought about the strong and handsome Cuauhtli Océlotl. Then I remembered my encounter with Snake Woman and the jadestone. "You would have fetched me a fine trade when it came your time," the old crone had said.

I tucked the jadestone under my sleeping mat, and forced myself to fall asleep so the Night Creature would pass me by.

I must have survived the terrors of the night, because I woke up just before the birds started to sing, before the sun god Tonatiuh loosed his arrows of light over the Desert Mountains and into the valley below. The heavens above were illuminated with brilliant pinks, purples, and blues.

I decided to make a buckskin pouch for my jadestone. While I was sewing the little bag, I couldn't stop thinking about Cuauhtli and what my father had said the night before. I figured my jealous father would never accept any marriage arrangement, so I might as well forget it.

I continued pulling the maguey fiber through the rabbit skin with the bone needle that Tomatl had made for me. Punch through, pull. Punch through, pull. Then it occurred to me that maybe I *could* convince my father that I should marry. It really would be the best thing. I started to think of ways to convince him; I would threaten to never speak to him again, I would run away, I would threaten to offer myself for sacrifice to Chantico, goddess of fire.

Just as I was finishing my pouch, the girls outside called to me to come down to the river for the morning bath. In our *calpulli* it was the custom that children bathed in the morning. After we married, we would bathe in the evening at the end of a day's hard labor. I'd heard that in other places people didn't bathe at all, that they sat in tiny rooms with steamy-hot stones and sweated themselves clean.

I shoved the jadestone into the little bag, glad that I'd put the fur on the inside to protect it, and tied it around my bare waist with a leather strand. Throwing my tunic over my head, I left the house and ran down toward the stream behind the other girls.

The sun began to warm the cold morning earth. Girls who had gotten there first had thrown off their tunics and stepped their way into the brisk cold water.

"Citlali!" they called, high spirited and free. "Come into the water!" They were splashing about and carrying on with screams of laughter and giggles, fully enjoying the fact that we were all children, and free from the social formalities of being serious and stern.

Reaching the river's edge, I threw my tunic to the ground and ran to join the other girls. My sense of security felt so real, but in reality it was as murky as a smoking mirror.

Vulture's Game

The noble lord Cozcacuautli Miquiztli woke up with a headache. He hadn't slept well, and normally would have slept much better if he didn't have to go out to the fields this particular morning to clear up the mess over his family's lands. He rolled over sleepily, pulling the embroidered cotton sheet over his head.

His newest slave girl soon appeared at his bedside. He could see her budding nipples through her gauze tunic.

"Not this morning, my love." He called his slaves 'my love' even though he hated them. If he knew one thing at his twenty-six years of age, it was that the young girls always responded better if he pretended to care about them. But they were just slaves, the lowliest of creatures. How could he possibly *love* any of them? He didn't even love his own wife, a distinguished woman of his own class. And also, they served to calm his insatiable desire, so he frequently availed himself of their nubile youth. He reached down and squeezed his awakening flint rock.

"Wait," he said, having second thoughts. He wasn't in that much of a hurry. "Come here."

"Yes, My Lord."

"Which one are you?"

"They call me Manah, My Lord."

"Have you flowered yet, girl?"

"No, My Lord."

Ah, he thought. Things that were forbidden and taboo made his blood rush all the more.

"Do you love your master?"

"Yes, My Lord."

"Look around you, Manah. What do you see?"

The girl nervously looked up around the stone walls and all that was within them. The early morning sun was beginning to come in through the open window. A gauze curtain gently fluttered in the soft breeze.

[41]

"I see your wooden table, My Lord, and your fine jewels, and copper bowls, and over there, a stone table with your copper vase of colorful dahlias."

"Yes, yes. That's a good girl, and do you know what?"

"What, My Lord?" Manah was beginning to relax and smile a little.

"All of this is here for you to enjoy, Manah. You aren't like the other slave girls who work doing the drudgery. No, no, no. You are here because your lord master wants to be with you."

She meekly smiled at him.

"Now all you have to do, Manah, is please your lord master. Do you want to please me, Manah?"

"Oh yes My Lord!"

"Oh, you are such a good girl." He reached his arm out from his sleeping mat and took her hand. "You sit here with me," he said, as he coerced her onto the edge of his platform bed.

All Manah could do was remember the words of the other slave girls that had encountered the same fate before her. *Whatever you do, don't let him know it hurts. It only hurts the first few times and after that it's not so bad. If he thinks you don't like it, he will turn ill on you, indeed.* This was the only advice she had received.

Manah forced a pleasant smile and looked at the man who was still covered in the embroidered, cotton bed sheet.

"That's a girl. Now we can make believe that we are in a big white cloud. Remove this bed sheet, my love. It's awfully hot."

She gathered up the embroidered cloth, holding it close as though it would provide protection against her predator. Somewhat startled, she looked at his naked, brown body, at his well-defined muscles, and at his manhood, a sight she had never seen before.

Miquiztli could barely restrain himself from violently taking her and thrusting himself into her fresh flesh, but he so enjoyed his little game that he continued on. He absolutely loved it when the girls didn't know what was awaiting them.

"My dear, throw aside that cumbersome bed sheet. It's in the way. That's a girl. Now, take off your dress. That's it. All the way off. Throw it on the floor. Go on. Nobody's going to punish you. Just throw it. That's better. Look at you. You're not so bad. Your nose is too big, but soon enough you'll have breasts that will be delicious.

[42]

Yes, delicious! That pleases your lord master. I know you want to please me, Manah, but do you desire me? Do you really want me, Manah?"

Manah sat next to him, vulnerable in her nakedness. "Of course, My Lord," she complied. She stared blankly at the floor. "You and no other."

The words rang sweetly in his ears, and flowed into the river of his blood where it satiated his unconscious need for approval.

The Vulture then grabbed her and proceeded with his pedophiliac conquest. When he found what he knew was the closed door to her secrets beyond, he tightened his hands around her. Then, with one forceful and violent motion, he broke her open, entering her forbidden chamber. Her pre-pubescent body was incapable of accepting the largeness of him.

Manah experienced a pain that she had never known. It was as though an obsidian sword was piercing through her, thrusting into her abdomen, and cutting her in two. Her eyes opened wide and her startled heart began to pound inside her chest. Her immediate reaction was to pull away from him, but she could not. She was pinned beneath him. He manipulated her as though she were a cotton doll. All she could do was bear it in disbelief. In all her agony, in all her fury, she said nothing; she showed no sign of pain. Only a single tear rolled down her cheek and dropped onto the woven sleeping mat.

Amidst the violent volcanic eruptions of pain, Manah felt herself filling up inside with warm *xinachtli*.

"There." he said. "All done."

With contempt he shoved her aside.

He sprang out of bed with a huge smile, leaving her there, crumpled up in the middle of the reddening bed mat. "Manah, darling." He said. "You did a fine job. I feel just splendid. Quite relieved. Now, run along. You'll get to see me again tomorrow morning." He paraded around the stone floor, taking in the fresh, morning air, stopping only to admire himself in his polished reflecting-metal. He was such a fine example of manhood, he thought to himself, so virile and strong.

Manah could hardly move, the pain from between her legs was so intense. Miquiztli turned around and noticed that she was still there.

"I told you to leave. Get out." His hidden hatred was beginning to show.

"Yes, My Lord." She said as she painfully got up. "It's just that I was thinking about how much I love my dear Lord Master, and how fulfilled I feel to have given him pleasure." Manah knew how to lie. Her words gave Miquiztli tremendous self-satisfaction.

"That's a good girl, Manah." He said. "Now, GET OUT!" He was tired of looking at this rodent girl with the over-grown nose.

"Yes, My Lord." Manah looked straight ahead and never once lost her dignity.

She picked up her tunic, and pulled it over her head. Slowly and painfully she walked out of the room, head held high, ignoring the blood running down her legs.

One Eagle Two Lives

"Are the men ready, councilor?"

"Yes lord." said the big bellied Pochotl.

"Good. They'd better be." Miquiztli couldn't stand incompetence. "Tell them I'll be right down."

"Of course, My Lord." Pochotl spun around and left the room.

"That turquoise broach, there." He pointed for his boy slave to see. "The one set in silver. Use that one to clasp my hair."

"Whatever My Lord wishes." The handsome boy slave fastened the clasp around his thick, black hair and stood back to admire the great Miquiztli. "You are ready, My Lord."

"I am ready," repeated Miquiztli.

He walked out of his chamber and through a vast central patio. When he reached the main entrance, a carved stone archway, he looked down the stairs where his councilor and personal guard were waiting below.

"I am ready!"

Miquiztli descended the four stairs of his father's house with all the arrogance of a Toltec noble. The sashes of his red loincloth ran twice around his waist and tied in the front, securing the *maxatlatl*, a V-shaped apron that covered his loins. It was woven of flaming yellow cotton, with bold red flecks all along the border. In the back, the *maxatlatl* was open, his buttocks exposed. He looked every bit the grand noble, but the great dorsal disc, the symbol of the highest Toltec nobility, was missing. It would have been attached to the back of his sash with a huge, red knot; but the informality of this day did not call for the dorsal disc. It was reserved for higher ceremonies at the pyramids in the city center.

His black chest cloth boasted the same red flecks, but also hosted an array of small shells evenly sewn into the fabric. The magnificent pectoral butterfly that should have lain atop his chest cloth was missing. This heavy jade adornment, honoring the Great

Obsidian Butterfly, was reserved for the greatest of Toltec warriors. Lord Miquiztli had not yet attained this honor.

His sandals had hard, leather soles, each with two leather thongs through the toes. They were embroidered along the heel and studded with turquoise, topaz and garnet gems, forming tiny images of Quetzalcoatl. He was wearing leg bands under each knee. Finally, a handsome arm cuff with long leather tassels hugged his left biceps.

Miquiztli was not wearing a headdress. The magnificent eagle feather adornments were reserved only for lords and high commanders of the army. Even though, his hair was neatly arranged. The top half was slicked back and folded into a tight bun at the back of his head, clasped by the turquoise broach. The rest fell, straight and black, just to his shoulders. He liked to wear his hair this way because it brought out his best features: broad forehead, straight nose, high cheek bones, strong chin. He was an extremely handsome man.

"I am ready," he announced. He stepped into the many-colored, six-manned litter that was on the ground waiting for him. The slaves hoisted him up, and he looked around behind him at the ranks of his personal guard. They were thirty in all. He then looked down at his councilor Pochotl standing on the ground beside him. Pochotl gave him a slight nod. Miquiztli raised his arm in a forward motion, his gold and silver rings flashing in the sun. The men began their walk out of the city of Tollan toward the north-east, toward the outlands of Actopán.

❧

At the river we were laughing and enjoying the favor of the gods. The birds were singing and a gentle morning breeze kissed our faces. Soon enough we paired off, washing each other's thick, long, black hair with cactus-root soap. Since Miyáhuatl and I were older we had to wash our hair and cleanse ourselves quickly, then turn to wash the little ones. So much of our lives revolved around work and survival, but mornings like these, when the sun warmed us, made the burdens of life even enjoyable.

I hadn't said anything to Miya yet about the council of the night before. I needed a better moment, when I could whisper, when no one would hear us, not even the gods. In the meantime, we listened to the other girls' laughter, their gossip and banter. We bathed the twins Axochitl and Oxochitl, as we did every day, playing and making a game out of it all. I couldn't contain myself anymore. I had to tell.

"Miya," I looked at her and felt very serious. "Wait with me after everyone goes. I have to talk to you."

Miya looked at me in surprise. "What about the water genies? Surely they'll come for us if we stay here alone."

Everybody knew the legend of *Matlacueyatl*. In the legend, *Matlacueyatl* had warned her beautiful daughter not to go to the waterfall, but the headstrong girl disobeyed her mother, and the water genies swept her away.

"They won't get us. They're at the waterfall, not here." As I said it, I willed it so, hoping my will would prevail.

"What would my mother say?"

"Tell your sister to tell your mother that you stayed behind to weave my hair."

"My mother would never allow that Citlali! You know that. She'll pelt me as soon as I come up to the hut."

"Tell her anything! Just stay with me, please. I need you to send a message to somebody." My desperation was obvious to her. I saw it in her face. She must have thought about all the times I had lied to help her out of a sneaky situation. Honor bound, she agreed.

"Itza!" she called to her nine-year-old sister who, by this time, had finished bathing and was trying to trap a fish with her friends.

Itza, whose name meant dream, playfully walked over to her sister wriggling like a fish, while her friends laughed hysterically. During the morning bath there were no adults to scold us, so Itza resorted to complete silliness. I often worried that Itza would end up with a bad fate upon her. She behaved in ways that displeased the gods. She wasn't the typical, docile turtledove that all little girls were taught to be. We were taught to walk with fixed eyes, to be hardworking and dignified.

She came up to us making a fish face.

[47]

"Itzacíhuatl! You have no self-control! What is to become of you if you are not serious and stern? Stop clowning around and listen to me." Miya forcefully grabbed her sister by the arm. Itza stood there, shaken and embarrassed in front of her friends.

Miya lowered her voice so the others couldn't hear. "I'm going to stay behind with Citlali."

Itza looked at me, wondering what could be going on, but I ignored her, finishing the braids in Oxochitl's hair.

"Yes, but what's mother going to think? You're going to get into trouble if you don't go back and grind the corn." Itza said, half threatening her sister.   "Mother's not going to think anything, Itza, because you're going to tell her that I'm collecting medicine plants with Citlali for her grandfather, and that I'm here with her!"

"Why should I risk my neck and lie for you? You know what she'll do if she finds out!"

"She's not going to find out, Itza. Besides, you owe me favors. I haven't said anything about who it was that smeared an egg on the effigy of the moon god Teciztecatl, nor did I ever tell who it was the time you and your friends ran through the mounds of corn husks, scattering them all over the place, and not once have I said anything about..."

"Yes! I'll do it, Miya." Itza wriggled out of her sister's grasp.

"Good. Now go back to the *calpulli*, all of you." She said, addressing everybody. "We all have things to do." The group of girls gathered up their tunics on the river bank, quickly dressed themselves, and headed off toward home.

"And Itza!" she yelled after her sister, "Make sure that somebody carries the twins so they don't get back dirtier than before we came. Their mother would make us wash them over again *and* give us a whipping!"

Miya always had to remind Itza of everything. Her little sister was so distracted, always with her head in the clouds.

Once everyone was gone, we made ourselves comfortable, stretching out on the giant rock slabs along the bank. We could tell that the gods were happy this day. We relished the sound of water splashing, the sun warming our naked bodies from the deep blue sky above. We felt completely safe, protected by the steep-sided banks of the ravine.

[48]

"So," said Miyáhuatl. "Are you going to tell me what's in that little pouch around your waist?"

"No." I said frankly, but Miya was used to my secrets. She knew that I was learning to become a Knower, and she never pressured me to tell her things. Being the good friend that I was, I had told her much, even the secret love potions that I had learned from the Ancient One. Surely the gods wouldn't be angered if I told my closest friend just a *few* secrets. I was positive I would never incur their wrath and end my days in the bloody death.

We lie stretched out and naked, looking at the sky above us.

"There was a meeting of the *altépetl* last night."

Miya looked surprised. I never told her the content of these meetings.

"So," Miya said, "they have meetings all the time. Wait a minute. I know." she giggled. "That old Coyote Dog, Itzcuintli Coyotl, finally croaked and died." She laughed, the only one amused by her joke.

"No, Miya. No." I said. Thus, I began to unweave the fabric of problems that had been discussed the night before. I spoke freely, confident that we were alone.

✂

As the noble Miquiztli and his men came upon the last mountain pass before reaching the *altépetl*, the noble, who had been talking the whole time with his councilor, motioned for his 30 men to stop. As the entire rank came to a halt, the slaves rested his ornately carved, brilliantly painted litter on the warm, sandy ground.

"I'm going to urinate." Miquiztli told his councilor. "Over there." He pointed to some mesquite trees at the edge of a gully. "Come with me."

The arrogant Miquiztli stepped down from his litter, and taking his councilor's hand, the two men walked toward the craggy trees. Leaving Pochotl at a respectable distance behind him, Miquiztli approached the gully's edge to relieve himself. He looked at his manhood and remembered the fresh young thing he had broken apart early that same morning. He smiled to himself, thinking about his virgin slaves. He hated them, the scrawny little rats, and they continually told him how much they loved and adored him. Now *that* was power.

Looking up around him, Miquiztli stretched and took a deep breath of sweet, desert air. An eagle flew over him in the sky above, letting out a shrill cry to all those who were listening.

The splashing of the river below sounded like children's laughter and Miquiztli experienced a sense of calm and tranquility that he wasn't accustomed to feeling.

Just then he noticed two golden bodies on the rocks below. He turned to see if Pochotl had noticed them, but his councilor was busy gathering up the savory pods of the mesquite trees, shoving as many as he could into his traveling purse, and into his mouth.

"Pochotl." He quietly said to his councilor. "You stay here with the men. I'm going down toward the river to have a better look." Pochotl would assume he meant look at the river. How could he have possibly known it was at the two girls? Besides, his councilor was happily gorging himself, so Miquiztli left him there.

He snuck down the side, hiding behind shrubs and bushes. Then he came to a mid-way point where he pushed aside the brush and foliage. There, before him on the rocks below, appeared a beautiful goddess with her maid-servant. His heart nearly stopped, and his breath almost ceased. Never before in his life had he seen such beauty. She lay there, enveloped in a thick, long braid that wrapped around her naked body as though it were Coatl, the serpent god, hugging her every curve. Her flashing black eyes sparkled in the sun as she smiled at her companion. Her full, red lips opened to emit a sound so sweet, so lovely, that it hardly seemed a real voice. Miquiztli was sure she was the goddess of the river. Then and there he vowed to adore and love her for all eternity. His body welled up with emotion, and tears came to his eyes, and he realized that this feeling was something he had never known before.

Regaining composure, and remembering his duties and the men waiting above, Miquiztli turned and crept back up the rocky bank as quietly as he could. The goddess never noticed him, and he was quite relieved that he had not disturbed her, an act that might have incurred her wrath.

※

Miya could hardly believe all that I was telling her. She was frightened. Was it true that the wrathful Noble Lord would come and burn their entire village? Or, worse, would the warriors of the Tlatoani come and destroy us all and sell us as slaves? Just for a few fields of corn? On top of all of this, the news of Cuauhtli Océlotl! His grandfather wanted to arrange a marriage! Miya was overcome with envious longing, even though she was excited for me at the same time.

"You must get a message to Cuauhtli, Miya. Tell him I *do* wish to be his woman. You can do that, can't you? You have contact with the people of the other *calpulli's* because you sometimes work in the communal fields."

I was begging. I could hear it in my voice.

"I do, Citlali. I see him. Sometimes my mother sends my brother and me to trade corn flour for rabbit skins. We go to his father, the elder Tecoyotl, directly."

"Can you get your brother to take you today? In the evening?"

"Oh, that's easy!" she laughed. "My brother lusts after a fat girl who lives in their same *calpulli*. He sneaks her candied squash and they go deep into the corn where she opens her legs for him. I know, because I've secretly watched them. Then my brother smiles a lot for two days."

"She does that?" I asked. I was truly surprised. "For candied squash?" We laughed so hard that our laughter rang out with the sound of the running river. An eagle flew over us in the sky above, letting out a shrill cry.

There was no way in that brief moment that I could possibly have known that the wind had carried my laughter to the ears of Cozcacuautli Miquiztli.

✖

"On to Actopán!" ordered the noble lord when he had comfortably settled into his litter, with the well fed Pochotl at his side. The slaves hoisted Miquiztli up and again began their burdensome march toward the *altépetl*.

✖

"Who is that yelling above the cliffs?"

"I don't know, Miya, but we'd better get out of here!" I said. We grabbed our tunics, threw them on, and raced each other back home. We ran over the arid desert earth, passed the prickly pear cactuses, and forged our way through the maguey fields, until we reached the little gardens surrounding our *calpulli*. We stopped, out of breath, in the corn field behind my home.

"Who was that, Citlali?"

"I don't know. I didn't recognize his voice. He speaks strangely. I don't think he's from here." I gasped to catch my breath.

"My mother probably sent him after me because I didn't go home to make the corn flour! Citlali! She knows!"

"You there! You girls!"

We jumped and screamed with fright.

"Now what have you gotten into?" asked Tomatl.

We quickly regained our self-control, seeing that it was the dear, little man-servant.

"We, uh, we were just returning from the river. We went looking for water frogs, but we didn't find any," lied Miyáhuatl as sweetly as possible.

"Well now, be off with you. You're in the middle of my vegetable garden!"

"Yes sir, of course, sir," we mumbled respectfully as we picked our way out from the stalks of corn. We spoke to Tomatl with respect, even though he was just a slave, not because he was older, but because he kept us well fed.

"Come Miya. I'll walk you home." I wanted to make sure Miya didn't get into trouble. I was also curious to see if her brother was smiling.

Miquiztli's Visit

Miquiztli and his men reached the *calpulli* governed by Quiahuitl, son of Ollin Ehécatl. As they approached the huts, Miquiztli thought about the stories he had heard about Ollin Ehécatl from his own grandfather, who, as a young man, had consulted the advice of the *macehuatl* Knower. As the story went, Miquiztli's grandfather, along with several army generals, had sought out the impoverished Knower for his advice about some military problems with the fearsome Chichimeca on the northern frontier. They had given him great gifts of jade and gold. The two men had made an agreement that in exchange for the Knower's wisdom, they would render a vast section of lands to the *altépetl* for the planting of corn. The Knower Ehécatl, however, after having gone off to the mountains to seek his vision, had come back with some ludicrous story about a frog and the birth of a woman child. As it turned out, the people of the *altépetl* encroached upon the lands anyway, and began to cultivate them. Now it was time to reclaim them, for his family and his king.

Miquiztli motioned for his men to stop. He looked at the mud-covered huts before him, and at the impoverished people who had come out of them to see what was going on. They were mostly mothers caring for small children or feeble old men, for anyone able to work the fields was off doing so. Facing the extreme poverty of the village, the noble and his men felt even richer and more glorious than back in Tollan, where they were constantly reminded of their status by the multitude of nobility richer than they. How pitiful, Miquiztli thought as he looked among them and at their primitive garments made of woven maguey threads.

"Pochotl," he said quietly, looking down to his councilor. "What do you advise?"

"Well, My Lord," Pochotl whispered, as he looked about at all the people who were quietly yet anxiously filling up the central area around them. "We ask for the Knower Ehécatl."

Miquiztli looked behind him at his personal guard, and then at the frightened people in front of their huts. From atop his high and mighty litter he announced, "We ask for the Knower, Ollin Ehécatl."

Behind the crowd a child dashed off, running as fast as two young legs possibly could.

"And who should we say is looking for him?" said a high voice, singing like a morning bird. And before Miquiztli's very eyes, the tall, slender goddess of the river emerged from the crowd.

"The uh..." he stammered in disbelief at hearing the river goddess speak, "The Noble Lord Cozcacuautli Miquiztli."

✄

"May we inform him of why the Noble Lord requires his council?" I asked, moving toward him and looking him directly in the eye. I fixed my gaze and held my head high.

"No!" said Pochotl firmly.

"No." said Miquiztli, repeating his councilor.

"Well then, Noble Lord Cozcacuautli Miquiztli, I will take thee to my grandfather, Ollin Ehécatl." I cast my eyes down, not wanting to push my luck. I was addressing a dangerous enemy, capable of destroying my beloved village for no more reason than a daring breach of respect.

It was only later, when the windows of everything that is, was, and ever shall be opened, that I learned the secrets of Lord Miquiztli's heart. Upon hearing my words, he realized that his beautiful river goddess was none other than a mere *macehuatl*, a child born of Dirt People. Even so, a seed of passion was then and there conceived in his heart. When he looked at me, the seed became a beautiful flower, brilliantly colored and sweetly fragrant, forever opening its infinite petals, but when he thought *who* I was, a mere *macehuatl*, the seed became dark and rancid. It putrefied and nearly died. Love and hate, born of the same seed. Right then and there, as this seed of passion was conceived, Miquiztli's heart entered a cavern of torment that he would endure the rest of his days and take with him unto his death.

He motioned for the slaves to set him down, gave instructions for some of his men to stay behind with the litter, and followed me (or was I the river goddess?) with his councilor at his side. A few of his armed men followed behind. We walked between the mud-covered huts, past the vegetable gardens, and along a narrow path lined with giant cane reeds. (These were the cane reeds we used to make the baskets and mats that eventually made their way to the houses of nobles like Miquiztli).

The reeds opened into a clearing, where we came upon a small adobe house, my house. Quiahuitl was waiting in front with downcast eyes, standing with little Itza behind him. I walked up to my father, looked at him, and then quietly and calmly took Itza's hand and led her into my abode, closing the maguey-fiber curtain in front of the doorway.

"I come to speak with the elder Ollin Ehécatl." said Miquiztli, approaching the area where, just the night before, the elders had had their council meeting. Posturing, the noble lord stood tall, arms folded across his chest, feet planted firmly in a wide stance.

"Yes, lord Miquiztli. My father knows of thy arrival." Quiahuitl began. "But he is old and feeble, and cannot leave his sleeping mat. He wishes to know if thou might speak to me instead."

Miquitzli and Pochotl whispered quietly to each other.

"No." replied the noble. "That will not do. I wish to enter and speak with him directly. I will take my advisor with me."

"My humble living is no sight for a great lord such as thee," said Quiahuitl, "but since thou dost wish to enter I invite thee and thy councilor. Come."

He led the two men through the maguey curtain, into our dark, room of a house. As the finely dressed Miquiztli entered through the curtain, he saw Itza and me sitting on a woven mat against the wall. Itza was shaking. I clutched her in my arms. He looked at me with penetrating eyes as I caressed her hair.

His advisor then pushed his way in, followed by my father. They cramped themselves into the room with the one window. Ollin Ehécatl was calmly puffing on the long pipe that Tomatl had prepared for him. I was glad to see that the nobles sat with their legs properly folded under them. Everyone in Cem Anahuac seemed to be respectful of age.

The four men spoke for some time, arguing the details of the use of the lands. Ehécatl explained his proposal for working the lands in exchange for a portion of the harvest so that the *altépetl* could continue paying tribute to the king. That way, he said, the noble lord wouldn't have to inconvenience himself by providing his own slaves to cultivate the corn. Unexpectedly, this infuriated the volatile Miquiztli, who said he could provide slaves anytime, anywhere, no matter what the number.

With fire in his eyes he softly said, "Why should I pay your people one part of the crops in exchange for working the fields? These are the words of fools. I can fill the fields with my own slaves and cultivate all of it myself." Hatred and disgust burned in him. "You and your people are wretches. You encroached upon lands owned by my grandfather. You don't deserve to live." His hushed vehemence was more frightening that yelling.

Ehécatl sat silently. Qhiáhuitl's jaw began to bulge in and out as he clenched his teeth. They knew all too well that the Vulture could swoop down on them at any time and devour them alive.

Then, unexpectedly, Quiahuitl raised his voice and barreled, "How dare you claim possession of any part of this sacred Earth as your own! There is no such thing as ownership of land! Why would I agree with you?"

"Grandfather," I said in my most feminine voice. I don't know what implored me to speak at that moment. It must have been Corn Woman working her magic, speaking through me in order to protect the *altépetl* and her sacred fields.

Miquiztli looked up and saw me in the doorway. My one long braid twined around my youthful body. It fell down the length of my slender neck, flowed over my tunic between my small breasts, down my flat stomach, around my hip, and wrapped around my thigh. Miquiztli sat there and stared at me, his fierce, black eyes penetrating my soul.

"Perfect!" he stood and triumphantly exclaimed, as though he had struck an eagle in flight. "Yes. I will accept your arrangement. The lands are mine, but you may remain on them and keep a portion of the harvests for yourselves." His handsome face smiled, showing his strong, white teeth. "In exchange for your granddaughter, Ollin Ehécatl. I will make her my concubine."

My heart fell to the floor. My father jumped to his feet and burst out with rage, "You cannot have her! You cannot have my Citlali!" I could feel his soul tear in two.

Miquiztli became indignant and repulsed, but instead of yelling, he lowered his voice to almost a whisper. "How dare you raise your voice to me? Don't you realize that I can destroy you with nothing more than a word? You're nothing. You're the scum that comes from the bottom of the earth, that which repulses the Filth Eater."

"Forgive me, My Lord." Quiahuitl said with down cast eyes, trying to save what he could of the grave situation. "It's just that...it's just that... she's not yet a woman."

"Very well, then. I won't take her as my concubine." Miquiztli said vindictively. "I'll take her as my slave."

Quiahuitl's face twisted and contorted. He realized that if he said any more, the Vulture was liable to impale them all with his mighty talons. My father stood there, helpless, and for all the thunder in his personality, he could do nothing. Absolutely nothing.

Miquiztli turned toward the doorway to leave.

"I want the little one, too. Pochotl, take the little one there." He pointed to Itza who was still crouched in the corner.

"Go with the man, Itza. Don't be afraid. Just do as he says." I barked at her.

"Don't touch the fruit, fat man. No one is to touch them. Do you understand?"

"Yes, My Lord." said the councilor, obediently.

Miquiztli grabbed me by the arm and led me toward the doorway.

"Lord Miquiztli," I pleaded in a state of disbelief and confusion, "Please, lord, might I have just one last time with my grandfather?"

Miquiztli looked down into my moist, brown eyes.

"Hmmph" he snorted. He pushed me back in and went outside.

That short moment that I spent with my father and grandfather were the last that I ever spent with them. It was the last time I saw my grandfather's long, white hair wisp in the gentle breeze that came through the one window. It was the last time I took his feeble, old hand in mine, and gently kissed his puckered little face. He had taught me everything I knew, shared the wisdom of his experiences with me, and I knew now that I would carry his spirit with me

[57]

forever. Miquiztli could take everything away from me, but he could never take away the fact that Ollin Ehécatl was my grandfather.

"You will see me again. Look for me in the changing wind." They were the last words my grandfather ever said to me. A tear gently rolled down his face.

The Birth of Ce Acatl

You might be wondering how it is that I am able to tell you of things that took place when I was not there. Well, it wasn't too much later that I learned of many things that came to pass. Soon I will get to that, but right now I shall tell you about our first warrior and the beginnings of our tribe.

In the most ancient of times the people lived in darkness. When they burst forth into the One World, Cem Anahuac, they were led by the great warrior Mixcóatl. Four hundred Mixcoa warriors were his loyal fighters. They came, fighting fiercely, from the nine hills in the north, by way of the nine Great Plains.

It was in this time, many grandfathers ago, that Mixcóatl and his four hundred warriors were fallen upon by the warrior goddess Itzpapálotl, the Obsidian Butterfly. With piercing terror she swooped down from the sky upon the unsuspecting men, engulfed them with her great black wings, and devoured them, brutally finishing off the last of the four hundred Mixcoas. Only Mixcóatl, their great war party leader, managed to escape her wrath and this just barely. He ran and hid in an enormous, earthen-pot shaped cactus, a *biznaga*.

The goddess, angered by his escape, attacked the thorny cactus, but Mixcóatl was safe inside his botanical womb, protected by its fertile juices. When he had fully renewed his strength, he burst out of the *biznaga* and shot his mighty arrow at Itzpapálotl, over and over again. Then, with the powers he gained from slaying her, he gave the life back to his four hundred warriors. They raised themselves up. They returned from the dead.

"Nobody will ever conquer my four hundred warriors while I live!" In triumph, Mixcóatl screamed his most terrifying war cry.

Then they all shot their arrows at the obsidian butterfly goddess, time and time again. After that they burned her. They painted a black stripe across their eyes and dusted themselves with her black ash in a sign of triumph over having conquered this most fearsome goddess.

Mixcóatl and his four hundred warriors led the people to the left of the setting sun. They wandered for many years and met grave affliction. In the year One Cane they reached a place in the desert known as Chicomótzoc, the Place of the Seven Caves. The people made the caves serve as their temples, and they made offerings there for four years.

Their priests told them about the first man and the first woman and the One World called Anahuac. They studied the celestial bodies and found that Venus, known as the god Tlahuizcalpantecuhtli, traveled through the Underworld more slowly than did the Sun, for every eight times that the Sun traveled through the Underworld, Venus traveled five. In time the priests learned that Venus sometimes appears as the Morning Star and other times in the starry evening sky. As Evening Star, Venus and the other forces of the night fight against the malign powers that steer the Sun toward the depths of the Underworld, where the great fiery shield is consumed by the Earth Monster at the very mid of night.

As Morning Star, he appears as a powerful warrior that, in the dawn of each new day, anticipates the Sun's rising, and attempts to assail the sun with golden spears. Venus is eventually defeated, ceding his place to the Sun, the true ruler of the diurnal sky.

The time came when the tribe left the Place of the Seven Caves. Once again Mixcóatl and his four hundred warriors led the people toward the region to the left of the setting sun. They traveled valley after valley, across the land. Along their journey they conquered the peoples they came in contact with, planning their strategies beforehand. When they had successfully killed the menfolk of a particular tribe, the warriors divided the plunder among themselves, riches, food, *pulque*, and women, so that no warrior would go without his proper share.

Eventually they came upon the region to the left of the setting sun, to Tepoztlán, place of the god Tepoztecatl, our god of *pulque*.

My grandfather told me that Mixcóatl had been pursuing the conquest of the Uitcnáuac, The Place Next to the Thorn, when he encountered an enchanting virgin whose beauty radiated like the warmth seeping out of fragrant, wild sage.

She was Chimalman.

[60]

She stood alone in the desert near the magical Hill of Tepozteco. Nothing at all clad her bare body except exquisite jewelry made of seashells, jade, and other precious stones. Upon seeing her, Mixcóatl, with all the warrior strength given him by the gods, marked his target, and readied his bow. He shot his arrows toward the beautiful Chimalman. The first arrow flew high and she only had to duck slightly to avoid its path. The second arrow struck her side but broke in two. The third arrow she captured in her hand and detained its course. Thus, when the fourth arrow was launched, the woman fled and hid among the magueys. When the fourth arrow had been shot, Mixcóatl turned and left. The woman ran to hide in the Place of the Red Caves.

Soon Mixcóatl returned to Uitcnáuac, The Place Next to the Thorn. He returned to shoot his arrow, but the beautiful Chimalman was not there. He was angered and took his fury out on the inhabitants of the villages.

The women at the Place of the Red Caves where she was hiding cursed her. "By your fault Mixcóatl comes and harms your younger sisters in his search for you." They took her to Uitcnáuac so that when Mixcóatl returned he found her there.

She was standing just as she had before, adorned in precious stone necklaces, her dark body radiating in the sun.

Upon seeing her, Mixcóatl marked a great circle in the earth. He set his arrows, and another time he fired at the beautiful Chimalman. The first arrow flew high above her. The second broke in two. The third she caught in her hand, but the fourth and final arrow flew between her legs, and the Virgin of Uitcnáuac conceived.

When the child was born he stirred four days in the womb, and his violent and prolonged birth caused the death of his beautiful mother. Ce Acatl was the day he was born, so he was named Ce Acatl Topiltzin.

He was raised by a crone named Cihuacoatl, Snake Woman, and when he was of age his father, Mixcóatl, took him and trained him in the things of war. He went to Xiuacan, the place of Hunting, and lived among his four hundred uncles, the great Mixcoa warriors.

Lamentably, as time went by, conflict arose among the warriors. Loyalties became divided, and it came to pass that when Ce Acatl was nine years old Mixcóatl was betrayed by his own brothers in the place called Xaltitlan. Ce Acatl learned of the treachery by way of a great bird, a buzzard king.

"Where is my father?"

Cozcacuautli answered, "The truth is that your father was killed. He was slain by your four hundred uncles and has been taken to his burial."

"Oh, my beloved father! The great warrior Mixcóatl!" the young Ce Acatl cried. In an act of loyalty to his father and the cult of Mixcóatl, he dedicated a cave as a temple where he kept his father's bones and sacred image inside.

His father's enemies were displeased by this and confronted Ce Acatl Topiltzin. "Why have you dedicated a temple to Mixcóatl, especially knowing it will anger us, your uncles, the Jaguar, the Eagle, and the Wolf?"

"It is true mine uncles. This deed I have done," was all that Ce Acatl replied.

Later he summoned his uncles to the sacred cave and the ground critters heard his ploy, "Oh my uncles, come. I rescind my loyalties. From now on I dedicate my temple to you. In truth, you, the Jaguar, the Eagle and the Wolf shall never die but shall live to conquer others. To those who are worthy I dedicate my temple, to my uncles!"

They distrusted the child Ce Acatl and even worse, they bound him by the neck and held him captive inside his temple cave.

Ce Acatl was not crushed by this action. With the special powers given him by the gods, he summoned the ground critters and said unto them, "Oh little friends, come and bore a hole inside my temple." The critters immediately began to gnaw. They gnawed him free and then bore a tunnel for him to escape from inside the temple cave.

When Ce Acatl's uncles awoke and became aware of his intended escape through a tunnel they formed a clever idea.

"We'll smoke him out of the crevice with flaming torches!" they said, and many were happy.

When Ce Acatl peered out through the opening, he saw his uncles the Jaguar, the Eagle and the Wolf howling with delight. When his uncle warriors burned the torches into the crevice, Ce Acatl, waiting below, knocked the torches down with a great club.

This angered his uncles, who then went in after him. First went the Jaguar who, in his hurry, stumbled into the crevice, but when he reached the cave inside, Ce Acatl was waiting for him and with great force smashed a huge rock down upon the Jaguar's head. In the same manner, Ce Acatl defeated the Eagle and the Wolf, who descended down the crevice behind the Jaguar.

Ce Acatl Topiltzin then took out a great conch and blew upon it, calling all the animals of the wild. They came to him in his defense against his uncles, and Ce Acatl, with all the animal warriors of the desert forests, escaped his enemies and survived.

Arrival

I sat holding Itza in the darkness, in a small mud and palm hut, where the rough hands of the guards had left us. It had been a long journey, much farther than the golden-green fields of Tlaloc and Corn Woman.

At first the guards placed heavy wooden slave-collars around our necks, and we walked surrounded by guards, alongside the noble's litter, trudging through the soft earth left wet by the rains. When I no longer recognized where I was, I gave up hope of escaping. I was afraid of becoming completely lost, or worse, eaten by the horrible god Tlahuizcalpantecuhtli, lord of the Earth and devourer of men.

After a long time the guards let us walk by ourselves, without pushing or shoving us forward. It was a grueling walk. When the rain ceased to pelt us, the sun beat down, and the dry wind parched our faces until they'd almost peeled off, like a snake shedding its skin. Onward we trudged, until our calloused bare feet began to bleed. Night came upon us as we reached the far side of a vast desert valley, but we continued walking, walking into the night. I later learned it was the Valley of Mixquiahuala. At last, we were shoved into a dark, little hut. We sat in silence for what seemed an eternity, not believing our fate.

"Why are we here?" Itza could hardly whisper, her voice trembled so.

"We are here because Quetzalcoatl wishes it." I hesitated, realizing that the young girl didn't understand. "We were traded, Itza. We were traded to the noble Miquiztli in exchange for peace among our people." Itza whimpered. "Miquiztli is a noble, Itza. A *pipiltzin*. He's so powerful that he can do anything he wants. If he becomes angry, he can destroy our village with no more than his command. He became angry with my father, Little One, but when he saw me in the doorway, Quetzalcoatl enveloped him, and gave him the idea to leave our people in peace in exchange for..." I cleared my throat. "...In exchange for us."

"Is Quetzalcoatl protecting our village?"

"Yes, he is."

"Will he protect us too?"

I chose my words carefully. "Our lives are a small sacrifice for the peace of our entire *altepetl*. All of our people will continue to live in peace because we are here. Quetzalcoatl has brought us here, Itza, to protect everybody else. We must honor him, Itza, that he hears our hearts."

"I want to go home, Citlali. When will we go home?"

"Oh, Itza...we'll go home when Quetzalcoatl wishes it."

We lay there, together in the cold darkness and finally fell asleep in our new and still unfathomed condition as slaves.

The Magueys

"Shsst." a voice hissed in the dark. I could see a massive woman standing over me.

"Wake up, lazy slugs!" yelled a woman with her hands on her weighty hips. Her brown, plump legs were covered with a tattered cotton skirt that accentuated her all-over roundness, and two long, black braids rested along her flaccid curves.

"Itza..." I whispered, waking her.

"I'm Tlatona. I'm in charge of you two dirt-groveling *macehualli* and when I tell you what to do, you do it." She pointed a pudgy finger at us. "Don't ever disrespect me. I hate disrespect from children. I have nine, and they all treat me with respect." She looked at Itza. "What do you know how to do?"

"What do you know how to do?" the fat woman repeated when she got nothing but a frightened stare.

Having just woken, Itza stuttered out a reply, "I, uh, grind corn and make *tlaxcalli* she said, referring to the round, flat cakes made of ground corn.

"Well that won't do you any good here. Here we make *pulque*. Our lives are dedicated to it. Besides, we live on boiled beans and raw corn. If you think anyone spends time making *tlaxcalli* for the degenerates that work here you're as stupid as you look."

Itza wasn't offended by the insult, distracted as she was, thinking about the size of the fat woman, and watching her shift her weight as she moved with her enormously long breasts that hung down the front of her over several soft, rolling, folds of fat. The two hanging breasts darkened at the areolas with cacao-bean nipples that pointed straight down to the earth, nipples that had fed her nine suckling babes and many more besides. The men in our world liked big women: sumptuous and fertile. No wonder she'd had so many children.

"And you! One Braid. What do you do? Grind corn and make *tlaxcalli* as well, I imagine."

"I uh..."

"You uh what?"

"I uh..."

"She's a medicine woman." interjected Itza.

"A what?!"

"Yes, right. I'm a medicine woman."

"You! At your age? What a lie. Anyway, if it's true you're completely useless as well," Tlatona curtly responded. "Anyway, it doesn't matter what you do, One Braid. The master's brought you here to breed."

I squeezed Itza's hand, a small comfort in such a frightening situation in this unknown place.

"Follow me," the fat woman ordered.

We quickly followed Tlatona and stood in front of the opening of the thatched hut where we'd slept.

The sun was beginning to rise at the far end of the valley, darkness giving way to an early morning glow. Hues of purple, green jade and rust spread along the horizon.

Maguey cactuses grew in the fields everywhere, with spiked, sage-colored leaves jutting out in all directions from the heart of the succulent plant. To the right of me, more thatched huts filed along the edge of an embankment that eventually lead to a small spring. Farther on the embankment became smaller and smaller, until it flattened out into the immense maguey fields.

In the open area in front of us giant straw mats lay on the ground where the largest maguey leaves had been opened and scraped clean of their slimy pulp. The leaves were then left to dry in the sun, and would later be separated into long, thin threads and woven into fabric. Beyond the drying mats, deerskin bags were hanging from 3-pole frames that were bursting full of *pulque*.

Fermenting the *pulque* in the deerskin bags was a skill passed from father to son. First the skin was removed from a carcass by blowing air into the animal which separated the skin from the muscle. The carcass was then slipped out of the skin and the extremities were tied closed. At this point, the skin was hung on a giant hook that gouged through the neck where the beast had been decapitated. After several days of drying, the inside of the skin bag was treated with wax from local bees. Once cured, the bag was ready to receive the sweet honey water which was left for several days to ferment into valuable, intoxicating *pulque*.

Everywhere thin, bony bodies were already moving to the busy rhythms of the morning's activities, separating threads with nimble fingers, weaving fabric, making baskets, rope, straps, and other household items that long-suffering porters would carry to the privileged class. There was an overwhelming sour smell of unwashed bodies that mingled with the surrounding filth, and the dry smoke of a cooking-fire drifted through the dusty air.

At this plantation the work was centered on the making of *pulque*. In Toltec society rigid rules were imposed for the drinking of *pulque*. The alcoholic beverage was considered by many to be the root of all wickedness. It was known to cause great misery and trouble, like a dark storm, a drunkenness that could lead to adultery, rape, theft, incest, or other serious crimes. The strong inclination toward alcoholism was controlled by severe punishment for offenders. Only the elderly were permitted to indulge, in addition to the priests and nobles, and they drank only a little, and in private, not wanting to become drunk.

If a drunken *macehualli* should show himself in public he could be punished by having his head shaved while everybody sneered and gibed. A second offense, however, would mean death; either by being beaten or strangled. This violent death was, of course, displayed for all to see, an example for all youth to avoid such delinquent behavior. Of course I didn't know any of this about *pulque* and drunkenness that day. The knowledge would be revealed to me later, when I came to learn the ways of being.

Each slave had a specific job, from diggers, who maintained the irrigation canals that came from the river, to porters who carried the final products to the city of Tollan in *petlacalli* baskets, suspended on their backs by a leather strap around the forehead.

Without delay we were put to work separating prickly threads. Tlatona was constantly watching us, threatening us with her stinging switch.

This was how we spent our first few days. We tried hard to avoid Tlatona's threatening switch, which occasionally stung us across our shoulders and backs.

Candied Squash

One night we lay awake, anxious and unable to sleep. "I hate that we don't bathe every day, Citlali. I miss our mornings at the river, and I miss walking around like a fish." Itza whispered. "And it smells bad here. I smell bad and I can hardly stand it." Slaves only bathed once a year, on the god Tezcatlipoca's day sign, in preparation for the grand festival dedicated to this god. We were feeling a deep repugnance toward the onset of filth.

"Well, at least you've talked to some of the others. I never talk to anybody with that big Tlatona always over me," I whispered back. I thought of how I missed Cuauhtli Océlotl. I thought about his bravery and the way his black hair fell down his strong body. I imagined that soon he would come rescue me from this hellish place and take me away. We would be married and have four strong sons that would grow up to become warriors, and two beautiful daughters, and I would be graced with my blessed destiny of motherhood. When I thought about my grandfather, Ollin Ehécatl, and his little, old, wrinkled face, his long, wispy hair blowing in the gentle wind from the one window, an uninvited tear stubbornly floated in my eye.

"Itza!" whispered a voice from outside our hut. We looked around. "Itza, it's me, Ixmitl."

Itza got up from her mat and went over to the side of the hut. Through the spaces between the slats she could see two friends that she'd met at the giant drying mats.

Oh, fine, I thought. Now on top of everything else, we were going to get into trouble.

"What are you doing here?" Itza whispered back.

"Come on out, Itza. We want to show you something fun." The two boys were squirming, trying not to giggle.

"What about the guards?" she wanted to know.

"All is well, Itza. They're busy." One of the boys quietly laughed.

Itza looked at me.

"What about the guards?" I said surprised, "What about the Night Creature!"

"Oh, come on, Citlali. Let's go."

"Itza, you know it displeases the gods to be disobedient..."

"We'll sneak. They'll never hear us. Oh, please, Citlali..."

"You go. I'm staying here."

I fell asleep with my jadestone around my waist, and dreamt about my beloved home. Only later did I learn about the adventure that my little friend had had.

Once outside, Itza met her two friends, Ixmitl and the handsome Pixahua.

"You have to be really, really quiet, Itza." said Pixahua.

"All right."

The night air was warm and the half sleeping moon gently illuminated the desert, casting the darkest of shadows around them. They crept along between the slave lodgings and the embankment, toward the west end, checking for guards each time they passed from one hut to the next. There was a larger hut at the end of the row made of wood slats, sounder than the rest. A flame was burning from inside, giving off a soft glow. From where they were crouching, the three mischievous children could see several of the guards in front, freely drinking *pulque*, laughing, and carrying on.

A young guard came out, looking as though he had just won a fight, sweating and smiling. He adjusted his loincloth under his protruding belly.

"Give me that." he said drunkenly to one of the others, grabbing the gourd full of *pulque*. He slapped the other on the back and shoved something into his mouth.

"What do they have?" whispered Itza, thrilled with the excitement of their adventure. The three youths were hiding behind the nearest thatched hut.

"Sssshhhh...It's food. Mostly *tamallis*, but also candied squash." answered Ixmitl.

Pixahua, being the older of the two boys, then ran behind the largest hut. He beckoned for the others to come. Having safely made it to the other side, the children crouched down around a small opening where they could plainly see what all the commotion was about. That was when Itza learned what some women would do for candied squash. The horrifying Tlatona, who was always terrorizing her and Citlali, was now on all fours, as the drunk, sweaty guards shared her vessel, driving themselves into the fleshy *cihuanacayo* that had them excited to the point of delirium. "Oh Mother Nature!" the one mounting her cried. "Fertility and Womanhood! I am your slave!"

"She takes the *tamallis* and candied squash to her children," said Pixahua. "Come on," he gestured, "This way."

They snuck back the way they had come, passing carefully from one hut to the next, cautious not to wake anyone. Once they had reached a safe distance, Itza realized that there were no guards around. They had all gone to partake of the great, massive Tlatona.

Pixahua walked out past the giant drying mats, the others following along. They reached the furthest side, where the *pulque* was fermenting inside hanging deerskin bags. Now a far distance from the slave huts, they could talk comfortably and move around. Pixahua took Itza by the hand and started dancing around her, and beneath the star filled sky he began chanting the ritual song of dreams;

> *Soon we will wake,*
> *We have only come here to dream.*
> *No one knows why*
> *We have come to live in this land.*
> *Our very being*
> *Is like a flower in the spring.*
> *Our heart gives birth*
> *To the flowers of our soul.*
> *Some of them open, some of them no.*
> *Some dry and die.*
> *And meanwhile we dream...*

Pixhua let go of Itza, for by this time Ixmitl had begun to dip into the fermenting *pulque*. The moon was now low in the night sky, and there the three friends sat and drank *pulque*, laughing and telling gossipy stories unto the wee hours of the morning.

[73]

The Axcaitl

Cozcacuautli Miquiztli lay stretched out among his exotic animal skins, fully enjoying the comfort of his terrace in the mid-morning air. Idleness was greatly frowned upon, but in the seclusion of his ranch home *axcaitl* he could freely partake in life's finest pleasures without the worry of some busy body priest spying on him. He sipped his fruit flavored *pulque*.

He had spent the previous day well. On an outing with a small hunting party looking for *tlaquatzin* opossums, he'd come upon a young buck, and had spent almost the entire morning chasing it. His personal servants had been there to help him, but they'd fallen behind and he alone had defeated the wild beast. No matter that he had not properly cleansed himself to hunt deer, he went ahead and gave the proper incantation at the kill. "*Ea, come to my aid, Spirits, Masters of the Earth, help me Four Winds.*" Although it had been incomplete, he decided it was sufficient enough to please the gods. Considering that hunting was generally a three day affair, this was a highly unusual kill. He lay there, gloating in his own noble and physical superiority.

The truth was, however, that Miquiztli wasn't all that he thought he was. His noble rank was relatively low, his grandfather having earned their noble title through an act of strength and bravery in an ancient battle in some long-forgotten war. Since that time, long ago, his father had managed to settle himself among the nobility, acquiring lands and a fine residence near the city center. Their mansion of a home, as exquisite as it was, however, was among the lesser of the noble houses, having only four pyramidal stairs, while the grander houses were raised much higher. The *axcaitl* country house was, by noble standards, modest as well. It was raised up on only two platforms, and while it had abundant rooms with thick, stone walls around a central patio, the roof throughout was thatched with reed and palm instead of the crossbeam and woven slats so common in the wealthier homes. Being an *axcaitl*, that is, a plantation estate, the house was sparsely decorated, with mostly bare necessities; an occasional table stone, *petlatl* mats that were strewn about, woven baskets full of dried fruits, nuts and seeds scattered around the floor, smatterings of earthenware and the like. The floor, being made of rock hard earth pressed solid with animal blood, was lavishly strewn with the skins of spotted deer. The softer pelts were reserved for bedding. The only chair in the place was reserved for the noble's receiving room, and used for more formal occasions. Out on the terrace reclining on luxurious animal skins, Miquitzli lay and relished in self thought with over abundant arrogance and pride.

"Lord Miquiztli." said Pochotl, coming out to the stone terrace.

"Ah, Councilor. How is your day?" Miquiztli raised his earthen drinking cup.

"My Lord, I am pleased to announce that today's meal will be fresh venison with a sweet-hot purée of pineapple brought from the hot lands." Pochotl smiled and patted his big belly.

"That sounds fine. Very fine. Sit Councilor. Here with me. I'll have the house boy bring you some *pulque*."

Even though drinking *pulque* was prohibited, and drunkenness punished by death, the attitude that laws are made to be broken transcends all time, and what a man does in the privacy in his own home is only for him and the gods to see: and so they indulged.

"Thank you, My Lord. You are so kind."

The mid-day sun, Tonatiuh, was directly above, and the two men were fanned with woven palm leaf fans that had been brought from the hot lands very far away.

"Tell me, Councilor, how goes the production of the *axcaitl*? Are things in order?"

"Yes, My Lord. I am told that the harvest is very productive this season." The two men discussed the details of the maguey production, and how all was to be distributed: cloth, baskets, gourds and other goods, as well as the savory *pulque*.

"And the slaves, My Lord..."

"Oh yes, the slaves." said Miquiztli, remembering his lovely river goddess.

"I am told that all is well, My Lord. No disturbance has been reported."

"Good." said Miquiztli, sipping more *pulque*. "That's good."

There was a long pause, and time seemed to stand still.

A cool breeze brushed over the terrace and a flight of tiny birds flew across the wispy, white clouds.

"Bring her to me when it is time."

"As you wish My Lord."

Music Walker

In our world time was not linear. There was no time before time, nor was there an infinitude of time to come. We saw time as a cycle where each point was both a beginning and an end. So the way we perceived time was through the present moment. This was the true essence of time, both its true beginning and its true end. As the cycle turned we watched how its movement created change.

The squash was now giant and orange amidst the late autumn leaves. The dry season would soon be upon the land. It was a time when many slaves fell ill. The cruelty of the guards worsened as the same amount of work was expected and forced. Itza had come to withstand the torturous place, working next to the fair Pixahua. As her name suggested, it was as though she were living in a dream, immune to all the misery around her. I passed my days telling myself oral histories, over and over. This was my desperate attempt to withstand the deplorable conditions.

Yé huécauh... I began one afternoon in my private language. It was one of my grandfather's favorite tales. *Once upon a time...long, long ago, before man lived in this valley, everything here was paradise. All the plants and animals lived happily together.*

I looked around at everything.

In those ancient times there lived a beautiful ocelotl who had golden fur, the color of the sun, and he had not even a single spot...

I especially loved the story of how the jaguar got its spots.

The day was so hot and dry I could hear the sound of the sun.

Suddenly there was a great commotion among the workers of the *axcaitl*. Chattering broke out like a swarm of cicada bugs.

"He simply fell down and died."

"How could he die just like that without the proper blessings?"

"First he turned into an eagle, and he flew above himself and looked at himself. Then he died."

The chatter was now growing into various versions of how he had died.

The slaves began to gather around the drying mats. Curious, I joined them. As usual, Itza was in the middle of the busy bodies, as engaged as anybody in her own version.

"Who died?" I asked an elderly man next to me.

"Why child, don't you know? The Knower." he said, his weak, old voice shaking.

I immediately thought of my grandfather, Ollin Ehécatl.

"Which Knower?" I poked his shoulder insistently.

"The Knower Music Walker." On hearing his words, I sighed a breath of awe. All the people were now gathered around.

The guards tried to put us all back in order.

"Back to work, vermin. Now!" They indiscriminately swatted their short leather whips at people's shoulders, arms and faces.

The crowd began to disperse.

The seriousness of his death was not taken lightly. The overseer had even come down from his hut atop the hill and was conversing with a few of the guards and several of the elder workers. I could hear them stating their different opinions. I eased over toward Itza to catch what they were saying.

"This will delay the production. If we don't produce, the evil master will beat us with stones!"

"We can't let the magueys flower! We must cut the hearts out before they flower! How is this to be done without the proper incantation to the gods?"

More elders raised their opinions. "If the hearts aren't cut out before they flower the plants will be wasted. It can be done without the incantation. The gods will understand."

"Hush you! How dare you attempt to perceive the nature of the gods! There must be an incantation!"

"Settle down, now, everybody," said a voice with authority. It was the overseer. "What we need to do is sit in council before we make any kind of announcement to the lord Master." He beckoned a few men toward a small hut where the body of Music Walker supposedly lay.

"Back to work! All *macehualli* and slaves back to work!" He yelled as he turned away.

"Citlali, what's..." started Itza, but in all the commotion, the guards were pushing and shoving us back toward our routine tasks.

One of them grabbed Itza and harshly threw her to the ground in front of her maguey threads. I looked up and by the embankment I saw a small, naked body heading toward the same hut that the Important Ones had just entered. Not wanting the toddler to accidentally enter behind them and thus risk an abusive shove or even a blow, I impulsively headed off after the tot. I neared the row of little thatched buildings and bent over to scoop the babe up. The child struggled as I picked it up, and as I fought to settle the wriggling lad on my hip, the rabbit skin pouch that I kept around my waist broke. The vibrant green jadestone was thrown to the ground. To make matters worse, before I could put the child down and retrieve the stone, it rolled into Music Walker's hut, the same hut in which the Important Ones had just entered!

Without thinking I loosed the lad and went in after my stone. Immediately the men looked up with stern faces, surprised that a woman should enter and spoil the sacredness and strength of their all-male affair. When they saw me standing in the doorway they were completely taken aback. Their mouths hung open, saying nothing.

"I've come in for the stone." It lay on the dirt floor in front of me.

"Oh, yes." One of them said with more breath than voice in his words.

In the middle of the small room I saw the lifeless body of Music Walker lying on a woven reed mat, blanketed in many colored flowers. His hands were closed around a turtle shell rattle that had been carefully placed upon his chest. The overseer, two elder workers, and several of the older guards were seated on mats in a circle around him. Rays of sunshine passed through the doorway where I was standing, casting my silhouette onto the cadaver. The ancient Music Walker's face, dusted with white lime, looked like dried white clay.

"I'll just take the stone and, uh..." I stuttered, but I was interrupted by a gurgling noise that came from the throat of the cadaver. Everybody looked in astonishment at the dead body lying there.

"Khkhkhh..." The noise became more noticeable.

"Music Walker lives!" Someone half whispered.

[81]

"No, he is cold and dead. His soul lingers before its journey to Mictlán," the oldest of the men whispered.

The sound of air was now coming out of the cadaver's throat.

All of a sudden the cadaver jolted up, casting flowers everywhere. It looked straight at me with its dead eyes open wide.

"The woman child must do it..." we heard it say.

It flopped back down like a rag doll, its once harmonious composure now twisted and crooked. Its mouth hung open and its wide-open eyes stared out into the rays of sun. I fell to my knees, astonished.

It was as though time froze. Everyone looked at the dead Music Walker.

Then slowly, I reached forward and took one of the brightly colored zinnias in my hand. The others followed, picking up the scattered flowers. Between us, we reverently arranged Music Walker's body once again.

Emboldened by the dead man's words, I said, "I too, am a Knower. I am granddaughter of Ollin Ehécatl." I was careful not to explain about the jadestone. Telling of magic diminishes its strength. I slowly picked it up and discreetly guarded it in the pouch and secured it around my waist.

It came to pass that I was asked to give the incantation of the giant magueys so that production could continue. I was qualified, they reasoned, by way of my training, but secrecy would have to be maintained because of my being a woman. Women did not partake in such occupations, but an exception could be made considering the grave circumstances. The elders would then search throughout the lands to summon another Knower. After they found a new Knower, they said, only then would they figure out how to inform the lord Master of the transition.

Cutting Out the Hearts

Early the next morning the overseer came to me accompanied by the two elder workers and several guards. Despite the early hours, I'd been grinding maize for some time.

"Keep your voice low," one of the guards said, as he pulled me up by the arm. The grinding stone I'd been using fell to the ground with a thud. They whisked me away so quickly I didn't see the frightened faces of the other women who were grinding corn.

Foreboding washed over me. Surely this was it. I was to be taken directly to Lord Miquiztli.

Instead, the men forced me out to the fields, pushing and shoving me along the way. The earth was dry and crisp. The morning air brushed my face.

We headed toward the section of five-year-old cactuses. The giant plants were ready to sprout their one long, yellow flower. If allowed to bloom, they would jut up toward the heavens and laugh with the gods. The *pulque* would be ruined.

In order to extract the juice for the *pulque* it is necessary to cut out the heart of the plant before it begins to bloom. Offering a prayer to the Sacred Spirit of the maguey appeases the gods, excites their fertility, and ensures more crops to come.

The process of making pulque starts with collecting the sweet water from the cactus. The center stems are pulled out and the heart of the plant is removed. Then a well is carved out in the middle. Daily, the sides of this well are scraped, farther and farther down the root. Each morning the bleeding honey water that forms inside the well is sucked out with a long, slender reed. The sweet juice that is extracted is then released from the giant straw into hollowed-out gourds, taken back to the work camp and transferred to deerskin bags. At this point the cactus juice, often called sweet water, begins the process of fermentation.

"Those cactuses there," said the overseer. He waved his whole arm to point. "They are ready to castrate."

The overseer had been in charge of the cactuses since anyone could remember. He was a stout, middle-aged man, who had contracted himself into slavery as a youth because of an accumulated debt that his widowed mother hadn't been able to pay. He'd worked among the maguey since that time, and because of his extensive knowledge of making *pulque*, he enjoyed special status and privileges among the workers and slaves at the *axcaitl*.

We walked up to the magueys.

"You there, Young Woman Knower, come." I felt a guard's hands on my shoulders, shoving me close to the first plant at the end of a very long row.

"Say something," ordered the overseer. He took an obsidian knife out of its sheath. It was chiseled to a fine, sharp edge, dark black and highly polished, and hook-shaped at one end.

I lowered myself to my knees and tried to recall the words that Ollin Ehécatl had once taught me. I knelt there in silence for a brief moment. Then, when the words came to me, I raised my arms to the pink and lavender heavens of the dawning sky. With all my spiritual strength I invoked the higher power, and began.

"*Ea, come hither, Spirit, whose happiness and good fortune lie within the sacred water.*" The obsidian knife was pushed into my hand. "*Now is the time that you enter the water of the maguey. Oh Woman of Order, whose spirit is the good fortune of rain, change your course and enter the heart of the maguey!*"

On saying this, I stabbed the knife down into the center of the maguey, and jabbed at the base of the giant leaves. One of the men took over and carved out the heart of the great plant. Then he passed the knife to the overseer who scraped the bleeding well of the freshly cut center. I raised my hands to the heavens and continued the prayer.

"*Ea, now is the time. Serve your purpose, O, Obsidian Knife. Scrape and cleanse your work inside the seed of the heart of the Woman of Order, so that later she may cry in melancholy and release a river of tears.*"

The eldest man inserted a long, hollow reed into the sweet water that formed in the freshly cut well, and sucked the juice up, extracting the precious liquid.

I yelled out with all my might and finished the prayer, *"Oh Sacred Spirit, whose good fortune resides in water, we have come to take out and raise the Esteemed Woman!"*

It was in this manner that I continued to give the daily prayers for the cutting of the first maguey, along with the overseer and his men. For several days I continued, blessing the cactuses early in the morning, and then returning to the work camp to spend my days painfully separating maguey threads in the scorching, hot sun and ending out my evenings by grinding corn.

I offered the prayers for the maguey for many days. In time the moon traveled across the night sky.

Then one evening my blood came down.

The secret had been easy to keep from my father, but I knew that I could not give the incantation when my body was in this sacred state. Blood, being the sacred fluid of life, was the holiest of holies. I lay awake waiting for Itza to sneak back from her nightly adventure with her two mischievous friends.

She finally snuck in, slightly inebriated. "Oh Citlali! I love Pixahua!"

"Itza, you'd better be careful. One of these days you're going to anger the gods, and they'll cast their wrath upon you. I worry about you. I really do."

"He's so gentle and kind. He kissed me tonight, Citlali. He did! His lips were soft and warm. When we came back he told me he's not going to let Ixmitl come anymore..."

I interrupted her exalted joy. "Itza, I have something I must tell you." My seriousness was all too evident. "They're going to find out that I bleed Itza."

"That's impossible. If you kept the secret from your father, you can keep it from anybody."

"No, I won't be able to keep it a secret, Itza. You see, I mustn't give the incantation during my sacred days. They're going to want to know why I refuse and I will tell them. I know that this is what Lord Miquiztli is waiting for, Itza. He thinks I'm still a girl child."

"He'll take you as soon as he finds out, won't he?" Itza suddenly looked as though she were about to cry.

"I am grateful the gods put you in my life, Itza. You must be strong and obedient, child. More than anything else, stay chaste

[85]

and honor the gods." I took my little friend's hand and held it to my cheek.

Itza looked at me with adoring eyes.

A Humble Visitor

Lord Miquiztli spent his days between practicing his military exercises and lounging around. First he engaged in throwing his long spear, sprinting at top speed, and swinging his great obsidian battle sword. Then he feasted on a variety of delectable stews that his cooks had created with his prize venison. He took advantage of his time at the *axcaitl* by surveying the lands and verifying that all his villages were continuing to pay their annual tribute. It was an extensive chore that the imperious Miquiztli took much pleasure in. At times he found himself needing to personally attend to some village *altepetl* or another, in which case he would have to use his special talents of persuasion to exact his rightly due taxes. Sometimes he only need arrive, and his mere presence would be enough to encourage payment or production. Other times, however, he was forced, by the sheer defiance of the Dirt People, to run havoc on their village, ransacking the place with his guards in order to teach them a lesson. These were the occasions that he enjoyed the most, actually, because he could justify the taking of new slaves to sell at the market in Tollan. He was, however, careful not to take too many as slaves. It could end up being counterproductive if the peasants lacked their strongest workers. If their production went down, so did his. Besides, he was cautious not to create too much of a scandal, that it might upset the royal palace. Miquiztli knew his limits within the law.

As a noble lord it was his lawful right to collect taxes from the several *altépetls* under his charge. However, he also had the unwritten responsibility to care for their people, mainly the chiefs and leaders, especially when production was in some way threatened. It was to this effect that one day he received an unexpected visitor.

At mid-morning Miquiztli was blissfully sitting in a large, stone bath, the water having been heated underneath with red-hot stones, and sweetened with the finest herbs and blossoms.

"Lord Miquiztli." barreled a man's voice. It was his round bellied councilor, urgently entering the room.

"Oh, fat man, really!"

"Please, noble lord. Excuse my vulgar interruption. There's a man who has arrived to the *axcaitl*. He claims to come from one of the *altepetl* villages under your domain, noble lord. He's accompanied by many others. They are clustered around outside. He says it's urgent that he speak with you."

"Errh!" grumbled Miquiztli, rising from his bath. Duty was, after all, the first priority. He threw on a white cotton tunic and belted it at the waist. His wet hair hung straight to his shoulders.

Outside the *axcaitl* a man waited, skin and bones, dressed only in a folded loincloth that was drawn up between his legs. With him were twenty or so people of his village. Word had spread that the notorious lord was currently residing at his country home, so these few *macehualli* peasants had taken advantage to come speak with him. For some time they waited, tired from walking the long distance, and hungry from the scarcity of rations they had afforded to bring. Finally the great Lord Miquiztli sent word to receive them.

The humble man was directed into the massive stone mansion, accompanied by only two companions. They followed a manservant through the courtyard and on into a great room where the noble awaited them. He was sitting cross-legged on a low wickerwork chair with no legs, with a high back that rose slightly above his head. Beneath him was an embroidered cotton rug, with images of jaguars, eagles, and other wild beasts. He tapped his fingers impatiently at the intrusion.

The three men reverently dropped before him, heads lowered, waiting for the noble to speak first, and thus give them permission to continue.

"What, what, what? What is it? Hurry up, now."

"Oh great and noble lord," said the humble man, using the formal speech required to address a noble, for there were several degrees of formality in our language, Nahuatl. "I come to beg thy mercy on our poor and humble *altépetl*. Our people are starving, great lord. Our corn has been infested with the *azcatl* ant, and as our shaman has been unable to control the plague; thy people hunger for lack of food." He reverently knelt with downcast eyes.

[88]

"So?"

The humble man looked at his two comrades and then back toward the noble's feet, still with downcast eyes. "I beg thee, great and merciful Lord Miquiztli, to save us from our starvation and misery."

"And?" Miquiztli did so enjoy watching peasants grovel in their abasement. He popped a candied grasshopper into his mouth and crunched it.

"We beg thee, great lord, to allow us to pay half our annual tribute this season, so that our children, thy children, who are now dying of hunger, may live." Even though the humble man had prepared his request time and time again, he now had tears in his eyes.

"Well..." Miquiztli said, dragging out the episode, "if I do this highly generous thing for your people, what can you offer me in return?"

"I can only offer you," the man said, with a lump in his throat, "my two most precious daughters. They are weavers, My Lord. They will work hard for you."

Miquiztli thought for a moment - two new slaves for the price of half a season's harvest. The harvest would be more valuable, true, but he could use new weavers. He would only be giving up half his tribute from this one village. He would still have plenty of tribute from other villages, more than sufficient to pay his share to the palace priests in Tollan. By trading half this harvest for the two daughters he would be acquiring the slaves at a fraction of their market value. While he often enjoyed stealing slaves, he couldn't always do so. It was a good trade.

"Well now, man. Don't grovel further. You know that your lord genuinely cares for the welfare of your village. So that your people no longer suffer in starvation and misery, of course I will concede to your humble request." He gloated in his own generosity. "And where shall we find these two maidens?"

"They await thee at the road with the others of my village, kindest of lords."

Miquiztli, who usually didn't participate in mundane activities like receiving new slaves, was spurred on by curiosity, and perhaps boredom, and thus, went outside where his counselor and a group

[89]

of guards were waiting. The humble man and his two companions followed behind the swiftly striding noble. They reached the intimidated villagers who were gathered together near a cluster of mesquite trees, shaded from the hot sun, waiting for his response. The skin and bones man went back among his fellow peasants and brought forth two recently bathed young girls.

"Take them, My Lord. They are good workers. They will serve you well." He steered the girls toward the noble and his men.

The two girls stood there, smiling, proud to be considered good workers, and excited to become part of a noble household, even if it was only as slaves.

"Welcome to my household." said Miquiztli, but upon seeing the beauty of their youth and because he was an impulsive man, he had a sudden change of heart. He pushed the weavers toward the group of guards. "Take them, Pochotl. They're yours. You serve me well. I give them to you to do with as you wish. Share them with the guards if you like."

The words stung the humble man with a horror that he'd never imagined. Pochotl beamed in delight and pulled one of the girls toward him, groping and sniffing at her.

"No!" yelled the humble man. "That's not what they're for!" He grabbed the other daughter and pulled her close to him. "They're my daughters! They're weavers! They deserve a respectable marriage!"

"How dare you insult me, you vermin, lowly, filthy dirt person!" Miquiztli's face turned red, his jaw pulsed in and out, and his hands began to tremble. He grabbed the second girl and shoved her at Pochotl. A commotion arose through the crowd of peasants.

"Please, Lord Miquiztli! They're my daughters! They're weavers!"

No one talked back to Lord Miquiztli.

"They are whatever I say they are! You bastard, son of a twisted wretch! I say they are little, round, wet holes for the satisfaction of my men!" Raging out of control, he drew out the obsidian dagger from under his sash and with one, violent sweep, hacked off the man's ear. "There! You see?" He said, holding up the ear for everyone to see. "This ear says that they are whores!" He flung the humble man's severed ear as far as he could, droplets of blood spraying off it as it spun through the air.

The humble man screamed in pain and horror, holding his hand to his blood-gushing wound.

"Leave! Go away! All of you!"

His explosive words ignited the crowd that had been frozen with fright. At once they ran off, carrying the wounded man along.

"Half the season's crops! It's a mighty fine deal!" Miquiztli yelled after them. "Ha! Ha, ha. Ha, ha!"

He turned and walked away, leaving the two most precious daughters amidst the groping men who were now smiling and grabbing their loins.

Such was the man I was soon to encounter.

Terrace of Stone

Several days passed and Miquiztli forgot about the ear episode. He came to live in a state of indifference toward his financial affairs, focusing more on his own immediate pleasures. He had a stone-cutter come from Tollan to carve an image on a slab of stone. The image was to pay homage to Tezcatlipoca, the Smoking Mirror, god of the Here and Now. Miquiztli was so self-absorbed that he was oblivious to the things going on around him, having no idea, for example, that a woman was giving the sacred incantation for his *pulque*-producing magueys, nor that his evil reputation was spreading throughout the valley inflamed by his recent act of brutality. He fantasized about his lovely river goddess, obsessed with an assurance that he could make even the most beautiful of women love him.

Early one morning, he woke to the sound of wild birds. An entire flock had filled all the trees and bushes surrounding the *axcaitl* and they were squeaking and squawking about this, that, and the other thing. Walking out onto the raised, stone terrace he looked out at the vast properties of his *axcaitl*. He took a moment to admire the color of the vibrant, orange squash blossoms - perfect morning to take his meal on the terrace outside. He called for a concubine to come sit with him while he breakfasted on a variety of delicacies; toasted *tlaxcalli* flat bread, sweetened *tamallis*, prickly pear fruit, and sweetened coconut milk that he'd finagled out of an old merchant in route to Tollan. He looked out into the distance, admiring this tranquility, only to see a tiny cloud of dust stirring up in the horizon. There would be visitors, Miquiztli thought to himself, but he never imagined who they might be.

"*Ma moyolicatzin Nohueltiuh*!" said a dashing young noble arriving to the *axcaitl* with nothing more than a small army behind him. "Greetings, older brother!" The young man had left his band of soldiers some distance behind, where they'd made an encampment, and he approached the terrace of the big house with only one companion. Miquiztli was waiting for him.

"Ah, young Nauhyotl. How good of you to come," Miquiztli lied. Having shrewdly sent the concubine out of sight, he was now sitting alone. "Please, bring your priest. Join me." He beckoned the men forward.

"I present to you my priest, Quetzalpopoca Smoking Feather, with whom I have the pleasure to be travelling."

Miquiztli noticed that the young priest had a stern face with chiseled features and an aquiline nose. It was a face of stone.

Nauhyotl looked around at the large, structure of a house as if inspecting it for flaws. He scrutinized the wide, stone walls, the recently added carvings around the bottom of the facade, and the thatched roof which would soon be in need of repair. He ascended the two stair terrace.

Nauhyotl comfortably sprawled out on the luxurious animal skins, but the priest sat at the far end of the stone terrace, folding his legs properly under him.

"*Nohueltiuh*, I come at the bidding of our father. He sends his best regards for your welfare." Nauhyotl said. He wasn't about to reveal the true nature of his visit, that he had really come to spy on his older brother's behavior. Rumors had been spreading through the military ranks about the Vulture's lack of discipline, but Nauhyotl made no mention of it. He was a shrewd man and formalities must always be respected. Like his father, he was a fine soldier, brave and just, with a special sensitivity for diplomacy.

The two brothers passed a good, long while talking about family matters, production of the land holdings, the latest news and goings-on in the royal palace, each man pretending to have a genuine interest in the other, and guessing the truthfulness of the other's words.

The sun reached the mid-way line in the blue sky.

"Word of mouth has reached our father that you cut off a man's ear." Nauhyotl finally said.

"Rubbish." said Miquiztli.

"That's what I thought." The younger replied, but in his mind he finished the sentence, "...*you'd say*."

[94]

Miquiztli looked at the young priest. "Acts of brutality have no place here."

The youthful priest sat stern and motionless. He wore a thick, black, full-length tunic, and his long, unkempt hair was matted with chicken blood, a practice which showed his dedication to discipline. Withstanding the hot, itchy mess of his hair and the stench that is produced was a small sacrifice that enabled a priest to adorn that most sacred and fertile of life's fluids; blood. Miquiztli wondered how it was possible that a man could sit motionless for so long and make no expression on his face.

Just then Pochotl came out to the terrace, approaching the men with all the proper salutations, and leaned over to whisper something in Miquiztli's ear.

The Vulture beamed in triumphant bliss and the seed in his heart began to bloom. "Have all the preparations made." He quietly said. His councilor turned and left.

"Well, now, young brother, it's so good of you to come. The west side is unoccupied." Miquiztli gestured toward some rooms beyond. "I'm sure you'll find everything you need there," He said, getting up. He then graciously excused himself. He would now have to be on his best behavior, with a priest around.

He went inside the *axcaitl* and barked at his servants to clean and polish the effigies of Ometecuhtli and Omecíhuatl, the first man and the first woman, and other idols in the *axcaitl* that suffocated under a blanket of dust.

That night, the evening sky turned from crimson to purple, to blue, and eventually to black. Miquiztli lay alone on his luxurious platform bed mat. What wonderful news Pochotl had whispered in his ear. The arrival of his lovely river goddess! Thinking about the first time he had seen her, he smiled. He relished in the thought planting his seed into this exquisite creature.

Smoking Feather Sees

When the sky eventually turned black, the heavens filled with an array of elegant Lady Stars. The gentle moon shone brightly upon the land. He had done everything he was supposed to do. He had solemnly blessed the fields. He had summoned the gods to bless the harvests and the residents of the *axcaitl*. He had cleansed and blessed the small temple shrine that housed the stone engraving of Quetzalcoatl. Then he carefully smeared fresh turkey blood across the tops of the doorways. Now he sat before a small fire behind the big house near a wikiup-style hut that was serving as his temporary shelter. The next day he would go to the slave camp to initiate a young Knower. Quetzalpopoca Smoking Feather was tired. He decided to sit and meditate.

The fire crackled.

How many times had he wondered what the fire and the sky were talking about?

Smoking Feather lit a long, clay pipe that he'd filled with the magic weed. He gently puffed, inhaled the smoke, and held it for as long as he could in order to receive the strongest effect. Upon exhaling, he felt lighter, and the world around him began to glow. He reached into the deerskin medicine pouch around his waist and took out his secret things. Were they powerful in and of themselves, or did they hold their power because of what they reminded him of? He thought about that and about other things. He continued puffing on the magic weed.

As he sat in meditation, Smoking Feather thought he heard a noise on the other side of the fire, but he couldn't see, blinded by the bright light it caused. Sparks shot off the flames in an up-side-down cascade toward the starry sky. Then, there it was again, a scratching sound, like a stick being scraped against the dry dirt. He set his pipe down, thinking he would refill it after seeing what all the noise was about, but just then a giant copperhead snake, as tall as he was, came slithering toward him from behind the brilliant flames. It coiled there next to the fire in front of him, swaying its massive head to and fro. He watched the magnificent creature, wondering if it was a god, an image of a god, or just a lowly instrument being used by a god. He crossed his hands upon his folded legs and waited. Smoking Feather was wise to be a patient man. His face remained expressionless, as if made of stone.

The snake jerked its head back and forth as though it were going to expel deadly saliva from its mouth. It opened its mouth wide, not to spit out poisonous venom however, but to release something extraordinarily different. The light flickered from the jumping flames of the fire, casting dancing shadows all around. Smoking Feather sat there and watched the snake open its mouth so wide that it appeared to come unbolted at the jaw. As though it were giving birth, it pushed and relaxed, pushed and relaxed. Then, a smooth, white object came protruding out of the snake's open mouth. The massive, white object fell to the ground with a gentle roll. There it lay, just in front of the stone faced priest. First it began to quiver, then crack, and finally it split apart, and up, from out of it there arose an indescribable vision for only Smoking Feather to see. He sat, with tears in his eyes, his heart filled with emotion and watched and experienced the inconceivable revelation of things to come. The screaming, howling images came pouring out of the giant egg, and swirled up toward the sky, where they meshed with the black smoke of the fire and disappeared into the night. Quetzalpopoca Smoking Feather then knew what he had to do.

Xochicalco

After the young prince Ce Acatl Topiltzin took out his sacred conch and blew upon it, calling all the animals of the wild, he escaped his enemies and survived. The loyalties of the tribes were severed, and bloody fighting among the people followed. In an effort to protect his life, Topiltzin was secretly taken to the palaces of Xochicalco, the sacred place of flowers and terraces of white stone.

At Xochicalco, massive sculptured walls fortified the city. To reach the restricted entrances, residents had to climb their way up narrow stairways and pass through stone porticos that limited access to two or three people at a time.

Legend tells that upon his entrance to the Kingdom of Xochicalco, Ce Acatl was confronted by a giant, four-headed snake that was being nurtured by the temple priests. Each head of the snake put before him a question. If he should answer correctly he would be allowed to enter the kingdom. If not, he would be destroyed by the Queen of Ignorance, who would tear him apart limb by limb, let the buzzards peck out his eyeballs, and feed his bones to the dogs.

The snake writhed high above him, her opalescent scales glistening with fiery intelligence. Her four heads lunged to and fro. Their forked tongues slithered in and out of their mouths, savoring the scent of the boy prince. The first head lowered itself just in front of the boy and whispered,

"Young one, I am the Queen of the Earth. All that you have, all that you do, all that you are, you owe to me. It is a gift I bestow upon you. Show me your gratitude and build me a temple. The roof shall reach to the heavens. Arrange the façade in a straight line. Consecrate the temple with a tortoise shell rattle in my name."

To this the boy answered, "What more holy temple can I consecrate to you than that of my own body? Oh holy Queen of the Earth, I walk in a straight line through time. My rattle is mine own

[99]

breath, housed within this sacred shell, which makes me at home in your temple no matter where I am."

The Queen of the Earth hissed and was satisfied. Then the next giant head lowered right in front of him.

"Young one, I am the Queen of Water. Go down to the caves at the edge of the valley, deep within the crevices, and there you will find a well. Bring me the golden sphere from the bottom of the well."

To this Ce Acatl Topiltzin answered, "The well that you speak of is the depth of my own consciousness, and the golden sphere is my in-dwelling heart. If you want it, you will have to eat me."

The Queen of Water hissed and was satisfied. Then the snake's third, giant head lowered right in front of him.

"Child, I am the Queen of the Sacred Winds. Bring me the heart of heaven beset upon an eagle feather."

"Oh my Queen of the Sacred Winds," the boy answered, "I did bring it. It is looking at you from within me and from without me, from all that abounds. Look among the trees, look among the animals, look among the rocks and you shall find the heart of heaven there. It is everywhere and in all that is."

Then the Queen of the Sacred Winds hissed and was satisfied.

Finally, the last of the giant heads lowered right in front of him, her forked tongue flickering to and fro.

"Child," she whispered, "I am the Queen of Fire. Bring me an eagle upon a *nopalli* cactus, while it is devouring a serpent." She cackled with laughter, "Ha! Ha-ha-ha-ha-ha!" because she knew hers was the greatest challenge of all.

"Oh fair mother, Queen of Fire," the boy replied, "I have here before you what you request. The *nopalli* cactus is the foundation of my soul. The eagle is my own illumination which devours the serpent, my own ignorance."

Then the Queen of Fire hissed and was satisfied.

In this way, the young prince Ce Acatl Topiltzin outsmarted the Queen of Ignorance at the gates of the Kingdom, freeing the entrance for himself and those who would follow.

Within the city walls there was an acropolis, a myriad of temples, and palaces, where the nobles lived in stone halls surrounding central courtyards. Ce Acatl lived his formidable years here, protected by the region's ruling family. He lived among the noble class, near the Pyramid of Stars, an elegant palace with its own temple where he enjoyed great panoramic views of distant purple mountains and the crimson setting sun.

In the central plaza of the city merchants from faraway lands traded exotic wares creating a plethora of different cultures. Foreign languages flew through the air. Anything could be found: shells from the ethereal waters, the dead and dried bodies of unknown sea creatures, musical instruments, slaves, colorful fabrics, earthen wares and basketry for the home. But foremost, Xochicalco was the leading spiritual center of our One World. Astrologer priests from all over the One World met here every 52 years to perform the New Fire Ceremony and facilitate the turning of time. They met secretly in an eerie, dank and deep cave, a cylindrical room through which a single beam of sunlight fell. It was here that they ushered out the end of days every 52 years, and prepared the way for the new.

The rulers of Xochicalco acknowledged Ce Acatl Topiltzin as the Prince of Mixcoatl, and he was given every opportunity to learn. He studied with priests and healers of the city as he grew into manhood. At night astrologers took him to the observatory and taught him the secrets of the sky. It was here that Ce Acatl had his great spiritual awakening.

One night while meditating at the observatory, he sat in silence to commune with the stars. He called upon the Great Spirit, that which gives light to all things. It filled up his entire being, radiating through his body as ethereal light. He touched the Great Spirit deep within himself and experienced the secret knowledge of the Heavens and the Stars. He was overtaken with joy, and an aura of light poured forth from his body from that day on. The people saw him differently in his new body of light. He radiated white light, and his eyes, filled with compassion, turned so black they appeared blue, like the plumage of a great tailed grackle. The people sang songs to Ce Acatl, and wrote poetry, and created wonderful works of art, for he taught them that artistic expression was the holiest manifestation of the Great Spirit within.

The people asked how the gods, who dwelled in the heavens, were related to the Great Spirit within. The Great Spirit is both Father and Mother at the same time, he told them. The Father is the force, the energy, which gives rise to all that is. The Mother is

[101]

everything that is manifest, everything that is. We are in the womb of the Mother and she is continually giving birth to everything that is, because of her sacred union with the divine energy of the Father.

The people directed their prayers toward the Heavens within themselves and began to achieve great things, which they had never done before.

Because of his lineage and immense spirituality, Ce Acatl Topiltzin, the Prince of Mixcóatl, became a leader among the people. They began to call themselves Nonoalcas, and word spread quickly throughout the One World about the Prince of Mixcoatl. Ce Acatl Topiltzin, the warrior priest lives! And so it was that there in Xochicalco, Ce Acatl set out to attain his rightful crown.

Darkness and Light

I found myself outside the door of a bedroom chamber, dressed in a long white skirt. It had gold embroidered borders and a matching white *huipilli* blouse. The edges of the blouse were bordered with gold thread that wove in and out of little yellow butterflies.

I'd been brought to the *axcaitl* the day before, thoroughly bathed, fed, interrogated, poked, prodded, checked for lice, and shoved into a small room with several other concubines. I'd been instructed on the form of speech to use and other courtesies when addressing the lord master. Now, just at sunrise, I stood in a corridor outside his room, dressed in white, while an elder woman fussed over me.

"Go on, now. Go in." A bony, old hand pushed me through the open doorway.

In the center of the large room there was a platform bed. Stretched out on top was an intricately woven *petlatl* mat where the man twice my age slept. A crumpled up cotton blanket lay in the middle of the mat. Along the wall there were several, elaborately worked wicker chests where he kept pieces of cloth, clothes, jewels and the like. Opposite these frail baskets there were two giant urns over-flowing with multi-colored flowers. One of the urns, I noticed, was made of a shiny orange metal and was not from anywhere I knew. It had probably been brought from some other land. The other urn was the *coyotlatelco* earthenware that I had seen at the *tianguis* in my village. Lines were etched through a red top layer down to a yellowish base, forming images of butterflies. The beauty of the two urns was enhanced as each overflowed with colorful, blooming flowers; zinnias, dahlias, bougainvilleas, sun flowers, marigolds, moccasin flowers, and even an occasional magnolia.

I softly walked across the limestone floor and around the bed to get a closer look at the man whom I was about to endure, but all

I saw was a pile of blankets. I stood there, in the soft morning light, looking at the empty bed.

"Ah, my child. Come. I've been waiting for you." said Miquiztli, standing at the window. "A very long time." He paused. "Sit there on the bed. There. That's a girl. I'm glad you like that dress."

Clothed only in a loincloth that was belted around his waist, he energetically stretched himself out across his bed mat, throwing the blanket aside. He propped himself up on one elbow and reached over to touch my arm. I winced, and he sat there, stroking the bed mat lightly with a boyish grin on his face.

"What's your name?"

I answered him, looking at him without casting my eyes directly on him.

He continued in his distorted delusion, "When I first saw you I thought you were the goddess of rivers." He mused. "Then I was deeply saddened to find out that you are just a peasant girl... and now you are a slave. Are you the river goddess, disguised as a lowly peasant, here to test me in some unforeseen way?" Then he changed the subject. "Let me see your hands."

I complied, raising my hands forward.

"You have beautiful hands. They're not working hands. Unheard of from someone of your class." I could tell he was trying to ascertain my true identity.

I knew he was in love with me. I could sense it with every part of my womanhood. Miquiztli looked at me for a short while, saying nothing. Then the Vulture got up and sat on the floor right before me.

He lifted his face to the heavens and spoke out, not to me, but to some god that he imagined was there. "The excitement of touching her for the first time gives me chills and my loins ache from the swelling! But see? Watch my self-control. Watch how I keep my hands between my knees!"

Suddenly he turned and looked at me. "I want you to love me, Citlali," he said almost pleadingly.

I was trapped in silence.

"Do you like the pretty things I've sent you?" he asked, referring to the dress and a few small jewels I'd received the evening before.

"They're nice," I responded without answering the question. My throat was dry.

I had no way of knowing that for the first time in his life the noble lord felt unsure of himself. He felt vulnerable, as though I would never accept him, and his masculinity depended on it. So he changed course. He decided to start with the usual approach that he used on all his first-time girls.

"Are you a virgin?" he asked.

"Yes, Lord Miquiztli. And you?" I refused to use the formal speech that *macehualli* were required to use with *pipiltzin*.

He didn't respond. He seemed prepared to ignore my insolence.

"Do you love your master?" he asked, smiling up at me.

Upon hearing the word "master" an arrow of revulsion pierced through my heart.

"I love the gods, and because the gods are manifested in humanity I am supposed to love you, too." I sat there, looking at the smiling, arrogant man. "But the truth is, I do not."

Miquiztli's face contorted. "Look at everything around you. All of this is here for you to enjoy, Citlali. You aren't like the other slave girls who work doing the drudgery. No. You are here because your lord master wants to be with you."

I felt myself glaring at him.

"All you have to do, Citlali, is please your lord master. Do you want to please me, Citlali?"

At this point I could care less about the consequences of my response. Hatred boiled up from deep within me and surpassed my fear.

"You have torn me away from my *altépetl*, my family, and my home. You are in control of my life, which has been sacrificed for the well being of my entire village. You can do whatever you wish with me, but you cannot make me love you."

Later when I came to see all things that ever were, are, or will be, I learned that Miquiztli had never in his life been rejected by a woman. Not even his wife. At first he was overcome with agony, but soon enough his strength of character came back to him. He had a new challenge now - to make me love him incessantly, so that I would beg him to take me, to ravish me. Yes, that was it. That's what he would do.

He hid his frustrated insecurity at my rejection, and managed control. He got up and pensively looked out the window, remembering the times that his mother had so harshly scolded him when he was a child. She'd told him that he was no good, that he was a wretched sinner, and that he would never amount to anything. He felt weak and vulnerable. The seed in his heart grew heavy. Not giving in to defeat and being the accomplished hunter that he was, he decided to change his approach yet again.

"You don't have to be a concubine, you know. I can make you my second wife," he said. His words floated around the room. I refused to capture them and take them into my heart. "I hate my first wife," he continued. "My father chose her in order to elevate our family's social position. She's the daughter of a Huaxteca war general. She acts like a nasty queen, you know, walks around with a haughty air." He gestured with his arm.

I didn't find his description amusing.

"I can have her anytime I want. She won't deny me. It's just that, well, I don't desire her." He looked into my eyes playfully. "She's got the face of a frog!"

I imagined his wife's human body with the head of a frog, and losing my self-control for a moment, I softly laughed.

He must have felt he was finally making some progress. He knelt before me again.

"Since we consummated our marriage I haven't lain with her," he whispered. "That was four years ago." All of a sudden his ideas twisted. He got to his feet. "I can get rid of her, you know. I can say she's barren! What a perfect idea!"

"Get *rid* of her?"

"Well, you know, by saying she's barren even her own tribe won't take her back. It's an excellent plan."

"Get *rid* of her?"

"Sure. There are lots of ways. I could publicly denounce her, and have her banished to the caves, or I could offer her to one of the merchant traders from the Zapotec lands of the south...oh, she might be offered for sacrifice in that case. Maybe better not." His mood intensified and a demented look swept over his face. "I could do it myself! I could cast her into the burning pit of Ometéotl the oldest god, the god of fire." His eyes were twinkling with excitement. "Oh, Citlali, my lovely Evening Star." He knelt in front of me, his face almost touching mine. The seed within his heart was now, more than ever, overflowing with blossoms of love. Then, for the first time in many years, and for many years to come Cozcacuautli Miquiztli made a request. "My lovely Evening Star, beautiful goddess of the river. I kiss the Earth and kneel before you." He looked up at me from where he was kneeling with moist brown eyes. He smiled, then took my hands and passionately kissed them all over. "Be my second wife and live by my side and love me forever."

I was overcome with fear at the thought of ending up with the same fate as the frog woman first wife. I looked at the pleading man before me and realized how dangerous he was. Then I thought about Quetzalcoatl and how my life had already been sacrificed for the well being of my people. Nothing seemed to matter anymore and I resigned myself to complete emptiness.

I said to him once again, not caring anymore about the consequences, "You can do whatever you wish with me Lord Miquiztli, but you cannot make me love you."

At that moment a strong wind blew in through the window, and knocked over the clay urn of flowers that went crashing to the floor. Miquiztli leapt up from the floor. The seed in his heart shriveled down to a cold, stone pit. He stood with his fists at his sides, rage and fury building inside him. His anger and frustration swelled at having been rejected yet another time by the river goddess. He slowly raised his fists above his head and yelled to the heavens.

"Raaaahhhhhh!"

His pain could be heard throughout the entire *axcaitl* and every living thing fell silent.

The wind whistled and howled as it swarmed through the room. It picked up objects that lay in its gusty path. Things began to fly around in the swirling air. The gusts chanted, "*Look for me in the changing wind.*" They folded into themselves, forming images of faces and things; first the stone faced priest, then a great palace, then a mighty lord dressed as Quetzalcoatl, the opulent, green jadestone, and finally a great city engulfed in flames.

My spirit left my body and I watched from outside myself at what happened next.

[107]

With no further warning, the wicked Vulture spread his great, black wings, and swooped down over the delicate Evening Star, bathing himself in her radiant beauty. Talons protruding, he took her from behind and plunged into her as though starved, and tasted her sweet juices, nectar of the gods. The Vulture penetrated deeper and deeper into her light, completely consuming himself in it, until he reached a point where he himself became full of light. Sparks and stars began to shoot out from him. The seed of passion passed through his body and planted itself deep within her, and the Star, which had previously been so brilliantly luminous, began to fade. The dark, black bird devoured her, violently planting his seed without end, quenching the thirst of his corrupt and evil will. In the midst of her excruciating defeat, the star began to cry, and her tears put out her light.

Miquiztli came out of his frenzied spell. "I'm alive!" he yelled. He arched his back and stretched his arms and chest. Oh, it felt good to have been born male! Warrior! Conqueror! Man!

I lay limp and lifeless in the middle of the mat. Blood and some other fluid flowed out from between my legs.

A torment of guilt overcame Miquiztli. Reality hit him like a cold wind. His psychopathic mind could hardly cope with what he had just done. He hadn't meant to do this. Really, he hadn't. He had planned the whole thing out ahead of time. He had wanted me to be his second wife! He had wanted to make love to me, not force me the way he did with all the rest. He looked at my pitiful body, crumpled up and folded over, face down, hair in disarray. But then I *had* rejected him, he remembered. He just hadn't the strength to control himself. He was weak. He gave in to his impulses. He had no self-control.

What if I really *were* the river goddess in disguise? A goddess' revenge could be devastating. The Earth Mother was the devourer of men, destroyer of all males. She who could strike a man down in the very midst of battle, he had defiled her!

He thought to hide me in some faraway place so that he could forget the fact that he had just violently and brutally ravaged the only woman he'd ever loved, and quite possibly a goddess in human disguise.

[108]

And that's exactly what he did. Anxiety ridden, he had me removed. I was taken to the farthest of rooms at the back end of the house where I was hidden from sight. There I would live out my fate. There my destiny grew in my womb.

Solitude

I spent my days in a cramped, windowless room, with a low ceiling. The only light came from the small, square entrance. Much of the time it was dimmed out, as the entry way was often covered with a buckskin hide. Day after day I lay on a woven mat, feeling revulsion and victimized. My purpose in this life was clear to me: to be removed from everything I knew and loved and brought to this Mictlán Hell so that I could be used and abused by its instrument of hatred and evil. This had been my sacrifice to the gods, but why this? I cried and prayed to the Plumed Serpent, Quetzalcoatl.

Days passed, but I stayed in the dark, solitary chamber. I sat numb, all day long, singing or talking to myself in some kind of fantasy world of my own, not bathing, not brushing my matting hair, until the time came that I began to vomit. I knew I was with child then, because an old woman had come and had sprinkled my urine on the petals of an ocelot claw flower, and the petals had changed from white to a stained red. Then my belly began to swell, and I began to tire easily and fall ill. During this period of loneliness I left my prison of a room only twice.

One of these times I mustered up enough spirit to venture out and roam the halls of the great house. I walked with pitiful steps along a stone corridor, looking at the orange and red friezes on the walls. They must have been stories of famous warriors in some long ago battle, for the men portrayed in them were elegantly dressed. They carried mighty obsidian swords and flint headed javelins. Some of them held the severed heads of their war victims up in the air. I knew how they felt, my spirit having been severed in two.

I came to a small room that housed several carved sculptures of gods and goddesses, and I thought about my most beloved goddess. What would Corn Woman be doing now? It had been so long since I had gone out to dance with Tlaloc and Corn Woman. I was sure that they had continued on without me.

At the end of the corridor I came upon a small yard. It was here that I noticed a triangular temple, dark inside, with only a single flame. As I sat and watched, I heard a mumbling noise, and could just make out a large, circular stone inside. It appeared to be carved and painted with the image of the Plumed Serpent, protector of society and the giver of knowledge, wisdom and peace. The priest inside was waving a small clay bowl of burning frankincense in the air, filling the little temple with a bluish-white smoke. Fixed in a trance, he would come outside just enough to circle in front of the stone, and then go back in again. I watched him there for quite some time, waving the smoke about, chanting, and circling the stone. Then a scrawny, hairless dog ran through the yard between us, breaking the trance of the stone faced priest. He looked up, straight at me and saw me spying on him. His eyes were outlined with black ash, and his long, black hair had been matted with the blood of some animal. The young priest stared at me, and for the first time in his long, long, career, perhaps the only time for many years to come, he smiled.

With my diminished strength I returned to my dark, little room, hoping that punishment would not come to me for having intruded upon a sacred ritual.

The only other incident that broke my long and painful solitude came one day when I received a visitor at the small door.

"Citlali, come out." he said. Pochotl reached in and grabbed me, now a disheveled woman, pulling me out of the tiny, dark room. "Word has it you're with child. Ah, well, look at you." He stood me in front of the door as if I were a cotton doll, shaking me to straighten me up. "Heh, heh, heh," he laughed, groping my crotch with his pudgy hand. "If you think there are any parts missing, I'd be glad to give you another throw."

I spat on the ground, a vulgar gesture I never thought I'd find myself doing. Pochotl angrily whisked me off.

As the councilor dragged me through the great house I could feel many eyes upon me. "She carries a child within her," the servants and other concubines commented when they saw my bulging abdomen.

Once inside the great receiving hall, the councilor presented me to Lord Miquiztli to announce my condition. When he learned of my pregnancy his feelings of guilt and shame subsided.

"A son! My son's going to be a great warrior! My son's going to be a powerful lord among men! My son's going to..."

"What if it's a woman child?" I interrupted.

Lord Miquiztli slapped me across the face, knocking me to the floor.

"If you do me the misfortune of giving me a woman child I will tear her heart out upon its first pulse. Then I'll eat it while it's still beating, and throw her empty carcass to the dogs."

After that incident I left the little room no more. An old woman cared for me, preparations that Lord Miquiztli had made in his effort to hide me from the watchful eyes of the gods.

A Ceremony Begins

By the religious calendar it was the nineteenth month, dedicated to Tlaloc, the god of rain. Normally slaves never attended religious ceremonies, but this time Cozcacuautli Miquiztli believed that the slaves' participation would teach them the value of discipline.

He planned to do several things while he was at the maguey fields: meet with the overseer, inspect the condition of the camp, and take part in the ceremony. It would be better if he could do all this in just one visit. He so detested going there.

The camp had been modestly prepared for a festival. As the sun began to rise, it illuminated the dried ears of corn hanging from the doorways. Their multicolored kernels, some yellow, some blue, some missing, looked like the teeth of an ancient, wrinkled face. The kernels represented both droplets of rain and the harvests that result from them.

The only other display of a ceremony was the crackling bonfire dedicated to Huehuetéotl, the Ancient One. The fire lay out beyond the hanging deerskin bags that held the fermenting *pulque*. It was a flat open area, with nothing more than desert brush scattered over a gently sloping, sandy hill. The slaves stood circled around the bonfire waiting for the festivities to begin. Near one part of the fire there was an unusually large clay urn, painted in the Coyotlatelco style, so typical of Tollan, with reddish designs scratched-out over a yellowish base.

Soon more people started to gather. Musicians from Miquiztli's personal household were now beating out rhythms on different kinds of drums. The most magnificent was the *huehuetl*, a large, upright, wood-framed drum with an animal skin tightly stretched over the top. There was a hefty man beating it, flaring his nostrils and jerking his head back and forth to the beat of the drum. He not only controlled the rhythm, but the quality of the tone, depending on where his long fingers slapped the hide. *Thump thump, tot tot, thump thump, tot tot*. Another man started in with a *teponzatli*, a piece of wood that had been hollowed out, the opening forming four prongs on top. He beat the two-tone block with rubber mallets, *tink, tunk, tink, tunk*. Seed-filled gourds and clay flutes then joined in, and finally, tortoiseshell rattles. Engrossing rhythm, rather than melody, was the achieved effect, making it penetrate into the very heart of all the gods who might be listening, and reverberate through the very soul of all those who heard.

Lord Miquiztli sat high upon a brightly painted litter that had been made especially for occasions such as these. From where he sat he could see the entire circle of participants. More importantly, they could see him.

An unknown priest then began the ceremony. He walked forward into the circle, dressed in a loose, black garment that was gathered at the waist with a rope made of braided lizard skin. Two enormous black earplugs protruded from his head, held in place by his leathery, stretched-out earlobes.

"The faces in the clouds are gods," he said, lifting his hands to the heavens. "They are worthy of adoration. The gusts of wind are gods. They live among the hills, the mountains, the valleys and the canyons. They are worthy of adoration. The rivers, ponds, and natural springs are gods. We give them our respect and adoration. But among the mightiest of gods is the giver of life, Rain. Tlaloc, god of rain. Ho! Ho-oh! Ho-oh-hai!"

He didn't mean that the rain itself was a god, nor that there was some god figure somewhere controlling the rain. He was referring to the essence of "rain-ness". That which makes up rain and allows it to *be* rain.

"...They are worthy of adoration..." the unknown priest continued. As he finished his oratory, people began to turn their attention toward the great clay urn. A youth pushed his way out of the circle, walked toward the urn, and reverently removed the bowl-shaped lid.

The Bloody

Battlefield of Birth

By the religious calendar it was the fifth month. The day was Eagle. As Venus, the morning star, appeared in the sky, day was born. Cooking fires that had been put out the night before were once again set to life. In a small, reed hut near the *axcaitl* I lay on a woven *petlatl* mat, shifting back and forth, getting up, walking around, squatting, anything that would alleviate the pain that I was now experiencing. I felt nervous and apprehensive. I couldn't imagine giving birth to anything the size of what was inside me. A panic overcame me that the creature would never come out.

"Call to the god Tezcatlipoca," insisted the scraggly-haired midwife. "You shall find protection in the god Tezcatlipoca!"

I coped with the intensity of my labor as three midwives meticulously fussed over me, preparing me for the birth. It was their job to thoroughly cleanse me, relieve my pain during the parturition, and help increase the flow of milk in my breasts. All the proper methods and remedies had to be adhered to, lest the gods be angered in some way.

"The wench is to be washed out with the juice of those plants." The scraggly-haired one said to the skinny one, gesturing to an earthenware bowl that contained a paste of herbs and healing plants. "Up inside her. Do it now!"

A stout and serious woman then sat down on the mat with her legs folded under her so that she could support the weight of me. I was to recline against her. She said nothing. She just ran her fingers over my matted, jet-black hair.

The scraggly-haired woman was now firmly massaging my vagina with medicinal oil that she had prepared ahead of time. She massaged, and massaged, so that the skin would properly stretch and not tear. All the while she hummed the sacred birthing chant, only stopping to give orders to the other two: "Keep the copal incense burning...Spread the smoke around with that eagle's wing...Hand me those leaves over there." She continued massaging and humming the sacred birthing chant.

They washed out my vagina with the juice of the medicinal plants, and rubbed it with sacred herbs, as they had been taught by their mothers and grandmothers before them. Finally, they dabbed inside me a perfectly measured amount of eagle excrement, all the while continuing to massage and sing, massage and sing.

✄

The stone-faced priest, Quetzalpopoca Smoking Feather hadn't gone to the ceremony at the slave camp. New life, the mystical enchantment of creation, was considered to be among the most important of blessings. The old crone midwife with the scraggly hair had insisted that he stay behind to help ward off evil spirits, lest the child be born a demon from the underworld, but enter the hut he could not. He could not even pass the circle of stones surrounding it, for his masculine energy might upset the harmony of the all female affair. So he resigned himself to patiently waiting outside, sitting on a little stump, analyzing the astrological sign, and thus the name, of the infant that was about to be born. The day was 5 Eagle.

The fifth month, he thought. Those born during this time are passionate, demanding and prosperous. They either learn their lessons by pleasure and enthusiasm, or they learn the hard way. There's no middle way. If they are able to control their explosive character and constructively channel it, they might achieve enormous rewards.

He puffed on a little pipe that contained the smoking weed. Eagle. Hmmm. Those born under this sign are dominant, and generally ambitious. They not only achieve what they set out to do, they manage to get others to do so as well. They are inclined toward organization. The great effort they make to better themselves and the world is recognized by others and gains them the respect and trust of others. Quetzalpopoca Smoking Feather drew on all knowledge and experience, concentrating his thoughts, trying not to forget anything.

The priest reasoned that the infant creature would be a man child and grow to be a great warrior, even though his visions had told him differently.

✄

Birthing was a woman's most dangerous battle. Just as men challenged death on the battlefield of war, women confronted it on the bloody field of childbed. I was not in labor; I was in battle, risking my very life. Moreover, I was presently abducted from my usual gentle state and was possessed by some great presence from far beyond. I was closest now to the Earth in Her fertile capacity. I risked possession by Toci, The Earth Mother, giver and taker of Life. If I should get too close to the divine forces, the Earth Mother and her malign spirits would surely take me and I would die in battle.

I was now squatting on the floor mat, supported by another woman, feet planted squarely on the ground. Sweat trickled from my forehead, and rolled down my flushed cheeks. The *petlatl* mat was drenched with the fluids of new life that were gushing out between my legs. I could feel the head come down into the birth canal, and as I pushed, I felt the life within me move.

Burning Peppers

At the ceremony, Miquiztli's excitement grew as the youth removed the lid of the giant urn. Then a grey haired slave came forward and handed something secret to the priest.

"I beg the gods to bless these items with their grace and divinity," he said. He then turned and placed the secret items into the great clay urn. The lid was quickly replaced. Within moments a white, hot smoke started to seep out of the lid of the urn, swirling around in a demonic-like dance.

"All of you! Slaves!" yelled the wicked lord master from his litter above, "Today is a day to rejoice!' He raised both hands to the heavens above. "Today you can be thankful that you have obeyed your master and the gods. For now you will witness what happens to those who sin. It has become public knowledge that among you there has been a sin so terrible and so vile as to disgrace the gods to whom we owe our very lives." Miquiztli got out of his litter. Several guards were pulling a couple of defiant, naked youths through the crowd. The two youths stood with their heads hung down, unable to lift their tear-filled eyes.

"These two slaves were caught in the act of fornication before marriage and *worse*, they were drinking the sacred *pulque*!" Miquiztli yelled, relishing in a perverse delight that he dare not let his face reveal. The onlookers stood aghast. "They are to be punished and delivered to the gods!"

"Yes, punish them!" yelled the onlookers. "We must appease the gods!"

The guards hefted the struggling youths up and held their faces directly above the urn. No longer a secret, the burning *chilli* peppers were sputtering and popping inside. Vicious white vapors seeped out from under the lid like snake tongues. They swirled up and blistered the screaming victims' eyes.

"Remove the lid!" ordered Miquiztli.

Itza and Pixahua then experienced a pain they never imagined possible, as the vapors from the burning peppers engulfed them and burned holes into their eyes. Their screams helped them none. Their gasps of air only sufficed to allow more deadly vapors into their mouths and lungs, burning and blistering them even more. Finally, after what seemed an eternity of torturous suffering, the guards threw them to the ground where they lay choking in blistering pain.

Salty tears rolled out of their swollen, bloody eyes.

"Fornication before the sacred act of marriage is a vile sin!" The unknown priest yelled out to all. "But penitence will help to purify the sinner's evil heart!" Taking a long, thick cactus thorn, he knelt down and sliced it through Pixahua's foreskin, twisting and turning it through the bleeding flesh.

"This is my penitence for my sin!" said the priest as he sawed the thorn back and forth.

"This.... is ... pe.....ence ...fff ....in." The blinded boy faintly repeated, coughing and spitting blood.

The girl suffered punishment as well. She was thrown back onto a stone slab for all to see, and before she was executed, the priest cleaved out her genitals with an obsidian knife, preventing her from enjoying the sexual act in the afterlife. She was then choked to death, not even able to let out one final scream. The boy was then stoned, and when he lay dead, the crowd stood in silence and awe.

The Crossroads

"Waahh!"

The infant took its first breath of life and wailed. Powerful, exhilarating, exalted life! The glory of birth filled the air and the cycle of life renewed itself once again. Hours of excruciating labor had come to an end. Cleansed and salved by experienced hands, the tiny babe was held over my head. The midwives rejoiced in the delight of the success that they had helped bring forth. I remember the deep look of joy in their old, penetrating eyes.

Then a miniature broom was placed into the infant's tiny hand and the scraggly-haired midwife began the ancient prayer foretold to all baby girls at birth;

> *"You shall be in the heart of the home,*
> *You will go nowhere.*
> *You will nowhere become a wanderer.*
> *You will become the banked fire,*
> *The stones of the hearth.*
> *The Earth Mother planteth you, burieth you.*
> *And you will become fatigued, tired.*
> *You are to provide water, to grind maize, to drudge.*
> *You will sweat by the ashes of your hearth.*
> *You are woman and thus you shall be."*

"Woman respond." the scraggly haired midwife was saying, slapping my cheeks. "She won't respond."

My bleeding would not subside. I lay on the mat, fatigued and listless. One of the women physicians swaddled the babe and the other two turned their attention to the slow and gentle extraction of the placenta.

Outside Quetzalpopoca Smoking Feather could hear the cry of the newborn child, and the commotion of the midwives. The curtain opened and a woman beckoned the priest through the entrance. Expressionless, the priest entered the circle of stones.

With all my strength I grabbed the priest's tunic as he crouched next to me. "Please, you have to help me." I whispered to him. I couldn't control the emotion that engulfed me, and tears rolled down my cheeks. "He'll kill the babe," I managed to faintly gasp in a breathless voice. Blood continued to flow out of my hemorrhaging uterus.

The stone-faced priest was expressionless.

"It's a girl child," said the old midwife, wringing her aged hands.

A feeling of doom filled the air. A hot breeze swirled into the dwelling through the slatted walls.

Quetzalpopoca looked at the infant born on this day 5 Eagle. She had strong features. Her thick black hair was mashed down and wet. "She shall be named Tonalnan, Mother of Light!" he boldly announced to all.

"Take her, priest, I beg you." I managed to say. "Here…" I said. Trembling from weakness, I touched the jadestone pouch that hung around my neck. "Give it to her…" and my breath was gone. Then I saw the ghost of Ollin Ehécatl standing there, smiling with arms outstretched, and I knew he had come for me.

Smoking Feather acted quickly. He tied the jadestone around his neck, and received the swaddled newborn into his arms. He hesitated for a brief moment to look deeply into my eyes and soul. Expressionless, the priest took the tiny bundle and ran.

That was when I died the bloody death. The more the blood gushed out between my legs, the more a great, warm light poured over me. I felt myself lifting up out of my body. I watched the midwives shake me. I saw Smoking Feather running through the brush with the swaddled infant. I saw many things that had happened in many places in Cem-Anahuac and beyond. My soul was sucked up into the Other Dimension and I was pulled into the Underworld of Mictlán. I tell you now, it is for this reason that I am a Knower of All Things, and this is why I am able to recount to you this story of my people.

※

Soon after, the gossips in the marketplace spread their poison about my death. "The parents indulged too much during pregnancy," they criticized. Everyone knew that the fluids shared during intercourse were needed to help the baby grow, not to mention to start the pregnancy, but after three or four months, the baby grew by itself, and if intercourse should continue, the extra fluids would make the birth long and difficult. If a woman consented and received more seed, the babe would be born coated in white *atole*, which might even act like glue sticking the baby inside. The tongues in the marketplace wagged, "Her childbed was the death of her because the baby no longer tolerated the seed!"

The news of my death sliced through Miquiztli like an obsidian knife slashing the soft flesh of a tender cactus. Pain radiated through him, not only for the loss of the one woman that he loved, but also for fear of the Earth Mother by whom I had obviously been possessed. Lord Miquiztli knew it had been the malign Earth Mother, Coacíhuatl that had taken my life. Coacíhuatl was not only a giver of life, but a destroyer and devourer of men.

In childbirth, the life of the woman was always favored over that of the unborn infant, and as such, Miquiztli assumed that the midwives had obeyed ritual duty and had cut the infant out of me, limb by limb, in an attempt to save my life. This is what they let him believe. While they had not understood the actions of Quetzalpopoca Smoking Feather as he took the babe, they did know to guard the secrecy of the priesthood. So they kept their knowledge silent. Fortunately Miquiztli was too distraught to question them.

The burial procedures began immediately after my death. In our tribe we usually burned our dead; burial was reserved for those unfortunate enough to die by the force of Tlaloc, to be struck by lightning or drowned, or for women taken by Coacíhuatl in the giving of life.

Everyone knew that my body was now highly charged with the spirit of the Earth Mother, devourer of men, and therefore was an immediate danger to anyone who dare come near. To ward off this dark and sinister magic, all those involved in the death ritual rubbed their joints -elbows, knees and ankles - with black ash, as this would help protect them against Her crippling power.

My corpse had to be removed immediately. Because my still and lifeless body was magically charged, they dared not take it out by the visitor's door. With obsidian knives they cut a hole in the back wall of the small reed hut where I'd died. Lord Miquiztli carried my body, now completely dusted with white ash, out into the night under a full-lit moon. My long, black hair hung almost to the ground. He was escorted by the midwives who screamed and howled sacred chants as they walked along under the night sky.

Not only were they on guard against the Night Creature and other cosmic forces, but they risked attack by warriors and thieves. Any part of my magically charged body could now be used as a talisman. My fingers or a lock of my hair might be used to cast a person's enemies into helpless convulsions, states of utter stupidity, or complete paralysis. A talisman was a powerful spiritual weapon. For protection, my mourners walked along brandishing daggers and shields. Not that anyone was foolish enough to approach the possessed old women. Their magic was far too powerful to challenge. When they reached the crossroads, a most lonely and marginal of places, my body was buried. As tradition dictated, Lord Miquiztli kept vigil over my grave for four nights as the magic power of my corpse slowly diminished. Then, with no ceremony or memorial, he was gone.

Book 2

Rise of an Empire

Dark Days in Tollan

Fires raged. Reed and grass rooftops hurled rolling, black smoke into the air. Women's screams, children's cries, destruction and devastation reverberated through the streets of Tollan.

Huemac and several warriors stood in the marketplace throwing wild glances around, checking for any raiders that might have stayed behind. Bodies were strewn about, lying in pools of blood. He recognized a crumpled old woman on the ground. "Grandmother Elder," he said, moving her white hair from her wrinkled face.

"It was the Chichimeca..." she whispered. Blood oozed from the wound in her stomach where an *atlatl* dart had plunged into her flesh.

"The Chichimeca are dogs! They will be cursed by the gods!" he replied.

"It is the will of the gods," she said. Her eyes rolled upward.

Huemac gathered the old woman into his arms. Her voice was so soft now that he had to put his face right in front of hers to hear.

"It is the will of the gods that there is Evil in the world." She took a shallow breath. If she had had the strength to finish she would have told him, "Good and Evil exist so that the people of the One World have the freedom to choose between them. This way we can discern. This way we can understand Good for what it truly is. We really only comprehend the divineness of Good if it is contrasted with the darkness of Evil." But she had stopped talking. Her ancient eyes turned to a blank stare and she died.

"Cacique! Naxac is... Our king is..." A young warrior ran up to Huemac and stopped just short of him, sending up a cloud of dust. "People are going to the Sacred House. There are people dying in the streets! Cacique! They're lying on the ground dying!" Rolling tears left tracks down his dirty face.

Trying to offset the raging of his pounding heart, Huemac gathered Grandmother Elder into his arms and headed toward the Sacred House of Healing.

[129]

The inner courtyard filled as those who still had strength carried their wounded relatives and laid them down on the ground. Kneeling, Tonalnan abruptly braced her hand behind the neck of a broken warrior and raised a gourd of bitter tonic to his lips. It would induce a heavy sleeplike state and relieve him of his pain. She would then wash out the gash in his side. This wound was more severe than some of the others, as it had been caused by an obsidian-tipped spear and not an arrow. As the warrior lay back, she considered whether to clean the wound and pack it with *huitlacoche*, the healing fungus that grows on corn, or induce the man and let him painlessly die.

She had escaped the flying arrows of the attack, protected within the inner courtyard of the Sacred House of Healing. As the onslaught began, she and the other women healers had rushed to prepare the tonics and remedies that they were now administering, while archers protected them from the rooftops, and swordsmen defended their door with massive obsidian swords.

The warrior winced as she patted the *huitlacoche* into his sliced flesh.

"Tonalnan!"

She turned stiffly around to see her father Huemac entering the courtyard, his arms full of death. "Father!"

"You there, lay out a mat," Huemac barked. A boy scurried over to a rolled mat and extended it out next to the wall.

Huemac laid the lifeless body along the mat and the boy reverently arranged her clothing. Together they placed the old woman's hands along her sides and spread her long white hair out in all directions above her head.

Tonalnan watched speechless in disbelief, her heart in her throat. Grandmother Elder had been the matron of the Sacred House of Healing, her mentor and her beloved friend. She was the Omecíhuatl of the clan.

Wails of pain and groans of misery danced their way into her ears as she slowly refocused on the wounded people around her.

She had been so immersed in packing the laceration that she hadn't noticed the courtyard filling up.

"Bring the zinnias from the medicine room," she told the boy. He dashed off. She addressed her father, "Elder Huemac ... I..."

Just then a woman appeared at the doorway of the courtyard, grasping the cold, stone archway with one hand, her other hand clutching her abdomen. Her long, matted hair hung unkempt and she was breathing heavily.

"The king... He..."

Her eyes were swollen with tears and her face and body was covered with dirt and debris.

"He..."

All those around her were now looking at her - the wounded lying on the floor and those kneeling over them.

"He was murdered in his bed!" screamed a young man who ran up beside her.

Gasps of shock reverberated through the crowd.

The magnitude of the raid was now beginning to sink in. Tonalnan looked at her father, Huemac. Sweaty and covered with blood, he stood over the body of Grandmother Elder. "The priest, have you seen him?" she managed to say.

"No one has seen him since he left for the caves four days ago."

The hardened warrior Huemac looked at Grandmother Elder who lay on the *petlatl* mat, her soul already beyond death's door. The courtyard was filled with wounded men and women whose cries pierced through the evening sky and through his heart. "She said it is the will of the gods that there is Evil in the world." He looked at Tonalnan and his eyes filled with tears. "It was the last thing she said before she died."

"She used to tell me the same thing. So that we can understand Good for what it truly is." Tonalnan sighed deeply and looked at the wounded who lay suffering and crying around her. "She would tell me that we really only comprehend the divineness of Good when it is contrasted with the darkness of Evil." She looked back at Huemac, her father. "I think I am beginning to understand."

Mictlán

You might be wondering how it is that I am able to relate these things to you, for I have told you that I died in childbed and now walk among the dead. But now has come the time that I shall reveal the sacred secrets to you from the Great Beyond.

Upon my death my body of light, that is, my spirit body, called my *tonalli*, started to tear away from my physical body. I felt my *tonalli* being lifted above myself, and absorbed into the cosmic energies that most humans never see. In that altered state I witnessed the events that were happening after I died. I stayed with myself for several days, watching over my own end and gathering the magical energies that would help carry my light body into the underworld of Mictlán, the land of the dead.

My journey to Mictlán was cold but it was not dark. The elders had always taught us that Mictlán was dark, but they could never know how it really is. They speculated and guessed because they were alive, and made us believe many things about the journey after death. In truth, however, they had little way of knowing if these things about Mictlán were true. They based their beliefs on the reports of their elders, and the elders who came before them, and those before them, in a seemingly endless chain of ancient authority. In our world we accepted what we were taught, and were not taught to question, so question we did not.

But they were wrong. In truth, the journey to Mictlán *is* filled with light. As I entered the realm of the dead, now in the form of my *tonalli*, I gradually assumed the knowledge of an ever-extending collective consciousness of everything that was, is and ever shall be.

As I descended farther and farther into Mictlán, I learned many secrets of our very being that humans do not know. Occasionally, though, these truths have snuck out of Mictlán, and elder humans have learned the happenings of the underworld through arcane sources. This was how our ancestors, many ages ago, came to know the secret truths about our world.

The Awakening of Itzpapálotl

The signal was a black stream of smoke that snaked into the sky. After dusting their bodies with white powdered lime, the people of the caves began their descent down the cliffs to the valley below.

There was much to-do and excitement this afternoon, as tribeswomen finished building four bonfires at the bottom of the rocky hill. The raid had been successful and their most honored goddess of war, Itzpapálotl, was sure to be appeased. Drummers gathered, and a flute player huffed and squeaked a rough tune, a very new and unusual event, as flutes were previously unknown to the people of the caves. (Several flutes had been stolen during the raid). The tribe's people began filling the side of the hill, sitting together with gourds of water and cactus fruits called *nochtli* to munch on.

At the base of the hill, Ichtaca of the Red Ant Clan stood proud as the *coyotl* headdress was placed upon his head in preparation for the ceremony: the hollowed out skull of a wild dog sported a wide open mouth and bared its deadly fangs as though ready to attack. The eye sockets had been filled with smooth, white quartz stones. The rest of the pelt hung over his neck and shoulders, covering his waist-length hair and would give him the magical protection of the *coyotl* in future battles. His muscular, dark brown body was painted with black, white and gray spots to enable him to channel the Great Coyotl Spirit, and he donned a *coyotl* fur loincloth. A few flint arrowheads hung from around his waist, as well as a collection of several, now-blackened fingers that he had taken from warriors he'd killed in battle. He was now ready to receive the ceremonial spear of victory.

"Titlacáhuan is coming!" someone shouted from the crowd.

The hoard of several hundred started barking and yelping, to invoke the gods, as their most feared sorcerer made his way down the hill.

Titlacáhuan the sorcerer was a force to be reckoned with. His magic was strong. His ability to foretell the future was as precise as a reflection on silent water. His self-control was far beyond that of any ordinary tribesman. He withstood the pain of self-sacrifice without the slightest flinch, capable of passing a cactus thorn through his tongue again and again, and of reopening the fresh wound every four days in order to collect the sacred fluid of life for burnt offerings to the gods.

Titlacáhuan walked through the crowd of people who prostrated themselves before him. His hands were outstretched above them, not as a blessing, but as a symbol of his authority over them. His slight body was adorned with a headdress of black-tipped eagle feathers and a multitude of amulets for his various shamanic rituals. His bear claw necklace gave him protection against evil spirits. He wore anklets covered with seedpod bells that jangled when he walked. His spotted leopard cloak had rattling snake tails sewn around the edges. His skin was dusted completely white except for a black ash band across his eyes, exaggerating his beak of a nose and high cheekbones even more. He reached the bottom of the hill, where four bonfires were burning and preparations had been made for the ritual that lay ahead.

Titlacáhuan beckoned to the tribal elders to be seated in the front of the crowd and then stared at Ichtaca, who stood at the other end, several juniper trees away, acknowledging his acceptance of the war party leader's successes.

Silence fell among the crowd.

The sorcerer planted his feet firmly and addressed the crowd. "The Omecíhuatl has taught us that since the dawn of time there always has been, and there always will be, grave persecution from the heavens," he began. All sat in reverence, with downcast eyes. "Devastation and Doom are upon us! The Omecíhuatl has seen the Great Planet that follows the people through the sky!" There were gasps throughout the crowd. "We are besieged by calamity and our children die of hunger. We suffer the peril of a great evil that is upon us." The murmuring continued. "But we will suffer no more! Raise your hearts to the heavens and call upon the goddess to rise up from the dead! Raise your hearts to her and call out her name!"

He raised his skeleton-like arms to the sky.

"Itzpapálotl!" he passionately summoned.

"Itzpapálotl!" everyone responded. They then started softly chanting the name of the obsidian butterfly goddess over and over, "Itz-pa-pá-lotl, Itz-pa-pá-lotl, Itz-pa-pá-lotl," bringing their voices and thoughts into unison. Their white, chalky faces were somber and expressionless.

"The Omecíhuatl says that we are to avenge the Obsidian Butterfly's death, and in so doing we will bring our goddess back from the dead!"

An uproar of cheers and clamoring of sticks, rocks and rattles broke out.

Titlacáhuan waived his hand across the crowd and a silence ensued. "Today we recognize our great war party leader, Ichtaca, for his bravery and strength against our enemies of Tollan."

A drum started beating, *Boom-bak-cha, Boom-bak-cha*, and a man began to sing in high-pitched wails, accompanying the rhythmic thuds.

Ichtaca, emboldened in his *coyotl* headdress, solemnly walked toward Titlacáhuan, along the length of the four bonfires.

"Ichtaca the Brave, Ichtaca the Strong, has made sacrifices for our mothers and all their children."

The throng was now silent.

"His sacrifices have been many and with powerful magic, for while all of you fed upon the flesh of this earth, Ichtaca fasted. While all of you indulged in your pleasures and passions, Ichtaca practiced self-restraint and chastity. While all of you conversed, Ichtaca sat in silence. Our war party leader has made these sacrifices to become Ichtaca the Strong, Ichtaca the Brave!"

Titlacáhuan placed his hand on Ichtaca's chest as the war party leader approached and stood in front of him.

"Ichtaca, I call upon you, through the magic of your sacrifices, to awaken our goddess Itzpapálotl, the Obsidian Butterfly, goddess of war!"

A young boy handed Ichtaca his quiver and bow.

Titlacáhuan turned and faced the spectacle that everyone had been waiting for. Behind each bonfire there was a giant post planted in the earth. A naked Tollan prisoner of war hung on each one, arms extended above and ankles below, tightly bound to the pole.

[137]

The crowd started again to softly chant the name of their goddess of war, "Itzpapálotl... Itzpapálotl... Itzpapálotl..."

Titlacáhuan walked over to the closest prisoner and screamed a high, shrill scream, "Ay, ay, ay, ay, ay, ay!" Then he thrust his face into the face of the prisoner and opened his eyes wide. "You will never again call upon the name of your god!"

With that, a man grabbed the prisoner's head from behind, prying open the victim's jaw. The sorcerer pulled out the tongue and cleanly sliced off the writhing organ with an obsidian blade. The prisoner screamed in pain and began to gag on his own blood, at which point his own reflexes bobbed his head forward and a red stream oozed forth down his chest.

Titlacáhuan leaned forward and licked the flow of blood spilling down the victim's breast. His eyes rolled back into his head and he smiled as he swallowed the blood and thereby absorbed the warrior's magical strength into his inner being.

Then he ceremoniously placed the slimy appendage in a gourd carried by the same boy who had given Ichtaca the quiver.

Looks of horror twisted the faces of the other three prisoners who were bound the same way. Titlacáhuan again began to scream his high, shrill scream, "Ay, ay, ay, ay, ay, ay!" as he walked over to the next prisoner. Again he thrust his face into the face of the bound warrior and opened his eyes wide. "You will never again call upon the name of your god!"

In this manner, Titlacáhuan cut off the tongues of all four prisoners who were tied to the posts, swallowed their blood, and took their magic into his own inner being.

The whole time the crowd kept chanting their eerie invocation, "Itzpapálotl, Itzpapálotl..."

At that point, Ichtaca and several of his warriors began to fire arrows upon the prisoners of war.

"Itzpapálotl, we sacrifice these humans to you so that you may nourish your strength with their souls," Titlacáhuan bellowed above the chanting crowd.

The hissing sound of the flying arrows ended with a thwack as each arrow penetrated the soft flesh of the victims. The bowstrings reverberated.

"May their spirit bodies feed you!"

[138]

From the depths of Mictlán, the goddess of war called the Obsidian Butterfly stirred.

Tulantzinco

Now a vibrant young man, Ce Acatl Topiltzin left the great metropolis of Xochicalco, with its massive stone fortifications and interior courtyards overflowing with exotic flowers and melodic birds. Ever cognizant of his lineage, his duty now resided in preparation for his royal accession. In the year One Calli Topiltzin headed north, and soon he and his 400 warriors arrived in Tulantzinco, where he remained for four years in a house of prayer. It was a time of deep meditation, when he came to understand many things.

He was very given to order, and when speaking to his followers on any occasion, he would present himself with the utmost care. His body would be painted black, but on his face he had only the stripe of black ash across his eyes, to honor his father Mixcóatl's slaying of the Obsidian Butterfly. From time to time he would appear before his people with his body painted in black and yellow stripes. On his head he wore a cone shaped hat made of jaguar fur. Woven into the chinstrap were the dazzling tail feathers of the yellow winged *cicique*, so that it looked like he had a yellow beard. It would wiggle as he spoke, and mothers would have to smack their small children to keep them from giggling. Often times he would wear spiral shaped gold earrings to honor the god of the Nine Winds. The V-shaped skirts that he would don for speaking were elaborately embroidered with precious stones and the most delicate of seashells that he had been gifted back in Xochicalco.

Often, surrounded by adoring listeners, Ce Acatl would speak about the divine nature of things. "The true spiritual warrior learns that he is dreaming reality," he would say. "Think about your sleeping dreams. When you know you are dreaming and can control your dream with your intent, this is called lucid dreaming." The people would nod and hang on every word. "So the spiritual warrior learns to control his dream of life, through his words and actions and by being deliberate with the use of his energy. This is called lucid living." He would smile and his eyes would turn to big blue-black pools of compassion.

The people had never heard such things and took much delight in the thought of deliberate living. Swift in their flight, they ran across the land and delivered his messages to others so that soon many people were coming to him in Tulantzinco to receive his council.

Greatly skilled men and women came to be near Ce Acatl in Tulantzinco, people of grace and integrity. There were carpenters, stoneworkers, painters, mechanics, weavers and people of the arts, like singers and dancers. Devoted men and great orators, warriors, poets and scholars came to see him and speak with him, as well as astrologers, midwives, soothsayers and healers. With so many people converging on Tulantzinco it became necessary for people to organize themselves and a structured society emerged.

Sometimes the prince of Mixcóatl delivered his discourses outside in the fresh air, on the side of a hill for all to hear. Other times he spoke to his inner circle, his closest friends, inside the calmecac, the monastery located in a long, rectangular, stone building. He always delivered his messages in the evenings, for the greater part of the mornings he spent in meditation and prayer.

At night he would venture off alone, accompanied by a million smiling stars or cloaked in misty clouds, to the river where he had his own private temple. On these nightly journeys he would wear a black robe, and his long hair would drape around his body. He reverently bathed himself, unabashedly naked beneath the admiring moon. In his nakedness at the mid of night he was at his most vulnerable against the night creatures and sorcerers who might cast demonic afflictions upon him, but this extreme state of fear only served to heighten his own sense of personal power, for in facing that which frightened him most, he was able to see the bigger truths; fear feeds on guilt and shame, and grows in the soil of loneliness. *What is there to fear*, he would wonder, *the events of life itself*? In these moments of facing his darkest fears he learned to forgive and love that which he feared most, that which he hated, and that which he detested. Through forgiveness, he reclaimed his inner grace, his vitality, and genuine acceptance of himself and the rest of the world.

[142]

After cleansing himself in the river, and in a heightened state of awareness, he would enter his small stone temple where he lit a ritual fire, never forgetting to say a small prayer of gratitude to the god of flint. As golden light bounced off the adobe walls and sparks swirled up to the dome shaped ceiling above, he would carefully lay out his altar with his most sacred magical weapons. As always, he would light his copal incense, pray to the gods, and begin his penitence to the god Quetzalcoatl, his protector, his defender, his god, his love, his light: Quetzalcoatl, god of energy, of creation, of vitality, of life.

Ce Acatl Topiltzin was a great penitent, whose austerity and self-control were greatly admired and imitated by other priests. They followed his example and over time his rituals were practiced all throughout *Cem Anahuac*, the One World. In front of his altar, in his private temple at the river, with the fire blazing and incense burning, he would slowly pass a cactus thorn through his body. Sometimes it would be his thigh, sometimes an earlobe, sometimes his foreskin, or perhaps he would pierce his tongue. On occasion he would be known to reopen a fresh wound that had not yet healed. Then, reverently and with extreme focus and self-control, he would capture the sacred fluid of life with a bowl made from the top of a human skull. After that he would slowly drip the divine substance over burning sage and pray through deep, resonant chanting as the now spiritually charged smoke dissipated into an alternate reality, the realms of the gods.

The pain of penitence was not to be mistaken for self-punishment of one's body for its impurities or transgressions, but rather a necessary means to obtain the most precious part of life: the sacred fluid, giver and sustainer of life itself. The pain endured was not believed to bring a priest closer to the Divine Spirit. It did, however, bring a priest closer to himself. Pain and joy were seen to exist together in a well inside the cave of one's consciousness. The deeper the pain carved down into the well, the more joys one's well could hold. Sometimes the pain of penitence would lead a priest into an ecstatic trance or hallucination, bringing an onslaught of prophetic vision. In enduring this extreme pain Ce Acatl exercised a level of self-discipline over his physical body that enabled him to achieve the highest states of consciousness, what he called pure radiant awareness.

These and other things Ce Acatl Topiltzin learned in Tulantzinco, and after four years the Toltecs of Tollan came to him, as he had foreseen. They came for the Prince of Mixcóatl, and asked him to be their king.

Funeral for a King

The attack on Tollan had devastated the people. The number of brothers and sisters, fathers and mothers who died could be counted four times across his hands. Huemac's tears wreaked havoc in his heart yet his face was dry and expressionless. As first general, he had many responsibilities swirling around in his head, widows and orphans left bereft from the onslaught, loss of skilled artisans who had provided essential wares for the community, funerary arrangements that now had to be made, but in all his brooding, what affected him most deeply was the disturbance this had caused in his eldest daughter's marriage plans.

In his own heart, he had wanted to offer his daughter Calli to the Patlachi nation of Pachuca, to form an alliance and get his finger into their mines of obsidian and lime. Eventually though, he came to yield to the counsel of a local hag who was a highly skilled and effective matchmaker. "Xolotl, son of Nauhyotl, is a perfect match for your daughter," the hag had said. "He has excelled in his education and has been promoted above all the other young men in the House of Warriors. He is a fine lad. His weapon handling is superb and he has recently proven himself on the field of battle."

What Huemac didn't know was that his wife and eldest daughter were in cahoots with her, paying the gray haired old woman with jadestones to convince him of this match. For additional payment – a basketful of quail eggs - she offered to display an ecstatic trance, shaking her fetid, gourd rattles and casting her fortune telling bones across the flagstone floor amidst high-pitched wails and ominous hysterics. It was effective indeed, as the entire extended family looked on, and when Huemac consented, Calli and her mother Itzali exchanged knowing glances.

Calli and Xolotl had known each other their whole lives, having always attended special ceremonies and festivals of the noble class, the *pipiltzin*. The population of Tollan numbered in the hundreds of families, and the enclaves of neighborhoods and closeness of extended families favored their chance encounters over the years.

After the marriage agreement had been made (a profitable prospect for the family of Nauhyotl, to marry their son into the family of the First General), old women of the neighborhood acted as go-betweens for the betrothed; They carried messages to and fro. On several occasions, servants from the young man's household presented themselves, laden with gifts, to the family of the bride. In an effort to show that his son Xolotl was worthy of the young maiden, Nauhyotl bestowed upon Huemac's household the finest of treasures including nine *petlacalli* baskets filled with beeswax oil lamps, food and flowers, painted gourds brimming with cacao, a hand-made long pipe with fragrant smoking herbs, a bright green and orange fan made from the tail feathers of a parrot, strands upon strands of tiny, precious stones, a reed trunk filled with knives and tools, bows, arrows, and shields, and a selection of necklaces and earrings made of emeralds and gold. The bride Calli was then at liberty to dole out the gifts or keep them for herself. She shared the jewelry with her mother, passed the smoking pipe and weapons to her father, and to her sister, Tonalnan, she gave the parrot fan.

Huemac grieved over the interruption of his daughter's betrothal. The following week he and his wife Itzali would have received the groom and his family in their home, where they would have presented their daughter, adorned in her finest weaving, to show off her extraordinary embroidery skills. She would have sat in silence, eyes cast downward, while her father and family would have duly proceeded to cast insults upon her, lamenting her laziness, her lack of grace and beauty, her shameful indiscipline, and her hopeless stupidity. After this age-old custom, the groom's family would have taken her with them and carried her off through the streets in a pseudo-abduction, members of both families pressed around, amidst joyous hoopla and yells.

In *Cem Anahuac* marriage was a simple affair. The celebrated couple sat together on a mat, and the corner of the groom's cape was knotted to the corner of the bride's skirt. The ceremony represented the transference of care of the young man from his mother to his new bride. The new mother-in-law would bestow upon the bride an inheritance of her finest garments, and feed her four mouthfuls of tamale. Then the bride would feed her new husband, and the festivities would begin. After much celebration, the newlyweds would be sequestered over four days, during which time they were expected to refrain from sexual intimacy. Years later, for Calli did eventually marry Xolotl, she would confess to her sister Tonalnan that Xolotl had been very diligent in honoring this abstinence and that his gentle demeanor toward her virginity earned him her loving devotion and respect.

But alas, Huemac had no time to think about marriages right now. This was a time for mourning. King Naxac was dead. Everyone in Tollan was focused on funerals and prayer. The main walkway had been swept for the procession that was to take place that evening. The small, stone houses that lined the thoroughfare were fragrant with ritual incense, and the street itself was blanketed with a plethora of petals and other plant life that the mourners of the dead king would walk upon in procession.

Quetzalpopoca Smoking Feather was to officiate the divine ceremony. He had had the fortune of surviving the attack due to the fact that he had been in the Cave of the Shadows in meditation and prayer.

Xolotl had survived, along with his father, Nauhyotl, whose job it had been to protect the dwellings of their extended family and all its inhabitants including, for better or for worse, his decrepit uncle Cozcacuautli Miquiztli, who had done nothing but sit in a corner and rock in delirium, picking fleas out of his hair.

Calli too, had survived, she and her mother and the other women of the family having been protected in a house of stone.

The brutal attack had not been expected. In the first place, it had taken place outside the season of war. Huemac felt cheated. Civilized people organized their wars in the off-season, never during the tilling of the fields. These intruders were savages, who knew nothing of planting and harvesting fields. Nor did they care. They stole in order to survive, and scavenged off remains like vultures. The attackers had crept into Tollan under the cover of a moonless sky, as dark as Mictlán itself. While the people lay unconscious, immersed in their dreams, several lone warriors snuck into the inner courtyard of the king, silently slicing the life out of his sentries and guards. Then, with the envied stealth unique to nomadic hunters, they entered the king's sleeping chamber, sliced open his chest and ripped out his beating heart before the old man could even utter a sound.

Huemac had woken to screams and yells, and an effective defense of the city had ensued, but not before the escape of the warrior who ran off with King Naxac's heart.

Huemac now stood, accompanied by a small entourage, and looked down the central walkway that was scattered with petals, blossoms and long grasses.

"The Chichimeca are our nemesis." Xolotl said.

"No, my young friend. Misfortune is our nemesis." He replied. "The gods feed on our retributions and punishments and the bones they cast away are our misfortunes. We cannot conquer Misfortune. We are her slaves."

Xolotl wasn't sure if he understood Huemac's rambling. He pretended he did by nodding.

As Huemac and the others stood in the main thoroughfare waiting for the procession to begin, the sun sank lower in the western horizon, casting a speckled display of crimson and gold through layers of stormy clouds in the evening sky.

"Any news from Tulantzinco?" Huemac wondered out loud.

"Not yet, my general," someone answered.

Huemac, Xolotl and the others walked down to the end of the central walkway called the Grand Ohtli, to the place where the dwellings stopped, where people were beginning to gather. Some men had painted their faces in black and white death masks, resembling living skulls, while others had painted skeletons across their entire bodies, as well. Wearing a death mask brought life to death.

The people gathered in bereavement and disbelief. After a time, a procession emerged from the Grand Ohtli. First came the old priest Quetzalpopoca, his waist-length hair matted with agave pulp and bright crimson dye. His stone face was as expressionless as ever, but was now painted in a black and white death mask. His fierce eyes looked like two deep, dark, brown pools that went on forever, and people were afraid to look into them, knowing his eyes could pierce their very soul. He donned the full-length black robe of a shaman-priest, and carried his magical weapons in a medicine bag around his waist.

Following Quetzalpopoca were the priestesses of the Sacred House of Healing, Tonalnan among them, wailing and ululating their high-pitched lamentations. They wore full length, black cotton dresses and high, coral-inlaid head ornaments with great, gold discs at the ears.

Behind the priests and priestesses came the body of King Naxac himself, upon a gem-incrusted litter inlaid with red jasper and black onyx and carried by the warriors who had failed to defend him. The king's body had been wrapped in several layers of his finest garments, and was bedecked with jewels of gold, silver and precious stones. Because it was considered the heart of the earth, an emerald had been placed in his mouth to serve as his heart in the underworld. Prior to the procession, during his four days of public viewing, locks of his hair had been secretly clipped, and the relics had been placed in a sacred urn upon his family's altar.

The women's high-pitched lamentations and wailing continued.

In the procession, the deceased king was followed by his next of kin, his wife and concubines, his children and extended family, his generals, priests and closest friends, all of whom carried special offerings to the cremation ceremony. Huemac and Xolotl and their families joined the procession at this place in the line. Behind them came throngs of musicians, artisans, family upon family, so that the hundreds of families of Tollan, lamenting and crying, made their way across the valley, under the setting sun, to the Field of Tears.

The people sat in a great circle around the edges of the field and watched as the litter with their king was placed on scaffolding that had been built up over an elaborately woven structure of branches and logs. His body was then reverently covered with an elongated *petlatl* mat.

Huemac looked on as the body of the man who had invested him with his position and authority lay upon the unlit pyre. Quetzalpopoca was now walking a circle around the deceased, cleansing the air with an eagle feather and burning purple sage, half chanting, half singing prayers to the fallen king. Several younger priests shook tortoise shell rattles, drums resounded, and flutes released eerie notes into the ethers. In the crowd, women mourned

[149]

and wiped their tears on specially prepared fragments of paper, which would be added to the burning pyre. The flames would carry their tears to the spirit world and relieve them of their pain.

In the world of Cem Anahuac, cremation was the most common rite of passage. Burial was reserved for those taken by Tlaloc, the god of rain, in deaths caused by water or for women who died in childbed. Only those fortunate enough to die by one of these sacred deaths could enter directly into the heavens of Mictlán. All the rest would have to be cremated in order to make the journey to transform their souls. The fires of cremation aided the transformation of the soul in its ascent to the sun. Fire, by its very nature, consumes that which is manifest and carries it through the sacred gateway to the world of the spiritual. Thus, it is a conduit of supernatural power between the living and the dead. It is for this reason that we people of Cem Anahuac cremated our dead.

A bowl of water was placed near King Naxac's head to quench his thirst in the afterlife. Bits of paper with drawings on them were reverently tucked into the *petlatl* mat bundled over him. They served as keys for his journey in the afterlife, and would allow him safe passage through the Twin Mountains, the roads guarded by the great serpent, and the realm of the great crocodile Xochitonatl. They would also open the gates of the Seven Deserts and the Eight Hills, and help him defend himself against the North Wind.

Quetzalpopoca Smoking Feather lit the fire and the sacred transformation began. As the flames engulfed the king, the sun sank below the western horizon. During the time of burning, the sky turned from a gentle purple to a velvety black, and filled with sparkling stars. Eventually the flames subsided into burning embers, but the families of Tollan remained camped out on the edges of the field, honoring their beloved king. Children had long fallen asleep. Some people were talking and visiting, many just lying on the mats they had brought with them, others still, sharing food and drink in one another's company.

"Look! An omen!" someone yelled with excitement.

Huemac lifted his gaze to the nighttime sky where he saw showers of shooting stars.

A restless reaction broke out among the crowd, especially among those who had experience with monsters and sorcery.

Then a commotion stirred among the people on the other side of the Field of Tears. "Huemac, Huemac the First General," people were starting to say. "Over there." Fingers pointed and the commotion moved its way toward the First General and his entourage, until a runner appeared among the faces around him.

"Huemac, First General of Tollan," the panting messenger said as he was pushed up to Huemac's inner circle.

Huemac looked at the runner's flushed face. Sweat rolled down his body caked with dirt from the road, forming streaks through the dust and dried mud.

"I bring news from Tulantzinco."

Everyone was quiet. Huemac's heart froze.

"Ce Acatl Topiltzin Prince of Mixcóatl has agreed."

Snakes and Sacks

Tohuenyo had been looking forward to the rattlesnake hunt for as long as he could remember. For season upon season since the time he'd quit sucking his mother for milk, he had practiced and trained. As a small boy he was given a wooden stick and was made to defend himself against the older boys who always ended up delivering crushing blows and giving him a good beating, but as he grew older, he'd learned how to defend himself and then he too, began to pound the other boys. When he had lived through ten seasons of the cold winds, he began his handling of the snakes. A white haired man of the tribe, now too slow for the hunt but highly respected for his knowledge and experience, trained him in the ways of the junior warriors. Several snakes had been gathered for his training. Their mouths were first bound and then sewn shut by the hands of the experienced elder. In this way he and the other boys had learned to pick up and handle the snakes without being bitten.

Just look at him now! Hunting staff in hand, he was ready to go on his first hunt. It felt oddly dreamlike. The young men were starting to gather down at the river's edge as the sun began to rise over the distant, flat-topped mountains. They would disperse in groups – each hunting party eager to bring back the biggest prize.

Tohuenyo was careful not to get his moccasins wet. Not yet. It was his first time to wear them, and he wanted to show them off. Since he wasn't married, his mother Nine Winds had made them for him. She'd used the heavy leather of the curly haired bison, a highly prized item she'd acquired through a crafty trade with a tribesman from the North. Using her magical powers of seduction, she and several other women of the tribe had lured a small band of northern traders into their caves. For several days, moans reverberated off the volcanic walls of the mountain's inner crevices while the talented women extracted the wares of the willing foreign traders, but by the fourth day, a grave silence ensued. The women's caves were full of the foreign traders' merchandise, but the tribesmen themselves were nowhere to be found. After that, there was plenty of meat to go around.

Tohuenyo stood proud in his buffalo skin moccasins. They went all the way up to his knees. The cording that tied them was firm and secure, and they still had the beautiful curly hair of the beast hanging off the top. He could see the other men in his hunting party admiring them. He could tell they were jealous, and he was emboldened.

"Tohuenyo, come with us," Ichtaca barked at him. He could use a hunter in his party from the Coyotl Clan. He'd had his eye on Tohuenyo for several winters.

The experienced hunters in Ichtaca's party took off at a lively pace and Tohuenyo was hard pressed to keep up with them. In all, about twenty hunting parties had departed from the rocky riverbank, each one with four to five men. Ichtaca was leading his men through the northern ravine to the place of the Enchanted Cliffs. As the sun rose in the morning sky, they ran past fragrant sage and juniper, leapt over arroyos, and jumped from rock to rock in dry river beds. After a half day's run, the earth's soft dirt gave way to rocky cliffs with ample crevices and abundant hiding places for the many creatures residing there. Birds of prey dominated the sky and cliff tops. Reptiles and ground critters lived below.

"Here we start searching," Ichtaca finally commanded at morning's end. His fiery black eyes were ablaze with excitement. He took a swig from his buckskin bag and tightened the belt around his rattlesnake skin vest. Tohuenyo knew the three other men in the hunting party only by their nicknames - a common practice exclusive to men since ancient times – Mazatl, goat, Cueyatl, frog, and Moyotl, mosquito.

The mid-day heat intensified the sound of the sun. Beads of sweat adorned their bronze skin. All was still and silent except for the in-and-out buzzing of desert flies. They walked through the cliffs carefully now, finding signs of the yellow excrement with tufts of hair and feathers, all the more recognizable by its excruciatingly putrid smell. Occasionally, Tohuenyo and the others prodded the crevices with their long staves, which were forked at one end. "I'm going to wrap my staff with the skin of my first kill," he said to anyone who was listening.

"If you even catch anything," Moyotl chided.

"My staff is long and strong," Tohuenyo retorted. "I shall be a prolific hunter."

Ichtaca and the others laughed at the double entendre.

Just then the buzz of a rattle went off.

"Don't move! Be still!" Mazatl whispered. He had stepped within a hand's length of a male diamond back, coiled and poised to strike. Keeping his feet motionless, he silently grasped the staff threaded through his backpack and wrested himself free of the pack. It was a silent and graceful motion. His feet never moved. Using the crook at the end of the staff, he reached down and gently lifted the snake at its middle. The snake's body went tense and bowed, as it tried to stretch out, which was when Mazatl deftly grasped it by its tail and let its head drop down. He held it there, arm's length away from his body. With his free hand, he opened the giant buckskin sack and dropped the snake, head first, into the bag. "Sacked," he said, triumphantly. Then he pulled the cord tight.

Tohuenyo stepped over to a stone slab that extended across a crevice opening. The others saw too, and they exchanged nods of approval. With non-verbal communication, the men arranged their next move. Using their staves as levers, Ichtaca and Tohuenyo pried the giant slab up from the volcanic crevice while the other three smoothly raised it and gently hauled it away. Careful not to cause any vibration or make any sound, they laid it down ten hands away, while Ichtaca and Tohuenyo stood stoically still. Then, with the stealth and silence the Chichimeca hunters were famous for they approached the crevice and peered down below – an entire den of tens upon tens lay below them. A treasure-trove indeed!

At the bottom of the crevice the pile of diamondback vipers about twenty hands wide squirmed and writhed. Some of the tails were starting to rattle. Their triangular heads bobbed and swayed as the snakes slithered closer to one another.

"Don't move your feet and they won't strike," Ichtaca reminded Tohuenyo in a soft voice. Tohuenyo nodded.

Legs planted firmly at the top of the crevice, the men proceeded to use their staves to gently lift the vipers by the middle of their leathery bodies, catch their tails, and lower them into their buckskin sacks, until each sack was full and tightly secured. A Chichimeca warrior in his prime could carry half his own body weight, so you'll believe me when I tell you that each man in Ichtaca's hunting party, including Tohuenyo, carried ten to fifteen vipers in his buckskin bag! Because they believed in the sanctity of nature and the wrath of the Mother Goddess, they reverently replaced the stone slab over the rest of the creatures writhing in the den.

The journey back to the village was slow and long. Preserving their energy, the men hiked at a steady pace. For a while, each man kept silent, lost in his own inner world. Tohuenyo had felt the true bond of brotherhood; acceptance from the older hunters from their hearty slaps on the back and their knowing looks of approval. Life was good. He was good. This was a good find, and they would return home with honor.

Tonatiuh, the god of the sun, looked down upon them from high in the great sky and tested their strength with his blazing heat. Not a single cloud graced the expansive blue of the heavens. Realizing he was starting to fall behind, Tohuenyo quickened his pace to catch up with the older men.

"I thought it would be harder to sack 'em," Mazatl was saying.

"Did you see their eyes? They looked like they were going to pop out of their skulls!" Cueyatl laughed, Ha! Hahahahaha," as he held onto the thick straps of his heavy load.

"It was hopeless for them to try to get away," Moyotl said. "We captured them. That proves that we are superior. The gods favor us."

"They writhed like the viperous creatures that they are. They deserve to die a serpent's death – with their heads cut off and their skin flayed."

"Mazatl speaks like a true warrior," Ichtaca interrupted.

"So what do we do now?" Moyotl asked.

What a strange question, coming from an experienced hunter, Tohuenyo thought. Obviously they were going to take them back home and empty the sacks into the viper pit. Any idiot would know this. Tohuenyo started to question Moyotl's character.

Mazatl, Cueyatl and Moyotl looked at Ichtaca.

"What?" Ichtaca challenged.

[156]

"Tell us," they chimed.

Ichtaca sighed. He stopped walking and looked at Tohuenyo, contemplating something, sizing him up and down. "Alright," he said. "Swear to secrecy."

"No problem!" the other hunters said gleefully, happy to be in on secret knowledge. Tohuenyo felt himself being pulled into the huddle of men.

Ichtaca pulled out his chert hunting knife and carved a thin line into the breast of each man. No man flinched. No man winced. The men pressed their palms to the small, dripping wound, and swore a blood oath to each other, promising to keep each other's secrets forever and always.

Ichtaca spoke in a low voice to the huddled men, his eyes shifting around to make sure that no birds were listening. "Titlacáhuan says that since it was so easy to sack the Place of Stone Houses that we will return and attack a second time." The men squirmed with excitement at the news. "We will do this in four moons. The elders wish us to exterminate the enemy and keep their stone houses for ourselves."

Mazatl interrupted, "How can you *keep* a place? It's not like we can just bring it back to the caves like we did with the prisoners and treasures."

Ichtaca looked pensively at the men, deciding whether or not to disclose the next piece of information. "The Omecíhuatl had a vision," he said, telling the secret that Titlacáhuan had confided to him. "We are to attack and destroy the Place of Stone Houses and take it for our own. We will move there. We will live there." He looked at his men. "It is the will of the gods that we no longer live in the caves."

Tohuenyo balanced his guilt of the betrayal of Titlacáhuan's secret knowledge with the excitement of the message it contained, but the other men in the hunting party reacted differently. "We are meant to know this, Ichtaca," Cueyatl said. "We are the first party of the warrior clan. We will make you proud and fight at your side!"

"Here, here," the other men agreed.

Their voices now dropped to a whisper, lest the Four Winds hear them.

Mazatl then said, "There were so few of them left among their houses. I alone killed seven. My only regret is that we left so quickly, but after Ichtaca killed the king, all I wanted was to get out of there."

Tohuenyo had heard that it was Ichtaca who had cut open the king's chest and ripped out his heart, and that Mazatl and the others had been right at his side. As a junior warrior, he hadn't gone on the raiding party. He'd had to stay behind and craft weapons, but now things were different, indeed. His successful performance in this morning's hunt would ensure him a place at Ichtaca's side in the next raid. "We will do this in four moons," Tohuenyo repeated, thinking out loud.

"Tohuenyo!" Ichtaca looked at the wide-eyed hunter with fierce, penetrating eyes. The men were still huddled and their sweaty faces were close. Ichtaca softened his voice. "Young Tohuenyo, I have always loved you as though we shared the same mother. You are the handsomest and boldest of all the lads in the tribe. You are clearly favored by the gods, but if you betray our secrecy, your fate will find its end. I will kill you and eat you myself."

The four of them towered over Tohuenyo who then belted out, "I will have your sister first!"

The men broke out laughing at Tohuenyo's audacity, slapped him on the head, pushed and shoved him, and then adjusted their heavy backpacks and headed home.

Snake Work

While Ichtaca was swearing his hunting party to secrecy on their way home from the Enchanted Cliffs, Nine Winds was leading the women in the huge task that lay ahead. There was much to do. Knives had to be sharpened. Tripods needed to be made for the smoking of the jerky. The bow drills and spindles used for starting fires needed to be tuned. Great stone slabs where the skinning would take place had to be laid out. Gourds needed to be gathered. It required intense organization, and the feisty, bony Nine Winds, daughter of the Omecíhuatl, would make sure it all got done.

First she and the rest of the women built wikiups, their summer lodges in the grassy clearing between the cliffs and the river bend below. They were dome shaped structures, built with poles, sticks, mud and hides that could be easily moved to follow a migrant herd. It had been many generations, though, since they had moved from the caves. So many life spans had passed that no one could remember moving the lodges to follow a herd. The elders' great-grand elders had told of such times in their stories and folklore, and the stories were still being told. At this point in their history, the tribe used the lodges in the warm season, when they moved out of the high cliff caves that they occupied during the season of snow.

Building a wikiup was a woman's work. Later, in centuries to come, people from far away lands would think that this was a way of demeaning a woman, a way of forcing on her the most difficult labor, but it was not that way with the Chichimeca. The lodge belonged to the matriarch of the family. A woman was highly respected because she was the giver of life. She was sacred. She possessed the magical power of creation. The matriarch owned the family property and passed it to the eldest daughter upon her death. Highly skilled and strong, women of a family could both put up their lodge and take it down in the time it took to eat a meal. Being proud women, they were not about to allow a man to meddle in their domestic affairs, and men were not welcome in the setting up of their wikiups or the arrangement of their caves.

Upon marriage, the man was welcomed into the lodge of a woman, and at her hearth in the caves. If a woman was not pleased with her mate she could choose to expel him. She would simply throw all his things out. (Usually when it came to that, it was in a fit of rage). Chichimeca tribal law would defend her. These were extreme measures, though, taken under the most difficult of circumstances, and rarely came to pass. The knowledge of such an expulsion was enough to keep a man grateful to have a shelter over his head and seasoned meals in his belly. Besides, the duties of a husband were simple enough: protect and provide meat. The Chichimeca had learned long ago that most of the time men desired the great pleasure more often than women, who were heavily burdened with infants. There was little problem in the event that his cravings exceeded those of his wife, however, for polygyny was universally accepted, and even expected of a healthy male. Most women encouraged their husbands to lie with their sisters and daughters, given the other woman's consent. The happiest of husbands seemed to be those who wed women with several sisters. Men who had been thrown out or who were too lazy to provide for a hearth, if not taken up by the least desirables of the clans, were forced to live on the fringes of society, alone, outcast, scorned and ridiculed.

While the lodges were being erected, the male elders, many of whom were leaders of their clans, partook in other activities with the junior warriors. The men and boys were engaged in weaponry and things related to war. Because these were the days of the great snake hunt, the elders were binding and sewing closed the mouths of a few snakes that had been caught for just this occasion. The boys would spend the day catching the vipers amidst the lashings and reprimands of the old men. When finished, the boys would turn to playing fetch or tug of war with the *itzcuintlis*, or rub their tummies and pull their tails.

With the lodges built, Nine Winds was free to organize the others, a duty that fell to her, as daughter of the Omecíhuatl. Assigning tasks was not a difficult job, though, because of the inherent structure of the tribe. There were different clans within the tribe, each comprised of several families. With time, the women of different clans came to perform the same tasks year after year. Nine Winds was acutely bossy, and never let events unfold as they may. She directed a group of women from the Elk Clan to tighten the sinew cords on their bow drills, even though they did it every year. Then she sent the daughters of the Black Forest Clan to collect tinder, and when one woman had the nerve to back talk her, saying that they already knew their duties, she slapped the woman upside the head and tore out a chunk of her hair while eliciting shrill screams. The survival of the tribe depended on performance. Laziness and indifference resulted in many deaths. This alone drove her intolerance.

Titlacáhuan and the other shamans of the tribe were up in the high cave with the Omecíhuatl and would be coming down to the event later that afternoon. Nine Winds wanted everything to be perfect for him, even though she abhorred him. Her hatred of him had started many years before. She wasn't about to let him find any fault with her work, whatsoever.

"First Mother," a small voice said behind her.

Yellow Skirt was unusually tiny and even though barely still a girl, she was one of the few females who had the courage to look Nine Winds in the eye. For this Nine Winds liked the girl, or was she a woman? Nine Winds did a double take and decided that Yellow Skirt now looked more like a woman than a girl.

"The slabs are ready and some of the hunting parties are returning. They've put the vipers in the pit," she spoke quickly and directly. Her voice was as tiny as she was. "If you don't mind, I'd like to gift you this knife. My elder brother agreed to make it for you. I think you'll find it very capable of slicing." In gifting the blade she assured herself a place next to the First Mother when skinning and gutting the snakes.

Nine Winds took the knife in her hands. The double-edged blade was carved out of shiny, black obsidian, darker than Yellow Skirt's hair. It was tightly secured to an elaborately tooled, elk antler handle with the head of a coyote carved on one side.

"Clan of the Coyotl," she sweetly said. "Your clan."

It was no secret that Yellow Skirt favored her son Tohuenyo. The girl had cleverly won his attentions over the past winter season,

[161]

taking advantage of the long cold months that the tribe spent together in the cavern, a great hall where the community would often come together.

"It's beautiful, Yellow Skirt. Thank you." She scrutinized the tool, wondering if her son returned the girl's... the young woman's affections. A spear of jealousy pierced her heart, for she knew that she could never have her son in this way. It was forbidden for women to lie with their own sons or brothers. Since ancient times it had been known that a horrible curse would fall upon them. The Great Spirit would plant loathsome monsters in their wombs, children with atrocious deformities that were so detrimental to the survival of the clan that they would have to abandon the newborns at birth. Men were free to lie with any woman other than their mother or sister, provided the woman consented. Since men bore no children, they didn't have to worry about the curse. The Chichimeca only had mothers. They did not know that men planted the seed of life during the great pleasure.

Nine Winds and Yellow Skirt walked from the lodges to the snake field, a vast expanse at the edge of the river's bend. At one end there was a snake pit next to a great, flat beheading slab. Volcanic boulders and a forested area lay beyond. Halfway down the field there was a skinning and gutting area along the riverbank, where nature had provided them with ample limestone slabs for easily rinsing the innards. The high ground above the field was strewn with three-poled drying racks where the flesh would be seasoned and smoked for long-term storage.

A hunting party from the Bow Clan had already returned and dumped the writhing contents of their buckskin sacks into the giant pit. The day started with a dozen diamondback vipers. The serpents slithered and furiously buzzed their tails, striking the air in vain.

As first mother, Nine Winds had the privilege of choosing the first snake. People gathered around as she peered into the pit and pointed, indicating the largest diamondback with an exquisite leathery sheen. One of the men from the hunting party reached into the pit with the crook end of his staff, hooked the beast in its middle, and gently lifted it. As the snake tensed its enormous body, everyone could see that it was longer than Mazatl, the tallest man in the tribe. "Oooh's" and "ah's" followed. Then another man, the tribe's best snake handler, raised a hollowed out sugar cane tube toward the snake. The viper instinctively started to slither inside. When the snake had moved a good two hand's length up the tube, the handler grabbed it, pressing the tube and the snake together with great strength, trapping the head inside. Slowly, with both hands, he released the body from the tube until he finally had control of the head. Since it was the first snake of the season, people pounded their staves, stomped their feet and yelped in triumph.

The handler forced the snake's jaw wide open exposing its lethal fangs. Then he deftly milked the venom into a clay urn and laid the writhing creature by the head on a giant stone slab.

Crunch! Crittiky-crackle, snap!

The bones of the neck popped as he worked his flint, ax-shaped blade to cut off the head. He tossed the head into a giant tortoise shell urn where it landed, still snapping. Then he reverently handed the freshly decapitated body to Nine Winds.

"Next," he said.

Yellow Skirt looked down into the pit and chose her diamondback, and in this manner the hunters and handlers prepared the vipers for the many women who were now getting into line. Soon there was an accumulation of snapping snakeheads in the giant tortoise shell. The deadly decapitated heads would continue to strike for some time before they finally died. The busy women were heavily put out by the naughty little boys throwing rocks at the striking severed heads. They laughed hysterically and then ran off, while the menfolk carried on with business as usual, unaffected by the ruckus. Heaven help any boy who happened to run within an arm's length of any of the women. He was sure to feel a sting across his backside. The fact that the men laughed it off irritated the demons out of the women even more, but they said nothing about it.

A Chichimeca woman would never contradict a man in public. It was considered a humiliation. If she was against something her husband did or said, she would tell him in private, and very carefully at that, for Chichimeca women knew that a man in control was a happy man, and whether feigned or sincere, a woman was intent on letting it be that way. A man who was in control of his life and

[163]

his world was a confident man, which made him a powerful warrior and a strong hunter - an intensely capable protector and provider. On rare occasions, if a strong willed woman was unable to control her domineering nature and belittled her man publicly, it never ended well. While there was respect enough among the people of the clans, a weak man who was nagged by a bully wife would invariably end up the laughing stock of the tribe.

More than previous years, this year's snake field was abuzz with fiery gossip. Second hand recounts of the attack on the Place of the Stone Houses and criticisms of others' appearances at the recent triumph ceremony flew through the air between sharp tongues and perceptive ears. Yellow Skirt, who knew everything there was to know about anyone and everyone, was delighted. She talked constantly in her tiny voice as the women set to work, and despite her small stature, she worked with amazing agility and speed. "Only a few escaped certain death," she said as she laid out her snake's carcass on the limestone slab at the river's edge. She then worked her skinning knife down its white belly, slicing the skin open to expose the pinkish-grey flesh. "...supposed to attack again," she said, finishing her thought.

Nine Winds wasn't listening. She was looking around making sure that everyone was doing what they were supposed to do. A few of the *itzcuintlis* had wandered over to the skinning area and a couple of women threw river rocks at them. The dogs yelped and ran away.

After slicing the skin down the belly of her snake, Nine Winds cut off the rattle and picked out the raw, fleshy meat from the end of it with the tip of her obsidian knife. She set the rattle aside to dry.

"First Mother, may we join you?"

Nine Winds looked up and saw two young women standing there with their snakes. Before she could answer, the women sat down, splayed out their snakes and started to cut the belly skins.

"We brought you these gifts." The taller girl reached over and laid a medicine bag in front of Nine Winds. "We're sisters," the shorter one said, "from the Elk Clan."

Nine Winds thanked them. "It is good," was all she said. The medicine bag was filled with turquoise stones. She raised her eyebrows, impressed. She understood the effect that her son Tohuenyo had on women. He had a magical charm that made women swoon and loose their breath. It had always been that way. She honored the young girls' efforts to catch her son's attentions. Women put every effort into getting and keeping strong hunters in their lodges, for their very survival depended on it.

By this time, Yellow Skirt had already cleaned and gutted the innards. She tossed the skin and innards into a buckskin bag where they would be safe for the time being. Later the innards would be used as bait for hunting turkey vultures. Immediately she was up and taking the flayed carcass to the women of the Black Forest Clan who were in charge of smoking the meat.

The Black Forest women had made the drying racks using three long poles that were bound together at the top with sinew cording. At about the middle, there were crossbars all the way around. The women were hanging snake meat in long chunks with thorny hooks. They had built a fire on the ground under each tri-pod meat rack. For each fire they had painstakingly started a burning coal using a bow drill and spindle. When they successfully created a hot coal, they put it in the center of a tinder bundle. Next, they blew on the bundle until a tiny flame burst alive, and then used the bundle to light the fire. The field was strewn with meat racks, with the smoking fires beneath them, and as the day went on, the air was filled with the woody smell of diamondback jerky. Once dried, it would last indefinitely.

The Black Forest women squinted their eyes at Yellow Skirt in disdain for associating with the woman who had slapped one of them earlier that morning. "It is the stupid she-wolf that follows the alpha female around," one of them said.

"You're calling me stupid?" She said in her sickly sweet, tiny voice. "Stupid is lighting each and every meat rack fire with a spindle and coal when you can just pass the flame after you get it started." She flung her freshly flayed hunk of meat over a rack, spun on her heels and walked off, her tiny butt shaking in its rabbit skin skirt.

The women of the Black Forest Clan had to think about that.

Gossip continued, ablaze like flames swallowing dry grasses, and Yellow Skirt picked up all kinds of news as she walked back to the river's edge.

"All the women are talking about the attack on the Place of the Stone Houses," she said in a matter-of-fact tone.

Nine Winds raised one eyebrow and continued pulling the skin off a carcass.

"Everyone knows that," the tall sister said. "It's been falling off everyone's tongues since Ichtaca's ceremony."

"Blessed be Itzpapálotl," they all said in unison and reverence, as was the custom after mentioning any sacred event.

Yellow Skirt continued, "Everyone's saying that the elders have decided to attack again and take their stone houses for our own." Before anyone could ask how they would get a stone house all the way back to the caves she added, "They want to *move us there*." She placed much emphasis on this last part, knowing it was the most provocative piece of her story. She retrieved the skin from the buckskin bag and pushed it into the river, rinsed it, and then shoved it into a gourd filled with urine, pressing it down and placing stones on it so it would be completely covered. "Who's ready to get another snake?"

The Omecíhuatl Arrives

The women worked under the hot sun, skinning, hanging the meat on the drying racks, fighting with the Black Forest Clan, talking about the next attack on the Place of the Stone Houses and what it would be like to leave the Place of the Caves. In four moons time their lives would be completely different. Women from the different clans elaborated with many details that which they had learned from their brothers and husbands. They'd heard that the people there dressed in woven *fabric*, but none of the Chichimeca women had ever seen any, and they could only speculate as to what *fabric* was. Supposedly the corn grew in rows as straight as the braids in Nine Winds' hair, but they couldn't imagine how this could be, for they had always and forever collected wild growth. Well, one thing was for certain. They knew their men were going to attack again, and they knew it was going to be in four moons time.

"Tohuenyo's back," the tall sister said.

The girls perked up and became alert.

Hunting parties had been returning all morning, delivering their catch and filling their rumbling bellies with *nopalli* cactus, cashews and roasted venison. The tired hunters would spend the rest of the evening hanging around the snake field resting before going out again the next day. The snake hunt lasted ten days. By the end, the tribe accumulated a hearty stockpile of jerky that they would store in the upper caves, enough to carry them through the winter.

When Ichtaca's hunting party came into the camp, the reception was welcoming. Cheers were hollered for Ichtaca, war hero of the tribe. Young boys ran up to him and touched his clothes and backpack, hoping his strength and bravery would rub off on them. The *itzcuintlis* ran around the hunters' legs, jumped, and barked at the commotion created by the excited boys.

While Ichtaca received a hero's welcome, Tohuenyo had the unabashed attention of the women. Sultry Tohuenyo was beautiful. He knew it. He knew the effect he had on women, so he puffed himself up like a grand turkey cock, even though he was carrying half his weight in a sack on his back.

As he walked past his mother, she gave him an approving nod. She was not a loving mother, but rather a fierce woman, a warrior, feisty and sometimes cold and cruel. She often slapped him upside the head as an expression of her twisted affection, but she was proud of her son, and with just a glance she told him so.

It wasn't long before Tohuenyo, Ichtaca and the three others overheard the talk of the circle - to think that they had just drawn their own blood and sworn themselves to secrecy for what was now flying freely out of the mouths of the women!

"Women's tongues are sharper and move faster than men's," Ichtaca said as he dumped his snake sack into the pit. In any event, the other four were sworn to secrecy and would still honor their warrior's promise on the very real pain of death.

Ichtaca could circulate close to the First Mother now that Tohuenyo was in his hunting party. It was not without calculating ambition that he had pulled the youth under his wing. With his newly won status as first warrior, he had the right to circulate anywhere among the tribe, but having Tohuenyo in his war party strengthened his position.

With nonchalance and an air of arrogance he moved his hunting party near the women of the First Mother, Nine Winds, shooing off a group of hunters who quickly gathered their things and cleared out. Mazatl and Cueyatl unloaded some tools and the men set to sharpening their weapons.

By this time, the number of people around Nine Winds had swelled. Work came first, and conversation with the men who had just installed themselves next to them was forbidden, as it would deter from the completion of the tasks at hand. Nine Wind's switch reminded them severely of that, but that didn't mean that glances weren't exchanged. Actually, there was ample non-verbal communication taking place - hand signals and gestures. Yellow Skirt and the Elk Clan sisters were vying for Tohuenyo's attention, but Tohuenyo was ignoring them. He was consumed in fine-tuning a flint arrowhead: all the better for the giant Mazatl, who had his eye on the feisty little Yellow Skirt. Secret messages flew between the young people when they thought the matron wasn't looking, but even though she was slitting snake bellies and tearing off their skins, Nine Winds hardly missed a trick. Then, unexpectedly, she received her own message. At one point when she caught Ichtaca's flashing eyes, he raised two fingers to his mouth and spread them apart with his long, wet, tongue. This was a most inviting proposition, coming from a man young enough to be her son, and Nine Winds decided to consider it.

The day's work had gone well, she thought. Many gourds were lined up with the skins soaking in either urine or a combination of wood ashes and water. "Tomorrow they'll be ready to tack up and dry," she said out loud looking at the gourds. The next morning, long before dawn and before repeating the entire day's process again, the women of all the clans would come down to the gourds, extract the skins from the urine, rinse them in the river, and remove all remnants of flesh from the under side. They would then stretch the hides out, sewing them to sturdy frames along the edges. As the stretched skins were drying throughout the day, the women would have to frequently massage them with acorn oil. This would make the leather supple and keep it from drying out.

"The Omecíhuatl comes!" someone shouted.

Nine Winds pulled herself out of her thoughts.

People were scurrying from other parts of the work camp – women from their drying racks, men from their weaponry. They sat in the middle section of the field, wherever they could find a niche to fit in. Punishment for late arrivals was severe, usually dismemberment of a toe as an example of a person's sloth.

Titlacáhuan and his entourage were approaching the snake field. He was not dressed as elaborately as he had been for Ichtaca's ceremony of triumph, but he was walking solemnly and with poised intent. The three shamans with him carried a large buffalo hide bundle. As they neared, Nine Winds could see the Omecíhuatl's age-old legs dangling out.

Everyone prostrated themselves in the direction of the Omecíhuatl, their legs folded neatly beneath them, their foreheads touching the ground. Only the clan leaders, both matriarchs and male elders, kept their heads off the ground. They kneeled on folded legs, but with their bodies leaning over and their heads respectfully bowed.

The shamans set the buffalo hide gently on the ground and propped up the ancient grandmother to face the crowd at the river bend. Titlacáhuan then began to shake his tortoise shell rattle in the air around her and call upon the spirits for protection by intoning their names.

The Omecíhuatl was a verifiable hag. She was said to commune with female demons and shape shift into beastly creatures at night. Adding to her savage demeanor was a massive amount of matted, waist-length hair, completely white and randomly adorned with metacarpals and phalanges from her recent sacrificial victims. Her crepe-like face was dark, the color of *chocolatl* and heavily wrinkled from decades of desert survival. This made her eyes even more frightening, for long ago she had gone blind in one eye, which was heavily clouded over with a thick white film. The other eye was all seeing, though, and swirled around in its socket landing on any and every detail. She was too old to walk or move about which explained why she was carried everywhere. Sometimes she would urinate or defecate on herself if she wasn't placed over a gourd in time, and there was great difficulty in cleaning her – not because of her brittle old bones, as one would think, but because she would kick and scream, and bite those who tried to bathe her.

For as horrid as she appeared (and smelled), the Omecíhuatl was wise beyond all measure. She was universally feared and respected.

Titlacáhuan was now burning sage around her and singing chants. He stopped and spoke to the tribe.

"The Omecíhuatl has had a vision!"

Not a person stirred.

The Omecíhuatl spoke in a dry and cracked voice. She was missing most of her teeth and when she sucked in a breath of air, a croaking noise came out of her fetid mouth. It sounded like she had a locust stuck in her throat. She raised a bony finger when she delivered her prophesy;

> *"To war we shall go,*
> *Not a battle will be fought.*
> *To take down our foe,*
> *Attack we shall not."*

[170]

Her eye swirled around catching the subtle dynamics of her surroundings, and the locust in her throat croaked again.

The shamans then picked her up in the buffalo hide and carried her back to the highest cave.

The people of the tribe resumed their work in grave silence, stricken with panic and fear.

The Inner Chamber

In the year 5 Calli the men, women and children of Tollan engaged in many days of ceremony and ritual to initiate the accession of their new first priest and military ruler, Ce Acatl Topiltzin. It was about this same time that I started manifesting my *tonalli*, my spirit body of light. By shifting my state of consciousness (remember that I now exist in Mictlán, the great void where the Sacred Spirit is unmanifest), I could drift among the beings in the One World, if ever so faintly. They could not see me, save for the exceptional few who had the gift of perception. In this way I followed the incredible events that were about to unfold.

I should tell you first that ours was not a world in which everything revolved around mankind, in which man was the center of all existence. To the contrary, all existence revolved around the gods. There was proof enough of this in the world around us: Nature, with all her botanical glory, the movement of the sun through the diurnal sky, the divine constellations in the celestial night. These were not the creations of humans. This proved to us that the gods were at the center of the One World. We humans were mere players of the gods' whims. In those ancient times, the driving force of my people was a profound religious spirit deeply inherent in our minds and in our lives. All that came to pass was a result of the will of the gods, and every outcome, whether good or evil was considered divine.

✾

"The gods have willed it thus," Calli whispered to her sister, fanning her with the betrothal parrot fan.

Tonalnan tried to calm her pounding heart, which had decided to beat in her throat, making it hard for her to swallow and breathe. "I'm ready," she told her sister Calli, as she patted her shoulder bag. She'd spent the better part of one moon searching for and gathering up the secret herbal remedy it contained.

They stood with several other noble women in the courtyard of the Sacred House of Healing, waiting outside the door to the inner chamber. This particular afternoon the sun god, Tonatiuh, cast his rays down upon the many urns throughout the courtyard that were filled with fragrant flowers - geraniums, zinnias, morning glories, dahlias, - planted especially for the coronation of Ce Acatl Topiltzin.

"Take a deep breath and remember that you are only a puppet being used by the gods to carry out their own divine plan," Calli reassured her.

Several bees danced on a gentle breeze that brushed passed them.

A monarch butterfly slowly opened and closed its wings on the crown of a potted marigold.

Humming birds prodded the trumpet shaped bells of a yellow and fuchsia bomarea that proliferated in the heart of the inner courtyard, while fiery bougainvilleas fingered their way up the columns of the surrounding open corridors.

Tonalnan waited at the entrance to the inner chamber, consumed by her thoughts of several nights before - Donned in simple white tunics and armed with sacred amulets and their most treasured magical weapons, a stolid group of middle-aged women had approached her in the Sacred House of Healing. They were the other women physicians with whom Tonalnan had spent her whole life, working, laboring, and studying together to strengthen the body of knowledge of medicinal herbs and healing powers.

"We've brought you a gift," one of them had said, masking grief and envy in her tone. She'd held up a strand of coral beads. Tonalnan leaned forward and the woman placed them upon her, pulling her long black hair through the lengthy, blood red strands.

"Grandmother Elder was the matron of our Sacred House of Healing," she said. "To all she was our beloved mother and friend, but you, young Tonalnan, you were her protégée. You are a young woman of most exceptional talents."

"We bestow upon you the office of matron," another said, "to be held in perpetuity, but until you yourself achieve the status of mother, we will, for the sake of appearances, collectively act as your regent." Her voice shook and her face contorted with emotion. "As thy regent," she self-corrected.

"We embrace thy bidding and will fulfill thy decrees, young maiden, while offering thee our best counsel," another of the midwives added.

"Be light of heart, mothers!" Tonalnan had jubilantly replied. "In return for this endowment I vow that mine will be a life of sacrifice and servitude."

Tonalnan now stood mesmerized in thought. Whether the professed loyalty of the older midwives had been authentic or a political ploy no one would ever know.

"Here," her sister said, handing her the orchid and breaking her trance. "They're calling for you."

A flock of musical blue mockingbirds descended as Tonalnan turned toward the threshold of the inner chamber to follow an unusually tall, slender slave whose face was painted green. He donned nothing more than a loincloth and a slave collar, and carried himself with a disposition of hopeless resignation. As she followed the slave down the dark stone hallway, the avian chorus faded. Her soft moccasins rhythmically padded the limestone floor. The room through the doorway at the end was aglow with the fanciful flicker of oil lamps, and white-grey clouds of smoke rolled toward her through the stone archway, enveloping her with the scents of cedar, juniper and sage. She could hear men's laughter.

The slave stopped at the door. She stood behind him upon the threshold between Then and Now. She had never met a prince before, nor come before the presence of an exalted one. The Grandmother Elder had attended King Naxac by herself when he was alive, with no other women physicians to aid her. "All things in their time," she could hear Grandmother Elder telling her. She heard a popping sound and a waft of *copalli* incense engulfed her.

"Let the medicine woman in!" hurrahed a joyous voice among the chatter.

The green-faced slave moved aside and Tonalnan stepped into the glowing, smoky room. It was about twenty paces long, with a dark flagstone floor and smooth stone walls. A lengthy floor mat lay stretched down the middle laden with a feast and occasional firepots, surrounded by Topiltzin's inner circle, the stone faced

[175]

priest and her father among them. Energetic conversations bounced between the men, filling the air with words like *limestone quarry, gold and silver, exacting tribute*, and *obsidian mines.*

At the far end behind the Exalted One there was a modest archway in the back wall. The darkness of the interior was acutely contrasted with the light emanating from behind the opening so that all she could see of him was the swaying silhouette of his elaborate feathered mask: velvety black shadows of twenty something quetzal tail feathers breaking the rays of light.

"My anticipated physician has arrived," said a delightful voice from behind the feathered mask. The shadow raised its arms welcoming Tonalnan, changing the formation of the rays cast by its silhouette.

Everyone fell silent.

Tonalnan walked down the side of the inner chamber, taking care to maintain her dignified composure, her stolid face, her steadfast self discipline so that every movement, every action, every thought was deliberate and controlled. The closer she got to the Exalted One, the more he appeared to change from shadow to man.

The guests threw cornmeal onto the fire pots causing sparks that glistened and popped.

As she approached this leader of thousands, eyes cast down, she knelt and reverently placed the potted orchid before him.

"A gift for thee, My Lord, from the Sacred House of Healing." She sat before him upon her heels with her legs properly folded under. Temptation got the better of her, and while she kept her head down, she lifted her eyes and cast her gaze upon him.

The prince sat cross-legged, placidly stroking an ocelot in his lap whose honey glazed eyes languidly deliberated between open and closed. The gold and black creature vibrated a husky rumbling sound she'd never heard before.

"It purrs," he said from behind his magnificent mask. It was predominantly blue, made with feathers from the inner wings of magpies, plumage of blue mocking birds, and the wing and tail feathers from blue jays of the Huachucan Mountains. It culminated in awe-inspiring blue quetzal tail feathers fanning out an arm's length above him. The masterpiece was highlighted with black and white woodpecker, iridescent blue-black grackle, and had accents of yellow and red.

"Why does our prince wear a mask?" she boldly asked.

"And you do not?" he said. "What is a mask but that which you put on to show the outside world? The mask we wish to present fulfills the role the world requires of us, but the mask each of us wears is the part of us most distant from our true selves."

She wondered whether he was a god impersonating a man.

As the afternoon stretched into evening they spoke of many things, such as plans for the building of the new city. Eventually, as the conversation turned toward the affairs of the Sacred House of Healing, words were shared about altered states of consciousness. Ce Acatl forbade the use of powerful medicines. He was adamant that the use of bewitching substances like *ololiuqui*, the cactus buttons *peyotl*, the *tlapatl* weed, and the *nanacatl* mushrooms were reserved exclusively for the priesthood to be used only for visions and prophecy. These plants had highly potent powers, and should be fiercely guarded. He also made it clear that drunkenness in public would be punishable by death for any *macehualli*, or by large fines for a *pipiltzin*.

"What better way to fill the coffers of the state?" someone chided.

Another round of *pulque* was then served. They were not in public, after all.

Many ideas for the new kingdom were exchanged above a melodic hum of flute players while they munched roasted peanuts and cashews. At one point Ce Acatl spoke to them about sacrifice.

"Everything is an exchange," he said. "Why look around you and you will see. If you want something from the marketplace, what do you do?"

"Trade something of equal value," someone answered.

"Or lesser, if your trading skills are honed!" Huemac interjected.

Everyone chuckled.

"That is right. You give something up. Something you value. And in this way, you are sacrificing something that you value to obtain something else. You do it because you are convinced that what you want is of more value than what you already have."

"What if what we wish to obtain is wisdom? What then? What sacrifice could we possibly make?"

"Ah, my dear Tonalnan. We see now why it is said your thinking is prodigious."

He studied his subjects in the room. "For things that are intangible such as love or well-being your sacrifice must be greater." He paused. "What would you be willing to give up to attain wisdom?"

The ministers of the inner council shifted and sat up, as though they were suddenly being scrutinized, their inner-most secrets revealed.

"If it is a prince's bracelet you long for, well you might have to sacrifice a portion of that delicious smoking blend you prepared. You know the one we're talking about, the one with tobacco, red willow bark and spearmint." Ce Acatl held out his turquoise and gold bracelet.

Tonalnan was obliged to humor her morrow's king, although she clearly felt she was getting the better part of the trade. Smiling, she reached into her shoulder bag and pulled out one of the pouches from within and handed it to him. She put the bracelet on her wrist.

"Let's suppose your desire is to obtain wisdom," he continued. "The question is what could you sacrifice for it? I ask you, where does wisdom come from? Can another man give you wisdom? No. This is not a trade that one can make with another. Wisdom is a gift from the gods, and as such, a man or woman must sacrifice their ignorance and bestial nature to attain it."

Water Is As Water Does

The lengthy conference of the Inner Chamber lasted way into the night, as Ce Acatl explained the plans for his new empire. To each of the council members present he assigned new responsibilities. As their sovereign, Ce Acatl Topiltzin would be First Priest and Minister of War. Tonalnan's father Huemac would continue as First General. Quetzalpopoca Smoking Feather was endowed with the powers of High Priest, and Tonalnan was given the title Guardian of the Sacred House of Healing. Other members present, some of whom had followed Topiltzin all the way from Xochicalco, would control the citizens and the development of streets and housing. Neighborhoods were to be built so that craftsmen and artisans of the same trade would live close together. Schools were to be built to teach religion and weaving to girls and hunting and war to boys. The mining industry would be given high priority for the expedient extraction of obsidian, calcite and gold. Commerce with subject nations was to be carefully controlled, with detailed management of required tribute. Magnificent pyramids would be erected to honor the gods, and most important of all, plans for a great palace, The Palace of Quetzalcoatl, would soon begin.

"Tell us, Quetzalpopoca, what best way is there to water the corn?" the Exalted One asked. Smoking Feather was now an elder and his wisdom was well regarded.

"Why lord, that would be by following the example of Tlahuicole."

"Do tell." The sovereign was now reclining, fondling a silver chinchilla. The elaborate blue feather mask had now been replaced by a blue-green gauze veil with tiny gold bells along the fringe. It was forbidden to look upon the face of Ce Acatl Topiltzin.

"Long ago," Smoking Feather began, "The god of thunder descended upon the village of a noble leader named Tlahuicole. 'Your people are desperate from the lack of rain,' the god said. 'I crave rain and love your people as though they were my own children. I have decided that upon my orders you will help them.'

Tlahuicole replied, 'Lord, I am your most humble servant. Command, and I shall obey.'"

"Oh that our subjects would obey us thus!" exclaimed Ce Acatl.

Everybody laughed except Quetzalpopoca Smoking Feather. True to his nickname, his face resembled stone.

"The god of thunder continued, 'It is thus, my son. Fill your urn with water from this fresh spring and go to the salty sea where you will hurl it into the brackish waters. Then, take the water from the sea, fill your urn, and return to pour it into the spring.

'As you wish, I shall do,' Tlahuicole replied.'"

Quetzalpopoca continued, "'Yes,' said the god, 'This is what you will do, my son, because the sweet water from the spring in the salty sea will not be content, and the salty water from the sea will be even less content in the middle of the fresh spring water. As both wish to return to their respective places of origin, they have no other remedy but to rise up in the form of a cloud. In doing such, the water from the spring will take the route of the sea, and the water of the sea, that of the spring. The two will be forced to encounter each other in the middle of their journey, crashing into each other and falling to the ground in the form of rain.'"

"Bravo!!"

"Hurrah!"

Sweetened coconut, wild strawberries and chocolate were passed around. When the delight with the story telling settled, Ce Acatl spoke, "We will no longer rely upon the rains brought to us by Tlahuicole," he said. There was a wave of astonishment. "We will change the watering of the corn. We ask you to look upon our plan."

Several slaves carried in a platform and placed it at the end of the room, near Topiltzin. The council members crowded around to look on. It was rectangular shaped, about the length of a grown man and about a hand's width deep. Inside was a soft, clay model of Tollan, with the mountains and valleys around.

"Observe, my great lords. Here, this section represents the fields of corn." He scraped a courtly finger adorned with a giant opal ring through the moldable clay to represent rows. "And this over here," pointing to a miniature canal that ran along the side of the platform, "is the River Xicocotitlan. Come, Chac. Pour the water."

A dark slave with giant braided buns on the sides of his-her head started to pour an urn of water into the canal.

"Watch the river water flow, My Lords!"

Before their very eyes, they witnessed how the water in the canal scurried through various channels toward the grooves meant to be the rows of corn.

"Thou hast moved the water from the river to the fields!" Tonalnan exclaimed.

"Yes, my darling physician, and this will be the strength of our nation."

The excited council members then spent immeasurable time discussing how they could build canals, divert the water and irrigate the fields.

Finally, when many topics of conversation had been exhausted, the king's anointing ceremony began. Any remnants of a banquet were whisked away by slaves, and all four walls were lined with black and red oil lamps, the flames flickering and fluttering in fanciful delight. Ce Acatl Topiltzin was placed on an ornately carved golden bench that was handsomely studded with topaz and jade.

After creating a sacred space with his tortoise shell rattle, and smudging everyone with an eagle feather and sage, Quetzalpopoca stood solemnly on one side of the youthful prince, with Tonalnan poised reverently on the other. The prince's favored slave Chac held out a ceramic bowl of sweet water from the River Xicocotitlan into which Tonalnan slowly poured a sacred herbal mixture from her medicine bag. The rest of the council members sat enraptured on the floor looking on. In their many hands now rested an assortment of finger drums and cotton seed bells.

Tonalnan emptied a vial of jojoba oil into the ambrosial solution.

"*Heh, na-nana heh..*" she began. "The Sun, the lord of the Sky will wash thy face."

The gentle *thumpity-thump-thump* of finger drums echoed through the room.

"Our Mother, Toci, Lady of the Earth will wash thy face." She then dipped a small swatch of moleskin into the water. Quetzalpopoca gave her a reassuring nod to proceed as they had rehearsed, but they hadn't prepared for what happened next, as the stoned faced priest lifted Ce Acatl's turquoise veil.

[181]

How each person saw Ce Acatl Topiltzin no one exactly knows, as the council members were sworn to guard the secrets of the Inner Chamber. Rumors later circulated suggesting that each person saw something different. It was as though Ce Acatl Topiltzin's face reflected what each individual's own psyche projected onto it, but isn't that the essence of seeing things differently? Some tales told that his eyes were blue, and his hair was yellow, while others said his skin was white. Rumors even circulated that sparkling rays beamed off his face and that his skin glowed with radiant light.

Regardless of how he was perceived, the task at hand continued on. The power of water to transform was employed as the High Priest Quetzalpopoca and Tonalnan performed the washing of the face ritual. When they finished, all she said was, "Thou hast taken a new face."

From that time on, the prince was referred to as king. From that time on, Tollan was to be called Tula. From that time on, they conferred upon him the prestigious title Quetzalcoatl, He Who Lives in an Exalted State. Ce Acatl Topiltzin Quetzalcoatl became their king.

Rulers do not become leaders on their own. They rise to lead because others choose to follow them. As such, the coronation of Quetzalcoatl was to be a public ceremony so that the people of the Nonoalca-Tolteca Nation could see the glorious coronation of their new king. News spread so quickly throughout the One World about the upcoming event it was as though the birds themselves had delivered it over all the land. The Prince of Mixcoatl was to be king! The warrior priest of Xochicalco! He of the cone shaped crown! Soon enough even more people from far and wide descended upon Tula and pledged themselves to the Nonoalca Nation, eager to call Quetzalcoatl their king.

The Coronation

You may have heard the saying "As above, so below." This was much the case in the days of the coronation. For the people, as instruments of the gods, began to manifest the will of the gods, who were at war for supernal domination. The gods played out their will employing the immensity of admixed forces and used mere mortals as pawns. The Dark Lord of the Here and Now, Tezcatlipoca was the god of destruction and catastrophe. Power and greed, secrets and lies, vanity and pride are all instruments of Tezcatlipoca, given to mortals to empower the demonic forces that strengthen the lord of the Here and Now. At the other extreme there was the god Quetzalcoatl, also called by the names of the Plumed Serpent and Lord of the Wind. The serpent lives its life forever pressed upon the earth, in the very midst of that which is manifest. The bird, however, soars in the heavenly realm above. As plumed serpent, Quetzalcoatl embodies the two, blowing life into all creation. Quetzalcoatl, the plumed serpent, is the divine force that enables the spirit world to unfold into creation and become material and manifest. Creativity and fertility, health and vitality, hope and felicity, these are the instruments of Quetzalcoatl.

The will of the gods seeped through the collective consciousness of the people of Cem Anahuac, the One World, and there were priests among them who held disdain in their hearts for Ce Acatl Topiltzin. "What will be your offering to the temple, noble lord? For if you offer only butterflies and flowers the sons of Tlaloc will be angered and bring calamity upon us all. It is necessary that you sacrifice a jaguar, an eagle, and a wolf. Take heed - these you must find yourself. Yes, yes!" They insisted. "This is befitting and proper for the coronation of a king!"

And so it was that after the ritual of the Washing of the Face, Quetzalcoatl left the people of Tula and walked into the desert alone; taking only what he could himself carry. "I will wander for forty days to find the jaguar, the eagle and the wolf," was all he said.

In Tula, the enormity of individuals that came together for the coronation was staggering. As had been agreed upon, Quetzalcoatl's counselors began to organize the throngs and hordes into constructive groups. There were as many different nations and dialects as there were professions: merchants and traders, hunters and warriors, stone masons and carpenters, midwives and healers, astrologers and prophets, artisans, weavers, potters and jewelers. There was even a multitude of prostitutes, thieves and slaves.

The people's sense of urgency for the coronation of their new king helped in the formation of their city plan, for in their excitement, they toiled with an intensity and cooperation as never before. As was the custom, the noble *pipiltzin* resided in great, stone mansions, two stories high that lined the central thoroughfare called the Grand Ohtli. Their homes were many generations old, built in the time of their grandfathers' grandfathers. Now, upon orders from Quetzalcoatl, all stone houses were to have a spiral trim atop their façades to honor the Lord of the Wind, he who blows life into all creation. So the great homes of the Grand Ohtli were covered with scaffoldings filled with masons and slaves, while the *pipiltzin* spent their time cleaning their central courtyards and beautifying their home décor for the festivities to come.

Flagstone paved streets latticed their way through the central neighborhoods of Tula's elite, and as one walked farther and farther away from the Grand Ohtli, the houses were smaller and less elaborate. Deals and family alliances were being made for wealthy new arrivals so that many homes had new extensions under way.

Artisans such as sculptors, potters, jewelers and weavers were afforded semi-accessible sections of the city, as well as weapon makers and masons. The *macehualli* peasantry lived in wikiups in the hills beyond, clustered into familial clans, where they tended the state's communal fields.

The city's preparation for the coronation had started before Quetzalcoatl left. "What's the point of bringing people together if they don't interact and make connections?" He had asked his heads of state. "I know this is a solemn ritual to honor the gods, but so too, let it be a time to be productive. Will my people learn that much

[184]

if they only sit and listen to talking heads, and then turn and go quietly home?" Many eyebrows were raised at this innovative idea. "Let all public ceremonies be combined with celebration!" Their reaction quickly went from astonishment to relief, and then to excitement at the prospects to be gained by this new custom.

The coronation of Ce Acatl Topiltzin Quetzalcoatl was to be loosely structured, with a central procession and offerings, yes, but afterward there was to be a huge *tianguis* bazaar with performances, concerts, dances, dinners, and exhibits where people could both market their goods and find whatever interested them.

The only difficult part in the planning was that the king was *gone*. After having set out on his mission to find a jaguar, an eagle and a wolf, no one had heard a word of him. The city leaders spoke nightly and passed messages back and forth, relentlessly tiring the legs of many runners, but nobody knew of his whereabouts. So preparations went on without him. It was decided that for the fortieth day the streets would be lined with brightly painted paper banners heralding the Nonoalca Nation, and strewn with burning incense and flowers. A sacrificial stone altar was prepared by master masons, dragged through the streets by forty slaves, and assembled on a mound at the far side of a great field just south of town. At the four corners of the field, giant structures of wood were carefully erected for bonfires, and decisions were made about the distribution of space for the great event. Prickly tongued crones quarreled with the authorities over the best locations, and feisty merchants fought for larger spaces to lay their wares, but in the end, preferences were determined by clandestine pay-offs.

Days and nights soon faded into one another and the two months of twenty days came to pass. The morning of the coronation finally arrived.

As the morning sun, Tonatiuh, peeked over the horizon, the sleeping Toltecs began to stir. Thousands had converged upon Tula, and many had slept for several days around the great field, in anticipation of the sacred event. Mats aligned the edges of the field, some with wooden frames for shade with colorful cotton fabrics draping over their wares. Not a single barter was permitted, nor the slightest exchange, not a song nor dance, nor an indulgence of any kind, until the ritual had been performed.

[185]

Silence predominated as the streets filled with onlookers, lest anyone should fail to hear the conch that would signal the coming of the king. Along the Grand Ohtli, nobles quietly waited upon their rooftops, leaning over their newly constructed spiral trims and drinking mugs of honey-sweetened *atolli*. Excitement permeated the silence in a way that only poets could describe.

Then, as the sun fully emerged and cast its radiance upon all the land, a most unexpected natural phenomenon occurred. Sweet, gentle monarch butterflies appeared and began to fill the air. There were just a few at first, descending upon the flowers that adorned the streets and houses. Soon more came, fluttering through the gentle breezes like laughter upon the wind, and more and still more, until there were millions. They playfully flirted with the Toltecs as if to say, "Wake up! There is nothing upon this moment that is lacking!"

As the people were mesmerized with nature's intoxicating kiss, the conch blew, long and loud. The people were drunk with the beauty of the monarchs, whose enchantment consumed their senses so that they were still and slow moving upon the arrival of their king. He came from the north, walking down the Grand Ohtli toward the great field. With him he carried not his sacrifices, but rather, they accompanied him! The jaguar to his right, the wolf to his left, and the eagle circled above. He donned a veil beaded with turquoise and coral, and white robes embroidered in silver and gold elegantly draped his dark, slender body. His waist-length, black hair flew out behind him.

The conch blew again and the sound of butterfly wings filled the air.

As he walked forth, the enraptured Toltecs gathered themselves behind him, and those along the rooftops threw out petals casting fragrant, multi-colored showers on the procession below.

At the great field he stood on a hill behind an altar accompanied by his first priest Smoking Feather to one side and his first general Huemac on the other. Two great heads of state would rule over Tula, the priesthood and the military, and he would be their crown jewel, the king of the greatest militaristic theocracy the One World had ever known.

Some people expected Quetzalcoatl to sacrifice the jaguar, the eagle and the wolf on the altar stone that day, perhaps the same people that demanded he sacrifice them in the desert, but he did not.

He blew upon a conch and looked out upon the masses sitting adoringly throughout the great field and beyond.

Glistening in the morning sun, the monarch butterflies continued to dance upon the wind.

Then Ce Acatl lit a sacrificial fire in a basin before the altar and raised his arms to the crowd.

"I am Quetzalcoatl, the son without a father! Can you not see me? Come here My Lords, I am waiting for you! I have brought my mother's dress and her sword. I will bury it in your throats, in your wombs, in your sides, so that you will know my mother is the One, Coatlicue, she who gives life to those who are dead!"

The erudite Toltecs who knew that Quetzalcoatl spoke in symbols derived a spiritual understanding of the words he spoke. They guarded the secret knowledge and passed it down to their children's children so that many generations after, the secret knowledge came to be called Toltec Wisdom.

Then Ce Acatl turned toward the flames in the basin and addressed the spirit of the fire. "I call upon you, my sister, Death! Here you will revive and be reborn. Come to help me, my father, the one of the burning canes, the one of the red hair, you who are father and mother of the gods! Sit on my mat of flowers – come and drink!"

Quetzalcoatl then laid a golden disc on the altar, burned *copalli* incense upon it, and reverently arranged other sacred objects around it - blood red coral, an eagle feather, a tortoise shell rattle, and a human skull.

Then the first priest anointed him with oil and the first general placed an obsidian dagger in his hands. So it was that on that day in Tula, Ce Acatl Topiltzin Quetzalcoatl became the Toltec king.

As quickly as they had come, the monarchs departed, leaving a profound change in those whose lives they had briefly embraced.

And Lord Huemac gave the anticipated command, "Let the festivities begin!"

The Gift

"Thank you, Great Father. My heart guards the knowledge you have shared and I respectfully leave." The words flowed out of her automatically.

"You see there?" Huemac said to the men gathered around him, "She is so composed you can see the femininity in her face!"

Nods of approval spread among the admiring chieftains and clan leaders as Tonalnan took her leave of her father's circle. Four seasons had passed since the coronation, and Tonalnan had ripened like the fruit of a cactus flower, full of life and vitality.

Huemac leaned toward his companions and whispered in a hushed voice, "All you vermin can forget any proposals of marriage that you might have. Forget it, I tell you. I will never let her go. Off with the head of any man who approaches her!"

There were too many people gathered in the central patio to form one circle for one conversation, which was the normal Toltec custom. When occasions called for large gatherings such as this, it seemed that people clustered in smaller groups with their own, private conversations.

I wonder what so many people could be discussing, she thought. *Does it matter what I say? Are they thinking one thing and saying another like I am?* As she slowly glided through the guests, she made every point of eavesdropping.

People were still talking about the coronation.

"The monarch butterflies were no trick of magic," the royal architect's wife said. "It truly was a gift from the gods."

"It proves he is the son of Quetzalcoatl," her society friend added.

"Well let's hope so," her husband Zolton interjected, "better from the gods than a trick of sorcery."

The next enclave was hovered around Cuilton, the agricultural engineer, whom she detested for his views on inheritances. Since the previous king, he had been trying to change the custom from matrilineal to patrilineal lineage. How oafish. Everyone knew that the only true proof of lineage was through one's mother. She would have to learn to tolerate him, she decided, because he was building the canals that were diverting water of the River Xicocotitlan throughout the entire valley. Because of the grandiose results of his canals, the city's grain houses were quickly filling.

"I hear his daughter Calli married Nauhyotl's son," she heard a man say to Cuilton.

"Yes," Cuilton replied. "I understand the lad is beginning to distinguish himself in battle."

"Deserves to be the First General's son-in-law," the man added. "Of course if you have your way, Cuilton, he stands to inherit the entire *pulque* production and not those sisters of his."

"Yes. Inheritances pass through women and we do all the work to manage the estates. Ah, well," Cuilton went on, "we know what part a man plays in spawning young." The men laughed. "You know his father Nauhyotl and I played together as boys. And the uncle, Miquitzli, too. Sad really, when you think about what happened to that decrepit fellow."

"Well Nauhyotl is the better man," another man said, "and he has taken over the *axcaitl* in a splendid way."

"Cheers!" The men raised their goblets and drank down their *pulque*, the favored intoxicating privilege of the nobility.

"I'm telling you," a woman at the next group of minglers was saying. "My whole trunk of clothing was gone! I couldn't find it anywhere."

"Well that's just absurd," a second woman said, eyeing the first from top to bottom, scrutinizing what little wardrobe she had left.

"No. I heard the same thing from one of the weavers at the *tianguis*," said a third. "She told me that her sister-in-law's niece's family befell the same misfortune. Lost all their clothes. It was theft, I tell you. Someone is ravaging the city and stealing decent people's clothes!"

"Attention everyone, attention!" Tonalnan could hear her mother clanging a golden goblet. "It's time for the performances."

Huemac's guests began to seat themselves on velvety soft animal skins that were being passed around by slaves. The elderly

[190]

sat on stone slabs at the back of the courtyard under the covered walkways.

An ensemble of flutists played, followed by a poet who told a story of a forbidden incestuous love. In their shame the siblings poisoned themselves and spent the rest of eternity in the land of tears. Everyone seemed to enjoy the entertainment, but Tonalnan could see her mother plotting and scheming in whispers with other crones. *What mischief is she up to now?* The matchmaker then went over and whispered in her mother's ear and she and the hag both looked straight at Tonalnan. *Forget it.* She glared back at them. *I will never marry and you can't make me.* She had her father on her side for this.

Just then a commotion could be heard in the Grand Ohtli. A group of drummers was coming down the street accompanied by several men blowing conches. Huemac's guests fell silent.

The parade got louder and louder. The guests then heard them coming through the halls of the house, their soulful rhythms bouncing off the stone walls. The musicians burst into the central courtyard with a flare of royal pomp.

The guests were elated, for in the middle of the drummers was the king's favorite slave. He-she was darker than any human in the One World, and his-her eyes were golden yellow. He-she had his-her waist-length hair arranged in two buns on the sides of his-her head. He-she was bedecked in golden jewelry, arm cuffs, ear plugs, and a golden butterfly chest plate. Around his-her neck was the collar of slavery, but it was gold. A dwarf held the other end of a chain-link rope that the neck ring was fastened to. The drummers pounded wildly and the slave Chac writhed and danced theatrically, swirling long ribbons in the air. He-she then collapsed to the stone floor and prostrated him-herself and the music stopped.

There was silence.

"Tonalnan, daughter of Huemac!" the dwarf holding the slave announced. "Mother of the Sacred House of Healing, the king favors you and presents you with this gift."

Will what I am thinking show? Can they tell that I now feel trapped? Many people suspected that the king's love for her was more than spiritual. Tonalnan stood up and all eyes were upon her. "Tell the king that I thank him for his gracious gift. Tell him that my heart worships the holy breath that flows from his sacred lips and that I am forever his loyal servant."

Some of the guests left the house of Huemac that day happy and contented, but others left with seeds of jealousy in their hearts.

Xipe Totec

"Don't go on!"

"No, really. I tell you. Everyone's been talking about it." Ichtaca's eyes gleamed with excitement.

"It's fantastical. They'll never believe you," Tohuenyo continued.

"Do tell us!" insisted Yellow Skirt, whose favor with Nine Winds over the past four seasons had opened her way into the Coyotl Clan.

"Well I will tell you, so you'll hear it from me before you see it on the cave walls," Ichtaca proclaimed. He looked at his closest comrades sitting around the fire, pausing to enhance the drama of his story. By this time the beautiful Tohuenyo was sitting against a great, flint slab of rock, with the bare-chested Yellow Skirt on his lap, wrapped up in his arms. Others were there, too, Mazatl, Cueyatl and Moyotl, and a few other young men and women that Ichtaca and Tohuenyo had agreed to include.

"Two seasons ago," Ichtaca started, "after the people of the Stone Houses crowned their king, he ordered them to bring him everything to build his royal palace. It was to be beautiful and spacious, elaborately ornate and worthy of a king."

Their eyes sparkled; some with envy, some with delight, some with greed. "They took him all he asked for, volcanic rock and limestone, clay and precious stones, even seashells, silver and gold. You know what he did next?" he asked his friends.

No one answered.

Ichtaca continued, "He ordered everyone to go home and lock themselves in their houses and reinforce their windows and doors."

Ichtaca took a hearty swig of mushroom tea from his buckskin bag and wiped his face on his arm.

"At sunset the wind started to howl through the streets, and all that night the people of the Stone Houses huddled inside their homes in fear, praying to their gods, as the violent storm rattled their windows and shook their doors. Then, in the morning, when

[193]

the conch blew, they came out of their houses befuddled and confused, as if waking from a horrible dream, for there before them, at the side of the giant field where the king himself had been crowned, stood an enormous palace befit for a king!"

Everyone was silent, except for Yellow Skirt, who let out a short gasp.

"You don't believe me!"

"Of course we do," said one of the women. She was grinding dried *nanacatl* mushrooms in a stone bowl.

A crashing noise came through the brush outside and a man barged into the cave. "Ichtaca! Tohuenyo! You are to come to the Omecíhuatl's cave!" Then the man turned and fled.

"Oh, but I am in another cave right now," cried Tohuenyo after him, "and am unable to pull myself out of it, but I will come. Yes, tell her I am coming!"

✣

The largest cave of the tribe was for the Omecíhuatl, Titlacáhuan, and the first mother, Nine Winds. It was a giant cavern filled with stalactites, off-shooting tunnels and chambers, and underground springs. In the middle, there was a pit with a fire, and a clay cauldron bubbled with the Omecíhuatl's stew. Tohuenyo entered with his comrades. Nine Winds was there alone with several of her hairless *itzcuintli* dogs. There were several human phalanx bones woven into the cornrow braids of her graying hair.

"Tell your companions to sit down," she barked, but she beckoned the youthful Ichtaca toward her and kissed him deeply. Tohuenyo stood, waiting for instructions. *Something's changed,* he thought.

"Where's the Omecíhuatl?" he asked.

"She's dead."

There was a brief disquiet as his companions stifled their initial surprise.

"I am Omecíhuatl now," she said sternly. She flashed a coy smile at Ichtaca who was obviously emboldened. Her face immediately returned to cold stone.

What will she do with me now? I am of the Coyotl Clan. She has plans for me, I know. "Mother, I..."

"Do not address me as Mother!" she shrieked at her son. Her voice echoed off the stone walls of the cave and scurried up the stalactites to the ceiling above. Several bats flew off. "From now on you will address me as Grandmother Crone."

Then she turned to his companions, "Prostrate yourselves," she demanded.

Ichtaca and the rest immediately dropped to their hands and knees and touched their foreheads to the cave floor.

"Not you," she said, slapping Tohuenyo upside the head. "You are my son. You remain standing and bow only your head." She folded his hands in front of him and kissed him tenderly on his bowed head. Then she went to Ichtaca and beckoned him to his feet. "And you, well, you are my..." and she leaned toward him and whispered something in his ear, then turned to everyone smiling and said, "...my war party leader."

She turned to Tohuenyo's comrades. "Get up. Dust yourselves off.

An old, frail woman came in and put more wood on the fire under the cauldron and stirred the Omecíhuatl's stew.

"Your uncle is coming," she said to Tohuenyo. "He brings a Toltec."

"Who is it?" Tohuenyo asked.

"Oh, I don't know. Some unsuspecting traveler they found on the road." Her mood softened. "He kept going on about following his king all the way from some place called Xochicalco."

Tohuenyo started to feel uneasy.

"Here, my darling. Drink this." She handed him a small dried gourd filled with obsidian wine. "Come now, all of you, have some tea." So Tohuenyo and his inner circle of friends sat on the rocks in the cavern and drank his mother's obsidian wine. It wasn't real obsidian wine. She was calling it that for some strange reason. It was as though she was trying to be pleasant, but she had had so little practice at it that when she tried, she came off as being deceitful and phony. Real obsidian wine was made with the blood of sacrificial victims. This was just *peyotl* tea. Better not drink too much of it. Oh, but it was so bitter and warm.

[195]

His mother emptied a thumb-sized vile of dust into his tea. *Ah, nanacatl powder*, he thought. *Yes, something's afoot.*

They sat on the rocks and drank the warm tea and after awhile began to feel a dream-like delirium drift through them. Nine Winds, the Grandmother Crone, spoke little and was actually being quite pleasant, save for the one incident when she swatted Yellow Skirt for trying to sit close to her treasure of a son.

Light flickered off the walls of the immense cavern from periodic hearth fires and a multitude of torches. It cast demonic images as its shadows danced upon the stalactites.

"You know today there is a full moon in the day time sky?"

"Yes Mo- Grandmother Crone. We saw it when we scaled down the cliff side to your cavern."

"That's a special sign for you, my Tohuenyo. The Lady Moon Metzli favors you. There was a full moon in the sky the day you were born. It's a sign, don't you see? And there will be one the day you die." She looked at him adoringly. "Really. Your uncle told me that all the significant days of your life there will be a full moon in the day time sky. He knows these things."

"Well," she added, "I suppose I'll tell you all why I've summoned you here."

She explained the plan to them.

"All of us?" Yellow Skirt was furious. She'd tried too hard for too long to get Tohuenyo. They'd even eaten *nochtli* together and drank its sweet juices, and that very morning he'd finally entered her cave! This couldn't be happening.

"Yellow Skirt, you will take Mazatl into your cave."

"But –"

"No objections. I insist." Nine Winds high cheek bones gave her a distinct authority. "Besides, Mazatl possesses a great quantity of flint. He can light the fires in your cave continuously! You'll stay so warm." Everybody laughed... except Yellow Skirt.

"You *will* accept, won't you?" Malice started to glimmer in Nine Wind's eyes.

"Of course," Yellow Skirt obeyed immediately.

"Good. So the only thing we have left is that Tohuenyo must be reborn. As a Toltec, of course."

"Xipe Totec," several of them said in unison.

[196]

"Yes, Xipe Totec." She confirmed.

"Oh, what an honor! Grandmother elder!" Yellow Skirt's mood suddenly lifted.

The effects of the tea were starting to get stronger. Tohuenyo felt a warm glow, as if everything was a dream. *No wonder she's calling it obsidian wine,* he thought.

He turned. A couple of men pulled along what appeared to be an intoxicated Toltec into the cavern. He watched as they climbed down the stairway of the precipice at the enormous entrance. *The precipice of my own transmutation,* Tohuenyo thought. As they walked toward them he could see that the Toltec had been reverently prepared. His skin was dusted white, but other than that he was without an outer garment. His nakedness was the Chichimeca's attempt to strip away his bestial self and move closer to his true, inner nature. He was heavily sedated and stood smiling, for over the course of three days he had been treated as a god, indulged in his every desire, and through awkward translations had been made to understand that he was going to the gods himself. For you see, admission to Heaven and eternal life with the gods did not depend on how one lived his or her life, but rather, upon the manner of one's death. Only warriors who died in battle, women who died in childbed, and those lucky enough to be chosen for sacrificial death would enter the celestial paradise of the gods in the Great Beyond.

Titlacáhuan walked behind them. As before, his slight body was adorned with a headdress of black-tipped eagle feathers and a multitude of amulets for his various shamanic rituals. He still donned the bear claw necklace that gave him protection against evil spirits. He wore the same anklets covered with seed-pod bells that jangled when he walked and the spotted leopard cape with noisy rattlesnake tails sewn around the edges. Once again, his skin was dusted completely white except for a black ash band across his eyes, exaggerating his beak of a nose and high cheekbones.

When they were all gathered together they laid the barely sentient Toltec across a long volcanic altar with grooves running along all four edges. Titlacáhuan had Ichtaca change to his vestments of First Warrior, the coyote skin headdress and his ornamental weapons, in the event that the goddess Xipe Totec unleash her fury against them. The rest of the companions wore blue painted masks, made out of dried pumpkins from the fields of the Toltecs themselves, with long, dried grass reeds protruding out of them in all directions. For they, too, would mask themselves in things Toltec.

Several crates of stolen Toltec clothing were passed around and the rest of Tohuenyo's companions rushed to cover themselves in the Toltecoyotl, or all things Toltec. *Now they think themselves Toltec, but in reality they become Titlacáhuan's sycophants,* he thought. *I wonder what is to become of me, when the goddess Xipe Totec descends upon me?*

Tohuenyo stood naked in front of the volcanic altar. Several old women were rubbing him down with jojoba seed oil that had been painstakingly prepared for just this occasion.

Torches and fires scattered along the ledges and crevices of the cavern provided the only light so that when Titlacáhuan shook his tortoise shell rattle and raised his arms, eerie, distorted shadows flickered on the back wall.

"Eh, goddess Xipe Totec, thou art the Tezcatlipoca of the red smoking mirror! Goddess of renewal and regeneration, it is thee who changes seasons and moves the cycles of life!

"Honor the Red Tezcatlipoca!" and everyone save Tohuenyo, who was still standing naked, banged slate rocks against the cavern floor.

"Xipe Totec! Xipe Totec!" they hollered and wailed.

Titlacáhuan slowly bent his boney frame over the sacrificial victim laid out before him on the stone altar and pushed a claw-like fingernail into the man's chest. "Xipe Totec," he whispered again, through half a mouth of rotting teeth.

Lifting the heavily sedated Toltec with one arm underneath his neck, the sorcerer poured a vile liquid into the victim's mouth. He pinched the man's facial orifice, forcing him to swallow and set the empty vial down.

The Toltec convulsed a couple of times on the cold, stone slab.

Then, with the needle-sharp point of a red obsidian dagger, the sorcerer began to carve into the victim's flesh at the top of the skull between his parted, loosely hanging hair. The dusted white Toltec jerked, and his eyes rolled up into his forehead. As the sorcerer sliced down through the middle of the man's face, blood from the top of his skull oozed out and onto the stone slab. The blade continued down, over his nose, parting his lips, and then his chin, separating the Toltec's face in two.

"Xipe Totec," Titlacáhuan whispered, "Descend upon us through this sacrifice." He continued his incision through the man's throat, down his chest, his torso and his abdomen, pulling the flesh apart and exposing the viscera within. The runoff of blood now began to fill the grooves along the edges of the stone altar, flowing toward the four corners where Nine Winds had placed four urns to capture the sacred fluid.

Titlacáhuan then held up a black obsidian ulu and commenced to flay the rest of the victim, skillfully removing his skin in one piece. The heavily sedated Toltec's body writhed in several violent convulsions, then lay stone dead, teeth and eyeballs projecting out through exposed musculature and tendons in a hideous grin.

After that the human hide was rinsed in clear water, and brought before Tohuenyo. The crones who had prepared his body with oil now fed his arms through the sleeves of the carnal cape. The split face and long hair of the victim hung about his shoulder blades and down his back. The hollowed out legs and empty feet dangled below.

"Xipe Totec surrounds you!" Titlacáhuan screamed. Tohuenyo watched as everyone smeared their arms and legs with the blood of the sacrificial victim. He'd been waiting for this moment, waiting to feel a change, something new. He stood there, wearing the flayed skin of the Toltec, drinking the obsidian wine that was now infused with sacrificial blood, waiting, waiting, hallucinating and dreaming.

"Dance!" the Omecíhuatl commanded. They placed a war bonnet on his head, and hung strands of deer teeth all over him. He was as high as he ever had been, ecstatic with euphoric delirium. Surely the goddess would appear to him now. He danced wildly and freely, calling upon Xipe Totec to deliver him into the Toltecoyotl so he could carry out Titlacáhuan's plan.

In the midst of his psychotropic experience he began to hear colors and see sounds. The colors of the Toltec clothing began to reach up into the air and swirl around him. He could hear them whisper.

[199]

"To-hueeeeen-yo," the colors chanted.

"To-hueeeeen-yo," They swirled above his head.

"We hear your prayers. Don the skin of a Toltec."

Everyone danced in shamanic ritual, shaking rattles and playing drums and flutes. Then they formed a procession and left the cavern to parade throughout the tribe. They entered everyone's lodges and demanded gifts for Xipe Totec. At the end, they returned to the great cavern, where they ceremoniously ate the Omecíhuatl's stew.

"Eat the meat of the Omecíhuatl," Nine Winds told everyone. "It has divine powers. Her magic will enter you."

When they finished their gorging, they fed the flayed Toltec to the *itzcuintli* dogs, lest the carcass begin to putrify and rot.

What's Yours Is Mine

Tula grew. The potential for expansion was strengthened by numerous rivers and tributaries that twisted and turned through two great mountain ranges on either side of the central high plains. To the east lay the mountains and rivers of the Coatepec, the Panuco, and the Tuxpán. Trade with these nations brought in shells and conches from the sea, as well as black and red coral and strands upon strands of pearls.

To the north were the far off lands of Aztlán beyond the Seven Caves of Chicomoztoc. Merchants from Tula were lucky to survive this perilous journey. It lasted several years, but if they were able to return, their slaves carried back with them baskets and baskets of turquoise and gold.

The dynamic expansion of the Toltecs resided in their conquest of distant places and the development of routes of communication through rivers and over land. They were clever administrators and, under the guidance of Ce Acatl Topiltzin, soon developed a keen system of production and exchange of obsidian. They started distributing the volcanic glass all through Cem Anahuac, the One World. They came to dominate the mines of the Knife Stone Mountains near Pachuca, those of Zacualtipán, of Huapalcalco, and Tepeapulco, as well as Otumba near the Valley of Texcoco. Eventually they would come to control the mines of Zinapécuaro in far off Michoacán to the west.

To the south, the Teotenancas were causing all kinds of trouble for Toltec domination. Located in the snowy reaches of the Toluca Mountains, they fortified their city of Teotenanco with a great, sacred wall. It was impenetrable, and they posed a mighty foe in the control of the obsidian mines of Cacamilhuacan.

In the mines there were vast workstations where skilled artisans prepared the raw cut rocks, called cores, which were then distributed by porters in *petlacalli* baskets to all the corners of the world. The cores arrived at the workhouses of Tula where they were received by lapidaries and transformed into magnificent weapons, and other brilliant works of art. They made arrow points, lance darts, spearheads, ulus, daggers and knives, and even the most feared *maquáhuitl* death swords – long, flat, wooden clubs outlined with razor sharp obsidian blades. The blades, embedded obsidian around the edges of the sword like jagged teeth, could slice completely through an enemy, making the obsidian death sword the most lethal weapon of all.

With the passing of time, the great leaders of Tula convened periodically to discuss important matters of state, especially control of the mines. They would gather at the home of the first general Huemac where they would inform him of the abundance of the One World's geological treasures, or the lack of, or inform him of new advances, such as the discovery of lime. It had been found in the rocky regions of the central high plains. When ground to a powder and mixed with sand it formed a new kind of mortar much stronger than clay. It was perfect for the commission of the new pyramid that would soon be under way.

It was on one such occasion that Huemac sat with Ozomatli the chief *pochteca* of the Cintéotl Clan and several of his associate merchants. Ozomatli's family had huge control of the mining trade, so much so that they occupied an entire zone far to the north of the urban center called the Saltpeter District.

Huemac and his guests met in an outbuilding of his palace at the south of town. The great room rested at the far end of a vast, flower-filled garden. The stone edifice was typical in that it had been constructed of uniformly cut basalt stones held together with lime-based mortar. The walls were then smoothed over with creamy white plaster. The one-room building sat raised on two small platforms the size of stairs. Along the façade, two circular pillars held up an extended roof that reached over the sculptured entryway, and in keeping with the new Toltec fashion, a lattice of stone spirals had been recently added to the rooftop along the front.

Inside, the room afforded a monochrome stone floor of expansive limestone slabs that fit together with perfect precision, and visually complimented the dusty rose plastered walls. Four ceiling-high windows along the back wall were so large that they might have been walkways, except for the built-in bench that stretched the length of the room beneath them. The windows, which allowed the room to swell with light, were decorated with white gauze curtains that gently wafted with each breath of wind. It was a perfect place for Huemac's meetings of state, far from the main mansion that was filled with curious ears. The men sat around on cushioned animal hides, playing board games and drinking refreshing chia tea.

"Tell me, Ozomatli," The rotund Huemac said, munching a fried grasshopper. After delighting in the initial crunch, he savored the sweet and fiery hot flavors of its chilli and honey coating. "How is it that one finds such mines?"

"The precious stones are not found the way you see them now, my friend," the honored guest began. "This is the way they are sold, resplendent and polished to a lustrous sheen. When they are found, they are crude and rough, with not the least appearance of beauty at all. They rather look like common rocks... to the common eye that is."

Ozomatli cracked a wide grin as he moved his cacao bean playing piece along the wooden board. Giant, turquoise earplugs made his ears look even larger than they already were.

"They are found here and there, way out in the country. Some in the cliffs and caverns, some in the hills. There are people among my family who know how to find the precious stones, that is, any precious gem wherever they may be. They say that where the earth exhales a gentle fog, a delicate smoking vapor that only disappears with the rising sun, that is where they will find them. There the precious stones were born and are hidden among the crevices and caves. Some are found deep in the veins of the earth, while others lay completely hidden, and there are some that dwell at the heart of other rough and crude rocks."

Huemac played his turn as his guest continued. He had every intention of letting Ozomatli win.

"There is another sign of precious gems." Ozomatli threw the stones and counted out the spaces with his marker. "Especially the *chalchihuitl*, the emeralds. They are found beneath the place of the herbs of ever-lasting green. You see, the brilliant green gems that are borne of these regions exhale a magical breath, fresh and humid, that saturates all that grows upon the earth above them."

[203]

Ozomatli took a sip of chia tea. "Now turquoise, that is a different matter. That is found in the great caverns of the north, and hides deep within the mountains of the Mother.

"The pearls, of course you know, come from the Coatepec by the sea."

In their symbiotic relationship each man benefitted. Huemac's military was strengthened by the demand for dominance and protection of the mining industry – and the enormous payments in kind that he and his household received. Ozomatli on the other hand, in order for his family's business ventures to thrive, needed the protection of Huemac's forces. If Ozomatli could form an alliance with the first general by marrying his youngest daughter, the pochteca's fortunes would be well protected, indeed.

"There!" Ozomatli said triumphantly as he cast the last play. "I've won!"

The assistant merchants and lapidaries politely applauded.

"We all win," thought Huemac out loud, "for we are Toltecs with a powerful king, son of Quetzalcoatl our god, and the mines of the One World are ours!"

"Praise be to Quetzalcoatl!" they cheered.

"Long live our king, Ce Acatl Topiltzin!"

"The mines are ours!" they all agreed.

"Yes, except for those stubborn Teotenancas to the south." Huemac grumbled. There was an awkward pause. "Oh, don't act so surprised my friend," for Ozomatli had not yet heard of the resistance. "I'm sure that son-in-law of mine can take care of them."

"Yes, send Xolotl," one of Ozomatli's associates chimed.

"Easier said than done, my fellow," the first general responded. "You know he is in Michoacán at the head of the king's army. Here, try this," Huemac told the companion, giving himself time to reflect on the Teotenancas. He handed the man a pipe with tobacco, red willow bark and mint. "My daughter makes it in the Sacred House of Healing."

"Hello, father."

Huemac looked up to see his daughter entering through the great, arched entrance. She carried a bundle in one hand. In the other she led Chac by a golden chain.

"Ah, Tonalnan. We were just talking about you. What luck. And now you are here," her father said.

"I think it was not luck, father," she boldly corrected. "You summoned me."

"Oh, yes. Yes, I did." Huemac was not bothered in the least at having been contradicted in front of his guests by Tonalnan, but let anyone else in the entire realm speak against him, and they should lose their tongue. Everyone knew this about the first general, though. It was common knowledge that he was the fiercest of all warriors, capable of pounding men down in the streets and cutting off their heads for crossing him, but he could not bring himself to say no to his adored daughters. They were both overly indulged.

Tonalnan steered Chac to some potted palms and laid him-her down. The languid, dark beauty with golden-yellow eyes reclined sideways on the cool, stone floor and assumed a pose of statuesque elegance. Tonalnan then took her bundle of copal and placed it at the foot of a stele of Quetzalcoatl.

"You remember Ozomatli, don't you my daughter?" The *pochteca* guest had all his attention upon her.

"Of course. Blessings of the First Lord and First Lady upon you," she said. She hadn't seen the chief *pochteca* of the Cintéotl clan in several years, since before the dark days of Tollan. She sat upon the cushioned hides with her feet properly folded under her with her eyes cast down.

Finally, after lengthy introductions and dutiful pleasantries her father addressed her. "How's your sister?"

"She's able. Her belly swells with the life inside her."

"I hear you're going to the *tianguis* tomorrow."

"Yes, father."

"You must take care of her. Make sure she doesn't walk too much or get too hot. Keep her out of the sun."

"Yes, father."

"Take enough slaves with you to carry everything."

"Yes, father."

"All is well. You can choose them now." The old general fumbled for some more tobacco. He never felt completely at ease in conversations with his daughters. It was as though they disarmed him somehow.

[205]

"Here, father, let me." Tonalnan daintily filled her father's smoking pipe.

"All right now, go pick out some gems." He brushed her away. "Be sure to get the same for your sister. I don't want rivalries in my own household."

Tonalnan walked over to the stone bench that was built adjacent to the wall. Swatches of black cotton lay along the length of it, each one containing a separate pile of spectacular stones and gems. The men stood and joined her. As she examined each pile, she was sure to comment on the exquisite beauty, the workmanship, or the luster, of each gem, and listen politely as the chief *pochteca* boasted about his efforts and labors in acquiring them. There were emeralds, lapis and turquoise, and red and black coral from the sea. There were pearls and fire opals, and bright green obsidian and many colors of jade. The blood red jasper was magnificent, and there were strands upon strands of golden-yellow amber, the beauty of which she'd never seen.

Ozomatli knew that whatever Tonalnan wore to the market place the following day would become a forceful fashion trend. "Take an opal bracelet," he said, and lifted the strand toward her.

"Thank you," she said.

Standing so close to the *pochteca* she couldn't help but notice the gnarled, scraggly hairs growing out of his over-sized ears.

He gently, if somewhat clumsily, tied the gems around her wrist.

"You know I have been recently widowed," he said, attempting to further his strategy.

Tonalnan was prepared, however. News of the woman's mysterious death had run rampantly off the tongues of nearly every woman in town albeit in utter secrecy. Some said she'd died of jealousy of one of her husband's concubines. Others said she'd been bewitched by a tortilla that she had negligently allowed to fold on itself when she was cooking. Still others said that she had accidentally stepped on a poinsettia, which, as everyone knew, is a certain cause of death. Then there were those who suspected that one of her husband's minions had murdered her to make way for a child bride. Tonalnan had thought that the folded tortilla was what ultimately caused the woman's demise, but now with the intensity of his attentions she began to wonder. In any case, she and her sister Calli suspected that the *pochteca* would be up to such tricks. They had spent the better part of an evening coming up with possible clever responses, but for all their efforts and speculations, in the end all she could say was, "Your loss bereaves us so."

The long row of gems was payment to her father. They were but a mere sampling of the fortunes the Cintéotl Clan had presented to him in exchange for military protection. She chose freely, taking whatever she wanted and however much she wanted, doubling each of her choices for her sister, Calli.

Then she left with her bundle of opulence and her adored Chac in tow.

The Great Tianguis

It was a fine day for the *tianguis*. The cold season was coming to an end. Recently, huge caravans of merchants and traders had been streaming into the city to sell their wares. Today's *tianguis* was sure to be a grand affair.

Tonalnan and her sister rode through the streets on individual chairs carried by four slaves each. As noblewomen, they had made every effort to look their best, for hundreds of eyes would be upon them.

Tonalnan had chosen to adorn herself in homage to Mazapa, a sacred goddess of fertility. She wore a full length, black and red cross-weave skirt. It had a wide yellow trim at the bottom that was elaborately embellished with tiger's eye beads. Her black and yellow *huipil* was sleeveless and tucked into a red sash that was pulled tight around her waist, accentuating her curvaceous figure. Nestled between her breasts rested a heavy golden disc suspended by graduated, gold and amber beads. Her face had been painted red, with thick, black lines outlining her eyes all the way to the temples. Her lips were painted black.

Staying true to the image of Mazapa, she wore an elaborately woven hat as wide as her shoulders, with a flattened front and back. It was short topped, and the length of the front band was expertly woven to look like yellow rows of corn. Two large golden discs adorned the sides, emulating the image of Tlaloc. Her hair fell loose and hung straight down her back.

Her sister Calli, now big with child, was dressed more modestly. She had decided to wear white and blue, the colors of the heavens. Her full-length shift was short sleeved, with a beaded lapis border at the bottom.

"We'll stop at the temple of Mazapa," Tonalnan ordered. The goddess was the patron deity of the agricultural workers, and her temple was located at the western edge of the city. For this reason, the temple was known as the doorway to the Valley of Fields. In

[209]

Tula's agricultural district, the humble adobe and stone dwellings were more spread out, separated by waist-high volcanic stone walls that crisscrossed the landscape. As they strolled their way along the dry, dirt roads, people came out of their hovels to look at the two noble women. Some of the residents gave them fruit and flowers. Some stared at Chac who accompanied them. Some waved. Young men, on hearing that the daughter of the first general and her attendants were approaching, engaged in mock battles, hoping to catch her eye.

At the one-room, stone temple of Mazapa, the women made burnt offerings of dried corn before an effigy of the goddess, and left bundles of sweet, nutty confections upon the altar. As was the custom, any child who would then pray and make offerings to the goddess was entitled to one of the sweets. With her temples a favorite among children, and with the help of molded figurines, the cult of Mazapa grew steadily among the lower classes of Tula. Because Tonalnan made it a habitual practice to leave offerings at the temple of Mazapa, she was greatly loved by all.

As the women headed back to the city center they could see the construction of the Pyramid of the Sun in the distance. It was progressing at a wondrous pace, and was covered with wooden scaffoldings all around. From afar, the hundreds of masons crawling all over it looked like thousands of worker ants on a mound. Streams of slaves laden with *petlacalli* baskets strapped around their sweaty foreheads reminded Tonalnan of leaf cutter ants, forfeiting their entire existence to perpetual suffering.

"Look, sister," Calli exclaimed. "We can see the full moon in the day-time sky over the pyramid. How beautiful she is!"

The litter-bearers hoisted them through the labyrinth of city streets. As they entered the populated market place, the crowd parted and people bowed, curtsied, or knelt, according to their station. Tonalnan was gracious and extended her hand to people, letting them touch her as they went by. Calli was reserved and did not.

"Let them take *ococintli*," she commanded. One of her porters was carrying a large basket of pine nuts. A woman slave scooped out the nuts and poured them into people's calloused hands.

After acknowledging her presence and declaring their heartfelt appreciation, the people then went on about their business, for it would have been considered rude to gather around her in a smothering throng. However, tongues quickly moved, and the news of her arrival buzzed along the market place. Before the sisters had set foot on ground, everyone knew they were there. "The princess Tonalnan is here! The daughters of Huemac have arrived! Look your best! It is sure to be a good day to sell!" Fathers counseled their sons on how to best sell their wares, and mothers pinched their daughters to perk them up.

The great field was given the name Yollotli, meaning *heart*, as it was the very heart and center of the city. It was vast, and most of the field lay empty, but since the coronation ceremony, construction of the city had progressed significantly.

To the south rested the Royal Palace of Previous Kings, but Ce Acatl Topiltzin had chosen not to reside there. It stood empty, and because it rested in front of Huemac's properties, the first general was at liberty to use it. He met there occasionally with his War Council and many chieftans. To express his gratitude, Huemac provided and cared for forty slaves so that the palace should be splendidly maintained.

From the Palace of Previous Kings, directly across the vast Yollotli stood the Palace of Quetzalcoatl in the north. Stone stairs extended the entire length of the palace, rising to a portico of forty arches. Quetzalcoatl's temple was located in one of the rooms of the palace. Tonalnan's father Huemac and other high-ranking officials often met in the Eastern Chamber to discuss matters of state. The king, Ce Acatl Topiltzin, would go there on occasion as well, especially to confer with chiefs from other nations, or their representatives. The king, as highest-ranking official of the Palace of Quetzalcoatl, would also sit in judgment over civil and criminal disputes. The Palace of Quetzalcoatl was the administrative hub of the Toltec nation.

To the right of the Palace of Previous Kings, in the east, construction still continued on the Pyramid of the Sun. Zolton, the royal architect, was designing a great stone stairway up the front so the priests could ascend into the heavens at the moment of the rising sun.

To the far west of the Yollotli, a new *ullama* ball court was being built beyond the edge of the field at the bottom of the hill, to the sufferings of many slaves who were driven beyond all measure by the impatient urgings of the king.

Market stalls extended down the length of the Palace of Previous Kings, and to the left, along the western edge of the field. More like scaffoldings than permanent structures, these stalls were used for the *tianguis* market. The frames of the stalls, mostly poles made from slender trees, were fastened with twine lashings. Some of the roofs were covered with flowing lengths of fabric: pinks and purples from elderberry, scrumptious oranges of alder bark, vibrant greens from black eyed susans, and brilliant blues from purple irises. Other roofs were made impermeable by spreading tar over woven mats, topped off with dried reeds. The stalls were for local merchants. Foreigners had to spread their wares on the ground in orderly rows in the middle of the great field.

The market was crowded and noisy. Flutes played. Birds squawked. Women bartered and haggled over prices. Vendors chanted out their goods in sing-song fashion, "*Tamallis*! Get your *tamallis*! Fresh *tamallis*! Get your *tamallis*!" Some vendors chanted just one word and stretched it out in the same way every time, "Cam-ooooohh-tli. Get your cam-ooooohh-tli," over and over in rhythmic, bellowing chants so that everyone knew where the roasted sweet potatoes were. The best *camotlis* were the ones that were salt roasted and then drenched in agave nectar with pecans and chewy chunks of honeycomb.

Tonalnan and Calli could hear the music of an informal drum circle coming from the north end of the market, in front of the palace of Quetzalcoatl.

> *Bam. Ba-dada, dada dum.*
> *Bam. Ba-dada, dada dum.*
> *Bam. Ba-dada, dada dum.*
> *Ba dada dum.*
> *Ba dada dum.*

Ocarinas vacillated between eerie shrieks, high-pitched wails, playful twitters, and soft melodic coos.

What they couldn't see were that the people inside the drum circle alternated between dancing in unison and showing off their athletic abilities, while energized onlookers clapped and yelped in excited expressions of joy. The sisters knew well what the musicians and dancers were doing, for every ten days they went to the *tianguis* market, and strolled along the same path. They always entered the market in the south-east corner of the Yollotli, turned left and frequented the line of vendors in front of the royal palace, then turned right at the corner and perused the stalls along the western edge. They usually stopped and ate a mid-morning snack at the end of the second row, but this they did sitting down on cotton blankets, for everyone knew that any young boy or girl who ate standing up was sure never to marry. To eat standing up after marriage would spoil the flavors of a marriage, which was worse than never marrying at all. The sisters would always end their trip to the market in front of the musicians and dancers, where they would sit on the steps of the Palace of Quetzalcoatl, with their attendants and slaves around them, and watch the entertainment below. Their parading through the market was always carried out with great pomp and pretentious noble arrogance. They made all the proper salutations to other nobles and ignored the foreigners spread out on the ground.

This day started out just like any other. The governor of the market, Matlal, welcomed them. He was the senior *pochteca* in charge of all other merchants. All the merchants obeyed him and treated him with reverence. Other tribal nations who traded with the Toltecs were ultimately under his command, and he saw to it that trade with other nations was carried out in an orderly fashion. He was fair and just and dealt severely with those who deserved punishment, unlike other senior *pochtecas* in the past who had served their own interests by cheating, swindling and abusing their power for personal gain. Topiltzin Quetzalcoatl was a wise king and surrounded himself with talented and capable people. Matlal was one of them.

They passed the lapidaries and gold workers first, nodding hellos to the eager sellers as they strolled by. They walked close and spoke softly, disguising their conversation behind broken sentences.

"I received a message," said Calli, referring to her husband Xolotl. "He sends word that they reached the far regions of the Tarascans in Michoacán." They stopped in front of the feather workers' stalls, where she leaned even closer to her sister and whispered, "They weren't able to subjugate them and are soon to return." She then coolly nodded to a passerby.

"We have any kind of feather for you today my ladies!" a merchant eagerly interrupted, trying his best to impress. "Any color, any kind of bird! Green, yellow, black, blue, red! I can cut them for you in your favorite design." The little man held up samples of masterfully cut feather fans.

"Thank you, Tototl, not today," said Tonalnan, as she indicated to one of her slaves to gift the feather workers a handful of *ococintli*. She lowered her voice and turned back to Calli. "What did father say? Was it failure or success?"

They stopped in front of the fabrics.

"If he was able to establish trade and returns with his forces strong, he will stay in good favor," Calli whispered. She then smiled at Zolton's wife who was passing by, followed by a handful of slaves and attendants.

"Good day to you Mother," Tonalnan said to the weaver. "We'll take seven blankets this day. Mind you, without flaws. They must have straight edges and be new. We want them to be smooth and thin. No lumps in them."

Several women weavers now gathered in the stall holding up *huipiles*. "Won't this blouse look stunning on you My Princess!" they said, holding up their work to show it off. "Take a *huipil* with blue hummingbirds today, My Princess!" Their eager faces showed their pride in their work, but even more proud they would be to have a daughter of Huemac wear their wares.

"Oh, yes!" The sisters delighted in choosing several *huipiles*, even though as noblewomen their own weaving was far superior. They then allowed the weavers to select an assortment of Ozomatli's stones.

The weavers and slaves folded the textiles into the *petlacalli* baskets, and the sisters went on their way, followed by their entourage.

[214]

They passed by the bulk foods - corn, beans, chilli, nuts and seeds – these their house servants would acquire, but they wanted to choose the irresistible fruits themselves. They stopped and traded for chicozapote, papaya, pineapple, sweet potatoes, honey, vanilla and *nochtli*, the sweet fruit of the *nopalli* cactus. Moving on they skipped some stalls, the cotton and the paper makers, which didn't interest them this day. At the end, vendors were selling giant bundles of wood. They turned the corner and continued past the first few stalls of pottery trays laden with sun-baked fish and basins full of fried, sweet-hot grasshoppers. Hunters sold dried meats and jerky as well as live birds in bamboo cages, while freshly killed turkeys hung up side down from their stalls.

Next the sisters stopped at several peddlers' stalls and traded for items that Tonalnan needed in the Sacred House of Healing. They took a variety of medicinal herbs, cactus thorn needles, candle bowls for beeswax candles, cotton wicks, and several dried gourds. Tonalnan's position as First Mother had been difficult at best, but she seldom confided this to her sister. As noble women, Calli and Tonalnan had been brought up exposed to matters of state – how to lead effectively, how to organize, how to plan – and their attitude toward difficult challenges was to take them on without complaint and solve them.

"How are things at the House of Healing?" Her sister often seemed to read her mind.

"Some spiders eat their young," Tonalnan answered clandestinely.

Trained not to discuss private matters in public places, the two young women often masked their conversations. Calli understood that her young sister was having difficulty with some of the crones at the House of Healing who envied her sister's position. She continued shopping, scrutinizing a small obsidian mirror for flaws. "Wolves abandon old and weak members of their pack," she said.

Tonalnan wondered how she should solve the conflicts with the jealous crones. Clearly, abandoning the old women to the wild, as would a pack of wolves, was not the honorable solution. Focusing on the responsibilities of healing, making house calls, midwifery, healings, medicines and new remedies all helped abate the tensions in the House of Healing and strengthened her resolve to persevere. She would give it more consideration.

Just then Chac, who, with permission, had wandered off to the dancing circle, came up and whispered something in Tonalnan's ear.

"We shall walk among the foreigners today," Tonalnan announced unexpectedly, "to honor the goddess of fertility." She smiled and turned to Chac. "Fetch me the sculptor and tell him to bring his figurines of Mazapa. He may bestow them upon the foreigners at my expense."

"Little sister, love of my childhood, clearly you push the limits of propriety," Calli said indignantly.

"Come now, my darling," Tonalnan said, "We shall spread the blessings of Mazapa out into the world."

Her sister, however, who was not so altruistic, said haughtily, "Let not the gods bestow the contagion of inferiority upon us for walking among the weeds." Despite her disdain, she agreed. "I will join you, little sister." Then she added, "Let us receive what we dare to bring upon ourselves."

Chilli Today, M'Lady?

In truth, the merchandise that was spread out on the ground of the great Yollotli wasn't very different from that of the locals at their stands. There were still potters who sold earthenware crockery like urns, jars, pitchers, flat griddles and mugs. They even sold candle bowls and oil lamps. What was different, though, was the style in which everything was made. Locally, everyone used red-on-buff pottery, called Coyotlatelco, just like they always had. It was simple – burnt red on a sandy background – there was no need for gaudy displays, but what the outsiders had done to their pottery, well that was a different matter.

The sisters lingered before an enormous ceramic wares display.

"It's tasteless and excessively showy," Calli said.

One of the merchants held up a painted, tri-pod vase and said something in an unintelligible language.

"Sister, you mustn't attest that you don't like it. Look how beautiful it is. How fanciful, how splendid!" The pieces were unlike anything she'd ever seen, beautifully detailed images painted in stark contrasts of black, white and red.

She addressed the little man. "Where are you from?"

The merchant responded in gibberish.

"Where is he from?" Tonalnan asked anyone who could answer.

"We come... Chupícuaro... kingdom near Guanajuato, yes," the second *pochteca* said in broken Nahuatl.

"Tonalnan, really. They can't even speak proper Nahuatl. Let's move on," Calli said impatiently, now starting to tire.

"From Chupícuaro... lines painted black and red. Make white background look raised." The *pochteca* continued, "We make good trade for Goddess of Mazapa, yes."

Standing at the edge of the earthenwares display, Tonalnan was bedazzled by the stacked piles of Chupícuaro crockery before her. The market was crowded and people moved behind her up and down the walkway, buzzing with conversations of business and trade. Interest was generating that the first general's daughter was looking at the foreign crockery, and people started to gather round.

Tonalnan opened her purse of stones. She took a handful and displayed them on her open palm. "Forty pieces of pottery, and I choose them," she proposed.

The two merchants haggled back and forth in their own vernacular.

"Green obsidian. All green obsidian," the second one said.

"Half green obsidian," she countered, "and half mixed."

The two *pochteca* again bickered amongst themselves. "Half green obsidian, half opal." They retorted. They stood firm.

Tonalnan looked away as if to indicate that she considered leaving. Then she turned back again as if to reconsider, "Half green obsidian and half mixed. Forty *four* pieces, and I choose them." She smiled pleasantly.

The merchants knew well that a trade with this noble woman would generate more business. They were not fools. They nodded.

Then Tonalnan's black lips spoke the words that would profoundly affect trade between Tula and the nations of Guanajuato from that point on. "Let the deal be done!" she ordered. "Fill the *petlacalli* baskets!" Then, after she went through the display and chose the best of the *pochtecas'* wares, a flock of buyers landed upon the two vendors, eager to emulate the household of the first general. They traded away everything the Chupícuaro vendors had, all that was painted black, white and red, and that is how raised white pottery came to Tula-Xicocotitlan.

As the sisters continued through the market they stopped and inspected different kinds of baskets, from the giant *petlacalli* baskets for transport to the smallest the size of half an avocado seed. Tonalnan traded for a yellow-headed parrot and they named it Panchotl. It squawked and carried on and they let Chac carry the bird in its maguey-fiber cage.

With so many people at the market this day it was preposterous to think it would be uneventful, and it was only a matter of time before a commotion stirred. As the women neared the drum circle at the Palace of Quetzalcoatl a huddle of people pushed their way through the crowd.

"What's all the fuss about?" a market lady asked.

People were pushing and shoving. Some were yelling.

"It's the egg seller," a man's voice said.

"The old hag is cheating people!" someone said. "She's trading crow eggs and telling people they're quail."

"No!"

"She'll get her punishment, she will!"

"And the duck eggs were rancid!"

There was more pushing and shoving and the woman was thrown on the ground close to Tonalnan and her sister. Tonalnan noticed that the market governor Matlal was standing nearby.

"Governor!" a man dressed like a guard said, "this woman is committing an injustice. Through cheating and trickery she trades not quail eggs, but eggs of crow!" He kicked the woman on the ground.

A vocal reaction buzzed through the crowd.

"Stone her!' somebody yelled.

"Who here has seen this to be true?" the senior *pochteca* bellowed.

Several people raised their hands. Somebody handed several crow eggs to Matlal. A duck egg whizzed past and cracked open on the accused woman's head, smashing on impact, splattering ooze and goo into her unkempt hair. The old woman winced.

Meanwhile, the music of the drum circle thudded on.

Matlal hesitated, carefully weighing the justice he was about to deliver in front of Huemac's watchful daughters– a justice that would seal the vendor's fate and possibly his own. He could take a stance of intolerance and if so, set an example for all to see. Yes, let the punishment be severe, and discourage further transgressions. The people will feel avenged. On the other hand, he could lean toward leniency and forgiveness for the poor old crone. Matlal the Merciful, the people would say.

Time stood still as the people awaited his decision.

The woman on the ground whimpered with her hands over her head.

"I'm watching you," Panchotl squawked, in a high, shrill voice.

Jolted by the bird's mysterious utterance, the governor raised his staff. "Burning peppers!" he proclaimed.

Several guards dragged the screaming woman away.

"Matlal the Merciful," Calli said under her breath.

Just then Chac came up and whispered something in Tonalnan's ear, again. He-she beckoned to the princess dressed as Mazapa to follow him-her, and handed her the golden length of rope fastened to his-her collar. She acquiesced and allowed her pet to lead her away through the crowd. The music of the drum circle faded behind them. They walked uncomfortably close to other people. Dogs, darting here and there, brushed their legs and barked and yapped. A little boy with snot running down his dusty face was crying. Roasted maize cobs crackled and smoked, adding to the crying boy's torment. Led by a burly trader, a chain gang of slaves trudged through the throng to the bidding platform at the northwest corner of the market.

As the last of the chained slaves passed them, Chac held the first princess behind her shoulders, positioning her so she could see.

"Look," he-she whispered in her ear, in a soft, feminine voice. "Feast your eyes on the beauty of manhood in all its virility!"

Standing erect on a crate in the middle of an enormous display of red and green chilli peppers was the most handsome example of maleness she had ever beheld. He was stark naked, except for the beads of moisture that glistened on his brown skin. Part of his waist-length black hair flew in the breeze; the rest fell softly down his pectorals and over his rippled abdomen. The creature was smiling with perfectly shaped, strong white teeth, as if to mock the blushing ladies who hurried by. Most men glared at him. A few smiled back.

"Look how erect he is," Chac whispered to Tonalnan.

"Yes, I see," she answered, as though in a trance.

Just then, magnetism seized the young man and he turned his gaze upon the alluring Tonalnan, and looked directly into her eyes, penetrating her very soul. They stood there, eyes locked, while all else faded into an immense blur. The intensity of the attraction took her breath away. She swooned and everything went black.

An Urgent Family Matter

"What?" Huemac's fist pounded the long table with a crack.

"She cries continuously, Father. She will not reason." Calli said, distraught.

"This is your doing, wife!" he yelled at Itzali, his first wife of many years.

"I know not why she cries, husband!" Itzali defended.

"Why she cries, why she cries. That is what I want to know. Tell me why she cries! Daughter! Calli! Tell me why she cries! You know my second daughter. You were with her last!" The first general trembled and his face flushed red. His jaw muscles pulsated. Sweat trickled down his brow. "I will NOT have discord in my house!"

Calli's face went pale.

Huemac began to pace back and forth across the flagstone floor. "Oh, I have armies to organize and villages to patrol, tribute to collect *and* protect, fields to police, mines to guard," his voice got louder and louder, "And now I am to have a daughter who is supposed to lead a house of government who does nothing but blubber and cry!"

A slave, who had the misfortune of proximity at an inopportune time, received a fatal blow from Huemac's heavy hand. "Do not dare to hear my private woes!" He yelled as he smashed the boy's head against a stone wall.

"What is it? What takes her so long? Why does she not speak?"

His outburst switched to molten silence. He plopped down on a sitting stone. "Wife! Make this madness go away."

Huemac's submissive wife was coolly instructing other slaves to clean up the murderous mess: remove the victim without being heard, wash the blood and clean up the pieces of splattered brain matter without being seen.

"Perhaps my wise husband will take time to let his anger settle and contemplate the situation," she cautiously said.

"Humph." the general said, again pacing around the room. This was a sign that he was calming down. "She cries for days and we know not why she cries," he repeated.

By this time, Calli was kneeling, trembling with fear. Then, with no warning, her eyes rolled back into her head, she swayed, and collapsed to the floor.

"Oh!" Madam Itzali screamed. "My darling!" She swept over to her full-bellied daughter. "We must take you away to the Sacred House of Healing!" Then she addressed her husband, "This is *your* doing! For killing your slave in front of her! We will retire her to confinement for the duration of her term, lest it have an evil effect upon her." She whisked her eldest daughter away, leaving Huemac alone.

Why must women be the most momentous of all my problems? He wondered.

Huemac then stormed through the palace to his second daughter's sleeping chamber.

He found her forlorn and looking out the window, staring at nothing. She looked haggard and drawn.

"Your mother tells me you haven't eaten in several days," he said brusquely upon entering.

She said nothing.

"You've shirked your duties at the Sacred House and you dishonor our family." His voice was rising.

Tears started to roll down Tonalnan's face. She sat stone still.

"I will not have a daughter disgrace our house! I command you to be well!" Huemac was now yelling.

"Oh father!" Tonalnan cried. She rushed to him and threw herself at his feet and hugged his legs. Sobbing, she mumbled something unintelligible.

Huemac reached down and put his hand on her head. She was burning with fever. His heart softened.

"Daughter," he said, kneeling before her. "What ails you?"

"Find him, Papi, find him for me, please!"

Thus it happened that lovesickness had taken over the young maiden, daughter of Huemac, to such an extent that it would have taken her all the way to death's door, but her father loved her greatly, and couldn't bear her pain, so he consented.

[222]

"Ticitl!" he called loudly, and when her nurse arrived he asked, "What ails my daughter? How is it that she has fallen into a fever? Of whom does she speak?"

"It is he who sells chilli in the marketplace, My Lord," the woman answered. "He has put the fire into her. He has planted a craving in her so deep that she is consumed with desire for him. She burns hot with passion, My Lord."

"Find him!" Huemac commanded, but the general didn't reveal to what end he wanted the chilli boy found.

New Lodgings

Life for the Chichimeca had changed quite drastically with the death of the Omecihuatl. Nine Winds was now first mother, though Titlacáhuan continued to rule over all the forces of their supernatural world. Having realized that battles were now futile due to the enormity of the Toltec military under Ce Acatl Topiltzin, Nine Winds decided upon a plan by means of infiltration.

They moved the tribe slowly, only chosen clans at first, to live on the outskirts of the city, just north of the Valley of Fields. Spies sent into the city watched and learned how to construct mud and stone dwellings, and soon they had a small village. They stole profusely, and expertly at that, things that they needed for survival, from among the thousands of families in the urban center.

Nine Winds insisted that several of her clan learn to speak the language, so Titlacáhuan chose the ever loyal Tohuenyo, Mazatl and Yellow Skirt to look for work in the city center, where they would learn Nahuatl and be the sorcerer's ears and eyes.

Yellow Skirt found work at a brothel where she delighted in her new accommodations. The madam lavished clothes and jewelry upon her, as payment for her burning work ethic. No one had the turnover rate of the new girl! She was rumored to have satisfied up to twenty-nine customers in a single evening. Yellow Skirt acclimated quickly, and even stained her teeth red.

Mazatl found employment in the construction of the *ullama* ball court, which was close to the brothel. He wanted to be near his woman Yellow Skirt, but since she was constantly working, he released his frustrations by learning to play *ullama* at the end of each day after the construction workers and slaves returned to their families. Proximity to the brothel favored him, but since the flower of his heart was consistently unavailable, Mazatl began to release his *xinachtli* into the vessels of the other women in the brothel who were not so occupied. Because of his great size and Chichimeca talents in giving pleasure, Mazatl soon became very popular at the brothel. In fact, it was so unusual for a man to give pleasure to a woman at the brothel that Mazatl was seized upon by the women who worked there and he soon got to enter for free. He lived a busy life – working construction at the ball court during the day, practicing and perfecting his game of *ullama* in the evenings, and giving and receiving pleasure at night. Life was good.

Tohuenyo found work in the marketplace selling chilli.

Titlacáhuacan's plan was in motion.

Finding the Foreigner

It came to pass that Huemac ordered the king's subjects to look for the lad who sold chilli in the marketplace. His soldiers stormed through the streets and pounded on people's doors. "Where is the stripling that was selling chilli on market day last?" they growled, but he was nowhere to be found.

In the garment district, textile workers spun fantastic tales about the incident. "The first general is looking for the chilli boy. His presence loomed before the princess and caused her to faint!"

"Yes," said another weaver, "his apparition rose before her in a great and portentous size. It nearly killed her!"

"He cast an evil spell on her, he did," they said, "What dread! I hear the general plans to stone him dead."

In the feather workers' district, people brooded over the matter as well. "What evil will hatch from this plight?" they worried.

In the Sacred House of Healing, mid-wives discussed the matter with disdain. "A curse upon this foreigner who brings bad medicine to our sister Tonalnan!" they decreed. For in spite of their occasional rivalries, the women physicians of the medicinal fraternity banded together in times of distress.

The Toltecs loved the genteel daughter of Huemac, for in both appearance and justice she was fair. They searched high and low for her confronter, but he was still nowhere to be found. Gossip spread like wildfire, and soon everyone had a say in the matter. Conjectures were made about the manner of his death, how the angry father would avenge his daughter's honor. Some residents placed bets on the outcome, and graffiti started appearing on public walls of a young man with a grossly enlarged and erect genital chilli pepper.

And so it was that word spread throughout the *calpullis*, all the inner districts of the city.

When Tonalnan learned that her father had sent his soldiers to find her truelove, her heart yearned for him even more, for she feared that her jealous father would surely order his execution. She now refused to speak in addition to not eating, and became as worthless as severed hands.

Huemac was left to manage the drama of his household by himself, as his wife was still overseeing their eldest daughter's confinement. He weighed the possible outcomes carefully of what to do about the chilli boy. Decisions of the heart weighed differently than battle strategies and conquests, especially those with consequences in his household. Whatever he chose to do with this scoundrel was going to affect the stability of his home.

On the tenth day after his daughter's affliction, the *tianguis* assembled once again. Huemac had spent the morning in council with the king and the elder priests to discuss division of powers between the military and the priesthood. Apparently some soldiers had quarreled with some temple priests over rights to temple offerings. The soldiers had helped themselves to quite a few scoops of maize and bean porridge from the altar of a local temple, when several priests arrived and caught them. A skirmish ensued. The leaders were called to convene at the Palace of Quetzalcoatl to discuss the matter. What followed was a heated argument between Huemac with his closest advisors and Smoking Feather, the aging first priest with his closest devotees. The blowup turned into a hot debate over with whom authority should be vested, the priesthood or the military, and while the men disputed and quarreled all morning long, the only resolution they reached was that the soldiers were to replenish the offerings they had consumed at the temple. Everyone left the meeting in a state of discord.

As he descended down the front stairway of the Palace of Quetzalcoatl, Huemac looked out over the Yollotli, filled with buzzing commerce. Everyone around him bowed and prostrated themselves. The drummers and other musicians at the bottom of the steps stopped playing and dropped to the ground. As he passed them, he motioned for them to rise and continue with their playing. All the people ahead, upon realizing that the first general and his highest council were walking among them, stopped what they were doing and dropped to the ground. As the general passed, he motioned for them to continue with their activities. This absolute reverence continued as Huemac and his advisors walked the length of the Yollotli, creating an undulating wave through the crowd as they walked to the Royal Palace on the other side.

Just as they were about to ascend the steps to the Royal Palace, Matlal, governor of the marketplace, came running up to the first general. There was much pushing and shoving and chaos behind him, and several screams could be heard.

"My Lord," the *pochteca* insisted. "He has been found. He is here!"

With that, several hands pushed a strapping youth before the general. He was covered in a white cotton skirt. His rebellious eyes were aflame with defiance and he bore a coy smile.

"Bring him to me alive," the general commanded. Then he turned and walked into the palace.

⁂

Tohuenyo found himself in a small stone pool in an interior patio. Three very large sentinels stood along the walls with obsidian swords. Two scantily clad virgins were laughing and attending him. A ravishing middle-aged woman was pouring jojoba oil and sage into the water. She was an aging goddess, he decided. He was startled when one of the virgins poured a large urn of hot water over his head, but he vowed not to let it show. A proud warrior would never become unsettled by a giggling girl. He sat tense and stern.

"Relax," the aging goddess told him. "This is not a pot of water to cook you in." The two girls giggled. Then she commenced to lather up his long hair.

While Tohuenyo was unsure of his fate, he couldn't protest to his present state, so he resigned himself to their will. One of the two girls was pouring hot water on his neck and shoulders. The other was massaging his head.

The seductive middle-aged woman slinked to the other side of the stone pool and let her tunic drop to the floor. The sentinels stood motionless, staring off into nothingness. Tohuenyo realized how hard the stone in the pool suddenly felt.

The aging goddess stepped into the small pool and sat on the ledge directly in front of him. Tohuenyo made a motion to grab the gorgeous creature and from out of nowhere an obsidian sword was at his throat. He released her and moved his hands back. The two virgins giggled. Together they rinsed his long hair and began to massage it with egg yolk, honey and fragrant oils.

Tohuenyo was given a smoking pipe with fragrant herbs. After several drags he began to feel completely relaxed. He felt the goddess reach down and begin to massage his feet on her lap. One of the virgins held the pipe for him and he took another drag. The pipe suddenly reminded him of Nine Winds. Then he thought of Ichtaca and the others and remembered his reason for being there, his mission.

Then the aging goddess stood up, turned away from him, and climbed out of the pool, flaunting her wet buttocks in front of him. She laughed as she jumped up to get a cloth.

"The stone in this pool is very hard," Tohuenyo confessed, "rock hard."

"Good," she said, drying his hair with a cotton cloth. "Know that we prepare you for harder times to come."

Tohuenyo wasn't sure what she meant, all he knew was that the flint rock climbed out of the pool with him and stayed with him the whole time while the three women attended him. They dried him off with cotton cloth, rubbing him vigorously. Then they massaged musky oil all over him and dressed him in fine cotton. He wore a black mid-thigh skirt and an off-white shawl wrapped around his shoulders that draped in front of his carved abdominal muscles, held in place by a black leather belt with a great, gold disc. In the middle of the disc was a green emerald the size of an egg. They strapped him into leather sandals that laced up to the knee, studded with turquoise and gold. Lastly, they cut his waist-length hair to just below his shoulders.

Tohuenyo wondered what kind of death they were preparing him for. In the back of his mind were inklings of what he was supposed to be doing here, remembrances of moving to Tula, learning their language, why he had sold the chilli in the marketplace, but the dreamy effects of the smoking pipe and the rock- hard stone he got from the goddess of the pool were far more present in his mind.

I know I'm supposed to be here for something, he told himself, but he couldn't remember what it was.

✂

When he was brought before the general, Huemac immediately questioned him.

"Where is your home?" he gruffly asked.

"I am a foreigner. I come from afar, where the full moon dances in the day time sky and the eagle flies over the mountain." Tohuenyo answered.

Tohuenyo's mind was in a fog. He had been given heavy doses of strong medicine in the stone pool.

"Who are you?" the general demanded.

Then Tohuenyo began to remember. Through the magic of Xipe-Totec he was to become a Toltec, but this he did not reveal.

"I am Tohuenyo," he said, "and I am he who you found, as you found me. Naked and in the absence of outer garments I am only my true self."

Then Lord Huemac said to him, "You have wakened a yearning in my daughter. You will cure her."

Tohuenyo answered, "My Lord, that cannot be. What are you telling me? Kill me! Finish me! Death to me!" for Tohuenyo longed for a warrior's honor. He remembered that he had accosted the fair maiden, causing her demise, and pleaded for his deserved retribution.

"No. You will go to her and you will cure her of this affliction that bewitches her.

Huemac hoped he was making the right decision.

✂

Tohuenyo was then taken to the maiden Tonalnan. As the guards escorted him down the long stone corridor, a wave of clarity flushed over him and he remembered why he was there.

I shall kill her slowly and quietly, he thought. *Perhaps by suffocation. Yes, by suffocation. Then I am to cut out her heart and take it to Titlacáhuan. Yes, I remember now. The magic of Xipe-Totec...the flaying of the Toltec... wearing his skin...*

[231]

The guards pushed him into the princess' sleeping chamber and closed and bolted the door.

Tohuenyo stood proud, feet apart, arms folded across his huge chest. The princess was on the other side of the chamber in a gauze tunic, sitting motionless, staring out the window at the evening sky. Her thick, black hair shimmered in the firelight of several oil lamps in the room. Her small waist spread into a fine, wide buttocks as she sat upon a stool. *I'll have her first, then I'll kill her,* he corrected. He studied her. *I'll bet she's a virgin. She's like a tightly sealed urn. I'll smash her open with this eager, rock-hard stone that those women gave me, and fill her vessel with my xinachtli. Then I'll cut her heart out. To the Hells of Mictlán with Titlacáhuan! I'll eat her heart myself.*

The Chichimeca warrior walked stealthily toward the maiden. She seemed dazed, out of sorts, and continued to stare out the window.

He lifted her hair. *She's a tiny, little thing,* he told himself, and he slowly placed his hand around the back of her neck.

Tohuenyo had a sudden change of heart. *Patience Tohuenyo,* he told himself, *if you oft her now it will cause a scandal and make it impossible to get to the old man.*

As if in a trance, the princess turned and looked up at him with her chocolate-colored eyes.

Then a most unexpected thing happened.

A swirling wind came in through the window carrying upon its breezes a multitude of glittering, burning fireflies. They filled the room, dancing and laughing in their ritual of courtship. Enraptured, Tohuenyo stood mesmerized by their delicate beauty and forgot his evil intentions.

Tonalnan, who was now coming out of her delirium, began to recognize the stranger before her and she started to glow. She stood, placing her hands upon his chest and looked up into his eyes. A golden radiance started to emanate from her chest, like a star, and soon she was engulfed in white light.

The Toltecs believed that the universe was filled with light, that there was no place where one physical object stopped and another began, because nothing was solid and everything was filled with light. Because the universe was filled with light, their bodies were

[232]

filled with light. Every person's physical body, their *nahual,* carried within it a light body, called a *tonal*.

Tohuenyo stood entranced in the radiance of her *tonalli*, letting the light transmission pass through him. It burned out his hatreds. It consumed his greed. It washed away his envy. It cleansed him of his pride. Xipe-Totec was answering his prayers of re-birth and renewal, but not in the way he'd expected.

The fireflies swarmed around the room.

A new emotion rushed through him, in and out of him, all around him, filling him with unity, harmony and concord.

He pulled her to him and kissed her soft, round lips, and from that moment forward, they made love. They swam through the juices of guava and pineapple, rolled in the aroma of spikenards, frolicked where dew glistens on grasses in the morning sun. They reached the stars, danced on the reflection of the moon, and harmonized with the stillness of midnight waters.

Tohuenyo introduced Tonalnan to the ancient Chichimeca teachings of giving and receiving, as the lovers devoured each other again and again.

Madam Itzali's Fury

Madam Itzali trudged through the courtyard, hoisting her skirts through the pouring rain. Rolling thunder pounded in the heavy, gray sky.

Her slapping moccasins echoed off the stone steps as she ascended the arched entrance of the first general's private outbuilding.

Barging into the great room, she encountered her husband with his closest friends, Cuilton, Zolton, Ozomatli, and Matlal, playing board games, drinking *pulque*, smoking fragrant herbs, and surrounded by several women from the House of Joy.

The men had been laughing, trying to explain to one of the pleasure girls, a foreigner named Yellow Skirt, the concept of paternity. Apparently she and her people hadn't figured out the role of men in procreation. Her people only had one parent - a mother - she had told them. No, stupid girl, people have *two* parents, a mother and a father. In fact, it is the father who plants the seed. The mother is only an empty vessel. They laughed in scorn at the ignorance of the foreign pleasure girl. "Of course you won't know what kind of corn your vessel will hold," they said mockingly, "as each of us intends to plant our seed in your fields." The men laughed, moved more pieces across their game boards, drank more *pulque*, and smoked more herbs.

It was at that moment that Madam Itzali stormed in.

"Out!" She screamed, panic stricken. "Out, all of you!" She barged over to Ozomatli and swept a wet moccasin across his game board, scattering the pieces. Then she grabbed Zolton's brand-new, raised-white drinking cup and hurled it across the room. *Pulque* sprayed everywhere as it smashed against the flagstone floor. Huemac's friends looked at each other in astonishment, for not once as far as they could remember, no, not ever, had Madam Itzali lost her composure. The first wife had always been a model of wifely dignity and submission. They quickly cleared out, dragging their pleasure girls behind them.

"Wife, you are way out of line!" Huemac roared, jumping to his feet. He raised his hand to strike her.

"How could you! How could you let him ravage her so!"

Huemac was now pushing his wife forward, she stepping backward, in a horrid dance of rage, toward the wall.

"First you deny the noble suitors who have pursued her, robbing her of her birthright, and robbing *me* of my *purpose* in *life*, to arrange for her a proper and befitting marriage," she was holding his arms, struggling with him to deter her beating, "Then, you allow her to be defiled by this... by this *thing* of a foreigner!"

"Woman, shut your mouth!" Huemac now had his wife pressed up against the wall, one hand over her mouth, the other poised to beat her.

She glared at him with a fire in her eyes that he had never seen from her, never imagined possible from his obedient wife.

They stared in fury at each other for what seemed like an eternity. Finally he released her, shoving her aside.

"Say your piece Madam, and be done with it."

Just before she spoke, lightning cracked outside the four windows of the back wall, and rolling thunder pounded across the sky.

Madam Itzali lowered her voice to almost a whisper. "Great and honorable husband, my love and noble lord," she said, struggling to regain her composure. "I am confused. Perhaps you can enlighten me." She glanced over at him to see if her tender voice was softening him. "I understand your intent to cure our daughter's ills. After all, he is the one who plagued her. He should cure her."

Finally the woman comes to her senses, Huemac thought. If he had murdered the boy, it would have dealt a crushing blow to his beloved second daughter.

"But husband, *now* what are we supposed to do? Our daughter has been compromised. She is polluted. Stained. She brings shame upon our house." She waited for her husband to speak the obvious answer, but he did not.

"Woman, what would you have me do?" Huemac had already decided, but pretended to consider his wife in the decision, lest his house divide permanently.

"I would that you not stone her, My Lord. She is a beacon of light in our family. She burns with more light and joy than a New Fire Ceremony. And the people love her. Imagine their retribution." She waited still for him to speak the obvious answer. He held his silence.

"Go on," he said.

Madam Itzali thought herself an expert at getting her husband to do what she wanted, and think things were *his* idea. She was always careful with the timing of her ideas, and the way she presented them to him. "Perhaps we can save her honor if they are *married*, My Lord. But that decision you would have to make, my noble husband."

A wave of relief rushed through Huemac's heart at hearing his wife speak the plans he had intended all along. *Best to let her think it was her idea,* he thought. He turned his back to her and crossed his arms. "Alright, Madam. Because you were the love of my youth and are the mother of my children, I shall agree."

Mother of my children... The words rang in Madam Itzali's ears as she remembered back to all those years ago when the Stone Face Priest had exchanged infants with her to keep her from being executed for delivering a stillborn son. Her midwives had secretly whisked away the lifeless creature, while the priest hurriedly placed a newborn upon her teat to suckle. "Her name is Tonalnan," the priest had said. It was her deepest, darkest secret.

"Yes," Huemac repeated. "I allow my youngest daughter, the love child of my own flesh and blood, to marry the lad."

"As you wish," was all she said. Madam Itzali did not dare tell her husband so, but she did feel vindicated. Her daughter's honor would be restored through marriage. It wasn't the match that she had longed for, but at least no one would find out about her daughter's misguided transgression in those wretched two days of fornication. Her absence in her own household had cost her dearly, but it was the price she had had to pay, as her eldest daughter's need during her confinement was the stronger.

Madam Itzali wondered which was the lesser of two evils: having her daughter fall into disgrace through an act of fornication, or allowing her to marry a lowly foreigner, a mere commoner, and openly bring mediocrity upon them.

Tying the Knot

Madam Itzali's sense of propriety had been challenged at every stage of preparation for the marriage ceremony. First, there had been no formal engagement agreement, as the boy had come from who-knows-where. Then, no servants had presented themselves at Huemac's household bearing gifts on the boy's behalf to prove him worthy of their daughter. To make matters worse, there had been no receiving of the groom and his family at their home to present their daughter in the Throwing of the Insults Ceremony. Normally the insults served as a way for a family to talk their daughter down, so that if a young husband should be unhappy with his new bride, the family could say "*We told you so*," making it difficult for him to return her. Madam Itzali was sure that the foreign-*thing*-soon-to-be-her-son-in-law would never try to return his bride. The weed had everything to gain and nothing to lose in this match. The worst part for Madam Itzali, though, was that after the sacred union, the groom and his family were supposed to carry her daughter off through the streets in a pseudo-abduction. This, of course, was not going to happen. Since the boy was a child of Lord and Madam Nobody from the unknown realms of Nobodyland, her husband had commanded that their soon to be son-in-law live with *them*!

One thing was for sure. Madam Itzali was going to make sure that nobody knew that the couple had already engaged in pre-marital intimacies.

Lord Topiltzin Quetzalcoatl officiated the mid-day ceremony in one of the gem imbedded, colonnaded halls of the Palace of Quetzalcoatl. The celebrated couple sat together on a mat in front of their modestly masked priest-king. The corner of Tohuenyo's cape was knotted to the corner of Tonalnan's skirt.

The ceremony represented the transference of care of Tohuenyo from his mother to his new bride. (Tohuenyo wondered what his mother, Nine Winds, would think if she knew he was performing this sacred rite). According to Toltec custom, his mother

[239]

was supposed to bestow upon Tonalnan an inheritance of her finest garments, and feed the bride four mouthfuls of tamale. People had speculated at how this was going to happen, since the foreigner was alone in the world, but the king himself stepped into the role and bestowed upon the bride not just a basketful of fine garments, but a room full of treasure. Lord Topiltzin then fed the bride her bites of tamale so tenderly that some people believed he was in love with her and would have taken her as his own had it not been for his strict adherence to celibacy, a requirement of a priest and a king.

It was then Tonalnan's turn to feed Tohuenyo four mouthfuls of tamale. As she did this, they gazed into each other's eyes so profoundly that the rest of the world faded away and disappeared. Then they hung their heads close together and cooed like lovebirds, ignoring everyone around them.

"Let the festivities begin!" ordered the king, standing up and clapping his hands together loudly.

Everyone cheered, and the feasting and music began.

The celebration enlivened with drumming and dancing.

Even Chac performed his-her beautiful feats of acrobatics and contortion with admiring agility and ease. All the while, the newlyweds sat on their mat looking into each other's eyes, and spoke in whispers and smiles.

After the performances, the king and heads of state retired to another hall within the palace.

Not all the guests were as happy as the newlyweds, though. Most disapproved of the match, but put on airs of acquiescence and approval. "I heard she's already been penetrated," they secretly whispered to each other in disdain. "Our darling princess marries despoiled." Then they turned to the general's wife and raised their new-fashioned Chupícuaro goblets, "To the bride! She is as radiant as she is pure!"

Some gossips hated the groom. "He integrates the filth of his inferior blood into our pure and noble race," they said. "He shall spawn a pack of runts!" but in courtly demeanor they turned around and honored him. "Good wishes to the groom! May he live long and die as an honorable Toltec with a sword in his hand!"

The nuptial pair was oblivious to the hornets' secrets that were buzzing around them.

In the Western Hall, Huemac and the aging first priest, Smoking Feather sat with Lord Topiltzin Quetzalcoatl. Other heads of state were there as well, including Zolton the architect, Cuilton the engineer, and Ozomatli, chief *pochteca* of the Cintéotl clan. Nauhyotl was there, too, and several of Smoking Feather's closest companions from his sacred inner circle.

They sat on built-in stone benches around the painted walls, with giant murals depicting battles of days gone by, and listened reverently to their king.

He set forth his directives of many present issues - *pulque* production, irrigation, construction of the great pyramid, progress of the ball court, plans of a second pyramid, and his vision for new schools. All this he declared in his soft, dry voice, imparting tranquility as well.

Because they were at a wedding, the benevolent king revealed his plans for the newlyweds as well.

"The girl will no longer be chaste, and therefore may no longer work among the priestesses in the Sacred House of Healing. She will retire to her household where she will honor her lineage by her diligence in womanly tasks and loyalty to her husband. May her labors and sufferings be in the name of Quetzalcoatl, god of wisdom and fertility. She shall pray and meditate four times daily and she is to assume responsibility for the maintenance of Quetzalcoatl's temple. This she will pay for out of her personal allowance."

"Our lord blesses my daughter with his grace," Huemac said. Secretly he was panic-stricken at the cost of maintaining such a temple.

Then the king decreed a sizeable income for the daughter of Huemac, including revenues from cotton and cacao. "This I proclaim, my friend Huemac, so that our houses shall be united."

There was no doubt that the first general and his family had protection of the king. There was also no doubt where Huemac owed his loyalties.

"As for the boy," the king went on, "I know there are those of you who despise him." Some of the men fidgeted, but all remained silent. "First he shall attend the Royal House of Learning where he is to acquire social graces and knowledge of sacred ways. After he is properly educated, he will attend all religious observances at the temple of Quetzalcoatl. And finally," the king added unexpectedly, "he shall be given a commanding position in my army. First General, see that these things are carried out."

"Yes, My Lord," Huemac answered.

Before any of the men could respond to this inconceivable preferential treatment of a foreigner, a woman's scream was heard, along with running footsteps smacking against the stone corridor outside the hall.

"Your Grace, Lord General..." a dirty, ill-dressed man ran, gasping for air, to the doorway of their chamber. Immediately two guards caught up to him and detained him with obsidian blades.

"Who is this thorn that risks his life to interrupt my daughter's wedding?" Huemac barreled, rising to his feet. "Get me a sword!"

The king and priests remained calm.

The guards threw the man to the floor. "Prostrate yourself before the king!" they said, as they themselves dropped to one knee and bowed.

Somebody handed Huemac an obsidian sword.

"A dead man cannot justify his actions," Topiltzin Quetzalcoatl coolly advised.

Huemac stayed his anger.

"Speak, humble man," the king gently commanded.

"My Lord general, th-th-th-they're c-coming!" The messenger said nervously, groveling on the floor.

"What! Explain yourself you fool or I'll have your head!" Huemac blurted.

"It's Xolotl and the king's army of four thousand! They're marching back to the city from Michoacán!"

The guests, including the king's council, were so thrilled and excited at the return of the soldiers that, after permission from their king, they fled the wedding and ran across the city to the western Valley of Fields to greet them. The people of Tula were eager to find out who had perished and who had survived.

Meanwhile, Tohuenyo and Tonalnan were still sitting on their mat in the Ceremonial Hall, unaware of their surroundings, now examining each other's hands. After a few moments, a gentle man came up and placed his hands upon their heads, one upon the other. They looked up and saw it was their king. Topiltzin gave them a spiritual empowerment and his blessing. Then he quietly turned and walked away.

Tied together and hand in hand, Tonalnan and Tohuenyo walked back home. After a marriage celebration, newlyweds were supposed to be sequestered over four days, during which time they were expected to refrain from sexual intimacy. Whether the lovers honored this age-old custom, nobody knows.

Return from Michoacán

Everyone who was able ran through the city to meet the forces that were coming back to the Toltec capital. Families were eager to find out who had survived the perilous endeavor. People applauded the returning soldiers, and yelled with joy, "Hurrah for the Toltec army!" and "Long live our warriors!" Women ran to find their long awaited husbands and lovers. "This is your daughter!" or, "This is your son!" the women would say. Xolotl's wife Calli was one of them. She exuberantly presented her husband with their newborn daughter, Quetzalli. Less fortunate women screamed out their lover's names, fraught with anxiety to encounter no reply.

Families carried bundles of food and new clothing to the soldiers, who, *en masse*, flooded down upon the River Xicocotitlan outside of town to cleanse themselves of the stains of war. By nightfall there were thousands of people up and down the river, spread out upon its banks, meeting, greeting, and reuniting in elated joy. Torches soon dotted the sandy beaches, and fire pits blazed and crackled with roasting turkeys and deer, as families settled into their campsites for the night. Less and less frequently, forlorn villagers would pass through the campsites, asking if anyone knew of or had seen their loved one.

To the Toltecs' great relief, not only did most warriors come back alive, but also their ranks had swelled. Under Xolotl's command, they had taken on a great number of battle ready youths along the way, eager to leave their villages and see the world beyond. They had also amassed a fortune in plunder and slaves.

When Huemac found his son-in-law the commander, he embraced him tightly and cried, "Victory shines upon our son of Tula!"

At midnight the king came out to the riverbanks to meet them. Everyone had expected him to come in high fashion, riding on a slave carried litter. He came walking, though, surrounded by his closest disciples. He was humbly dressed in the black robes of a

[245]

priest, and had matted his long hair with turkey blood. A carved, wooden mask covered his face.

When he encountered the young commander Xolotl, he presented him with a quetzal feather war bonnet, one of the highest recognitions of war. A more formal ceremony would take place in several days, after the king had assessed the triumphs of the campaign. In the meantime, he performed a ritual blessing for the returning four thousand warriors. Then he retreated to his private temple for meditation and prayer, leaving Xolotl sitting at his campsite, holding his infant daughter, with Huemac and their wives.

Huemac was exceedingly proud of his son-in-law. He could not have made a better match for his eldest daughter. Hadn't it been his idea to marry her to this exceptional young man? Yes, he was sure it had been his idea. He gloated and boasted of this fact all night long, "See how triumphant my son-in-law returns. I chose an excellent match for my daughter!" His wife and daughter said nothing, letting him revel in his bragging. They could not forget, however, the high price it had cost them to get the matchmaker to cast her fortune telling bones and convince the stubborn old man of the union.

In the days that followed, the warriors returned to their homes throughout the city, and shared their stories and spoils of war with their families. There were festivities in people's homes, as they celebrated the long-awaited homecomings. Then, there were celebrations between neighbors, as old friends reunited with one another and caught up on each other's lives. Even new matches were made as triumphant warriors were rewarded for their conquests in battle - fathers eager to strengthen their family's protection offered their prettiest daughters to the warriors who brought back the largest spoils of war. With these new alliances, even more festivities took place.

Several days after the army's return, a formal celebration took place in the Royal Palace of Previous Kings. Xolotl was praised by the king for his successful campaign of establishing trade and commerce throughout the lands. He did not conquer the nations of the P'urépecha speaking peoples by force, and this, Topiltzin Quetzalcoatl said, was a great feat indeed, as it opened the routes of commerce and trade. Mercy and justice were the qualities of a fair and noble king, and Xolotl had embodied these qualities in the name of his lord, Ce-Acatl Topiltzin. Xolotl had used good judgment in recognizing that the Tarascans at Tzintzuntzan were a force to be reckoned with. Instead of attacking the Tarascan capital and risking the lives of his warriors, he had negotiated an economic and political alliance.

Huemac secretly disagreed. Whether he had thought of it himself or whether he had overheard some soldiers talking, no one knows, but he was of the idea that the kingdom of the P'uréchepa speaking people should have been attacked and forced into the Toltec empire as a tribute paying nation. Part of him felt betrayed by the young commander, for wasn't *he*, Huemac, the one who had promoted Xolotl in the first place? Hadn't he placed the war party leader in his present position and ordered him to conquer the peoples of Michoacán? To think that the king was rewarding him not for conquest and subjugation, but for merely establishing commerce and trade annoyed him beyond all reason.

Ce Acatl Topiltzin Quetzalcoatl presented Xolotl with the great, dorsal disc, the *Tezcacuitlapilli*, the highest recognition of a Toltec warrior. Everyone cheered. Huemac applauded, but secretly he seethed.

Plots and Schemes

The sorcerer Titlacáhuan foresaw many things. With the power and knowledge that he received from his magical weapons, he prophesied of a time to come when the People of the Caves would find it difficult to remain where they were and they would leave their cavernous dens. They would come to live among their enemies, they and all their progeny, while the Great Cataclysm had yet to appear. In the meanwhile, a comet would burn across the sky and a reign of destruction would begin. These and many other things the necromancer Titlacáhuan declared.

Titlacáhuan sat cross-legged before a small fire with his eyes rolled back into his head. Nine Winds was shaking a tortoise shell rattle around him, calling upon the goddess Itzpapálotl. *Eh, mother of war, awaken from your slumber in the depths of Mictlán. Hear our prayers, oh mistress of inextinguishable power, that we may rise and rule.* She then used an eagle feather to fan burning sage and copal over Ichtaca and the others around the fire. The small wikiup was soon filled with a smoky haze.

For some time, Ichtaca the warrior, who was sitting next to Titlacáhuan, had been training as the old sorcerer's apprentice. He had been learning to break his attachment to his distorted version of reality through near death experiences devised by the old man. He had come close to death by being buried alive in a crevice in the earth. Then the old man hung him upside down in a tree. After that he was given uncommonly high doses of hallucinogenic plants. These experiences had served Ichtaca to tame his mind, master awareness, and begin to understand the great mysteries of transformation. He now sat next to the master sorcerer and fed the old man soaked peyote buttons.

He raised a drinking gourd of water to wet the old man's lips.

Mazatl and Yellow Skirt were talking softly on the other side of the fire, Yellow Skirt in the comfort of her lover's arms. They were discreet and spoke in low voices to respect the master's journey.

He was preparing to seek a vision, and they were there to protect him from harm. Titlacáhuan had already consumed a gourdful of fresh peyote buttons. By the end of the night it would reach twice that amount.

Nine Winds sat down in the circle on the other side of Titlacáhuan. She was silent, but looked annoyed. She transferred some scorpions from one vessel to another and closed the lid. Then she cast her fortune telling bones on the dirt floor and poked through them. She scooped them up and cast them out again. She did this several times before she sighed, gathered them up frustrated, and tucked them away in a buckskin bag. She picked her teeth for a while. Ichtaca fed her brother another button.

"Where is he? Why doesn't he come?" Nine Winds finally whispered.

"He'll be here, Grandmother Crone," answered Mazatl softly, confident of their warrior's bond of brotherhood. "I saw him on market day last. They turned him over to the general."

"Good," Nine Winds said.

The fire crackled and the old man ate several more buttons before Yellow Skirt offered the next piece of information. "The general's daughter became ill when she saw him in all his nakedness and she fell to the ground." She sneered.

Nine Winds was expressionless. She was mending a belt with a cactus thorn needle.

"The general made Tohuenyo couple with his daughter to *cure* her of her sickness."

"What a remedy," said Ichtaca, pushing another cactus button into the stoned sorcerer's mouth. "Grandmother Crone," he whispered to Nine Winds, "I can cure you of your ills."

She threw a scorpion at him. He captured it as it was crawling away and tossed it into the fire. It sizzled and popped.

"What happened then?" Nine Winds prodded.

"The mother of the girl set off in a rage and forced her daughter and Tohuenyo to make a formal union."

"Why was the mother mad?" asked Ichtaca.

"They believe the great pleasure is evil, brother, but only sometimes." Mazatl interjected.

They all sat in silence for a while.

[250]

The old man started to hum.

It was hard for them to understand how something could be evil sometimes and not evil at other times, when the thing itself went unchanged.

"You see, young Mazatl, they *are* confused. I told you so." Nine Winds confirmed. She tied off her sewing and bit the thread.

"There's something else, Grandmother Crone," Yellow Skirt said. She looked at Mazatl for confirmation. When he nodded she continued, "They say that babies come from *xinachtli*. Men plant them into women through the woman's *cihuanacayo*." Nine Winds was raising her eyebrows, but Yellow Skirt went on. "That means that people have two mothers. We have our mother, and a man-mother that planted us in her. They call the man-mother a fa-ther."

Nine Winds was silent. It was something she had always suspected in the back of her mind. Hearing it made her panic. Not wanting to show fear, she froze.

Ichtaca became pensive. The implications of such a truth were staggering.

"We shall speak of this later." Nine Winds curtly commanded.

"The whole tribe is here," Ichtaca told Mazatl, pulling himself out of deep thought and changing the subject. "There is no one left in the caves." He fed the humming sorcerer another peyote button. The old man was starting to talk to himself in unintelligible gibberish. His eyes were rolling all around, following invisible entities.

The door flap shook open and Tohuenyo came in, carrying bundles in his arms. He quickly assessed the shamanic ritual and quietly dropped to his knees and bowed his head. "Grandmother Crone, I have come. You see I have not failed you." He softly said.

Nine Winds got up, walked over to him, and smacked him on the back of his head.

Tohuenyo sighed. *She's happy to see me*, he thought. *What a relief.*

"What detained you?" she hissed.

"The army returns from Michoacán," he answered. "Everyone is crazed. The streets are filled and hard to pass through."

It took time for Tohuenyo to unpack the gifts he had brought back from Huemac's palace. They sat in silence watching as he

[251]

presented his mother with an assortment of stolen weapons and jewels. He even brought back an obsidian dagger for Ichtaca. The whole while he unpacked the gifts in silence, but by this time the old necromancer was wailing something incomprehensible.

Tohuenyo looked different, nervous, like something was bothering him. "How much has he had?" he asked.

"Somewhere near twenty." Ichtaca answered. "It's going to be a long night."

They cared for the sorcerer the whole while he was in his altered state. They kept him from reaching into the fire. They comforted him through his screams of fear. They watched as he laughed himself into hysterics that ended in tears. They gave him sips of water and cleansed him every time he vomited. At one point, a giant crow hopped into the lodge and sat on the sorcerer's shoulder. It squawked, and he talked back. This dialog went on for some time between the necromancer and the crow. Then the shiny black bird hopped off, squawking indignantly, and strutted away with tiny, waddling steps out of the lodge.

They whispered of many things during the sorcerer's journey, of all the new things they were learning in the City of Stone Houses. Tohuenyo told them about everything Toltec he could think of, but refused to talk about his new bride. Mazatl shared his experiences and Yellow Skirt told of hers. Then they recalled the prophecy of the old Omecíhuatl, *not a battle will be fought to take down our foe,* and recognized its unfolding.

When the necromancer Titlacáhuan came out of his altered state, only then would they finalize their plans to infiltrate. This came to pass after several days. The death-defying necromancer came to his senses and revealed the essence of his vision. "They, their kin, and all of humankind will be sustained by the plants of the earth only if the gods are properly fed with human blood," he said.

Then, on blood oath, Titlacáhuan swore his accomplices to secrecy, and began to reveal his plans.

The Princess and the Weed

Celebrations continued privately in people's homes for several days. Within the first general's palace, extended family came and there was much to-do, as excited relatives listened to marvelous tales of battles and glory. Xolotl presented his wife with an exquisite collection of shiny, green ceramic urns that were sculpted into exquisite shapes like pumpkins and pineapples and corn. Nobody had ever seen such masterful workmanship in pottery, not even the black clay vessels of Oaxaca could match their beauty.

On several occasions throughout the celebration Xolotl held his infant daughter up to the heavens and exclaimed, "The heavens have blessed us with Quetzalli, Princess of Tollan!"

People gathered in the great room amidst music and feasting, and almost everyone was there – aunts, uncles, cousins, nieces, nephews and in-laws.

"Where's Tohuenyo?" Calli asked, almost unable to mask the distaste in her voice.

Upon hearing his name, everyone fell silent and looked at Tonalnan.

"He left for a spiritual pilgrimage," she said forthrightly. "He told me he would be several days in the caves to the north to meditate and pray." She was proud that her new beloved had a spiritual nature.

Xolotl's uncle, Lord Cozcacuauhtli Miquiztli had been crouched on the floor against a wall keeping to himself. "When a man starts entering caves, there's no good that will come of it!" he loudly interrupted. People barely noticed Lord Miquiztli anymore, as he mostly sat rocking and picking his fleas. In fact, his family hardly ever took him out, but this being such a huge occasion, he was brought along by his brother, Nauhyotl. Then the decrepit old man started making comments to the effect that entering women's caves was habitual. He then reached into his loincloth, grabbed his genitalia, and started pumping himself into ecstasy.

[253]

Eyeballs opened and eyebrows raised as Miquiztli made a spectacle of himself.

"You disgusting old pervert!" Tonalnan yelled. "Father, who is this man that he can insult me so?"

Xolotl jumped in to stave off the escalation. "He means nothing by it, my princess. He lost his wits long ago when his beloved died in childbed. He is nothing but a withering, wretched old man." Xolotl picked up the old fool and started to drag him off.

"Curse him!" Tonalnan said feistily. "I curse the day he was born!"

Xolotl's half-witted uncle was laughing to himself, still masturbating.

"Can't you see he is already cursed?" Xolotl said, and he dragged the pathetic, detested old stink-bag out.

Reactions were mixed throughout the room. The family loved Tonalnan dearly. She was the darling of the empire: ravishingly beautiful, intelligent, and full of grace.

This made the foreigner all the more unbearable. They didn't like him. In fact, in recent days, people had come to nickname him The Weed. They were taken aback by the old man's offending Tonalnan, yet many people thought the criticism of her husband, The Weed, was funny.

In any case, the whole episode served to remind people to gossip secretly, planting their wicked little comments between rows of normal conversation, like weeds among corn, lest the princess be further offended. Even so, Madam Itzali did a fantastic job of keeping the conversation lively and gay, and provided periodic rounds of entertainment. There were poets and musicians, and Tonalnan brought out her talking bird, Panchotl, whose repetitive verbiage had everyone laughing. Her slave hermaphrodite performed unbelievable contortions and everyone applauded. In spite of all the gaiety, secretive, malicious prattling still prevailed. Irritated with the hypocrisies, Tonalnan retired early to her private room.

When Calli found a moment alone with Xolotl in the courtyard, she told him the whole story of her sister's ill-fated betrothal. Instead of calling her new brother-in-law by his name, she too referred to him as The Weed. Xolotl hated Tohuenyo. He hadn't even met him yet, but he hated him.

✄

Tohuenyo walked through the desert fields in the moonlit night with his dagger at the ready. Only the bravest of warriors would venture out after dark and risk the wrath of the night monsters and demon creatures that roamed the earth at night. Mazatl and Yellow Skirt accompanied him. They were returning from their ordeal with the Omecihuatl and the sorcerer.

They walked through the fields in silence, from their Chichimeca encampments north of town toward the city center. None of them wanted to say much. Each of them was reflecting on the intensity of their experience over the last few days – the exhausting exchange of information, caring for the necromancer during his vision, bearing the weight of Grandmother Crone's insults and criticisms, being forced to memorize her plans and instructions. They walked back to the city in silence, except for the occasional hooting of hunting night owls and coyotes' howling.

When roads started to appear, they ducked behind a volcanic stone wall at the edge of a field and changed into their Toltec clothes. It had felt so good to wear animal skins and go about half naked, but camouflage was necessary if they were to be successful. Cloaked in Toltec cotton, their cover-up could proceed as planned.

When they reached the paved streets and stone houses, they proceeded with caution. Not wanting to be seen together, they hid behind corners and alleyways, stealthily running down streets when the way was clear. Soon they came upon the lively brothel. Light was flickering from inside the windows, and the rooms bustled with merriment and laughter. Tohuenyo stayed hidden in the shadows of the stone buildings across the street as Mazatl and Yellow Skirt went to the door. The couple turned back and gave their clansman one last glance. Then they opened the door curtain and went in.

Tohuenyo heard hooplas, and hurrahs and several women squealed with delight.

He was quickly on his way.

[255]

He moved from shadow to shadow until he reached the palace that was supposedly his new home. He reasoned that he could probably walk in through the main entrance, but he didn't want to raise any suspicions over arriving in the dead of night. Better to jump the wall, he decided. He crept along the perimeter of the buildings, careful to avoid any guards. When he came to the giant *ahuahuete*, he climbed up its branches until he reached the top of the palace wall.

He was in.

He crept along the roof of the palace buildings until he came to the courtyard behind Tonalnan's sleeping chamber, and silently slithered down one of the portal columns. Dark clouds rolled in front of the moon, and shadows started to play tricks on him. He slipped in through the open window and found his bride stretched out in deep slumber. The clouds went along their business, and the moon's glow poured in through the window, kissing her with its soft light.

Tohuenyo knew what he had to do. Grandmother Crone had made him memorize it over and over the last several days. He was to kidnap the general's daughter and take her to the north, to the caverns where the Chichimeca used to live. There, Ichtaca, Cueyatl and Moyotl would guard her as they pleased, while Tohuenyo would return to the palace and head up the search for her rescue. With the old general debilitated from the loss of his daughter, and Tohuenyo proving his loyalty by leading the effort to save her, they could proceed with the next part of their plan.

Tohuenyo looked at his new bride in the moonlight. She looked so perfect, so pristine. She had captured his heart with a single glance the first time he saw her at the marketplace.

There had to be a way out of this, somewhere he could take her where the two of them could escape the world and be alone. If only they could reach the velvety clouds and live upon the threshold of the kingdom of the gods.

He decided to go outside for some fresh air. He secretly ascended to the rooftops of the great palace. Maybe the lady stars would make this nightmare go away.

※

Madam Itzali couldn't sleep and insisted on barging in on her husband and one of his concubines. It was only because the man had finished his business that he tolerated the intrusion at all. Exasperated with his wife's involvements as of late, he ordered his lover to withdraw.

"Woman, my patience is tried with you," he said. Huemac knew his limits with his wife, though, however impatient he may become. Ultimately the wealth of their fortunes was hers. He thought about his friend who was working for political changes to transfer inheritances out of matrilineal lines and make them the birthright of men. "You request my audience at a most inopportune time," he added bitterly.

"Dear husband," Madam Itzali said, heaving her skirts to move toward the window. Melancholy seeped out of her and drove her gaze into the moonlight. "I wonder if we have greatly erred in marrying our daughter to the... *foreigner*." Madam Itzali was above name-calling and couldn't bring herself to call him The Weed.

The general sighed. He got up from his sleeping mat and stood naked behind his wife. He thought about how he used to love her. He still loved her. He just didn't love her the same way. "Go on," he prompted.

"Nobody accepts him, My Lord," she said frankly. "The people ridicule you because you allowed your daughter to marry a nobody foreigner instead of a suitable Toltec noble."

Now Huemac understood the severity of the matter and forgave her untimely intrusion.

"They ridicule *me*?" he voiced, draping himself in white cotton robes.

"Xolotl tries to defend you. He protects your honor by explaining away your reasons for allowing the marriage. But in truth, Xolotl despises him. He hasn't even met him, and he loathes him."

This time Madam Itzali had no plans to manipulate her husband. She had no ulterior motives; no ideas to plant in his head making him think they were his own.

"Husband, I cannot bear the thought that the people ridicule you. I cannot bear it!" She turned and put her face into his shoulder.

[257]

For the first time in many years, the general encountered the mother of his children in his arms. He embraced her and held her head in his hands.

"Gentle madam," he said, ever finding solutions. "There is a way yet to save our honor."

His matronly wife squeaked in his arms, innocently betraying her years.

"I will send him into battle to get rid of him," he whispered to the wind. "I will entrust Xolotl to this charge. Xolotl will finish him."

This was the best news his wife had heard all evening.

Outside sitting on the rooftop, Tohuenyo heard it, too.

The Plumed Serpent

Revealed

Huemac needed to rid himself of this son-in-law problem once and for all. The plan of sending the chilli boy off to battle seemed an excellent way to take care of the situation. The boy would die a respectable warrior's death. His daughter Tonalnan would have to be proud of that, since it would bring her much honor, but even better, she wouldn't be able to find fault with her father. Huemac would then lavish his daughter with empathy and condolences, and restore both his public image and the harmony of his household.

The decision, however, was not his to make. It was the king's, and in order for the king to send his great army into battle again, there had to be good reasons – political and economic reasons. The people of a nation will easily fight for ideals. Kings fight for power and wealth.

Huemac immediately thought of the Teotenancas of the Toluca Mountains to the southwest. Up to this time, the Toltecs had been unable to penetrate their great city because it was fortified with a massive, stone wall. Some said the wall was guarded by a great demon that possessed any outsider attempting to intrude by force. The Teotenancas controlled the nearby obsidian mines of Cacamilhuacan in the foothills of the snowy Xinantécatl Mountains. Possession of these obsidian mines could justify risking battle with the Demon of the Sacred Wall. Once defeated, the Teotenancas would have to surrender control of the mines.

After much deliberation, the king Topiltzin Quetzalcoatl agreed to the campaign. His motivation wasn't so much the obsidian trade, but rather the magnificent grandeur of Teotenanco itself. The city, his informants had told him, was a great metropolis that rested amidst green grasses, atop the Hill of Tetépetl, and it was fortified by a magic wall. It contained a multitude of resplendent, stone palaces, courtyards, a main road about two thousand paces long, a ball court, and even construction of a pyramid was under way. In spite of all this glory, the Teotenancas engaged in human sacrifice. The Toltec king wanted to bring Teotenanco into his flock of nations devoted to the august deity Quetzalcoatl, god of wisdom and love, and put an end to their ghastly human sacrifices. Control of the mines, he said, would be the blessing the Toltecs would receive for converting the misguided residents within the city's sacred wall.

Preparation for the Toluca campaign would take several months. An arsenal of weapons had to be created. The smallest weapons could be made by family members, but larger, more formidable weapons were carefully crafted by skilled artisans who were masters of their trades.

Every warrior's knife was unique. There were flint, chert, jade, chalcedony, bone, and many more. Sometimes a warrior had his knife made. Sometimes they were gifted. Sometimes he made his own. Many times the handles were ornately carved and covered in mosaics of turquoise, shell, or other precious stones.

An *atlatl*, or dart thrower, was a long, thin flexible shaft, capable of propelling darts with maximum force and accuracy.

Some warriors used maces and stone-headed clubs with a rounded, stone strapped tight at one end that could crush an opponent's skull. Maces with a pointed stone head could gash through flesh and bone.

Hooked lance heads and swords were particularly deadly. They could twist around an enemy's entrails and pull them back out through the entrance wound.

Obsidian toothed spears were used at the forefront of battle before hand-to-hand combat set in. They typically had a broad, wooden head twice the length of the user's palm. The point was usually edged with jagged obsidian blades like crystalline fangs.

Bludgeons and clubs were more rudimentary and carried by the lower classes.

The deadliest weapon of all was the *maquáhuitl*, a broad sword– like weapon made out of wood, studded with pieces of razor sharp obsidian glass to create a blade. It was an arm's length long, and a hand's length wide, and when wielded with enough force, could cut of the head of a deer.

Warriors' wives and families devoted their time preparing the warrior's armor. The most prevalent defense was the *chimalli*, a round shield. Some shields were animal skin with feather trim. Others were wood, while others still were metal alloy with mosaic, inlaid stone. Metal shields were heavy and impractical, though, so when they were used, they were small. Almost all shields were painted with spiritual symbols that served as powerful talismans and enhanced the magic of a warrior's weapons.

Body armor consisted of a thick, heavily padded cotton vest called an *ichcahuipilli*. It was worn under a warrior's outer clothing, and gave him a formidably stout appearance. Helmets were carved from hardwood in a variety of heraldic shapes including jaguars, eagles, and wolves.

High ranking nobles who could afford more equipment also invested in pounded metal arm cuffs and protective leg bands.

Preparation of all these weapons took time, and Huemac could not help but dwell on the words spoken by the king at his daughter's wedding;

"As for the boy," the king went on, "I know there are those of you who despise him." Some of the men had fidgeted, but all remained silent. "First he shall attend the Royal House of Learning where he is to acquire social graces and knowledge of sacred ways. After he is properly educated, he will attend all religious observances at the temple of Quetzalcoatl. And finally," the king had added unexpectedly, "he shall be given a commanding position in my army. First General, see that these things are carried out."

"A commanding position in the army," Huemac kept repeating to himself. Reluctantly, he was going to have to see what he could do.

✁

In the days that followed the wedding, Tohuenyo started his schooling at the Royal House of Learning. The schoolboys and adolescents who went there made fun of his thick accent and broken Nahuatl, until he secretly pinched them and pulled their hair.

Discipline at the school was tough, physical, and immediate. Priests administered most of the punishments, but deferred to the headmaster for more serious crimes. Physical castigations included enduring multiple perforations with cactus needles while sitting in a corner, or lying bound and naked in an icy puddle outside. Priests would lacerate a pupil's fingers for botching manual labor, or a tongue if they misspoke their lessons. The worst punishment, though, was the burning peppers – being bound and held, choking and coughing, over a smoking fire of blazing, popping chilli.

Tohuenyo was lucky, though, or maybe he just knew how to stay out of trouble. Because he was older, and taller, than the rest of the boys, it wasn't long before he was able to intimidate them. He started by pinching them. They held their complaints in silence, lest they be punished for whining. Soon he started making faces at them to scare them. One time he brought a scorpion and, forever his mother's son, quietly slipped it into another boy's bag. The boy, an upper-class bratty snob, had antagonized Tohuenyo long enough. The condescending whelp went into hysterics when he reached into his bag and got a scorpion sting. Screaming, he flung the arthropod across the room without thinking and it hit the attendant priest in the head. The bratty snob boy spent the rest of the day in the corner with cactus thorns stuck under his fingernails. He never disrespected Tohuenyo again.

Their lessons included practicing the skills of battle and weapon making in the morning, as well as learning the indispensable social graces of appropriate behavior for nobles. After a mid-day meal, they studied oral histories and their sacred obligations as heads of families. They were made to memorize the twenty day signs and eighteen months of the calendar and were expected to know the pantheon of gods that ruled the cosmos from the thirteen heavens above.

Tohuenyo learned fast, and it wasn't long before the headmaster singled him out one day and invited him to attend a private gathering of priests who were going to hear Topiltzin Quetzalcoatl reveal the teachings of the deeper mysteries.

Tonalnan was so excited that she spent three days and three exhausting nights weaving and embroidering black robes for him. When Tohuenyo arrived at the exclusive secret meeting, the priest-king was preparing to talk about the nature of the cosmos and Quetzalcoatl the god. About twenty black-robed priests sat reverently before him, Quetzalpopoca Smoking Feather among them. They placed Tohuenyo in the back and swore him to an oath of silence and secrecy.

The priest-king and his companions met in a private temple atop the Pyramid of Coral northwest of town. Dedicated to Ehécatl, god of wind, the pyramid was circular, as well as the temple built upon it where they now were. They'd had to climb the great stairway of the pyramid in formal procession, chanting the Song of Ehécatl, and make burnt offerings on an altar before they were allowed to enter the sacred space at the top. Inside the circular room, a fire blazed in the center, and the walls around them were painted with beautiful murals that elaborately explained their origins and cosmology. The cone-shaped ceiling had an opening at the top to allow the escaping smoke of the fire to reach the heavens.

Tohuenyo sat with his legs crossed on the floor in absolute silence, with his head hung down. The pungent odor of the dirty priests around him was almost overpowering except that the aroma of *copal* was starting to fill the room.

The melancholy melody of a lone flute echoed off the walls, while the firelight flickered, bending the light and causing the painted gods on the murals to warp and writhe as though they were breathing.

Now unveiled, with black and yellow stripes painted on his face, Topiltzin Quetzalcoatl stood up and began chanting a strange verse that Tohuenyo had never heard before. His chanting was resonant and loud. It echoed off the walls and reverberated back into Tohuenyo's heart. All the while, the priest-king shook his tortoise-shell rattle;

> *"I come from Quetzalcoatl,*
> *I go to Quetzalcoatl.*
> *I came to play the sacred drum,*
> *In the hearts of the People I play my drum.*
> *I came to blow the holy breath of Ehécatl*

[263]

Into the flute of a thousand sounds.
I am Quetzalcoatl."

The priest-king raised his rattle to the four directions and prayed to each of the four Tezcatlipocas; north, south, east, and west, inviting them to enter the sacred space. Then he used a black and white eagle feather to spread about the fragrant smoke of burning sage to purify the circle of unclean energy.

He sat down and took his time before he spoke.

"The sun, the human one, the flower, and the bird... are at the vital center of consciousness. They are found upon the wind, the wing, and the cloud, carried by Ehécatl. From the sacred waters of rain, consciousness becomes manifest in the corn which, fed by the sun, sustains the flower, the bird and the human one.

"This is Quetzalcoatl.

"The thunder that plants the metal of its voice into the throats of birds and the human one, this too is Quetzalcoatl.

"The jewels and precious stones that have captured colors and taken them prisoner, that are found in the sparkling rivers and caverns of gold, these jewels that speak to us with flutes as voices, they too, are Quetzalcoatl.

"Quetzalcoatl gathered the bones of woman and the bones of man from Mictlántecuhtli, and the human one was born.

"Quetzalcoatl has no form, but we paint his image as a plumed serpent so we can understand the deeper mysteries of our god.

"When we are naïve we are like the serpent who spends her life forever connected to the earth, looking for nourishment and hiding from predators. She slithers along gracefully, but spends her life only seeing what is immediately in front of her.

"When the seeker of knowledge grows in spiritual awareness and rises above the pyramid of consciousness, he soars, like an eagle in the heavens above. The spiritual warrior only reaches this great height when he surrenders his attachments to the mundane. This consists of judgments, fear, and lies that have been programmed into his mind by others, confusing him with rules and agreements about who he is and how he should live his life. The more he eliminates the distorting lies in his mind, the less susceptible he is to their power. He becomes an eagle, a seer. He

[264]

flies free from old judgments and fears, soaring high on his own currents and living life effortlessly and impeccably."

The priest-king sat quietly and let his companions reflect on what he had just said.

One of the priests scattered some copper pieces over the burning coals, turning the flames a brilliant green.

Another priest tossed some fire sand into the flames causing a myriad of tiny, popping sparks. The brilliant light show soon fizzled out, but the copper infused flames stayed green.

Topiltzin Quetzalcoatl continued his instruction.

"We use the symbol of a plumed serpent to represent the dual nature of the Sacred Spirit. The serpent, with its body ever connected to the earth, is the material aspect of our world. The bird, which flies among the heavens, is our divine nature, the sacred Spirit in our world. Existence is ruled by this duality. If you observe with spiritual eyes, you will see that the earth forever breathes the ethers of the sky, and the sky, that is, the heavens above, are ever drawn toward the earth below. What this means is that the divine Spirit and all that which is manifest are forever engaged in an interplay that is the Sacred Dance of Life."

Topiltzin Quetzalcoatl paused.

"Master, how does the god Ehécatl participate in the Sacred Dance?" a disciple asked.

Topiltzin looked at Quetzalpopoca Smoking Feather, and held up his palm, offering the honor of response to his first priest.

Quetzalpopoca's words were slow and his voice was soft and dry from age. "Ehécatl is the god of wind," the stone-faced priest said. "But the spiritual warrior sees beyond that. In the deeper mysteries, Ehécatl is the holy breath that breathes the divine Spirit into everything that is."

"Quetzalcoatl is the dual nature of our world. Quetzalcoatl is found beyond the serpent and the bird," the priest-king reiterated. "Quetzalcoatl is found beyond the heavens and the earth. Quetzalcoatl is the divine Spirit that is blown into all of manifestation by the holy breath of Ehécatl, the wind."

Topiltzin the priest-king then went on to explain how each of us lives in our own dream, our own separate reality. "The dream we each live is like a smoking mirror," he said. "Everything that happens to us in our life is a reflection of our inner being. That's why life is like a mirror. If our hearts are pure and unclouded by fear and judgments, we will reflect that in our dream and the world outside ourselves will be filled with abundance and prosperity.

"When our hearts are filled with perplexities, our dream of reality becomes clouded. That is why we say *smoking* mirror, for we do not see life as it really is. We see reality through all the beliefs, judgments, opinions, fears and pain that are part of our personal dream." Then Topiltzin Quetzalcoatl added as an afterthought, "What the world presents to us is a reflection of what we hold in our hearts within."

"Master, whose is the real one, my dream or someone else's?" another disciple asked.

Topiltzin replied, "Tezcatlipoca is the god of the Smoking Mirror. He feeds on our conflicting nature as we go through life thinking our own dream is the only perception of reality. Brothers and sisters kill each other to prove their dream is right and fail to understand that they are only fighting about the dream they were born into. But the more we purify our hearts with wisdom and love, the more we fight off the cloudiness of Tezcatlipoca the Smoking Mirror, and our dream of reality becomes clearer."

Everything was quiet. The priests of Quetzalcoatl's inner circle sat in contemplation for some time.

Then the priest-king Topiltzin added, "Tezcatlipoca feeds on evil and fear in the hearts of men. Quetzalcoatl is strengthened through wisdom and love."

By this time, Tohuenyo was feeling overwhelmed with emotion at the beauty and intensity of Topiltzin Quetzalcoatl's teachings. His eyes filled with tears and he began to cry. Somebody must have noticed, because soon he felt the tug of a priest pulling him to his feet and escorting him outside into the mid-night air.

He wiped his eyes, and ran down the pyramid stairs, but his tears continued to flow. A great sadness overcame him, unlike any grief he had ever known. He cared not about the dangers of the Night Creature, cared not about any demons that might be lurking in the dark shadows of the night. All he could do was run and cry, and cry and run. He ran and ran, in a flood of tears, back to the city of Tula, through its empty streets and *calpulli* neighborhoods, out the city and across the Valley of Fields until he came to the River Xicocotitlan. There he collapsed on the banks of the river and released a lifetime of sorrow and pain, his tears falling into the waters of the river.

He cried out his memories of evil and pain.

He cried out Ichtaca's *coyotl* headdress ceremony when Titlacáhuan cut out the victims' tongues, licked the oozing blood for its magical powers, and ordered their sacrifice by the bow.

He cried out the Xipe-Totec ceremony when his kindred flayed the skin of the Toltec while he was still alive so he could make the sacred dance for rebirth and renewal.

He cried away his plans to kidnap his wife and murder his father-in-law.

He cried because he knew, deep down in an unseen part of him, that everything he had learned his whole life, and the people who were closest to him, that he cared about the most, were wrong for him. They were like the Smoking Mirror, evil servants of Tezcatlipoca, motivated by wickedness and fear.

He cried the most when he realized he didn't want to be like them anymore. Instead, he wanted to swim in the spiritual sea of Quetzalcoatl, the greatest god of all.

So it was that there, on the banks of the Xicocotitlan, under a blanket of stars and in a river of tears, Tohuenyo became a spiritual warrior for wisdom and love. And from that time forth, Xicocotitlan was secretly transformed into a River of Tears.

The Toluca Campaign

Two months passed and the preparations for war were successfully coming to an end. Arsenals of weapons were stockpiled, warriors had sufficient armor and shields, and enough *petlacalli* baskets had been woven to carry provisions for months. The time had finally come to send the army to the Valley of Toluca to liberate the city of Teotenanco from their wicked ways. While Huemac and his cronies like Ozomatli were motivated by the burning desire to control the mines of Cacamilhuacan, the people's motivation was more idealistic. Most of the Toltec families were passionate about spreading their cultural values throughout the One World, especially the absence of human sacrifice - the fewer nations that practiced this wicked evil, the better.

Huemac had still not settled the question of assigning his son-in-law to a commanding position. He kept putting it off, not knowing how the dynamic would play out with his other son-in-law, Xolotl.

Xolotl was to lead the army. A thousand warriors had been called upon for the Toluca campaign. It wasn't as large as the expedition to Michoacán, but it wasn't as far, either.

On the morning they were to leave, floods of warriors danced through the streets, yelling and screaming out powerful war cries to let everyone know they were ready for battle.

Small bands of soldiers, in their own, private war parties, went from house to house, pounding on doors and screaming in people's windows, demanding roasted maize cobs, scoops of spicy-hot bean paste, bags of sweet-hot, fried grasshoppers, or anything else they could elicit from defiant matrons, armed with brooms, intent on protecting their kitchens. This resistance was mostly for show, however, as the women of Tula had been cooking for days in preparation of the warrior's departure.

After the plundering and raiding of homes and neighbors all morning, the conches in the Yollotli finally started to blow. Warriors and their families made their way to the great field surrounded by the Palace of Quetzalcoatl, the *ullama* Ball Court, the Royal Palace of Previous Kings, and the almost finished Pyramid of the Sun.

The warriors organized themselves first by families, then by clans, then by neighborhoods. Families and friends surrounded their men who were going off to battle, some engaged in last-minute necessities – don't forget this, don't forget that. Others shared last-minute words of wisdom or gifted the warriors personal items like talismans or magical potions.

The army was accompanied by several hundred porters who were in charge of the vast supplies to be carried in the *petlacalli* baskets. Soon there were too many people to fit in the Yollotli, so slowly, the army and the people who accompanied them to say their goodbyes started to make their way west toward the Valley of Fields. As they walked through the city streets, people lined along the rooftops showered them with fragrant petals and tiny, brightly colored feathers that wafted to and fro, twisting and flittering all the way to the ground.

Over the past few months, Tohuenyo had kept busy studying at the Royal House of Learning and attending all the religious observances at the Temple of Quetzalcoatl. He had also spent his nights with his wife, the fair Tonalnan, and he left contented at knowing that his seed grew inside her luscious womb. The idea of being a father had never occurred to him, and now that he was aware of this divine empowerment, his mind was set on having as many children as possible.

Those thoughts would have to wait, however. Tohuenyo had a burning desire to prove himself in battle and win over the affections of the Toltec people. The Chichimec-turned-Toltec walked out of town toward the River Xicocotitlan accompanied by his wife and a dozen porters that carried his supplies. Soon the army converged on the banks of the River Xicocotitlan. An enormous number of canoes waited for them on the other side.

The warriors were accompanied by their kin, much like they had been when they returned from Michoacán, but this time there would be no staying overnight. The soldiers were anxious to leave. Today the riverbank would serve only to host their waves of goodbyes.

Huemac had accompanied Xolotl and his entourage of battle leaders to the riverbank, along with their families and wives. He had paid no attention to Tohuenyo whatsoever, who was still considered the dirty foreigner and was socially ostracized.

When most of the army reached the riverbank, the conches sounded once again and it was time to say goodbye.

Both cheers and tears went around. Lovers engaged in deep kisses. Fathers held their babies, and ruffled their children's hair. Mothers embraced their sons, uttering sacred incantations that would protect them in battle.

Tonalnan had vowed not to cry. She would cleave to hope, and not let doubt enter the door to her heart. She fussed over the padded, cotton under armor that she had so painstakingly made for her beloved.

"Your most powerful weapon is your inner strength," she firmly said. She removed her gold medallion of Quetzalcoatl and tucked it into the folds of his sash.

"I will return to you, beautiful woman," he said, holding her head in his hands. "I will return and we will have many children!" Only death could keep him away from her now.

As Tohuenyo and Tonalnan embraced for what might be the last time, Huemac approached them and gruffly said, "You go with Xolotl. He will assign you a command."

The Toltec warriors then turned and crossed the River Xicocotitlan. As they waded through the river, a wave of sadness that no one could explain overcame them. Men sighed and reminisced over melancholy memories of their lives, but as soon as they were out of the spellbound waters and reached the canoes on the other bank, their grief vanished. They hollered and cheered, high-spirited and ready for battle. The Toluca campaign had begun.

Journey to the

Jilotepec Mountains

The army rowed down river all day until they came to the nation of the Tepehí. When they reached Tepehí of the River, the tribes received them with much fanfare and excitement. The Tepehí peoples were subjects of Tula, and highly praised Quetzalcoatl their king. When they had received word many days before that the Toltec army was going to be camped on the shores of their river, they reached into their stores of maize. By the time Xolotl and his army arrived, the villagers descended en masse upon the warriors, and lavished them with an endless variety of delectables made with corn. Previous trade arrangements had already been made as well, and Xolotl delivered a sizeable supply of textiles, lime and stones for weapons to the local governor. In exchange, Xolotl received a chain gang of slaves and one of the governor's daughters as a concubine. He thanked the governor profusely for this most generous gift, and went on and on about how useful the delicate daughter would be to him during his perilous journey. The maid stood proud and smiled as Xolotl elaborated - she could tend his wounds like a surrogate mother, cook for him, mend his clothing, set up his camp, and keep him properly nourished with her sweet juices by night. Later, back at the camp on the shores of the river, Xolotl was heard saying, "Damned to all Mictlán if I didn't get stuck with a skirt during a campaign!" After that he secretly sent the virgin to his wife back in Tula, escorted by several guards. He didn't even bother to wave goodbye as they rowed away in their canoes. The virgin of Tepehí and her escort were never seen again.

From Tepehí of the River, the army rowed west, toward the foothills of the Jilotepec Mountains. Over the next two days, the landscape was changing into many shades of green, as the rainy season was finally upon them.

When the river started splitting into tributaries and became too shallow to navigate, they knew they were coming into the country of the Taxhimaya tribes. The Taxhimaya people lived in scattered villages throughout the mountains. Their tribute to Tula consisted mostly of animal skins, as they were expert hunters of the large game in the mountains. If anyone wanted bone antlers for a knife handle, an antelope hide, or an even more exceptional jaguar, it was the Taxhimaya they would turn to.

At the foothills, Xolotl ordered his army to dry dock their canoes in the hills high above the river, as everyone knew that the river surged with floodwaters during the rainy season and would wash away anything in its path. He then paid the Taxhimaya a valuable amount of obsidian to protect the canoes.

They spent several days in the foothills while they prepared to cross the mountain pass. During this time, the army of a thousand warriors started forming into bands. Except for the high-ranking nobles, leadership positions weren't assigned. They were fought for, so that there, in the foothills fights started breaking out among the warriors. Not only did the nobles place high stakes bets on the winners, they were also able to determine how to divide the resulting leaders into companies of war parties, and then decide who among the nobles was going to command each one. Because of his success in the Michoacán expedition, and because he had incurred the king's favor, Xolotl had been given the assignment of High Commander of the Toluca campaign. He was then in charge of sixteen commanding nobles, including Tohuenyo, who all held the title of chieftain.

It was during this time that rumors started spreading that there was an undefeated giant in their midst. Tohuenyo had been mostly keeping to himself, surrounded only by the silent company of his porters. He'd been ordered by Huemac to go with Xolotl, but managed to follow him along the journey at the discreet distance of a stone's throw. Even so, the news of an undefeated giant was irresistible, and Tohuenyo soon found himself in the chiefs' camp, listening fervently to the excited accounts.

"He's bigger than any man I've ever seen," a chief named Cuauhtémoc said.

"And strong, too. He can pull a tree right out of the ground!" somebody else added.

"He's a giant, I'm telling you," Cuauhtémoc said. "I'll pay the Commander a hundred baskets of cacao to have him in my company," he boasted.

"Let's see if he survives," another chief said.

"He looks destitute. The poor bastard is bereft of proper armor and weapons. Doesn't even have an *ichcahuipilli* to keep himself from getting hacked up," somebody else said.

"Well I saw the thug with my own eyes. This very morning. He hacked a man up with a *maquáhuitl*, he did," the chief named Cuauhtémoc said. "I'm placing my bets on the giant. Anyone who wants to bet against me can, but you're a fool if you do."

Nobody said a word.

"In fact," he went on, "I'm so sure that my feisty giant can beat any man, I'll pay four times the wager."

"Let's see what he looks like, first," Tohuenyo objected.

"Yes, let's see!" The others agreed.

Down the hill in a flat expanse of dirt, dozens of warriors were gathered round in a ring. They were screaming and hollering, cheering for and against the two men thrashing each other in the middle. As the nobles arrived, they could hear the *crack-crack* sound of colliding spears.

"Spear fight!" one of the chiefs surmised.

As the noble chiefs approached the ring, the onlookers obediently pushed themselves aside, in deference to the nobles' superiority. Tohuenyo was surprised to see that Xolotl was there, watching from atop a boulder a few paces away.

As soon as Tohuenyo got close enough to see the two men fighting, the giant had his opponent on the ground. He raised his spear and thrust it at the man's throat, stopping just short of the kill.

Tohuenyo's heart skipped a beat.

The giant was Mazatl.

"The giant wins!" a battle veteran with one eye yelled. He pushed up Mazatl's arm.

[275]

Hoorahs were heard all around as payments were exchanged. Most payments were tangible, such as precious stones, or pouches of smoking weed. Some warriors had bet on promises of future payments, like a basketful of maize cobs when the next crop came in. One man even bet his wife against another man's two concubines. The wife had an inheritance. The two concubines had beauty and youth. Tohuenyo didn't see which man won. He was fixated on the fact that the giant was Mazatl.

Mazatl, his eyes grazing across the spectators, looked up and saw Tohuenyo. They locked eyes.

Tohuenyo, forever quick to think, used Chichimeca sign language to tell his friend not to speak. *Don't let anyone see we know each other*, he signed. *Lose the next fight and I can come up with a load of weapons and armor for you.*

The chief named Cuauhtémoc, so sure about his feisty giant, was now laughing and waiving his purse in the air. "I'll double the wager on the next round!" he was yelling. "Who will take me on?"

There was a lot of fidgeting and head scratching, but nobody answered.

"I will," Tohuenyo announced.

"Ah, the son-in-law of the first general!" Cuauhtémoc said sneering.

"What a good bet you've made, Cuauhtémoc!" one of the other nobles said. "You'll be sure to get your payment. No lack of funds there."

"Add your wives to the bet, Cuauhtémoc!" another chief said.

All the nobles laughed. "You'd have to wager more than your wife to win the Princess Tonalnan!" somebody yelled.

"First we shall see the opponent! Then we'll settle our wagers," Tohuenyo yelled. "Who challenges the giant?"

A hardened battle veteran with a scar across his mouth and many feathers in his hair stepped forward. Everyone called him Yauhtli. He always licked his sword after a kill.

Tohuenyo smiled a big, handsome grin.

"Wager?" Cuauhtémoc asked.

"Alas, Cuauhtémoc. I will not wager wives," Tohuenyo said mockingly. "My wife is the most beautiful of wealthy heiresses in

[276]

the land." Then he added, "How could I consider bringing your hairy beast of a wife into my bed after I win?"

Everyone laughed.

Cuauhtémoc's brown face turned deep red.

By this time the giant was sitting at one end of the dirt expanse, drinking water and wolfing down a few bites of maize and bean cakes. He snorted as he ate and then wiped his mouth with his sweaty arm. He belched and then farted.

The challenger Yauhtli was at the other end, surrounded by his supporters and friends.

From his elevated vantage point, Xolotl had been watching the entire deal. He couldn't resist a bit of interference. "Gentlemen," he interjected. "Why not wager porters? Four each, and the porter comes with the contents of his *petlacalli* basket. Winner's choice." It was obvious that the giant was going to win. He'd been winning all morning. If Xolotl could get Cuauhtémoc to disarm Tohuenyo by choosing his baskets of weapons, his sinister obligation to Huemac would be easier to carry out, as it would leave his filthy brother-in-law unarmed.

"Agreed," both nobles said in unison.

"No weapons!" the one-eyed veteran yelled. "Let's see what these warriors can do on their own!" Then he added, "The fighter who wins gets to handpick the warriors for his own war party! Let the challenge begin!"

The two warriors ran toward each other screaming their most terrible war cries. They pounded each other like thunder, twisted and contorted and dropped to the ground and rolled. Then they got up and dealt each other harrowing blows. With his left hand on Mazatl's chest, Yauhtli pounded his fist into the side of Mazatl's head. Mazatl dropped to the ground. As quick as that it was over.

There was a wave of shock as the spectators gasped. Then Yauhtli's friends and supporters started to cheer.

Cuauhtémoc stood, mouth agape, staring at his fallen giant.

✄

Yauhtli was given a position as a war party leader, and permitted to choose ten of the strongest warriors to serve him.

Cuauhtémoc paid Tohuenyo the *petlacalli* baskets and the slave porters as promised. The winner didn't choose all weapons, though, as everyone had expected. He also chose tools, provisions, blankets, and clothes.

Mazatl was left where he fell. Then the spectators disbanded and returned to their camps. People wanted no more to do with the fallen giant who had so excruciatingly disappointed them.

Tohuenyo stayed with his now outcast friend until he came to. Then he half-carried half-dragged the big man back up the hill to his own, private lean-to a comfortable distance away from the noble chiefs' camp.

Mazatl slept for hours. When he woke, Tohuenyo winked at his friend, and gave him the winnings. "Not bad for a couple of savages, eh?" he said. Mazatl smiled, then winced and put his hand to his head.

Bones of the Two

Several months passed and Tonalnan was settling in to her new routine of caring for the Temple of Quetzalcoatl, religious observances, and prayer. At first, when she'd learned that the king had mandated that she no longer oversee the Sacred House of Healing, and dedicate all her time to being a dutiful wife, she was elated, for then she had had a husband at her side to take care of. Now she lived in solitude and often felt useless.

She paid for and oversaw the maintenance of the Temple of Quetzalcoatl, and went to the temple to pray and meditate four times a day as the king had decreed. She always took Chac with her to help her sweep the temple and light the burnt offerings.

One morning, her adored slave seemed particularly quiet. Chac was always quiet, and only spoke to Tonalnan, and in whispers, at that, but this day, Chac was withdrawn and forlorn.

As they were sweeping the floor with hand brooms, Tonalnan said, "Lonely Chac, you wear a face of despair."

Chac only looked at Tonalnan, his-her golden eyes burgeoning tears.

"There, there, Chac," Tonalnan soothed. She picked up her pregnant belly and went over to her pet, taking Chac's hands in hers. "You must tell me what troubles you," she said.

Chac was not accustomed to speaking and sat quietly, looking sad. He-she glanced one way, and then the other, avoiding words.

"Find your courage, Chac. I know you have plenty," Tonalnan encouraged.

Chac's words were barely audible. "I... we... I..."

"Go on,"

"They laugh at Chac." Chac's golden eyes lowered. "They ridicule Chac for both male and female and say Chac a demon."

"Who said that, Chac? Who said you're a demon?" Tonalnan lowered her voice. They were verging on a forbidden topic inside a temple. Talking about demons in temples was to tempt sacred forces.

Chac's tears began to silently fall onto the flagstone floor, where they immediately absorbed into the porous stone.

In whispers, Chac explained the hurtful experience he-she had had at the *tianguis* market the day before. Tonalnan was infuriated by the experience, but didn't let it show.

"Chac, you come with me. I'm going to take you to someone who will tell you the real story of people who are born into bodies that are different. Don't you listen to those wicked tormentors in the market, Chac, not even for a moment."

Tonalnan took her slave by the hand, not his-her golden leash, and led him-her out of the one-room temple and down the stairs of the Pyramid of Quetzalcoatl. They walked past the Palace of Quetzalcoatl. The grand Yollotli to their left was practically empty.

Tonalnan led Chac north of town through twisted streets and alleyways, neighborhood past neighborhood, until they came to an obscure one-room stone hovel with a single window.

"Grandfather Elder!" Tonalnan said at the cotton padded door curtain. "Grandfather!" she repeated.

"Who goes there and disturbs my meditation!" squawked back a dry, old voice. "You ought to know better than to disturb a priest in prayer! I'll have you lashed for this impudence!"

The door curtain opened, and Smoking Feather poked his face out, squinting his eyes from the sun. His face was more wrinkled than ever, and his unkempt white hair shot out in all directions.

"Ah, Tonalnan, my child, why didn't you say?" The stone-faced priest's expression softened. His tongue fidgeted around in his mouth where he had lost several teeth.

Quetzalpopoca Smoking Feather had always loved and lavished affections on Tonalnan, ever since she could remember. He was almost like a second father to her, although she never knew why.

"Well, come in, don't just stand there like an idiot!"

Quetzalpopoca's kindnesses were always laden with a few cactus thorns.

Tonalnan and her slave sat down with their feet properly folded under them.

After a lengthy silence she spoke, "My heart grieves, Grandfather Elder, for cruelties toward those who are born with bodies that are both male and female." She was already pulling out her smoking blend and searching the small, dark *chantli* for his pipe.

"Cruelties toward those who are born in duality?" the ancient priest repeated whilst sitting his old bones down on a mat next to the table stone. "Why that would be the doing of the Queen of Ignorance. Everyone knows that the maimed and crippled children among us are the closest to the gods." He raised a pointed finger in the air, as if to strengthen this truth. "It's because of their courage. It takes great courage to live in a body that is different or that doesn't function in perfect strength and health."

Quetzalpopoca Smoking Feather puffed his bone pipe and made several smoke rings in the air with his wrinkled, old lips and grinned a toothless smile.

Tonalnan placed a handful of opals on the table stone.

He then agreed to share his wisdom;

"The ancient voices tell us that many ages ago, after the gods had assembled at Teotihuacan and the sun had been created, they asked themselves who would inhabit the earth. The gods turned to Quetzalcoatl and gazed upon this most powerful god, keeper of wisdom and things related to maize. Quetzalcoatl, who is also the White Tezcatlipoca and therefore one of the children of Ometéotl, oldest of old gods and creator of the universe, rules the ends of the earth where the sun sets over the celestial waters. It is the land of experience, wisdom, fertility and life. Because Quetzalcoatl possesses these qualities, it was decided that he should make the trip to Mictlán to search for the precious bones of man and the bones of woman so that humans could be created and inhabit the earth.

It came to pass that the god Quetzalcoatl went to the Underworld, to Mictlán, below the nine levels of the Underworld. He approached Mictlántecuhtli and Mictláncíhuatl, the Lord and Lady of the region of the dead, and he spoke to them. "I come in search of the bones in your possession. I have come for them."

"What shall you do with them?" asked Mictlántecuhtli.

"The gods are anxious that someone should inhabit the earth." Quetzalcoatl said.

"Very well," Mictlántecuhtli replied, "Sound my shell horn and go around my circular realm four times."

The shell horn had no holes, so Quetzalcoatl, because he was a creative and wise god, called upon the worms, which made holes in the shell. Then he called upon the bees, that went inside the horn and it sounded.

Mictlántecuhtli heard the sound, and he said anew, "Very well. Take the bones." Then he turned to those who served him and told them, "People of Mictlán! Gods, tell Quetzalcoatl that he must leave the bones."

Quetzalcoatl heard him and he said to himself, "Indeed not. I shall take possession of them once and for all." He then turned to his *nahualli*, his double. "Go and tell them that I shall leave them." he whispered.

His *nahualli* said in a loud voice, "I shall leave them!"

Then, Quetzalcoatl went and took the precious bones. Next to the bones of woman were the bones of man. Quetzalcoatl took them all.

Then, once again Mictlántecuhtli said to those who served him, "Gods, is Quetzalcoatl really carrying away the precious bones? Gods, go and make a pit."

The pit having been made, Quetzalcoatl fell in. He stumbled and fell and suffered such a fright that he fell dead. Oh, the precious bones were scattered! A quail flew down and chewed and gnawed on them. Then Quetzalcoatl came back to life. He was grieved and he asked of his *nahualli*, "What shall I do now?"

"Since things have turned out badly, let them turn out as they may," his *nahualli* answered.

So it came to pass that Quetzalcoatl gathered the bones and he took them away. He took them to Tamoanchan. As soon as he arrived, the woman called Quilaztli, who is Cihuacoatl, took them and ground them to a fine dust with her heavy, grinding *metlatl* stone. When she finished, she put them in a precious vessel of clay. Then the gods and Quetzalcoatl did penance, and Quetzalcoatl bled his member upon the bones, thereby giving his fiery spirit to the bones of dust. Then the gods said, "People have been born, oh gods, the *macehuallis*, those who were given life through penance!"

Since the bones of woman and man were scattered in Mictlán, and were mixed together, and since they were ground together to a fine dust, there is no complete woman, and no complete man. A man has woman inside him, and a woman has man inside her. Each is both masculine and feminine and thus a manifestation of the dual nature of Ometéotl, the oldest of old gods. Humans are made of the bones of the two.

When Quetzalpopoca finished relating the story, weary from the telling of it, Tonalnan said, "Thank you, Grandfather Elder. My heart guards the knowledge you have shared and I respectfully leave."

❈

Later, when Tonalnan and her slave were alone in her sleeping chamber, she repeated the lesson they had learned from the ancient priest.

"A man has woman inside him. A woman has man inside her. We are all made of the bones of the two."

Chac smiled.

The Bride of Jocotitlan

In Jocotitlan there was an aging governor named Blue Hummingbird who had four wives. Restless for youth and beauty, Blue Hummingbird arranged for himself a fifth wife, the beautiful virgin daughter of the famous Otomí warrior Anyeh. The virgin's name was Andoeni.

The people of Jocotitlan were happy, and made many preparations for the marriage. They celebrated with feasts and dancing, and the radiant Andoeni was pampered and given many special privileges.

It so happened that several days before the conjugal vows, a blind sorcerer came to Blue Hummingbird with news of a prophecy.

"I have had a vision, O Great One," the decrepit, sorcerer said. "You shall lose your precious bride forever," he divined, "before you can consummate your marriage."

The people of Jocotitlan were shocked.

"Why that's impossible, old man," rebutted the governor, "we are favored by the gods."

"And there's more, O Great One. Your love will die," the sorcerer added, his white eyes rolling back into his head.

Andoeni, frightened by the sorcerer's prediction, looked at his white eyes and asked him directly, "Can you tell me, what will be the cause of this misfortune?"

Then the diviner said, "A handsome warrior will come who will bewitch you with his honey-colored eyes. He will charm you and seduce you and you will lose yourself to him." The blind, bag-of-bones sorcerer raised his voice. "Beware fair maiden! You will forget yourself! You will forget your love to your betrothed! His eyes will be your demise!"

When the governor heard this, his rage was volcanic. He ordered at once that the blind prophet be bound and dragged to the farthest reaches of the forest where the coyotes would tear his flesh apart and the vultures would pick it clean to the bone.

Then the sorcerer sarcastically said, "The governor will never spread the limbs of his young sapling! Hear me now! Beware!" and with that, the decrepit, old sorcerer vanished into thin air.

�֍

"You know you've reached the summit when you can see the Hill of Xocotitlan in the distance," a veteran warrior reported to Xolotl. "The people of Jocotitlan live just beyond the hill."

From the Taxhimaya foothills, the men had started hiking up to the Teconaltic Pass, a two-day's journey through rough, mountainous terrain. It was named Teconaltic because of the vast amounts of carbon deposits found there. Graphite tended to be a popular favorite, as it could be used for murals inside houses. It tended to wash away on the outside of buildings, though. Nobody was much interested in diamonds. They were colorless and boring.

Despite all the valuable graphite to be had, no one wanted to pick up rocks and add them to their loads on the way into battle. That would be for the return journey home.

Tohuenyo had spent most of the two days listening to Mazatl's explanation of *ullama*. Before Mazatl joined up with the army, he had become rather adept at the game. He boasted so passionately about it that soon the two friends had a following of admirers.

Tohuenyo thought long and hard about telling his friend Mazatl about his change of heart, about how he'd decided to break with his mother and her malevolent plans and never go back to the Chichimeca tribe. He thought about explaining to Mazatl that human sacrifice was evil and went against the most basic human nature of creation and survival.

He wished he could explain things the way Topiltzin Quetzalcoatl did, but in truth, he didn't even understand all of what the wise sage had taught his disciples that night he heard him speak in the Pyramid of Ehécatl. He knew in his heart of hearts, though, that Quetzalcoatl was good and right, and he wanted Mazatl to be a part of it.

"We are at the summit, My Lord," Tohuenyo heard the veteran guide tell Xolotl at the end of the second day. "Just beyond the crest of that hill you'll see the valley below."

[286]

"Make camp!" Xolotl yelled. "In two day's time we shall cleanse Jocotitlan of its vile inhabitants who practice human sacrifice and offend our beloved Quetzalcoatl!" The warriors cheered, and conches began to sound.

Their last night in the Jilotepec Mountains was uneventful, save for a vicious coyote attack on a couple of shiftless, dimwitted warriors who thoughtlessly ventured beyond camp to scout around for *nanacatl* mushrooms.

The next morning they rose before the sun, and started their trek down the mountain and across the valley below. They spent the day traversing the dry grasslands and reached the eastern foothills of Xocotitlan Hill by nightfall.

The army settled in around the base of the hill and the men set up camps by war parties, with companies now taking shape under the different noble chiefs. Xolotl still had not assigned Tohuenyo a commanding position, so he continued to camp near the High Commander with his friend Mazatl, their porters, and several *ullama* fans.

For some reason that Xolotl couldn't explain, they hadn't encountered any scouts or spies from Jocotitlan. That evening, the High Commander sat in council with his chiefs discussing the lack of resistance.

"What could be the reason for it?" Tohuenyo questioned. He had been emboldened from winning his bet a few days before, and decided it was time to incorporate.

"They would not see our approach, as their city lies on the other side of this hill," Cuauhtémoc speculated, "unless they had scouts. So why don't they have any scouts? It all seems so strange."

"Perhaps their city is abandoned," one of the chiefs offered.

"Or better yet," another man said, "What if they're all dead?"

"Then we wouldn't have anyone to kill, would we?" Cuauhtémoc retorted. The two men glared at each other.

"Cuauhtémoc," Xolotl ordered, "You will go ahead and scout around. Take no one with you. We can't risk being seen and you're our best spy."

✖

One morning Andoeni decided to bathe in the river like she always did. She wasn't afraid, since her betrothed, the powerful governor, had arranged a special place for her along the river, a hidden cove, an impenetrable refuge, with calm waters and a gentle pool. This morning the nubile maiden was particularly happy, humming in anticipation of her upcoming betrothal. She dropped her white cotton shift to the ground, and stepped into the crystal clear pool. No sooner had her supple breasts submerged under the welcoming water than she realized that a strange warrior was watching her by the side of the pool. He was gorgeously handsome and she was immediately captivated by his honey-colored eyes.

The strange warrior held out his hand. As if in a trance, Andoeni walked out of the pool, water rushing off her radiant body. Then, without looking away from her black eyes, the warrior gathered the naked maiden into his strong arms and kissed her fresh lips deeply. She responded with hungry passion. The gorgeous warrior was everything she'd ever dreamed of. He was her savior, the hero who had come to rescue her from an arranged marriage to that old man, she-forgot-his-name. She forgot herself. She forgot everything except his honey-colored eyes. Then the strong warrior roped her around the waist, and led her deep into the forest.

As the day progressed, Blue Hummingbird started wondering what had happened to his lovely betrothed. For many hours he waited restlessly for her to return. What could have happened? Had she been attacked by a wild beast, or was she bitten by a venomous snake?

By nightfall, Blue Hummingbird left with several of his warriors to find her. They spread out through the forest, calling her name, "Andoeni! Andoeni!" but there was no response. The absence of a moon made the night even darker, and the search for the maiden was all the more terrifying.

The governor was at his peak of fear. An owl howled. What if the prophecy of the sorcerer was true? What if she had already died? They searched for her all night, but nobody found even a trace of his beloved maiden.

At dawn, feeling defeated they turned to go back home, when the owl howled again. The pathway through the forest seemed to stretch out before them. They were in the thickest part of the forest now. Blue Hummingbird looked through the foliage and thought he saw a dark force of nature wave at him. It seemed to be a demon of some kind.

He pushed forward through the thick leaves and branches, and there before him was his beloved Andoeni, naked with all her petals open in full bloom, underneath a foreign warrior with honey-colored eyes. They were in the climax of deeply impassioned love.

Crazed with fury, the governor grabbed the man by the hair with his left hand, lifted him off of her, and plunged his obsidian long knife through the man's stomach and up into his lungs, lifting him into the air.

The woman screamed and cowered back, paralyzed with fear.

Then the governor, in a jealous fit of rage, cut out the man's eyes and hammered them into the trunk of the nearest tree. "There! Take that, you scoundrel! You won't be bewitching any more women now, will you!" he screamed.

He turned toward the woman. His love for her had completely died. "I hate you, you vicious slut!" He stood, soaked in blood from the murderous hacking, with his long knife dripping at his side.

Andoeni scrambled to her feet and started to run. She ran and ran, through the forest, pushing limbs and branches out of her way. Her heart was exploding in her chest. She could hear the governor's feet pounding behind her. She was barefoot. She was naked. She was desperate. She was about to die.

✄

Xolotl sat deliberating over the absence of Cuauhtémoc. Maybe he shouldn't have sent his most trusted chief out the night before, but Cuauhtémoc could survive anything. He was favored by the gods. Surely he'd gotten himself into some heroic situation that he had to solve. Back in the Michoacán expedition, Cuauhtémoc had come across a raided village and rescued a handful of frightened widows and orphans. He'd protected them all the way to Tzintzuntzan, where he'd delivered them safely into the care of the women's temple.

Xolotl still waited. A whole day had passed. Soon it was going to be night and his chief had not returned. Then the general had a clever idea. Why not send his filthy brother-in-law out, now that night was upon them, to find his trusted friend. It was a moonless night. How perfect. Maybe idiot Tohuenyo would fall off a cliff, or get eaten by a wild beast. Then his problems would be solved. Without the chilli boy to contend with, Huemac would regain the love of the people. His wife's sister would restore her respectable position, and he would strengthen his future entitlement to the first general's office. There really was no reason to like Tohuenyo. None at all.

"Go find Cuauhtémoc," he ordered Tohuenyo. "You can take your pet ram with you." Since the fight, men had started referring to Mazatl as the pet ram, even though to his face they still called him Mazatl, the goat.

Tohuenyo and Mazatl set off from the foothills into the forests of Xocotitlan Hill. It was a dark moonless night, filled with sounds of scurrying creatures and a hooting owl, but the Chichimeca were fierce warriors and lethal hunters. The two brave men ventured forth. At dawn they decided to split up their search. Mazatl went off into the thick of the forest.

Tohuenyo followed a creek until he came to a small cascade of falling water. The dense forest at the sides of the creek was thick with branches and leaves, making it hard for him to see. Where could Cuauhtémoc be? Just then he turned, and - *WHACK!* - A naked woman came flying out of the foliage and pounded right into him.

The hysterical woman hadn't seen Tohuenyo any more than he had seen her. He held her, writhing in his arms, and looked up to catch a glimpse of a crazed, blood drenched man in the foliage, breathing forcefully, long knife drawn. Then he turned and disappeared into the forest.

Before Tohuenyo could settle the woman down and make sense of what had happened, Mazatl came walking down the creek, carrying a carcass in his arms, but it wasn't a bear or a deer. It was Cuauhtémoc, and his butchered corpse had no eyes.

[290]

The Battle of Jocotitlan

Tohuenyo and Mazatl returned to the campsite to find it all but abandoned. Their return journey had been somewhat arduous. Mazatl had cradled Cuauhtémoc's body all the way back in his great arms. After some time, when the girl's bare feet had started to bleed, Tohuenyo hoisted her onto his back. Thus burdened, the two men slowly hiked through the dense forest, up and down hillsides, over creeks and riverbeds, and in the late afternoon, finally reached the camp.

Dozens of porters stoically sat around the campfires eating maize-bean flat cakes and poking the embers, keeping the fires barely ignited. Free from their heavy burdens when their masters were fighting a battle, the porters were at liberty to move around the camp. While most porters in the One World were slaves, the porters who went into battle were not. Their indentured servitude into the military was an oral agreement sealed by a facial scaring, which made their prospects of escape very grim. A porter who did escape would not only cut off his own food supply, but would also extinguish his ability to find more work, as anyone thereafter would recognize his facial scar.

They watched quietly as Tohuenyo and Mazatl hefted their loads to the back of camp toward the *nahuallis*. The *nahuallis*, whose name meant "physical form of the human one," were the king's private collection of spiritual sages. Neither priests nor warriors, *nahuallis* were in a class of their own. They were often sent into battle to bless the outcome with their divine presence, but were highly protected and not allowed to partake in any activity that might endanger their lives. Sometimes, when marching long distances, the white *nahuallis*, called *iztacs*, would walk under a shaded canopy. Carried by devoted warriors, it protected them from the blinding sun. The *tlatoque nahuallis* would often ride on the backs of warriors if the trek became arduous, and the *xolome*, the most revered of all, was hoisted along on a type of stretcher, the long handles of which rested on the shoulders of enduring porters.

The *nahuallis* turned from their jovial conversation as Tohuenyo and Mazatl arrived.

"Treachery has befallen our brother," Tohuenyo said, the traumatized woman still clinging to his back.

Mazatl laid Cuauhtémoc's body on the ground before them.

Instead of speaking, the *xolome* pointed with his copper walking staff for the three white *iztac*s to attend to the body. He often used gestures to communicate, as his physical condition made it difficult for him to speak. They simply called him Xolome, because he was the only one of his kind in the group of *nahuallis*.

"When did they leave?" Tohuenyo asked, helping the woman to the ground. A white *iztac* draped a cotton blanket around Andoeni, then went to attend to the corpse.

"Just this afternoon," an outspoken *tlatoque* called Miztli answered, "when the sun was over there." He pointed with his shortened arm. They called him Miztli, which meant lion, because of his bravery despite his small size. "We could hear the conches of Jocotitlan sounding their alarm." Miztli hoisted himself onto a small boulder and stoutly sat down. "That's when the first commander ordered everybody to arms."

Xolome raised his copper staff to Tohuenyo, and twisted sideways to look up at him as he spoke. "You have women's clothing amongst your belongings."

Tohuenyo turned to his porters who by this time had gathered around. "Is this so?"

"Yes, My Lord," one of them answered. "Your wife had us include it. And images of the goddess. A whole basket full of them."

Tohuenyo had fervently objected when his wife insisted that he carry along a load of the cult of Mazapa. It would be too heavy and burdensome to take into battle. How could she even think it? Apparently, not only had she thought it, but she'd managed to sneak the religious paraphernalia into his supplies as well.

Xolome continued, "Find attire for this woman and get her decently covered. And heal her feet," he added. "She is going to need them."

After that, Xolome stopped talking. His severe kyphosis sometimes made it difficult for him to breathe, and he easily tired.

�֍

Decked in his recently acquired war bonnet and laden with weaponry and padded armor, Xolotl crawled with his ranks through the cornfields toward Jocotitlan. Apparently, earlier that morning something had tipped the Jocos off to the Toltec presence, because suddenly the conches had begun to sound throughout the town. That's when Xolotl had quickly assembled his men and headed to the fields for battle.

The morning sun beat down upon them from a cloudless sky. Xolotl could see the warriors of Jocotitlan forming behind giant stone and wood blockades, lying behind makeshift breastworks, and lining the roofs of their humble buildings on the outskirts of town.

The High Commander hunkered in the cornfields with his chiefs around him and assessed the situation. There appeared to be about five hundred enemy warriors protecting the town. A sweaty informant pushed his way into their circle.

"Sir! Four hundred Atlacomulco warriors come from the north. They're heading to Joco to join forces, My Lord." The informant breathed heavily, gasping for air.

Xolotl the High Commander brooded pensively. It would be just about level, as the Toltec army numbered just under a thousand.

Finally he looked at his noble chiefs and ordered, "Pole bearers at the front, *atlatls* behind. Anyone who's capable of wielding a *maquáhuitl* shall. Other than that – men with swords, knives, bludgeons, stay with their war party leaders. Standard bearers remain with me." Then he raised his voice, "Kill or be killed. Take as many as you can. Better to die fighting, my brothers! If they capture us, they'll feed us to their gods on the sacrificial stone!"

Xolotl, easily identified as the high commander by his magnificent war bonnet, stood and yelled to his warriors who were crouched, hiding in the corn, "We are the Toltecs of Tula-Xicocotitlan! We do not feed humans to the gods! Any prisoners we capture, we'll take back to Tula as slaves. We will cleanse these savage Jocos of their unclean practices and bring culture and knowledge to their measly existence! We will show them what the edge of a Toltec sword feels like, then we will plant our seed into their fertile soil to strengthen their race with our Toltec blood!"

On hearing this, the warriors were emboldened, for the thought of coming into spoils of war excited them greatly.

"Rahhhh!" they yelled, raising their spears and shaking their shields.

Xolotl turned toward the Joco warriors poised to defend themselves and their flesh-eating gods. On his command, the Toltec pole bearers lined up in front of their war parties that were now clustered into their prospective companies.

A lone pole bearer came forward and stood next to Xolotl at the edge of the field.

Xolotl nodded, and the pole bearer ran through the clearing toward the enemy and launched his weapon into the air. It soared in a smooth arc, and then landed in the grassy dirt, the obsidian spearhead completely submerged in the soft earth.

The Joco warriors laughed, mocking the measly distance of the pole bearer's throw. With that, dozens of Joco warriors came running forth toward the clearing, stopping just short of the landed Toltec pole. They tightened their position and covered themselves with their shields, weapons at the ready.

Xolotl then motioned, and a high flute sounded. The pole bearers dropped to one knee, revealing a line of *atlatl* throwers behind them. At that same instant, a surge of *atlatl* darts whizzed through the air, arcing over the field, and plummeted into the surprised Jocos. The darts' barbed obsidian points penetrated their padded body armor and drove deep into the chests of any warriors unlucky enough to be in their trajectory.

Dozens of Joco warriors fell.

Another wave of *atlatl* darts whizzed into the air and plunged into the flesh of more Joco warriors.

The conches sounded, and immediately hundreds of warriors from both sides of the field ran towards each other, screaming violent war cries, with weapons raised.

The bloodbath that ensued was a measure of physical strength, as warriors fought for their lives and their gods. Xolotl's Toltecs delivered serious lacerations and dealt chopping blows to their enemies. Brains went flying through the air as the heads of Joco warriors were broadsided by heavy, swinging *maquáhuitl* swords. Xolotl's army fought their way toward the defenses at the edge of town. The Toltecs then used flaming arrows covered in tar to burn the wooden blockades. Screaming Jocos ran out from behind them, their flesh crackling and popping in flames. Swords lacerated arms, exposing dangling brachial arteries that spurt forth red blood.

Not even the reinforcements of the Atlacomulcan army could stop the mighty Toltecs. By the time Xolotl's army reached the houses at the edge of town, the Atlacomulcan warriors fled, abandoning their Joco allies to their own deplorable fate. Within the city, the Toltec warriors continued their assault. Anything that could burn was set ablaze.

Yauhtli had taken to using a bludgeon and heaved a deathly blow to an opponent's abdomen, causing the unlucky man's entrails to violently expel from his body in transanal evisceration.

When there was no one left willing to fight them, Xolotl's potent warriors turned their attentions and violently plunged themselves into the defenseless Joco women, as the elderly and feeble desperately tried to cover the eyes of their screaming children. "We shall cleanse your race of your vile and wicked ways by planting our superior seed within you," they justified.

The defeated remaining warriors of Jocotitlan were rounded up and restrained in wooden collars and then tied into chain gangs. The governor, Blue Hummingbird, had been found alive, hiding in the temple of his flesh-eating god, Huitzilopochtli. The Toltec warriors who found him brought him to Xolotl in the middle of town and threw him to his knees.

"You can kill me Lord Xolotl but you will not win!" the defeated governor defiantly said. "Huitzilopochtli will avenge us! Huitzilopochtli will rise up one day and become the strongest god in all the One World!"

Xolotl and a few chiefs who were now gathered around him laughed and mocked the destitute man.

"Says the defeated loser," somebody said fiendishly.

The warriors laughed above the echoes of women's screams. There was still a great degree of chaos throughout the town as most of the warriors were still plundering and raping its inhabitants.

"Kill him!" the onlookers prodded.

"No." Xolotl said. The governor of Jocotitlan Blue Hummingbird was an important trophy of war. This capture could be the very accomplishment that would win Xolotl the position of Protector of the Palace of Quetzalcoatl, making him the next in line as Tula's First General.

"We take him alive," he told the men.

✴

The following morning a messenger came running into camp. "I'm looking for the foreigner who married the princess. I bring a message for his ears alone." he said. He was a messenger sent from Xolotl in Jocotitlan. When he found his man he dropped to his knees and said, "Lord Tohuenyo, I bring a message from the High Commander Xolotl."

Tohuenyo liked being addressed by his new title, Lord. "Go on," he said.

"The Commander has taken Jocotitlan. The city surrendered peacefully without a fight, and their governor Blue Hummingbird has agreed to serve our king Topiltzin as his loyal and faithful subject. As a sign of good will, the governor will journey to Tula with a gift of slaves and treasure." What the messenger didn't divulge, however, was that Blue Hummingbird would be escorted to Tula with his arms bound to a beam resting across his shoulders.

Tohuenyo wondered how much of this story was true. "Your words are heard, messenger," Tohuenyo said. "What more?"

"In several days time, the High Commander will turn north to Atlacomulco, to pacify the peoples of that nation. They too, worship flesh-eating gods and our High Commander says they need to be taught to love the one, true god, Quetzalcoatl. In the meantime, he wishes you to away to the Valley of Toluca. You are to commence an attack on Teotenanco to weaken their stronghold. In several days time, the High Commander and the rest of the Toltec army will reach Teotenanco to reinforce you."

Tohuenyo listened carefully to the messenger's words.

"And finally," the messenger continued, "your command will be the army of *nahuallis*."

Some army, Tohuenyo thought. *An army that can't fight. Three white iztacs, five tlatoques, and one xolome.* In addition, he had picked up the stray woman. Well, at least he had Mazatl, an invincible warrior and faithful friend.

"Is that all?" Tohuenyo asked.

"No, My Lord. One more thing. You are to leave at once, and journey by way of the marshes of Ixtlahuaca in the center of the valley."

"Thank you," Tohuenyo said. "You can tell the High Commander that his wish is my command. Tell him that I will go directly to Ixtlahuaca and then on to Teotenanco and commence the attack at once." Tohuenyo looked at the messenger who stood there, staring at him. "Well, go on! Tell him! Tell your master that his brother Tohuenyo loves him and will do as he wishes."

With that, the messenger scrambled to his feet and ran off.

Tohuenyo then gathered his porters, all the *nahuallis*, his friend Mazatl and the woman Andoeni they had rescued, and bid them to sit around his fire.

"Here, here," he said. "We are to away this very morning. The High Commander has ordered us to attack the walled city of Teotenanco at the end of the Valley of Toluca." A wave of uncomfortable fidgeting rolled through his comrades. "I am to be your commander, and the *nahuallis* are to be my army."

"But lord, the *nahuallis* never fight," Grey Iztac protested. He was the eldest of the three *iztac*s, who were siblings. The brothers had simply been named for their eye color, grey, green, and blue. He flung his long white hair back over his slender, pale shoulder.

Tohuenyo ignored the protest. He knew that Huemac and Xolotl had been plotting to kill him. He knew this was their attempt to cause his untimely demise. Xolotl probably figured that Tohuenyo would die trying to protect the sacred *nahuallis*, but that the *nahuallis* would be safely captured and ransomed back to their king. Tohuenyo continued, "To get there, he has ordered that we journey by way of the marshlands of Ixtlahuaca."

"Hmmm..." one of the *tlatoque*s uttered. Everyone had heard the stories of the marshlands of Ixtlahuaca. They were famous for their delectable frog stew. *Pochteca*s high and low never failed to mention that they had partaken of this incredible delicacy when they shared experiences of their merchant adventures abroad.

Before they departed, Tohuenyo forced Xolotl's personal porters at knifepoint to empty the contents of their *petlacalli* baskets. He then "borrowed" the baskets, stacked them and tied them to a travois, that Mazatl was put in charge of dragging. He also tied on the loads of four of his own porters, who would now be in charge of transporting the Xolome.

"The High Commander has ordered us to go to Ixtlahuaca," he said to his small band of warriors, "so naturally we will go the other way."

Madam Itzali's Secret

At first, married life presented her with a huge challenge. The king had ordered her to give up her position as a physician at the Sacred House of Healing. Women physicians, like priestesses, swore themselves to a life of self-sacrifice and chastity. Tonalnan had broken those vows, so she'd had to swallow her pride as she handed over the strand of blood-red coral to the new matron, who stood beaming with pride and smirked with an *"I'm the head matron now"* gleam in her eye.

The newly wed bride had grown up always expecting to live out her life in virginal chastity, free from the burdens of dependent children and a husband's demands, and thus able to devote the whole of her existence to medicine and healing. Though, while she loved her husband dearly, shortly after her marriage she came to realize that she loved knowledge and power even more. How could she spend the rest of her life with nothing more than the drudgery of a dutiful wife to sustain her? Her mother and sister, on the other hand, had exclusively and intensively given their lives of labor over to their husbands – but also, being the well-bred noblewomen that they were, their labors were devoted to the realm of textiles.

"That's it," she soon realized, "textiles!"

Legend tells that during the reign of Topiltzin Quetzalcoatl the crops were so abundant and the cotton so plentiful that it grew magnificently in many splendid colors – blue, black, brown, red, yellow, green, even purple and orange, not to mention glorious white like the clouds of the sky. Shortly after she was married, Tonalnan discovered this bounty and saw it as an endless opportunity.

In Cem Anahuac, noble women were highly skilled craft producers, and in the House of Huemac, they devoted themselves to weaving. Some noble men, and most often kings who were not also priests and therefore chaste, sought to marry many wives so they would not only forge new alliances, but also enrich themselves through the artistic creations produced in their own households. Huemac had never taken more than one wife, but had immersed himself in concubines, so that craft production in his household was relatively low.

The income from cotton and cacao that Tonalnan received from the king was barely enough to maintain the temple of Quetzalcoatl. She began to see textile production as an opportunity to strengthen her house, that is, the royal house she was encouraging her husband to build. In her mind, she was not going to live with her husband in her parents' house for long. No, she and her husband were soon going to have their own residence. She had no idea how, but she would either make it happen or die trying.

The first thing she set out to do was to further master the skills of weaving. There was much to improve – combing the cotton to remove the seeds and undesirable fibers, then spinning the silky fluff into thread using a tri-pedal distaff and a horizontal spindle. Then there was the mastery of the back strap loom, a simple construction that consisted of sticks, rope and a strap worn around the weaver's waist. Light and mobile, they could be set up almost anywhere, inside, at the marketplace, even used while watching small children. It wasn't long before the persistent Tonalnan mastered the back strap loom and learned how to brocade designs into the fabric as it was woven. Soon she was turning out her own *huipilli* blouses, flowing curtains, and lavish bed coverings.

She reasoned that if she had more women to help her comb, spin and weave, she could increase the wealth of her household. Then the thought occurred to her that if her husband were to take more wives of noble rank, not only would they acquire fortunes through dowry, but also they could enrich themselves through artistic creations and establish gift-giving networks with other kings. If her bride-sisters worked diligently, they could even engage in fierce, competitive merchant networks, and enhance their alliances. Tonalnan fantasized that one day she would come to dominate the textile trade throughout all the One World, Cem Anahuac. She would send a runner to find her husband in battle and communicate her plans to him.

"What are you thinking about, daughter, that you are so consumed in thought?" her mother, Itzali said one day. They had been sitting under the porch of the patio all morning spinning cotton thread with distaffs and spindles.

"Mother, why did Father never take more wives?" Tonalnan asked.

"Hush, daughter. You aren't to talk of such things," Madam Itzali replied sternly, pulling her spindle back and forth. After a few moments her mother then said, "You know, if your husband should return alive and choose to take more wives, you're just going to have to bear it." Then she stopped pulling her thread and looked her daughter straight in the eye, "You are his first wife, and by law the matriarch of the estates. You and only you would attend royal festivities and manage affairs, not any of the others." She waved her spindle at Tonalnan. "Jealousy is unbecoming of first wives. Don't succumb to it."

The ambitious Tonalnan wasn't about to succumb to anything that would impede her new plans. The thought of sharing her beloved Tohuenyo with other women didn't bother her now. To the contrary, she saw it as an opportunity to gain bride-sisters and further her ambitions. This was how the detachment between Tonalnan and Tohuenyo started.

"Sister!" Calli yelled, as she scurried across the patio floor, hiking up her skirts so she wouldn't trip. "Sister, come!" Calli approached her sister and practically grabbed her, pulling her from her spinning. As the spindle pulled taught, the strand of thread she was spinning ominously broke in two.

"Don't worry. You can fix it later," Calli said desperately. "You must away with me, sister. You must come with me now!"

Madam Itzali dropped her spindle. "Come, mother," Calli added. "Come quickly. You are being summoned to appear before the king."

As the three women hurried down the hall of their palace, Calli pulled her sister along by the arm and spoke in hushed whispers. "They are saying terrible things, Tonalnan. They are spreading false and wicked rumors about you, about mother. It's terrible. Don't believe them. Not for one moment. They're lies."

As they reached the arched front entrance of their palace, the women encountered Huemac and Xolotl's father, Nauhyotl.

[301]

"Will somebody please tell me *what* is going on?" Madam Itzali insisted indignantly.

"Silence Madam!" her husband barreled. He gruffly grabbed her arm and led her along. "You stay here!" he ordered his daughter, Calli.

Calli stopped in her tracks, panic stricken.

The women were hard pressed to keep pace with the men folk, Tonalnan slowed by her progressing pregnancy, her mother with age. They crossed the grand Yollotli, marched up the stairs, and entered the palace's Western Hall.

The dark interior appeared black until their eyes adjusted from the brightness of the sun. The colonnaded room was filled with burning candle bowls and they could see an ornately carved screen at the front of the room, made of a white cotton sheet stretched across a finely crafted frame. The king was sitting behind it amidst an array of small candles, casting his silhouette onto the screen. The shadows of the exquisite, long tail feathers of his headdress swayed across the screen as he moved.

Stone benches lined the painted murals on the walls, and many grandiose pillars sustained the ceiling throughout the room.

The ancient priest Smoking Feather was sitting on one of the stairs to the side of the screen, smoking a long peace pipe. He then passed it off to the king behind the screen.

A pair of basins blazed with green flames at the bottom of the stairs.

"House of Huemac will take the north wall. House of Nauhyotl will take the other," the king commanded.

Huemac, Madam Itzali and Tonalnan took their seats on the benches, their backs against the walls. Nauhyotl paced around a bit and then sat down against the other wall. Tonalnan looked at her mother in angst. Her mother's lips were pursed and she was unusually pale. Her father Huemac sat glaring furiously at the floor.

"As of yesterday evening," the king began, "Lord Cozcacuautli Miquiztli is dead." His voice was smooth, and his words flowed like honey.

The king took a puff off the long pipe and exhaled.

"I understand there is a dispute between your two houses over the inheritance of his estates," The king said.

Tonalnan had no idea what he was talking about, nor why she was there.

"The inheritance in question," the king continued, "includes the *axcaitl and altépetl* of Mixquiahuala, including all revenues and complete control of the *pulque* production, as well as those of Actopán."

The old priest took the long pipe from the king and with much effort sat back down on the stair.

"It has come to our attention that Lord Huemac, our highest and most honorable general, claims the inheritance of Lord Miquiztli."

This was most unusual news. Tonalnan and her mother sat perplexed. What was all this about Lord Miquiztli? Hadn't the half-wit Miquiztli committed social suicide with his perversions after her wedding? Why would her father claim the inheritance of that flea-infested, monster of a man?

Madam Itzali had no idea why she was there either, and sat impatiently, feeling imposed upon and waiting to leave.

Topiltzin Quetzalcoatl's shadow shook on the screen each time he moved. "Our beloved First Priest, Quetzalpopoca Smoking Feather shall speak his piece," the king announced.

Smoking Feather laid the long peace pipe down. "I was at the birth of Tonalnan," he said.

Tonalnan could see her mother's eyes widen.

"I was standing outside the circle of stones as the mid-wives attended the long and heavy labor. I remember casting spells to ward off demons and bless the sacred affair," the old priest explained.

Tonalnan's mother sat looking terrified. She tenderly placed her hand upon her mother's, but the woman flinched and pulled her hand up to her bosom.

Huemac continued glaring at the floor.

The old priest continued. "The mother died in child bed. Before she took her last breath, she begged me to save the life of her babe."

Tonalnan felt numb.

"I took the babe and ran. I left Mixquiahuala and ran all the way back to Tula, then called Tollan. In the Sacred House of Healing they told me of a noble woman who was about to deliver, who might suckle my new burden. When I arrived, she had just delivered a stillborn son. She took the crying Tonalnan and latched the hungry infant onto her teat. Then she bid the midwives to dispose of the lifeless bundle and swore me to secrecy thereafter."

Huemac shifted in his seat.

Madam Itzali sat white-faced, looking terrified.

Tonalnan could feel tears falling out of her eyes.

"The child Tonalnan is the fruit of Lord Cozcacuautli Miquiztli's seed," Smoking Feather confirmed. The stone-faced priest had held Madam Itzali's secret for years in fear of retribution by the evil Lord Miquiztli, but with that threat gone, he released the truth into the world and let the forces play out as they may.

Huemac nodded in acknowledgement. He had heard the old priest's confession that morning's eve at the deathbed of Lord Miquiztli. Understanding Tonalnan to be the only recognized girl child of the deceased lord meant she was entitled to his inheritance. Matriarchal lineage was ancient law, passed down from the ancestors since the time before time. Huemac was as quick as a wolf in seizing this opportunity to obtain additional wealth for his house.

Tonalnan felt like she wanted to slip off the stone bench and melt into the floor.

The king then spoke from behind his screen. "The House of Nauhyotl contests the legitimacy of inheritance claimed by Lord Huemac on this day, Seventeen Monkey. Lord Nauhyotl, you will now be heard." His voice was dry and unemotional.

Nauhyotl stood up, walked past the giant pillars to the middle of the room, and sat facing the screen at the bottom of the stairs.

"Great and mighty king Topiltzin Quetzalcoatl," he began. "I beseech you to put into effect the new ruling of ten days past." He was talking about the new law that Quetzalcoatl had finally agreed to, put forth by a determined group of noble lords. According to the new law, wealth would now be transferred through male lines, from father to eldest son. In the event that the eldest son had no male heirs, the wealth would transfer to the next eldest son. "Oh gracious king," he continued, "Under the new ruling, I am to rightfully inherit the estates of my elder brother upon his death."

[304]

Nauhyotl then returned to his place along the wall.

Lord Huemac, you will now be heard," the king said.

Huemac moved forward to the middle of the room.

"Great and mighty king Topiltzin Quetzalcoatl," Huemac said. "The House of Huemac begs you to honor the decision that the ruling shall not take effect until the end of the ritual year." There were nine days left before the end of the ritual year.

Huemac turned and walked back to his seat against the wall, casting a murderous look at his wife as he sat down. He sat stiffly, staring straight ahead.

Tonalnan sat grasping what she was hearing, her head reeling with the new information. Huemac, her father, was not her father. Her mother was not really her mother. Her real father, now dead, had been a disgrace to all. Was she still the same Tonalnan? Was she the same human one, knowing that her blood was now different?

"Madam Tonalnan," she heard the king command. "Come thee forth and sit before us as we deliver our justice."

Tonalnan, on the verge of losing her composure, sat on the stone floor at the bottom of the stairs before the king. She hoped no one would notice her trembling hands.

"It is the decision of this king," Topiltzin Quetzalcoatl said, "That the estates in dispute of the Noble Lord Miquiztli shall pass completely and with full royal protection to the young Madam Tonalnan, daughter of Huemac and wife of Tohuenyo."

Huemac sighed. Thank the gods for the king's love of his daughter.

Nauhyotl grunted and clenched his fists.

"On this day, Seventeen Monkey," the king continued, "to be administered by whom she wishes."

Huemac assumed that his daughter would declare him legal administrator of her new wealth. After all, he had always been her father, even if she hadn't been his seed.

Tonalnan thought carefully of the consequences of her decision. If she requested that her father administer her inheritance, she would be repaying him for a lifetime of fatherly love and stay in his good graces. If she did that, however, she would be sweeping the entire income away from the House of Nauhyotl, which depended heavily on the wealth generated from the estates and tribute. On the other hand, if she requested that Nauhyotl administer her wealth, it wouldn't be any different than giving the wealth back to him. Surely her father would expel her and her husband from his house, and they would be dependent on the House of Nauhyotl. Then, if she chose her husband, she would make enemies of both Nauhyotl, father of Xolotl the High Commander, and her own father, First General of Tula. She was not so foolish as to distance herself from the most powerful Toltec military leaders, and of course, she could not, by ancient law, administer her estates herself because she was a woman. Since time immemorial, the transfer of wealth was matrilineal but administered by men. That was soon about to change.

"I choose you, My Lord," she declared. "I choose my fair and noble king, Ce Acatl Topiltzin."

This was most unexpected.

Madam Itzali was now fanning herself with the small fan she kept in her sash, looking very nervous indeed.

"Clever girl!" laughed the old priest. By choosing the king, she would maintain a degree of control over the inheritance, as the king was impartial to courtly power struggles and too disinterested in wealth to care if she administered the estates herself.

"Madam Tonalnan proves her sensibility," the king said warmly. "As for the pending castigation..." He motioned for her to return to her bench at the wall. "The wife of Lord Huemac shall be sentenced for the crime of lying to her husband in a vile act of treachery."

Huemac was now grabbing his wife by the arm. She had started sobbing uncontrollably. He pulled her over to the center of the room. Tonalnan sat frightened, watching the horror unfold.

"Madam, you know that the punishment for adulterous women is social banishment, but your crime seems heinously worse. I know not what to do with you, Madam Itzali, for you have always been dear to me, a pillar of strength, the very perfection of womanhood. And now to find out that you have lived with this lie for all these years..." The king's voice trailed off.

He'd stopped himself to contemplate her punishment carefully.

Madam Itzali was sobbing in the aggressive clutches of her husband.

"Please do not banish me, My Lord, I beg thee!" She dropped to the floor and crawled halfway up the steps, reaching toward the glowing screen. The shadow of the king hung its head low and sighed heavily. The woman continued her plea, "I can withstand a beating, My Lord, or even death, but please, I beg you, do not have me ostracized," she sobbed into the stairs.

Social banishment was a hideous punishment for women adulterers, and Madam Itzali feared she might suffer the same fate. Women were physically thrown out of their houses into the street and were forevermore forbidden to have any contact with anyone. Everyone knew that if you looked at a woman adulterer's eyes it would immediately cause vomiting and illness. Women adulterers were so heavily shunned that they couldn't even find work in a house of joy. They ended up crumpled up in a corner on the streets, their only chance of survival being to steal food from stray dogs or extend a begging hand.

Tonalnan couldn't bear it any longer and rushed to her mother and held her. "Father, do something!" she pleaded.

The king, distraught and apparently no longer able to bear the gravity of the painful situation then said, voice trembling and uncommonly slipping into first person, "I defer the punishment to you, noble Lord Huemac. She is your wife. You shall administer justice as you see fit." Then, by the looks of the shadow on the screen, it appeared that the king lowered his face into his hands and cried.

Nauhyotl was now looking on with great sympathy. "Have pity, Lord Huemac, on this poor woman. Her crime was no worse for want of a child."

"Tonalnan shall remain my daughter," Huemac said, his voice laden with emotion. "It is through no fault of her own that she has falsely lived as my daughter all these years. I claim her as my own!" There was no doubt that Huemac loved both his daughters.

"As for this woman here," he shoved the downtrodden Madam Itzali with his foot, "since she begs for mercy against ostracizing, I sentence her to death by strangulation!"

"No!" Tonalnan started sobbing. "No, father, no! That cannot be!"

Madam Itzali wailed into the stairs.

[307]

"This very day, so that her inheritance passes to my eldest daughter, Calli! There will be no arguments! This I do decree!"

Quetzalpopoca slowly got up and mournfully crept out of the Eastern Hall with the small pain-filled steps so characteristic of the elderly. Revealing the truth as he had, ended up having two faces. The bright face was that Tonalnan was now protected with her own wealth. After all, the room full of treasure the king had gifted her for her dowry wouldn't last forever. The dark face, though, was painted with the inevitable consequences of Madam Itzali's lie. In either case, Quetzalpopoca had to release the truth - especially before his death, which he could feel slowly approaching. Carrying that lie to the afterlife and having to justify it to the gods was *not* something he was willing to do.

Before Quetzalpopoca Smoking Feather left the dark hall, he beckoned the sobbing Tonalnan behind a giant pillar and into the shadows. "Here," he said, placing a small pouch into her hands. "This was your mother's."

Tonalnan opened the pouch and a glowing green jadestone rolled out onto the palm of her hand. "Keep it close to you always."

Tonalnan never saw the stone-faced priest again. Some said that he turned into a hawk and flew away, others said he strayed into the forest where the water genies whisked him away, and others still said nothing about his disappearance, but just cried.

Jiquipilco

Tohuenyo hadn't been able to stop thinking about Andoeni's breasts pressed against his back, or her soft *cihuanacayo* brushing against him with her legs wrapped around his waist as he carried her out of the forest that day. Even so, his fidelity was immaculate. He'd honored the sanctity of his marriage through fierce devotion and immense self-sacrifice.

You won't be surprised then when I tell you that he was thrilled and much relieved when a runner found him and delivered his wife's message encouraging him to strengthen their wealth through an additional royal marriage.

If royal alliances were what she wanted, sister-wives she would get. He had suffered through enough nights of protecting the sensuous Otomí princess while restraining his overwhelming cravings. He approached her and asked, "Can you weave?" The Otomí princess assured him that her brocading was admired throughout all the land. He then confessed that her beauty disarmed him, and from that time on, Tohuenyo took Andoeni unto him as his woman.

Tohuenyo and his makeshift army left the camp at the foothills of Xocotitlan Hill with all haste and headed east, back to the Jilotepec Mountains the way they had come. Instead of ascending into the mountains, though, they turned south when they reached the foothills, and quietly hiked their way down the length of the valley to the *altépetl* of Jiquipilco. There they encountered the Otomí speaking Jiquipillis. Their governor was a cousin of Andoeni's father, the famous Otomí warrior, and the tribes allowed Tohuenyo and his band to hide in a secret cavern in the mountains behind their communal lands.

The Jiquipillis had four times been raided by the oppressive Teotenancas, and their haggard governor was much relieved to receive the envoy of Toltec *nahuallis* with their charismatic leader. Through the translations of Andoeni, the governor wasted no time in offering his allegiance to the Toltecs, although he was hard pressed to provide additional warriors, as most of the men of fighting age in the *altépetl* had died defending their villages or had been taken prisoner for sacrifice to Teotenanco's flesh-eating gods. What he *was* able to offer, though, was the secret cavern and warm cauldrons of steaming, hot *pozolli* stew.

From Jiquipilco, Tohuenyo sent two of his fastest porters back to Jocotitlan as spies. He instructed them to find Xolotl, without being seen, and report back to him of the High Commander's secret plans. From his trusted spies, Tohuenyo learned that Xolotl's army had turned north after the sacking of Jocotitlan, and had plundered and pillaged the town of Atlacomulco, tumbled the effigies of its flesh eating gods, captured over a hundred prisoners as slaves, and raped and ravaged its women as they had in Jocotitlan, justifying their violent actions as an ethnic cleansing.

Through his spies, Tohuenyo also confirmed that Xolotl had no intention of sending reinforcements south to Teotenanco, and intended for Tohuenyo to meet a grizzly end.

The Jiquipilli women were so taken with the *tlatoque* little people in Tohuenyo's band of travelers that they insisted the travelers extend their stay. Several Jiquipilli widows then journeyed down into the marshlands of Ixtlahuaca and traded *petlacalli* baskets of maize cobs for enough frogs to make a feast of famous Ixtlahuacan frog stew. Accompanied by a couple of Ixtlahuacan matrons who would prepare it for them, they carted the live frogs all the way back to Jiquipilco by night, and the next day, they feasted Jiquipilli style, as only the Otomí of the Jilotepec Mountains know how to do. Their women sang beautiful songs of days gone by, of the time of the ancient ancestors, when the lovers Iztaccihuatl and Popocatepetl moved heaven and earth to be together for eternity.

Xolome was so moved by the song that he cried, and for the next several days it rained and rained.

During their stay at Jiquipilco, the governor offered his youngest daughter to Tohuenyo as a wife to form an alliance to the Toltec empire. Instead of asking about a dowry Tohuenyo was heard asking, "Can she weave?" When he saw the girl's samples of brocaded fabrics, he promised to come back for her on their return journey home.

When it came time to say good bye, the people of Jiquipilco begged Miztli to stay behind with them. The lion-hearted *tlatoque* had to gracefully decline. The *tlatoque* little people enchanted the hearts of everyone they met in the One World, making farewells particularly sad.

Trail to Teotenanco

Tohuenyo and his army of pacifists left Jiquipilco, and hiked south through dense pinewood forests. The Otomí speaking people of Temoaya received them peacefully, after realizing that they were a band of *nahuallis*. The people of the Temoayan nation were fiercely spiritual. They highly esteemed sorcerers and priests of any god, but they especially revered *nahuallis*. They called white *iztac*s Spirit Walkers, and while the travelers didn't stay in Temoaya, the name Spirit Walkers stuck.

As they marched south, they encountered the *altépetl* of Xonacatlan. Like the Temoayas and the Jiquipillis to the north, the Xonacas lived on the fringes of Teotenanca territory and managed to escape, for the most part, Teotenanca suppression. The Xonacas were expecting the Spirit Walkers, for they had received news of their coming. They hid the travelers in a sheltered cove beyond a hollow recess in the forested mountains, where a crystal waterfall rushed into an enchanted pool and chirping *centzontlis* mocked them with their songs of four hundred voices. They stayed more time than they might have in Xonacatlan, charmed by the sheer beauty that surrounded them. They spent their days frolicking with the monarch butterflies and caught and caged several *centzontlis*. The three *iztac* siblings ran freely and chased each other, laughing in the cool shade of the pinewood trees. Spellbound as they were in the majestic forest, the travelers almost forgot the purpose of their journey, but Xolome finally reminded them of their mission. The Teotenancas controlled the obsidian mines in the snowy Xinantecatl Mountains. Control of the mines, he told them, would be a blessing the Toltecs would receive for converting the misguided residents of Teotenanco who worshiped flesh-eating gods; but first they would have to face the demon of the wall.

After many days in the enchanted forest, the Spirit Walkers left Xonacatlan and made their way to Ocoyoacac, where the expecting tribe awaited them. The Ocoyoas had already received secret

[313]

messages of the arrival of the *nahuallis* of Ce Acatl Topiltzin, and they hid the travelers in the crater of a sleeping volcano. From the top of their volcano, Tohuenyo and his small band could look east and see the snowy peaks of Ajusco. Toward the west, they saw the rolling Toluca Valley with vast, fertile green landscapes, undulating with forested hills. In the distant horizon of the setting sun they could even see the purple Xinantecatl Mountains. From their vantage point they could also see the Tetepetl Hill to the south, where they would find the imposing city of Teotenanco.

The crater afforded Tohuenyo and his comrades a place close to the stars, where they could spend their evenings talking quietly, close to the protection of the heavens. Miztli said that the stars were little holes in the sky that the gods looked through to watch the human ones at night. Xolome said that the stars were goddesses who bestowed blessings on children who live in fear. Mazatl said the stars gave strength to the athletes who played *ullama* in the form of physical empowerments. Tohuenyo said for everybody to quit talking about the stars, because it was time to come up with a course of action.

So it was that in the crater of the sleeping volcano at Ocoyoacac, the small band of Spirit Walkers devised a plan to penetrate and subdue their thousands of blood thirsty enemies behind the fortified wall in the menacing city of Teotenanco.

The Demon's Eye

At last the Spirit Walkers reached the edge of the forests of Techuchulco and beheld the walled city of Teotenanco, as it came into view in the distant horizon. They had been successful in both skirting the marshlands in the center of the valley as well as avoiding the smaller towns that were allies of their Teotenanca enemies, and in so doing, had avoided many great dangers.

Now Tohuenyo, Mazatl and Andoeni walked in the full view of dawn, straight toward Teotenanco, accompanied by their nine *nahualli* friends and followed by some twenty *petlacalli* porters. At Xolome's insistence, they had searched the contents of Tohuenyo's cargo and had found things he didn't even know he'd had. To Andoeni's delight, there was a trove of goods related to the cult of Mazapa – women's clothing, figurines, nutty confections, even a priest's black robes – and most spectacularly, the sacred vestments of the goddess that had belonged to Tonalnan. The items had been intended as a peace offering. Tohuenyo decided to use them in his plan of attack, instead.

They made quite a show of themselves as they approached the walled city. Tohuenyo had cast off his warrior's attire and donned the priest's black robes. He wore his hair loose, down to his chest, but refused to smear it with turkey blood. The huge, muscular Mazatl sported a dark leather loincloth and black hip band, with nothing more than sandals and a wide, gold collar around his chest and shoulders. He also wore the painted death mask of a black and white skull, and a pyramid shaped headdress on his head. Andoeni walked along in the sacred vestments of Mazapa, including her painted red face and blackened lips, as well as the brocaded Mazapa crown.

The three of them were followed by Xolome, who was carried along on his stretcher, with his simple tunic and copper staff. He was playing a clay flute with eight holes. A couple of porters carried the caged *centzontlis* next to him, and he chimed back and forth with the majestic little birds.

After Xolome, came the three *iztac*s. They walked under a shaded canopy that was held by adoring Xonaca worshipers, who had insisted on joining the expedition. The *iztac* siblings played small drums and tortoise shell rattles, and raised quite a spectacle with their chalky white skin, their long, yellow hair and their gray, green, and blue eyes.

The five *tlatoque*s weaved in and out of the line of Spirit Walkers, walking around freely, some of them juggling, some of them occasionally throwing nutty confections to the curious onlookers they were now beginning to draw.

The porters walked behind them at the end. Their loads were greatly lightened, as Tohuenyo had ordered them to bury the weapons and armor in the crater of the sleeping volcano two days before.

By the time they reached the great wall of the city on the hill, they had quite a crowd gathered around them. They stopped and looked up at the massive structure, studying it, each in their own way.

The wall was the height of about sixteen men, one standing upon the other. Plastered gray, it was slanted, and inclined back toward the Tetepetl Hill with a huge staircase going right up the middle. The stairway was so wide that six men could easily stretch their arms across it. At the base of the stair, there were two enormous reddish-brown basins, ablaze with burning fires, even though it was morning. The guards of the city eyed the band of *nahuallis* as they approached the stairs, but stood back and let them pass.

The Spirit Walkers continued their procession up the great stairway, the porters helping the little *tlatoque*s ascend. At the top they saw the Eye of the Demon, a dark gray monolith crowned by a carved hematite, five-pointed star. In the middle of the black and reddish-brown star was a silver-gray disc, a shiny circular eye that looked out over the entire Valley of Toluca. To the east were the great peaks of Ajusco, to the west, the Xinantecatl Mountains, and far to the north, as far as the eye could see, was the Hill of

Xocotitlan next to the Jilotepec Mountains. They had journeyed that far.

Tohuenyo shuddered as they walked past the iron ore monolith with its Demon Eye.

At the top of the stairs there was a flat expanse that stretched out before them, filled with merchants and bustling shoppers in the midst of a *tianguis*. They saw many of the same wares that were sold in Tula – firewood, textiles, feather work, pottery and ceramics, not to mention a whole variety of foods. It was quite different than the *tianguis* in Tula, however. This market had an assortment of morose and aggressive merchants with bone nose plugs and sinister looking amulets of blackened phalanges dangling around their necks. There were shrunken heads hanging from vendor's stalls, and fried blood cakes of questionable origin. In the center of the field there was a *tzompantli*, a giant rack filled with dozens of whitened, human skulls.

Many of the inhabitants of Teotenanco had painted themselves blue to varying degrees and in an assortment of styles. It was obvious that there was abundant wealth in this place, even if it was displayed with excessive morbidity.

The crowd parted and let the *nahuallis* through, backing up so as not to be touched by them. *Nahuallis* were sacred and not meant to be touched by hands other than a king's. While they appeared reverent to the *nahuallis*, the Teotenancas glared with suspicion at Tohuenyo, Andoeni and Mazatl.

An old man tugged Tohuenyo's arm and said, "Beware of the women of this place. Here there are she-demons who drink the blood of children. At night before they go out to do their evil deeds, they pluck out their own eyes and tear off their own legs. They bury their eyeballs and legs underneath their hearths. Then they grow wings like great woven mats and fly out to plunge themselves into demonic carnage. They eat the flesh of men!"

Tohuenyo examined the blue faces of some women merchants in a nearby stall. They snarled back at him. When he turned around, the old man had disappeared.

"Mazapa! Pray to the goddess of Mazapa that your crops shall reach toward the heavens!" Andoeni yelled, valiantly. She motioned for Miztli to distribute some of the confections. The tension eased.

[317]

Tohuenyo sent Andoeni and the white *iztac*s through the market to proselytize the cult of Mazapa. He and Mazatl then escorted Xolome and the *tlatoque*s to the edge of the market where they could rest under the shade of an *ahuahuete* tree.

Tohuenyo turned to Mazatl. "Let's talk," he said.

They walked away from the crowd to the solitude of an empty *ullama* ball court and sat along the edge.

Tohuenyo hadn't had any time alone with his lifelong friend since they'd had their chance encounter back in the Jilotepec foothills. They reminisced about the fights that day, how Mazatl had kept winning all morning and how they'd rigged the final fight to walk with the winnings. They talked about the capture of Andoeni and the fate of Cuauhtémoc. He was contemptible, they agreed, but it was unfortunate that he had been murdered. Tohuenyo had been waiting for an opportunity alone with his friend who was like a brother.

He took a risk and decided to confide in him. He told Mazatl about the teachings of Topiltzin Quetzalcoatl, and about the god of harmony and wisdom. He told him that he'd had a kind of awakening that he couldn't explain and that he no longer wished to carry out his mother's evil plans and be her soldier of treachery. Then he told his friend his biggest secret – he no longer wished to be Chichimeca. He now considered himself a Toltec and a follower of Quetzalcoatl.

Mazatl said he understood, but he never said whether he agreed.

Back at the tianguis they found the *tlatoque*s dancing around Xolome and the *centzontlis*, juggling and making people laugh. Miztli was flirting with women, as usual, and he often took advantage of the fact that his face only reached the height of people's bottoms to get a good laugh.

Entering the city had been much easier than they had expected, so Tohuenyo decided he no longer had to bear the scourging itchiness of the priest's tunic he was wearing. He decided to change into the other garments that his adoring wife had packed for him: a noble's princely robes and jewels. The soft cotton would be a welcome relief after donning that course maguey fiber robe.

About the time Andoeni arrived with the three *iztacs*, a messenger ran up to Tohuenyo and his band of travelers under the tree.

"King Black Snake is ready to receive you," the messenger said.

This was the news they had been waiting for. They knew the king would have been informed of their arrival since they'd left the protective forests of Techuchulco.

On their way to the king's palace, they passed the blood soaked stairs of a pyramid and shuddered to think of the causes.

✄

Black Snake was the fiercest man Tohuenyo had ever seen. He had a black stripe painted across his eyes, and a shortened human rib through his septum, another bone through his lower lip, and a multitude of other facial piercings. His headdress was pyramid shaped, with gold and obsidian inlay. Glossy, black crow feathers hung at his temples. His robes were brocaded black on black cotton, and he was laden with gold and obsidian jewels.

Tohuenyo and Mazatl, who had grown up with Titlacáhuan, were accustomed to a sight such as this, but Tohuenyo could tell that Andoeni was hard pressed to maintain her composure underneath her Mazapa crown. He could see that she was trembling.

Black Snake's queen sat beside him. She was half his age and sat so still that she looked like a carving of human stone. Her black hair was adorned with a net of lustrous white pearls from the sea. Her face was dusted completely white. She was wearing thick black eyeliner, and her lips were painted crimson red. Bare breasted, she was strewn with blood red coral necklaces, golden arm bands, bangles and bracelets, all embedded with precious jewels. Her name was Itzpapálotl. She'd been named after the goddess of war, the Obsidian Butterfly. She was known to her people as Madam Butterfly.

"Who are you, and what is your purpose here?" the king finally said. His voice was unusually high and he was soft spoken, not at all what they had expected from his ferocious features and nefarious reputation.

The inside of their palace was dark, and very different from the palaces at Tula. While the palaces at Tula had murals on the walls of their gods and heroes of days gone by, the walls of Black Snake's palace had morbid paintings of warriors cutting off the heads of their conquered enemies, and pulling the hearts out of sacrificial victims. A great stone sculpture of Huitzilopochtli, the Blue Hummingbird, stood at the end of the dim hall.

"Lord Black Snake," Tohuenyo said, still kneeling as they all had been since they'd entered. "I humbly request permission to be in thy presence."

Black Snake pounded his scepter on the floor four times.

Tohuenyo rose.

"Lord Black Snake, I am here as a messenger of the god Quetzalcoatl, one of the four children of Ometeotl, highest of all gods, He-She who created Himself-Herself before creating any of the other gods."

Everyone bowed their heads reverently upon hearing the sacred names of Ometeotl, God-Goddess on High.

Tohuenyo spoke forcefully and with the confidence of a Toltec noble. "Lord Black Snake! You are to worship the one true god, Quetzalcoatl, god of wisdom and love. In so doing, you will also honor Mazapa so that the maize of your realm will grow as high as the heavens and your people will not know hunger. Hear my words, lord of Teotenanco. You are to banish your flesh-eating god, Huitzilopochtli!"

Black Snake stood up so violently that his throne shook. His queen flinched.

"Messenger of Quetzalcoatl!" the fierce king began in his unusually effeminate voice, "I am obliged to believe that you speak your truth, as you are surrounded by *nahuallis* and are therefore understood to be of impeccable character. But who is to say that your truth is also mine? By what means shall you convince me that your god is stronger than mine?"

"On the court of *ullama*, My Lord. Let your strongest player match ours," Tohuenyo answered.

Thus it came to pass that the great and strong Mazatl played a one on one game of *ullama* at the ball court the following day against the champion of Teotenanco. When Mazatl won, the king was furious and stormed off so violently that the heavens felt his sting and began to rain.

Tohuenyo and his Spirit Walkers again came before the king.

"Lord Black Snake, I am the messenger of Quetzalcoatl, god of wisdom and love. Banish your flesh-eating god Huitzilopochtli and tear down his temples. Worship Quetzalcoatl, Lord Black Snake, the one true god!"

The king, distrusting the Toltec noble then said, "And how am I to know you are a true messenger of Quetzalcoatl?" as it continued to rain.

"My *xolome* can speak to thunder and move lightning at his own command!" Tohuenyo attested.

To see for themselves, the king and his court went out into the rain under the dark, stormy clouds and watched the fearsome lightning storm.

Thunder rolled across the sky as dark clouds crashed together. "There they will fall, the sons of Tlaloc," Xolome predicted, right before two great, twin lightning bolts powered down upon the summit of the Tetepetl Hill – exactly as the *xolome* had just foretold.

More thunder rolled and the rain streamed down like strands of beads, but then, an insurmountable catastrophe occurred. Another bolt of lightning cracked and crashed into the iron ore monolith at the entrance of the city, exploding the Demon's Eye of Teotenanco to smithereens.

"Our protector!" the onlookers yelled in fright.

The king, in his fury, grabbed the goddess of Mazapa and ordered the Toltec and his *nahuallis* to leave his kingdom.

"My god, Huitzilopochtli is weak. I will nourish him with the blood of your priestess of Mazapa!"

"Beware, Lord Black Snake!" Tohuenyo threatened, "For the gods are at war. In two day's time your god, Huitzilopochtli will try to hide the moon, but Quetzalcoatl will prevail! Quetzalcoatl will save the moon! This is a bad omen for you, Black Snake!" This the *xolome* had prophesied.

"Leave my city, evil mischief maker! Leave my city now!"

Then King Black Snake took the beautiful Andoeni by her hair as though she were a doll of rags, and dragged her off. Her crown

was expected to be a warrior, expected to kill to prove their worth to other men and the gods?

You are free to relax and be yourself. The words rolled over and over in his mind.

"Do you suppose they have guards on the other side?" Mazatl asked, bringing Tohuenyo back to the moment.

"I don't know," Tohuenyo answered him, "but I think our best strategy is to scale the wall and get to the rooftops." He shifted his heavy load of weapons.

Mazatl tightened the belt that held his *maquáhuitl* sword and slung his bow crosswise over his shoulder, pulling it tight under his quiver. "Ready, brother!" he said.

Mazatl stood on Tohuenyo's shoulders first and pulled himself up to the top, then grabbed Tohuenyo by the wrist and pulled his friend up to him. It was a clumsy ascent. Their weapons shifted and threw them off balance, but they'd gotten extremely lucky. There were no guards in sight. Where was everybody?

Next they snuck onto the roofs of the palace, careful to walk along the tops of the walls, as this would hide the sound of their footsteps. They finally came to a courtyard where they could hear several priests talking and preparing the maiden for sacrifice.

"This will appease Huitzilopochtli. Our god will then devour the evil mischief maker, you will see," they heard one of them say.

From atop the dark roof Tohuenyo used sign language to tell Mazatl to wait. They were so close.

These were the priests who were going to cut out her heart and feed it to their blue god. They still had time. The ceremony hadn't been performed.

Just then, they heard a woman's shrill scream, and then another one, and then more.

They flattened themselves against the roof as more people started to scream.

"Come brothers, come quick!" they heard somebody in the room yell desperately. "It is happening! Huitzilopochtli is devouring the moon!"

Tohuenyo and Mazatl looked up to see that the moon was beginning to darken on its lower left side. The battle of the gods had begun.

[324]

They slipped down to the patio in one agile leap, and entered the room that the priests had just vacated. Mazatl shoved a table stone in front of the woven mat door.

They were surrounded by the priests' religious paraphernalia for the impending sacrificial ceremony. In the middle of the floor lay a massive, solid gold headdress. The front band was triangular-shaped, with golden discs and dangling, stepped pyramids that hung from the sides. Most impressive of all, were the brilliant, giant plumes that shot out in all directions from the golden crown. They faded from deep crimson red into a brilliant orange, and culminated in fiery yellow at the ends. Tohuenyo had never seen anything like it.

He glanced up at Andoeni who lay heavily drugged and sleeping, extended on a stone altar at the end of the room. Mazatl was now over her.

"What are you doing?" Mazatl demanded.

Tohuenyo strapped the High Priest's headdress onto his head and pulled it tight.

"I'm stealing the golden crown."

More screams and mayhem could be heard from outside. It sounded like hoards of people were now in the streets, screaming and cheering a hellish delight.

"And the High Priest's royal cape, I see." Mazatl picked up the sleeping Andoeni, draping her limp body in his strong arms.

Both of the men were taken aback by her stunning beauty. Tohuenyo had been right. The Teotenancas had meticulously prepared her for her journey to the gods.

Her full, voluptuous breasts were covered with nothing more than sheer, white cotton gauze, gathered in the middle by a gold clasp embedded with opals and pearls. Around her hips there was a wider strip of white gauze, tied together on one side so that it covered her hips just to the tops of her smooth thighs. The ends of the long piece of material draped over her and hung down, almost to the ground, the edges finished in brocaded gold. Around her throat and bare waist were strands of gold beads, and her loose black hair was crowned with a delicate diadem of pearls. She smelled of gardenia, and her dark skin had been oiled with gold dust, giving her already beautiful skin an intoxicating sheen.

"Let's get out of here," Tohuenyo commanded.

They snuck out the back patio into the night, watching suspiciously for guards. It was unusually dark.

"You go up first then I'll hand her to you," Mazatl said.

Once on the roof they could see what all the screaming was about in the streets below.

In the night sky behind them, the moon was blood red.

Emboldened, Tohuenyo walked straight to the edge of the palace, carrying Andoeni draped across his arms. He looked down upon the frenetic crowd. People were carrying torches and relighting the bonfires at the bases of the pyramids. King Black Snake and his nobles were in the street outside his palace in the midst of a crowd.

"Huitzilopochtli has devoured the moon!" someone in the crowd yelled.

Women screamed, grasping their heads.

A man ran through the streets shouting, "Huitzilopochtli will be reborn as the moon! See his bloody birth!"

Tohuenyo, forever the brave challenger, stood at the rooftop staring at the Teotenanca king.

Then someone noticed him.

"It's the messenger of Quetzalcoatl! There, on the rooftop!"

Everyone turned to look at the Toltec noble. The sleeping goddess lay across his strong arms. Behind his plumed crown, the moon glowed blood-red in the sky. Then slowly, the red glow started to fade, and the left side of the moon burned once again with brilliant, white light. Then gradually, the white light pushed its dark intruder out, proving that Quetzalcoatl, the god who rules the color white, was the strongest of the four sons of Ometeotl.

"You see there, Black Snake?" Tohuenyo yelled to the Teotenanca king. "Quetzalcoatl has once again defeated your god, Huitzilopochtli! Give up your flesh-eating god, King Black Snake! This is your last warning!"

"Seize him!" the king commanded.

Tohuenyo turned and walked along the roof toward the north end of the palace, effortlessly carrying his goddess. Arrows and *atlatl* darts whizzed past him, but he did not run. He was confident that his god would protect him, confident that his state of grace was enough to deflect the deadly projectiles.

Mazatl wasn't as spiritual about the onslaught. He was grasping arrows from his quiver and firing them as fast as he could, while dodging a volley of darts and arrows and trying to keep up with Tohuenyo at the same time.

"We should have used snakes on that snake of a king," Mazatl said, as they reached the back of the palace. To their great fortune, there was a stairway leading down the back wall of the king's residence. To their great misfortune, three guards were heading up the stairs.

"Let me take them!" said Mazatl, pulling out his *maquáhuitl* sword. He then heaved the colossal weapon and sliced the three guards open, each in turn, their innards spilling from their bodies as they toppled off the stairs and splattered on the ground.

Mazatl pushed forth down the stairs ahead of Tohuenyo and the sleeping girl, bloody *maquáhuitl* raised, ready for the next onslaught of warriors. He peeked around the corner to see where they were and who was coming. He did not tell Tohuenyo how many warriors were approaching. He only said, "You'll have to exit the city through the main entrance. It's ahead to the left. I'll hold them off for you."

"I'll put her down and fight with you!"

"No! You must save her, and you must save yourself. If they get to her..." Mazatl broke off his thought and looked at the woman in Tohuenyo's arms. He put a hand up to her forehead for an instant then said, "Now! I'll cover you!"

Then the gentle giant Mazatl turned into a fierce fighting machine. As Tohuenyo walked confidently out of the city with the Otomí princess in his arms, Mazatl shot his arrows and launched his *atlatl* darts in an impassioned frenzy. When he ran out of projectiles, he came out from behind his corner wielding his *maquáhuitl*. In the light of the moon now shining full and bright upon him, he held back twenty Teotenanca warriors who were trying to get at him - bashing in heads, cutting off limbs, slicing through abdomens and thighs, and ripping through his enemy's self-confidence. The rest of the warriors, too frightened to advance on the furious war machine, stood back, hesitating.

At last Tohuenyo reached the crumbled ruins of the monolith at the city's entrance. He turned to see his lifelong friend only twenty paces away, finally being apprehended by the king and his

Teotenanca warriors. They shrieked and howled, and disrobed him. First they castrated him with a jagged-toothed spear head. Then they sliced open his abdomen and pulled out his entrails with a hooked blade, the whole while slapping him in the face and insulting him to heighten his torture. After that, they cut off his limbs, and while he was still alive and conscious, King Black Snake plunged a sacrificial knife into his chest and ripped out his beating heart. Then Black Snake shoved the quivering organ up to his mouth and voraciously devoured an enormous bite of Mazatl's heart. He then screamed his most terrifying war cry.

Tohuenyo's own heart exploded in his chest as he witnessed the demonic butchery of his best friend. Frozen with fear, he stood where he was, watching them.

The king and his warriors then turned toward Tohuenyo.

Tohuenyo felt like he was in a dream. They advanced toward him, but he couldn't move. He stood petrified as they came closer and closer.

"Messenger of Quetzalcoatl," King Black Snake said. "You come to my city and offend our god." The king's face was bloodied from eating Mazatl's heart. "It is you who will now give your heart to our Huitzilopochtli, along with your Otomí bride!"

The king raised his sacrificial knife and took a step toward Tohuenyo.

Tohuenyo realized it would do no good to run. He was about to put the sedated Andoeni down, when all of a sudden his aggressors froze in fright. They stepped back and lowered their weapons.

Behind him, having just ascended the stairs, came the boy Blue Iztac. Whether it was an apparition or reality, no one ever knew, but they all saw him.

"A plague upon your house, Black Snake," the boy child said chillingly. "That which you worship so dearly will be the death of you."

Black Snake said nothing. He'd fought many battles and won many wars, even delivered hundreds of sacrificial victims into the hands of the gods, but he wasn't about to engage a nahualli. Especially not an iztac. Iztacs were the incarnation of Ometeotl, God on High and father-mother of Huitzilopochtli, Quetzalcoatl, Tezcatlipoca and Xipe Totec.

He watched in fear as his Toltec foes disappeared into the night.

Snake to Snake

Once again Tohuenyo had fought a battle without raising a weapon. How was he going to explain to Andoeni what had happened? What was he supposed to say, that he'd mastered the art of running off while letting Mazatl fight his battles and die for him?

He missed his gentle giant friend. He'd always been quiet and never complained about the life the god's had given him. It was hard to think that he would never see Mazatl again.

He couldn't think about that now. He had an evil opponent to defeat. Besides, Teotenanco was the gateway to the tropical lowlands of the south. If he could subjugate them, it would bring much commerce to Tula, including salt, exotic fruits and precious stones and pearls from the sea. No, he wasn't going to dwell on losses. He forced himself to focus on that which moved his objective forward. What was it that Mazatl had said to him? *You are free to relax and be yourself... be yourself... be yourself.*

Over the next several days at their hidden encampment at the Eye of Water, he contemplated this and other things Mazatl had said to him. Then he remembered something Xolome had said back in the enchanted forest of Xonacatlan – *Use the gifts the gods have given you. They come in the form of natural talents. Use those talents, and you will prevail in the greatest of undertakings.*

Of course!

Tohuenyo took his porters, left Andoeni and the *nahuallis* behind with their four Xonaca worshipers, and disappeared for many days.

It was a time of anxious waiting and intense labor for Andoeni, who spent her days preparing food for the all male band of travelers. She toiled silently, and was able to make meals out of the fish and frogs that the Xonacas hunted in the rivers and the marshlands.

When Tohuenyo finally returned, he ordered that no one touch the heavy *petlacalli* baskets, on pain of death.

Ten days had passed since the murderous night of the blood moon. The night was now moonless, which made it possible for them to sneak through the forest of Tetepetl Hill, detected only by watchful owls. When Tohuenyo and his many porters reached the edge of the tree line at the city's back wall, they found an arched doorway with two guards standing on either side. The guards alone stood between the palace wall and the haunting forest of the dark night.

From behind the trees where they were hiding, Tohuenyo took out a small clay flute and blew upon it. The flute released its voice mimicking a hooting owl.

The two guards at the door stirred.

Next he took out a larger, round clay flute in the shape of an animal's head. When he blew upon it, the second flute released its voice, mimicking the shrieking voice of a jaguar.

The guards nervously glanced around, and backed up against the wooden door.

Then Tohuenyo took out a flute that resembled a human skull. When he blew upon it, the flute released its voice, mimicking the most horrific deathly scream imaginable.

"The Night Creature!" one of the guards yelled.

"She has come to feast on our entrails!" the other guard said. When they saw that there were no witnesses to their cowardice, they opened the wooden door and escaped inside.

They bolted the door behind them, but as so frequently happened, Destiny smiled upon Tohuenyo, for there was a gap about a hand's width between the stone threshold and the bottom of the door.

Tohuenyo and his loyal porters stealthily crept up, and one by one, laid the *petlacalli* baskets next to the bottom of the door. Carefully lifting the lids, they freed scores of venomous vipers, watching the carnivorous reptiles slither silently within. By the time they were done, hundreds of rattlesnakes were quietly crawling within the city walls.

❋

They say that Black Snake woke up amidst a mass of cold, leathery serpents that had curled up next to his body for warmth. In horror, he'd jumped from his sleeping mat, startling the vipers into instant attack. Several of the snakes managed to bite him before they all scurried off, fanning out in all directions from his bed, coiling themselves against the walls of his room and threatening him with their rattling tails.

His queen, sleeping naked beside him, had frozen with fear, petrified and unable to move, and unbeknownst to her, it is what saved her.

By mid-morning, the anxiety-ridden king was in excruciating pain and lay semi-conscious in his own vomit. Tight, hard swelling pustules stretched his skin at the bites, turning them silvery and shiny. The venom spread over his body in dark red streaks. Soon, blood started to ooze out of the bluish and blistering puncture wounds. When the hemorrhaging set in, he started leaking blood from his nose, mouth and anus. Finally, blood began to seep through his skin in a rash of hundreds of red thorn pricks.

The whole time, his horrified queen crouched naked in the corner, surrounded by the coiled vipers with their rattling tails, witnessing the torturous extermination of her husband, watching helplessly as his life painfully slithered away.

Help was not forthcoming.

The plague of serpents spread throughout the city and inflicted the same painful death on a multitude of followers of Black Snake's flesh-eating god, Huitzilopochtli. In just the short span of a single morning, more than half of the city's inhabitants were afflicted.

✳

It took Tohuenyo several days to collect all the snakes and put them back into the *petlacalli* baskets. As he ventured through the devastated city, the frightened people called to him, "Help us, Quetzalcoatl!" They prostrated themselves to him when he cleared their homes of the venomous monstrosities. Then they solemnly attended to their dead, cursing Huitzilopochtli who had forsaken them, and swore their devotion to the new Toltec god.

[333]

When the queen composed herself she summoned Tohuenyo to her throne in the great hall.

Again she appeared with her face dusted white, wearing thick, black eyeliner, and her lips were painted bright red. She was still bare breasted, but this time her erect nipples were pierced with dangling ornaments of gold. Instead of a net of pearls in her hair, she wore a gold headdress crafted into the shape of a jaguar, thickly adorned with black and yellow plumes. Around her wide hips she wore a black strip of cloth, tied in a knot at the side of her hip, with its long trails culminating in a gold brocaded border. Her neck and slim waist were lassoed together with tiny gold beads.

"Messenger of Quetzalcoatl," the queen, Madam Butterfly said, swallowing back her pride. "You have proven your god superior to Huitzilopochtli who has forsaken us." She paused and looked at Tohuenyo who was now dressed in full Toltec regalia, with the exception of the high priest's headdress, which he donned to flaunt his victorious conquest. She continued, "I rightfully resign our independence and decree our allegiance to Ce Acatl Topiltzin Quetzalcoatl, king of kings." She then pounded her late husband's royal scepter four times on the floor.

"As a sign of our allegiance I present you with my two sisters, Yaretzi and Anayel." The whole of Cem Anahuac knew of Topiltzin Quetzalcoatl's ultimate sacrifice of celibacy, which is why she offered the princesses to Tohuenyo and not the king, Topiltzin. "May your betrothal unite our two houses," she decreed.

Yaretzi and Anayel were not particularly beautiful, but because they were twins, they were considered an immeasurable blessing. Their combined dowry was a formidable treasure, and the queen assigned four hundred warriors and their families to return with them to Tula for their protection during the journey. Upon their arrival to Tula, the Teotenanca warriors were to swear their allegiance to the Toltec king.

In the face of this undeniably generous gift, Tohuenyo's heart grew cold and his face was expressionless. "Can they weave?" he asked. When the Toltec was brought samples of their exquisite brocaded lengths of cloth, he was pleased.

And so it was that Tohuenyo captured the magnificent city of Teotenanco and brought it within the control of the Toltec empire.

The obsidian mines of Xinantécatl were now under Toltec control. He had earned the devotion of the king's *nahuallis* and, unexpectedly, gained his incredibly wealthy third and fourth wives, the royal twins.

Later it was rumored that Madam Butterfly summoned Tohuenyo to her inner chamber and compensated for her inability to betroth herself to him, constrained as she was by her office of queen. They engaged in an ancient fertility rite that lasted many days, until he was sure that he had planted his lineage deep inside her womb. "Give me a Toltec child!" she said, in the throes of passion, enamored senseless by his godlike masculinity. What the queen didn't know, however, was that Tohuenyo's seed wasn't Toltec. He was Chichimeca. She also didn't know that he could care less what cursed offspring she spawned. He was devouring her as the ultimate insult to his greatest enemy, Black Snake, who had murdered his best friend. What went through his mind as he exploded inside her was, "Look now, Black Snake! See how your woman begs to be my slave! Who is her master now, Black Snake? Who is her master now?"

Before he left, Tohuenyo ordered the Teotenanca survivors to demolish their images of Huitzilopochtli throughout the city. In four month's time, he informed them, a Toltec army would arrive to rebuild their city in the magnificence of Quetzalcoatl. In addition, he trusted that Ce Acatl Topiltzin would want to form a proper alliance, and assured the queen that the Toltec king would with all certainty send her a Toltec prince to be her king.

Warriors' Return

The homecoming at the River Xicocotitlan was glorious and welcoming. News reached the city of Tula long before Tohuenyo's return. Most of the city turned out to greet the hero who had conquered Teotenanco with no more than a handful of *tlatoques*, *iztacs*, and a *xolome*. They had come back with scores of porters carrying their spoils of war; mostly obsidian from the mines of Xinantécatl. After crossing the Xicocotitlan River, the mysterious River of Tears, the army camped up and down its sandy eastern banks. Reunited with family and friends, and onlookers curious to see the foreign Teotenancas, the soldiers built their fires in the sand and told stories of near death adventures way into the night. When the warriors exhausted their stories of Teotenanco, they reminisced of battles of long ago and far away, and made themselves the heroes.

Blue *Iztac* told the story of a great storm, and how the Sons of Tlaloc had appeared to them as twin lightning bolts at the top of Tetepetl Hill. He showed off a copper scepter, a gift that the Sons of Tlaloc had left behind after the storm. After the torrents had subsided, he and Miztli found copper rods exactly where two great lightning streaks had crashed into the earth. After hearing about this magnificent display of sorcery, the people marveled and said, "The *xolome* can speak to thunder and move lightning!" They were in awe.

The lion hearted Miztli, together with the other four *tlatoques*, told the story of their return journey through Jiquipilco where their commander Lord Tohuenyo had returned to collect his fifth wife Xochitl, the governor's youngest daughter. The poor, destitute governor had been unable to offer a dowry, so he'd allowed several of the village's widows to leave with the *tlatoques*. Miztli sat purring with pride in the lap of his buxom Jiquipilli woman, and told the story of his adventures with animated and charismatic exaggerations.

[337]

The story of Andoeni's rescue became so famous that different versions eventually appeared throughout the One World. Some even came to tell that in absolute heartbreak, the fair Andoeni jumped off a cliff into the raging waters of a river below and killed herself after the violent murder of her lover with the honey colored eyes. The relatives of Cuauhtémoc were beside themselves with grief. They'd learned of the news because Xolotl had already returned.

One of the most talked-about stories was the night of the blood moon and the heroism of an unknown warrior named Mazatl the Giant. In a valiant show of super-natural strength, Mazatl the Giant had defended his lord, Tohuenyo, and fought off twenty Teotenanca warriors so that the commander could escape with the Otomí princess, Andoeni. The tale ran rampant through the crowd along the riverbank, and was told and retold for many generations after.

Yellow Skirt, who had been roaming from campfire to campfire searching for her lover, heard the news from a particularly brutal Teotenanca warrior who had witnessed the scene with his own eyes. He elaborated on the details of Mazatl's disembowelment to such a degree that the devastated Yellow Skirt walked off into the night and lacerated her breasts with chips of obsidian in a sign of mourning.

The most heroic story, though, was that of Lord Tohuenyo himself, who could obviously communicate with snakes. This was proof that the god Quetzalcoatl smiled down upon him. If the gods favored Lord Tohuenyo, the Toltecs reasoned, they would, too.

Many people sought the war hero, but Tohuenyo was nowhere to be found on this night at the sandy banks of the River Xicocotitlan. He had headed directly back to Huemac's palace where he was received by his first love. She introduced him to his newborn daughter, Quetzalpétatl, meaning *she who walks on feathers*.

After a passionate embrace, Tohuenyo looked at her and said, "Wife, first you love me to the point of death. Then you would have me take other wives. Your change of heart confounds me."

Tonalnan suspected her desire for sister-wives might be misunderstood. But in her mind, her change of heart was the truest meaning of sacrifice. She would share his love, even risk losing it, in exchange for the chance to build a family dynasty, *her* family dynasty. Loneliness was a possible outcome. Success was inevitable.

She answered him not, but raised the infant before him, "Look, her eyes are the color of green jade," was all she said.

It was true, and the people of Tula took it as a sign from the gods that the child's life was meant to serve the holy and the divine as a priestess of the high temple.

✄

Several days later, in a grandiose celebration with festivities throughout the Yollotli and all of Tula, Lord Tohuenyo received the great dorsal disc of the Toltec warrior nobility. The king Topiltzin Quetzalcoatl also bestowed upon him the golden pectoral butterfly, encrusted with emeralds and jade. He was then given residence at the Royal Palace of Previous Kings where he would now reside with his five wives. Finally and most significantly, he was given the title of High Chancellor, and was instated as Protector of the Palace of Quetzalcoatl, highest administrator of justice in the Toltec realm.

Xolotl had also received the golden pectoral butterfly from the king for his military accomplishments two months earlier. His defeat of the northern Valley of Toluca and subjugation of the two towns of Jocotitlan and Atlacomulco were immensely significant for the control of trade to the far reaches of the northwest. The king, Ce Acatl Topiltzin, officially recognized Xolotl as Huemac's successor as First General of the Toltec empire. Xolotl and his one wife, Madam Calli, would continue to reside in the First General's palace, under the tutelage of Lord Huemac.

Xolotl now had to publically honor his brother-in-law Lord Tohuenyo, but secretly his bitter envy filled him with hatred. He didn't know when, he didn't know where, but one day he would take part in Tohuenyo's demise.

Book 3

Trail to Xipe Totec

Ollín

In days of old before Mixcoatl defeated the Obsidian Butterfly, the first astrologer Hueman predicted many things to come. He taught the People that great calamity and devastation appear on the eve of every golden dawn.

Listen then, Oh my children, tribe of Mixcóatl, to the wisdom of our ancestors, for they will tell. Call upon the spirit of your ancestors, upon whose shoulders you stand. The ancient ones have preserved our origins. Guard this wisdom, young apprentice, seeker of knowledge. Learn it well and keep it in your heart for you, some day, will be an ancient one, expected to share this song and prayer.

My voice is old, yet I, Citlali, Star from the Great Beyond, speak of truths that should always be told. So, listen now, not with just your ears, but with your eyes and your heart. Listen to what our ancestors have left for us to know:

In the beginning there was nothing; nothing at all. No light, no life, no consciousness, no movement, no breath. Here in this void the Oldest of Old Gods, Ometéotl, formed. Ometéotl, Creator of the Universe, is both masculine and feminine and this is why this Supreme, first god was able to create himself-herself out of the dark emptiness that was nothing.

In Ometéotl all opposites unite. The Creator is both generator of chaos and giver of harmony and order. Ometéotl is spirit and matter, fire and water, black and white, stillness and movement, life and death, creator and destroyer, and the embodiment of both good and evil. Because of this, the Oldest of Old Gods is called the god of duality, and is the divinity where opposites converge in a supreme manifestation of The All.

The oldest god creates and destroys in order to generate *ollin*, the sacred movement in continuum, which gives impulse to our world and everything that is.

Once created, the supreme god Ometéotl, being both masculine and feminine, spawned children, the four Tezcatlipocas, who became the ministers of the creation of our visible, palpable, physical and changing world. Then they created the gods destined to the preservation of this world, the sustaining of all natural phenomena, and the unchaining of the life forms. These four gods, children of Ometéotl, have ever since served as the guardians of humans, and as our guides, it is they who administer both rewards and punishment.

At the ends of the earth where the sun sets, there is the sun's home. This is the region of the White Tezcatlipoca, who is also known as Quetzalcoatl, keeper of wisdom and things related to maize. There in the sun's home is the land of experience, wisdom, old age, light, fertility, life and holy breath. Quetzalcoatl who rules this land rules over these qualities.

Opposite the region where the sun sets, there in the east, that is the land of the Red Tezcatlipoca, the Goddess of Renewal who is called Xipe-Totec. If one were to ever reach there, and it is doubtful because it lay at the ends of the earth beyond many perils indeed, one would find the region dominated by springtime and rebirth. There the seasons are forever changing, the leaves of trees constantly falling, and new buds continually sprouting forth. Xipe Totec rules over renewal and change. As the Earth casts off her old and dying leaves, and then blossoms forth with new foliage, she goes through a process of dying in order to be reborn. Xipe Totec is also said to rule over time.

In the area to the left of the setting sun, there is the land of the Blue Tezcatlipoca, the God That is Eaten, Tonatiuh, the sun. This god is the God That is Eaten because day after day the sun descends to the Underworld and falls into the shadows of darkness, while in the heavens the moon and the stars reign. Fighting against the Night in the underworld, Tonatiuh is weakened and loses energy, but the nutrients of the blood of life that we spill in penitence help fortify him to win the battle against the Night. Each dawn he emerges from the Underworld and at this moment he becomes the Eagle of Fire Bolts, a symbol of his victory against the treacherous Night. This land at the end of the earth to the left of the setting sun is associated with blue because the trajectory of Tonatiuh is a great circular path that begins with the parting of the immense Celestial Blue.

[344]

If you look to the north, to the right of the setting sun, you will be facing the land of the Black Tezcatlipoca, the lord of the Night Sky. The Black Tezcatlipoca is also known as Tezcatlipoca, as Lord of the Here and Now, and as the Smoking Mirror. The god Mictlántecuhtli reigns in the land of Tezcatlipoca. This is the bitter cold and fleshless Land of the Dead. It is said that when one dies, one goes there; one goes directly there, and from that land do the dead set out.

Know then, that after the four Tezcatlipocas created the earth, the heavens and the underworld, long ago, before the first Age, Tezcatlipoca and Quetzalcoatl became rivals in a chain of destruction and creation that was to unfold and would characterize the existence of five different worlds throughout time. Each world was an Age, dominated by the great burning disc in the Celestial Blue, and therefore, each Age is called a Sun.

Quetzalcoatl created The First Sun, the Age of Water, and molded man and woman of ash, but the jealous Tezcatlipoca interfered and all was carried away by water. The people were turned into fish.

Tezcatlipoca then brought into existence The Second Sun, the Age of Jaguar. In this Sun there lived giants. The ancient ones told that the giants greeted one another thus: "Fellow, do not fall, because he who falls, falls forever." It came to pass that the heavens were oppressed and the sun did not follow its path. Darkness came, and the giants were eaten by jaguars.

Quetzalcoatl created The Third Sun. It happened that during this age it rained fire and those that lived were burned. It also rained rocks and sand. This sun came to be known as the Age of Rain of Fire.

Tezcatlipoca responded with The Fourth Sun, the Age of Wind, but during this time all was carried away by the wind. The people were changed into monkeys and were scattered into the mountains to live as monkey-men.

Quetzalcoatl then created The Fifth Sun, the age we live in now, called Ollin, the Sun of Movement. In this Age, the sun follows its path and there is continual movement. All that ever was, is, and ever shall be, is in a constant state of change. At the beginning of

[345]

this age Quetzalcoatl journeyed to Mictlán to retrieve the bones of woman and the bones of man.

Tezcatlipoca's envy brewed, as the jealous lord of the Here and Now vowed to intensify the powers of the night – poverty, misery, war and disease - for, only evil and devastation can bring about about real change.

And so it was that these two forces, Good and Evil, were now at war. In the greatest days of the Toltec Empire, Quetzalcoatl reigned supreme in divine glory. The people loved and adored their god and their king. All of the inhabitants of the land had access to him. He was just and wise and heard their pleas with righteousness.

They say the Toltecs revered Ce Acatl Topiltzin Quetzalcoatl as a god and offered him prayers and built altars and temples in his name. The Palace of Quetzalcoatl became a radiant example of the magnificence of the empire. Inside the great palace, columns were carved by highly skilled lapidary artisans and inset with brilliant, precious stones. The walls, even though they were painted with richly textured murals, were adorned with tapestries of expert feather working and inset with precious stones. In the king's inner chamber one wall was entirely inlaid with emeralds and green jade, another with turquoise and gold, the third with coral and red jasper, and the fourth with white shells and pearls from the sea.

Next to the palace they built a pyramid to Venus the Evening and Morning Star. They called the colossal wonder the Pyramid of Tlahuizcalpantecuhtli to honor the Toltec king because Quetzalcoatl was also seen as Venus the Morning and Evening Star. At the top of the pyramid they erected giant atlases, sculptural figures of warriors, used as columns that were as tall as four men. In this way, they thought to revive the fallen giants of the Sun of Jaguars of the Second Age. Along the north side of the pyramid there was a beautifully detailed, long-running frieze filled with jaguars, coyotes, eagles and hawks. Behind the pyramid they constructed another sculptured wall that they called the Coatepantli, the length of which depicted a series of serpents devouring human skulls. All who gazed upon the Coatepantli recognized it as Venus, the Evening Star, being devoured by the great, super-natural forces of the Earth.

In the reign of Ce Acatl the Toltecs became very rich. Food was so plentiful that it came to be of little value, and was available for all. Storehouses had to be built to accommodate the overflow where maize cobs hung from the wooden beams and giant urns of dried beans crowded the floors. The pumpkins and other winter squash were so huge that they could hardly be carried in a person's arms. Amaranth abounded, and it is said that the cotton grew naturally in every color. Flowers proliferated profusely - fuchsia, hydrangea, dahlia, marigolds, wisteria, sunflowers and poinsettias that grew as tall as trees. Jacaranda towered to the heavens, and magnolia perfumed the air. Birds were so plentiful that they lived in the city among the people, inspiring poetry and song. Cenzontli mockingbirds sat on rooftops and serenaded humans with their four hundred voices, and iridescent hummingbirds frolicked around bougainvillea with butterflies and bees.

As the empire of Tula expanded and the great Pyramid of the Sun reached its completion, the people celebrated their bounty with festivals of worship and praise. Ritual celebrations lasted for days, during which time the citizens would decorate their doors with bouquets of bulrushes and brightly dyed cornhusk flowers. They aligned the streets with giant botanical arches overflowing with fragrant, colorful blossoms. Painted paper banners that stretched from rooftop to rooftop across the city's streets created playful canopies that masqueraded the heavens in a veil of merriment and goodwill.

Before ritual processions, women would prepare enormous quantities of food including honey-pineapple *tamallis* and smoked *chipotle* bean cakes. The people would gorge themselves and offer edibles and goodies to anyone who came to their homes. There was dancing in the streets and in the Yollotli, with singing and flute players and drums. Everyone wore their finest regalia – men adorned with feathers and women bedecked with jewels. They would dance way unto the night and then return to their homes where they would imbibe great quantities of *pulque*.

When the eve of a ritual would come everyone would carry baskets and urns full of vegetables, legumes and grains to the base of the Pyramid of the Sun to sacrifice part of their bounty as an offering to the gods.

The people would ask their king Ce Acatl Topiltzin, "Why must we sacrifice part of our bounty?" and the king would answer, "In

[347]

sacrificing, or giving up, our wealth we are reminded to be grateful for everything that we *do* have. When we are in a state of gratitude we are in harmony with the gods and reap their favor."

The people asked their king, Ce Acatl Topiltzin, "Must we also sacrifice ourselves to appease the gods?" and the king would answer, "No, my children, for human life is the most precious creation of the gods." Ce Acatl Topiltzin Quetzalcoatl would answer thus because he loved his people and abhorred human sacrifice. He saw it as a vile sin.

On the morning of a ritual, Ce Acatl Topiltzin would lead the procession before sunrise and the throng of thousands lining the streets would prostrate themselves before their king and kiss the ground. At the top of the pyramid, priests would light fires in giant, shallow urns, and together with their king they would burn the vegetable, legume and grain offerings of all the citizens of Tula.

As the seasons turned to years however, the people of Tula grew accustomed to the wealth and bounty that Quetzalcoatl bestowed upon them, and their hearts became careless. Their awe and gratitude of their blessings turned to expectation and a sense of entitlement.

This is when I watched from the Underworld, from the land of Mictlán, the unfolding of atrocities that were to come. For, it was at this time that Tezcatlipoca descended from the Heavens, sliding down on a glistening rope of spider thread, with the mission of destroying Quetzalcoatl's people so that he himself would become their king and favored god. Ce Acatl was in his thirty-eighth year.

Ullama

It so happened that one day, many years after the coronation of Ce Acatl Topiltzin, the king himself was granting audiences in the colonnaded Western Hall of the Palace of Quetzalcoatl. Lord Tohuenyo had long since been instated as Protector of the Palace of Quetzalcoatl, and as such, was the senior chief of judicial affairs, but on occasion the king would grant appointments to the nobility, preside over hearings, pass judgment on international concerns, or attend other matters of business required of a king.

On this day, *Nahui Tecpatl*, there arrived twin lords before the king, both handsome and strong, unlike anyone had ever seen. Their waist-length hair fell over great blue heron feathered capes that draped all the way to the floor, and their blue-black tunics were embroidered with silver thread and garnished with pearls from the sea. They donned heavy strands of lapis and jade, and upon their heads they wore coronets of downy white egret plumage that resembled the clouds. Most captivating of all were their eyes, for their immense blue-black irises where like mesmerizing, watery pools that shimmered with reflective light. One of the lords carried a crystal spear and the other a rattle made from an enormous black gourd.

When the twin lords spoke, the brother with the crystal spear spoke first. Then, in the middle of the sentence, the brother with the enormous black gourd rattle finished each thought, symbiotically vacillating the dialogue to express a single stream of thought. Their voices enchanted everyone who heard, having the calming effect of a gentle rain on all those who listened.

"Hail to –

"the King!" they said.

They summarily bowed gingerly with a dignity and composure known only to gods and kings.

Ce Acatl, seated upon his throne with his chief administrator Tohuenyo standing at his side, looked down upon the twin brothers. The masked king nodded to acknowledge them.

"Who are you?" Lord Tohuenyo demanded, pounding his staff of office on the stone stair.

"We are the sons of –

"a magnificent lord." they said.

"Whose reign is predominated by his obsession to –

"fertilize his penetrable wife, our Lady and Mother who sustains us," they said.

Through an archway in the far wall they could see rolling gray clouds churning in the sky.

Their black, shimmering eyes glistened like pools of water reflecting the light of the stars, and the pitter-patter sound of gentle rain could be heard landing on the stone patio outside.

"We come to invite you, oh lord, Ce Acatl Topiltzin –

"to *challenge* you to a sacred game."

Threads of blue-white light seemed to radiate through the crystal spear and the black gourd rattle began to stir. At the same moment, thunder rumbled in the sky above.

"If we accept this challenge," said Ce Acatl Topiltzin, "what will you give us if we win the game?" for Ce Acatl Topiltzin, King of Tula, was known far and wide for his excellence in the ball court of *ullama*.

"Well that depends," the brother of the crystal spear said.

"On what you, oh Mighty Lord, are willing to bestow upon us if we win," the other brother finished.

"Ha!" laughed Ce Acatl proudly, for no one had ever defeated him in the sacred game. He exuberantly added with all confidence, "If you win I will bestow upon you my most precious stones and my green quetzal crowns."

Whereby the brothers then said,

"It is well, oh lord. If you defeat us –

"We will give unto you our most precious golden gems and our finest green feathers."

✂

It came to pass that the whole of the city of Tula bustled with preparations for a sacred ball court game. Neighbor told neighbor from rooftop to rooftop, "The king is to play *ullama* in ten days time!"

Structures were built around the rim of the court where the priests and *pipiltzin* could watch the game under cotton canopies shading them from the sun. Huge scaffoldings were erected behind these for the *macehuallis* who would have to sit on, or in most cases hang off, them to see the game. Tall poles were erected at each of the four corners of the court displaying giant flags that were woven from the very finest maguey paper and painted to honor the gods of the four winds. Behind the scaffolds, the Yollotli's grounds were set up with stalls for vendors. Streams and streams of cut paper hung between the stalls, filling the sky with vibrant colors and festive cheer.

The court itself was cut out of the earth below ground level. A long central alley, where the players would commence the game, was flanked by two inclining walls down the entire length of the court that ascended to almost the height of the outside walls. As the game progressed, teams would run up these inclined walls, passing the ball back and forth between them. At the top of the lengthwise walls, and in the very middle of the court, there were two protruding giant rings, one black and one white, about the length of a man's outstretched arm. The object of the game, very simply, was to pass the ball through the ring. At the ends of the central alley, and running perpendicular to the court, there were two smaller open alleys, where teams could entrap each other in the midst of play for added humiliation or prestige.

Families celebrated private rituals in the days before the game, and priests of the Order of Quetzalcoatl were sent out through the city to sweep out peoples' homes in a gesture of servitude and humility. People gave the priests toasted maize cobs and again decorated their doors, lined their streets with flowery arches and displayed their family crests outside their homes with banners and flags. Some had butterflies, others wolves and jaguars, and others still, turtles, turkeys or stags.

Nightly there was celebration and joy. There was music and laughter and dancing and song, all of which was intertwined with reverence and prayer to the gods, especially Quetzalcoatl, diviner of creation who lives in the nine heavens above. The people would pray, "Come you, divine inhabitant, deity of the holy breath and the divine winds, infinite being of the four directions. Come you, the one from the highest heavens, and illuminate our spirits, Lord Quetzalcoatl, come and rule over the Nine Winds!"

✠

On the day of the game, people began to gather around the court, priests and nobles sitting on padded chairs under their shade and commoners filling the scaffolding behind them. Above the white ring on the far side sat Huemac, the aged first general, with his two daughters Calli and Tonalnan. Their shade structure was draped with sheets of white cotton gauze, studded with golden rings. At their feet surrounding them on blankets spread out on the ground were the rest of Tohuenyo's wives and his multitude of children.

Tohuenyo's first-born daughter, Quetzalpétatl, was among them. Her jade-green eyes had set her apart at her birth, and since then she had devoted herself in body and spirit to the devotion of the gods as a temple virgin and priestess in training. She was a favorite of the people and had the adoration of her king. Ce Acatl called her Little Sister, and often lavished exquisite gifts upon her. When she was little, the king had even been known to eat at Tohuenyo's table stone and spend hours instructing her upon his knee about ancient prophecies and tales of heroes of days gone by.

The *nahuallis* had a tent of their own, covered in feathered tapestries that had been brought from the private lodgings of Ce Acatl Topiltzin. The ground inside was covered in animal skins and soft, furry pillows, and did not have chairs to sit upon, but like the other nobles, they had a table laden with delectable fruits, roasted grasshoppers, chocolate covered ants and exotic beverages.

Zolton's tent was not far from Huemac's, and it too, was teeming with his much expanded family. As royal architect and chief engineer, he had amassed great fortunes after the completion of the Pyramid of the Sun; lavish properties and estates had been bestowed upon him by the king. In honor of Tonatiuh, god of the Sun, the gauze drapes of his shade structure were vibrant blue,

[352]

delicately brocaded with golden suns. Tonalnan had overseen the execution of the weaving herself.

Cuilton's tent was farther down the length of the court and was covered with green cotton gauze with brocaded yellow maize cobs, as he was still agricultural engineer. On the other side of Huemac was the ever so wealthy Lord Ozomatli, still chief *pochteca* of the Cintéotl Clan and Controller of Trade. The fabric of his shade structure was bright yellow embedded with black obsidian beads. He now had two wives of his own, the most recent of a very tender age so that the people questioned his scruples and gossiped behind his back.

The high ranking priests and other nobles aligned the extent of the far side of the court along the white-ring side, filling up their colorful stalls, laughing jubilantly in expectation of the impending feat. The scaffoldings behind the stalls were filled with the servants and slaves who attended the priestly and noble class.

On the Yollotli side of the court, the side of the black ring, sat a multitude of new arrivals, foreigners, the lesser-knowns, and those whose new-found wealth didn't include titles, properties or estates. Their shade structures, for those who had them, were crude and lacked color, being assembled with dull mats and dried grasses. As was custom, one noble who had been elected by the high council was in their midst – Xolotl – to give credence to the appearance that the Toltec nobility was on the side of the people. Xolotl's tent, covered in black tapestries and encrusted with red gems, had been set up right above the black ring, directly across from his wife and her family. He sat in his warlord regalia proud and straight, with his hands firmly upon his knees. At his side sat an unknown foreigner, someone he had befriended at the House of Joy, and while the unknown man was dressed in the vestments of nobility – black cotton tunic, clustered, waist-length coral beads, leather sandals, shoulder length hair – the man had not the refined demeanor of a noble upbringing.

Farther down the court on the black-ring side was the only other elaborately covered structure. It shaded the women of the House of Joy. It was covered with tapestries of flowers that had been painstakingly woven into maguey-fiber lattices. The carefree women inside the structure, their teeth seductively stained red, were scantily clad, bejeweled, and smelled of spices and perfume. Messengers and slaves discretely streamed to the back of their tent, bringing them small gifts and favors to guarantee preferential treatment and reserve appointments for their masters.

The other shaded tents on the black-ring side were cruder structures housing mid-level artisans, market vendors, mining administrators, *pochteca* tradesmen, weapons masters, over-seers of the pottery guild and the like. Everyone in the realm was allowed to attend the *ullama* game, so that the scaffolding on the black-ring side was quickly filling with laborers, field workers, foreigners and slaves, cheering and rowdy in excited anticipation of seeing their king.

Tonalnan looked across the court and caught her brother-in-law Xolotl's eye, offering an aloof nod as an appropriate gesture of acknowledgement. "Who is that unknown who sits with your husband?" she asked her sister, Calli.

"I know not, younger sister," the elder replied.

Standing behind the foreigner there was a hooded, ancient man hunched over a quivering cane that had a snakehead handle with black obsidian eyes. While the ancient man was hooded in a spotted leopard cloak, she could see singe-tipped eagle feathers and a multitude of amulets hanging from his loose, white hair. He wore a bear claw necklace and anklets of seedpod bells. His hooded leopard cloak had rattling snake tails sewn around the edges, and his face was dusted completely white except for a black ash band across his eyes, exaggerating his high cheekbones and beak-like nose.

A chill ran down Tonalnan's spine.

"Over there, dear Chac," she whispered, "I see a sorcerer standing among them," but when she looked back he was gone.

A band at the far end of the court began to play - flutes, whistles, ocarinas, rattles and drums – lively ghost songs recounting tales of famous heroes and battles between the gods.

The sun approached its zenith in the cloudless sky.

A commotion stirred at the other end of the court as the players approached. Then, in an exuberant craze, everyone cheered and roared as four players climbed down the walls and into the central alley. They paraded around, with arms raised high, showing off their mighty strength and power. They were elaborately dressed in high

[354]

headdresses and exotic capes, their faces and bodies painted black with white skeletal bones. Bones were the symbol of the creation of humanity in the Fifth Sun, and for this reason the players donned not only death masks, but had their whole bodies painted like skeletons, as well.

The band played excitedly, while fans from both sides threw flowers of all kinds down upon the parading players.

Then, in a silent remission, Lord Quetzalcoatl raised his hands in prayer. The crowd fell silent.

"Good people of Tula!" the king bellowed, "We gather here today before the gods to honor them through what mortal strength we may!"

The crowd was still, heads reverently bowed. Only Quetzalpétatl dared to cast her gaze upon the king during his prayer, a disobedience that occasioned a swift and bloodletting pinch from her mother.

Still dressed in full ceremonial attire, the king continued, "Oh father, Mixcóatl, slayer of the Obsidian Butterfly and protector of the Nonoalca-Toltec Nation, speak on our behalf to Cintéotl, our revered goddess of maize and all that is precious. Advocate on our behalf to The One for Whom We all Live so that we may continue to glorify the gods. Eh, White Tezcatlipoca, Quetzalcoatl! Eh, Black Tezcatlipoca Yayauhqui! We honor you as sons of Ometéotl the highest and most supreme god. You are the opposing twins, sustainers of movement through time. Blessed are the opposing forces of black and white. Blessed are the opposing forces of perfection and chaos. Blessed are the opposing forces of darkness and light!"

The crowds murmured, and slaves hurriedly began to clear the flowers from the court.

Ce Acatl Topiltzin then announced the three other players.

"Lord Tohuenyo!" The spectators went crazy with excitement and praise for their warrior hero and more streams of flowers flew into the court, whereby more slaves scurried to retrieve them. A couple of attendants removed Lord Tohuenyo's headdress and ritual vestments, revealing his painted body adorned only in a wide, leather-banded loincloth and sandals.

[355]

"And our guests," the king continued, "the sons of He Who Penetrates the Mother Who Sustains Us!"

People cheered.

As the slaves reverently removed the capes of the godly twins, the spectators cheered even more, for who could not be aroused at such an introduction? They too donned the painted death masks, and their bodies were painted to look like skeletons.

"And I, your mother, your most chaste and humble king. I vow to protect and watch over you, my children! May you suckle my breast for true guidance and knowledge and grow to prosper and thrive!" With that, Ce Acatl Topiltzin prostrated himself and kissed the ground. Upon disrobing, the king commanded, "Let the game begin!"

He was then handed a rubber ball the size of a human head, and the band resumed its lively playing.

The players took their positions and Ce Acatl slowly raised the ball to the heavens above. After reverently lowering it to the earth, he heaved it across the court to the twin brothers, commencing the game.

Once in play, the ball in *ullama* is never allowed to hit the ground, and must be volleyed between the teams by striking it with a hip, a foot, or a knee. Also, hands were forbidden to have contact with the ball. If such a move should occur, a wave of violent protests would break out among the crowds, replete with heckling and boos.

Ce Acatl and Tohuenyo played against the twin brothers for some time in the central alley and even managed to trap the brothers in their corner for several rounds, but were startled by an unusual sound of thunder that no one could explain as there was not a cloud in the sky. Then the king and his teammate were pushed back in a series of exchanges to the central alley.

Next the brothers began passing the ball to each other, which was also completely allowed. May the stronger team take control of the ball, and let the defending team try to take it away. The brothers then worked the ball up the incline toward the black ring, but try as they may, they were unable to protect it from being taken by Ce Acatl, who, in a magnificent athletic display, captured the ball with his foot and hoisted it backward, over his head to Tohuenyo standing below. Then he sprang down the incline to the middle of

[356]

the alley and was able to retrieve Tohuenyo's pass. They kept control of the ball this way for some time, and even managed to work themselves up the side of the incline toward the white ring, to the amusement of the raving fans above. As they approached the ring, the twin brothers struck them by surprise and washed away their moment of glory.

The game continued this way for some time, with exchanges of control of the ball, entrapments in corners of the court, and amazing displays of athletic feats.

Then, after what seemed like unending attempts by either team to insert the ball through their ring, Ce Acatl, from three-fourths the way down the central alley, slammed into the ball with his hip in a lengthy skid sending it high into the air, soaring toward the white ring where it spun several times in the center of the ring, and then jutted through, the penetration of the ring winning him the game.

Those who were sitting bolted to their feet and everyone hollered and cheered in a frenzied hysteria, ecstatic at the end result of the game.

Ce Acatl and Tohuenyo raised their arms in triumph.

Tonalnan turned to her sister and said, "Who are those lords, who so very nearly brought our king to defeat?" and her sister replied, "I do not know."

✖

The next day the twin brothers again appeared before the king. When Ce Acatl demanded his prize, they brought the accorded gifts, but instead of emeralds and pearls they presented him with grains of corn and instead of quetzal feather crowns, they laid before him the green leaves of maize.

"We offer you – "

"the most precious jewels of our kingdom, oh great king." they said.

Ce Acatl stared at the heap in dismay. "Is this what I have won?" he asked indignantly. "These are not precious gems and fine feathers. I will not accept these! You are liars!"

Upon hearing this the twin brothers had their maize and corn leaves removed where they were cast away in a hidden spring.

[357]

They then addressed the king and said,
"If that is what you wish, oh Lord Ce Acatl Topiltzin –
"We rescind our golden gems and green feathers."
They admonished him for his hubris.
"Go you now from the eternal springs to the dessert, –
"and walk among the thorns."
"Your kingdom shall wither, its children will mourn -
"You will plead for water and scavenge for corn.
"We, the sons of Tlaloc promise you this, oh prince! –
"Misfortune will be yours for years to come!"
With this, the Sons of Tlaloc disappeared.

Victory Festivities

The victory celebration was a grand event, held in the great hall of the Palace of Previous Kings. Tohuenyo had graciously agreed to host the event, and the whole of the Toltec nobility had been invited, as well as nobles and statesmen from provinces throughout the empire.

Ce Acatl was seated at a far end of the great hall, on a gem-incrusted throne-like chair with a giant bejeweled snake's head rising from the back of it. As visitors came, they paid their respects to the king by kissing his feet and leaving precious gifts and tribute before him, so that soon, the stone floors around him filled up with exquisite woven trunks filled with treasures and jewels, great urns of the finest the fields had to offer, piles of textiles and pottery from far away lands, *petlacalli* baskets filled with obsidian from the mines of Cacamilhuacan in the snowy Xinantécatl Mountains and rubber from the distant forests of Yucatan. There were even gifts of pearls, shells and dried hippocampus and other sea creatures from the ethereal waters at the ends of Cem Anahuac.

By mid afternoon the Palace of Previous Kings was filled with people from many lands, speaking all sorts of languages and dialects.

"Hail to our king, Ce Acatl Topiltzin!" They cheered, and raised their goblets in admiration.

They lounged and visited, listened to music and poetry, strolled about the palace admiring the giant murals and tapestries covering the walls, and strutted through the gardens, fiercely displaying their finest wardrobes of the latest cottons, the rarest feathers, the tiniest bone beads, the most fiery opals, and the highest and most elaborate hairstyles or head coverings. They ate and drank, discussed anything there was to talk about, and ate and drank even more.

"The king is the object of perfection," they said in their conversations. "We must strive to be more like him."

[359]

"He truly is the incarnation of Quetzalcoatl!" others claimed.

The people loved and adored their king, Ce Acatl Topiltzin.

Except for a very few, for off in an obscure corner, the seed of the voice of dissent was germinating.

"Tohuenyo, my brother!" Xolotl exclaimed, slightly bowing to his host and the Madam Tonalnan. Despite his hatred for Tohuenyo, the son of Nauhyotl was not about to jeopardize his position as successor to Huemac due to negligence of social formalities. He was surrounded by his wife and entourage. "Let me introduce you to my dear friend." It was the same man who had sat at his side at the *ullama* game. "This is Ichtaca of the Red Ant Clan."

Lord Tohuenyo grasped the dear friend's forearms in a formal embrace, and the two men stood intensely fixed upon each other's gaze while a lifetime of memories passed between them.

"So nice to meet you," Tohuenyo lied. "Welcome! Welcome to my home."

They spoke of inoffensive trivialities until Xolotl's entourage dispersed out of boredom.

"Leave us." Xolotl snapped at his wife, Calli. He had long since soured toward his wife for cursing him with a useless, dawdling, flute-playing whelp of a son.

"Sister, I shall show you the butterfly gardens," Tonalnan graciously said, steering her away.

"So, brother," Tohuenyo said to Xolotl. "Where did you *really* meet this Ichtaca of the Red Ant Clan?"

Xolotl and Ichtaca laughed boisterously.

"We share a common interest, you might say," Xolotl answered, "in the House of Joy." What he refrained from saying was, *often simultaneously*.

The men held their laughter so as not to draw more attention upon themselves.

"Yes, I see," said Tohuenyo, feigning naïveté. For he had long since known that Xolotl frequented the House of Joy to the great suffering of his devout wife. Many *pipiltzin* men found the talents of Madam Yellow Skirt's courtesans too irresistible to deny.

"How many children do you have now, Lord Tohuenyo?" Xolotl asked in an effort to sway the conversation, lest it turn lewd.

"Ah my man! You ask your brother such a difficult question, for I cannot keep count, but that my first wife, Tonalnan has only one. My first-born, the daughter with green eyes." He touched his lips with a kiss, indicating his love for the child. "But the gods seem intent on keeping that female from germinating my seed." He hesitated, reflecting on memories of days gone by. "I long ago gave up trying with that female... but my other wives? Now they are sumptuous and fertile indeed! I must say that I have upwards of forty children between the rest of them!"

"Lucky man!" Ichtaca said, slapping Tohuenyo on the shoulder in an unexpected display of familiarity.

"Well it is no secret that I have but two," said Xolotl. "And you, Ichtaca? How many do you have?" he truly was curious, for he had never asked this of his intimate friend.

"Well now, gentlemen," Ichtaca said, clearing his throat. "It has been my fate in this life to be the consort to the queen of my people, a beautiful but aging woman who, when I first joined with her, had but one son."

A dagger of melancholy pierced Tohuenyo's heart.

"Soon the queen gave herself over entirely to her medicine and sorcery. She tired of me and cut me loose, so I found refuge in the folds of disgraced women's skirts. And here I am, your lords." He bowed his head in subtle subordination. "Surely I have little bastards running through the streets of Tula by now, but none that I would claim as mine own," he added whispering.

"And the queen's son? Asked Xolotl, for now his curiosity was piqued.

"Ah, alas. She sent her son away, Lord Xolotl, so that he may spread her teachings and mysteries throughout the land. She sent him on a quest to conquer our enemies, who claim false wealth and deny us of our birthright."

"How intriguing my friend," Xolotl interjected. "Tell me more..."

"The heart of her son went astray, Lord Xolotl, for instead of bringing back the severed head of the enemy king, he married a princess of that evil realm." Ichtaca was now staring directly into Tohuenyo's eyes.

"Treacherous!" Xolotl exclaimed.

[361]

Then Ichtaca added, "But my queen pines for her long-lost son. I'm sure that if he were to return to her she would hastily forgive his transgressions, for she loves him so."

Ichtaca was the only one that noticed that a tear swelled and fell out of Tohuenyo's eye.

Satisfied that he got his point across, Ichtaca changed the subject. He turned to Xolotl and said, " Gentlemen, I wonder if we are not incurring the wrath of the gods upon us."

"Really man," said Xolotl. "Whatever do you mean?"

Ichtaca lowered his voice. "I have it on good word that the king's opponents were the Sons of Tlaloc and that he refused their gifts as being unworthy."

"What did they offer?" Tohuenyo asked, relieved that the conversation had turned.

"I heard they offered him grains of maize instead of precious stones, and the green leaves of corn instead of cherished feathers."

"Why that's deplorable!" said Xolotl, indignantly.

"The king was incensed at the worthlessness of their reward and refused their gift." Ichtaca added.

"As any man would," asserted Tohuenyo in defense of the king.

"Don't you *see*?" insisted Ichtaca. "They had their precious stones and fine feathers taken away and cursed the king for his pride."

Tohuenyo and Xolotl were silent.

Ichtaca was now emphatically whispering. "The Sons of Tlaloc have been insulted and will withhold their pluvial bounty."

Just then Madam Tonalnan approached, laughing in merriment. "My Lord, more guests have arrived and we must greet them."

"Of course! Gentlemen, please excuse me. Xolotl, my brother, so good to see you again." He turned to Ichtaca. "Nice to meet you," he lied.

Tohuenyo then addressed his first wife and said sincerely, "Lovely Lady, I shall follow you. I will go wherever you go," but his sweet affections for her were of a spiritual nature, for with the taking of additional wives, his lust for her had waned. He took her elbow and walked away, raising his goblet to his guests in honor of the king's success, but in his heart, doubt mingled with his joy and a bitter longing prevailed.

[362]

Ichtaca then whispered in Xolotl's ear, "Surely Tezcatlipoca will seize this moment for revenge. Whose side will you be on?"

The Wood Porter

Now it came to pass the following year that Tlacatl, son of Calli and Xolotl, had reached his manhood years and often took it upon himself to leave the city to wander the forest and play his flute. He was a slender fellow, of slight build and delicate mannerisms, and carefree in his thoughts and intentions.

One day, Tlacatl went into the hills away from the city to play his flute and enjoy the fresh breezes and sounds of nature under the golden sun. He found a boulder next to a receding stream, where he played whimsical melodies surrounded by a chorus of birds.

"You there! Young Toltec!" a rough and scratchy, ancient voice interrupted.

Tlacatl stopped his playing and turned around to find an ancient porter dressed in nothing more than a loincloth and a bear claw necklace, loaded with a *petlacalli* basket on his back that was strapped around his forehead. The basket was filled with kindling, and Tlacatl supposed he was on his way to market in Tula.

"Grandfather," Tlacatl said in a welcoming tone, "salutations to you this fine day."

The ancient porter stood there staring at him and sniffed, leaning on his walking staff.

"What relief can you provide for a weary old man, my son?" the porter asked.

Tlacatl passed the elder his deerskin bag of maguey honey water. The fertile juice that comes from the plant is greatly nourishing before it ferments and turns to *pulque* wine.

The ancient grandfather took the bag with a shaky, bony hand and drank freely. When he was done, he wiped his dripping, toothless mouth with the back of his hand and stared at Tlacatl with penetrating eyes.

"My son, do you know Ce Acatl, the priest?" The ancient one asked.

[365]

"Why yes grandfather, he is our beloved king." The youth answered.

"My son, go to him at once and tell him that a great priest brings him a message from his father who now dwells in the land of the undead."

Tlacatl did not want this errand, for he suspected the ancient one to be a necromancer who communed with the dead. He protested, "I cannot do this deed that you ask, grandfather, for the king would never believe such an incredulous tale." Tlacatl thought himself courageous for his emboldened challenge.

Mysteriously the old man's black eyes began to glow. Pointing to the contents of his basket he said, "Not everything is as it seems, my son." With that, the ancient porter touched the wood, whereupon the branches began to quiver and move, turning into great snakes that slithered out of the basket and fell to the ground. The ancient porter quickly stabbed one of the escaping snakes with his staff, and it immediately turned into a twisted wooden cane. The top of the cane was an intricately carved snakehead with black obsidian eyes.

White with fear, Tlacatl leapt to his feet and ran away to tell the Toltec king that he had encountered a necromancer with a message from Mixcóatl, the king's long-dead father.

Ce Acatl's advisor's were suspicious and cautioned him insistently, "You must not go, venerated priest. It might go badly for you. It could be an ambush, or even worse, you might be bewitched by sorcery or trickery!"

But the king's curiosity had been whetted and his decision was made.

On the day Twelve Monkey, they returned to the boulder next to the receding stream. They found the ancient porter dressed in nothing more than a loincloth and a bear claw necklace, loaded with a *petlacalli* basket on his back that was strapped around his forehead. The basket was filled with kindling. Ce Acatl and his entourage supposed he was on his way to market in Tula.

Ce Acatl approached the decrepit creature and said, "Little grandfather, I am told that you bring me a message from my father, Mixcóatl the king."

The old wood porter looked at the king and with a toothless grin answered, "Beware, priestly king, for whilst you fast in seclusion and prayer, your enemies feast at your abandoned table, devouring your empire's greatest banquet – the loyalties of her people."

On hearing this, Ce Acatl was dismayed and his heart became heavy and burdened.

While returning to the city a two-headed deer crossed the path of the king and stared at him before bounding off into the woods. It left Ce Acatl with a grave foreboding that the workers of darkness were stirring their evil brew.

Sisters of Zapotlán

One night, as was often his custom, Ce Acatl ventured off, accompanied by his personal guards, to his own private temple under the stars. He wore his usual black robe, and his long hair draped freely around his body. As was his custom, he would reverently bathe himself, but on this occasion, another year had passed and still there was no rain.

Instead, he ceremoniously dusted himself with the soft sedimentary sand of the dry riverbed, unabashedly naked beneath the admiring moon. In his nakedness on such a dark night he was at his most vulnerable against the night creatures or sorcerers who might cast demonic afflictions upon him. His two guards stood watch, and knowing this comforted him.

In the middle of his ritual dusting, he could hear the whispers of feminine voices.

"Who goes there?" the king calmly said. Walking with the grace and confidence of nobility, he cloaked himself in his free fitting tunic once again. He pulled his long, graying hair out from under his tunic and flipped it behind his shoulder.

Two modestly dressed women humbly approached him, heads covered with shawls, eyes cast down. They took tiny steps to show their humility, but Ce Acatl's two guards rushed up to impede them, crossing their obsidian spears to block their way.

"We are thy servants, oh gracious king, sisters traveling from Zapotlán. We have come to thee to beg thy counsel and deliver unto thee a great message from our lord," they said. As the women made no aggression toward him, he beckoned his guards to lower their spears.

"I cannot receive you here, fair maids," the king replied, "for you must request an audience at my palace." Upon which, the twin sisters dropped to their knees and clasped their hands. Faces wet with tears, they pleaded, "Oh fair and just king, we beg thee to receive us that we may deliver our sacred message!"

Because of their desperation, the king took pity on them and acquiesced. "Very well then, on the morrow I shall receive you at the Palace of Quetzalcoatl. Let my witnesses be my guards, who, on tomorrow's day will grant you entrance and escort you in."

The sisters thanked him profusely.

"Now be off! Both of you! I am to continue my penitence in solitude. Your womanly essence is not welcome here!"

With that, the cloaked sisters clambered to their feet and scurried away.

That night in his private temple, as he passed a cactus thorn through his foreskin, collected the sacred blood, and presented it to the gods in burnt offering, Ce Acatl prayed for strength to maintain his chastity. As high priest of his people, it was expected of him, as chastity was considered sacred and divine. He was unspoiled, a virgin, and his purity was what inspired his people to follow the teachings of Quetzalcoatl, son of Ometéotl, God on High. He must be strong. He must remain chaste. He was the Mother of the Toltecs, and their welfare depended on his leading by example.

✻

It so happened that the next day there was a *tianguis* market in the Yollotli. The city center was bustling with people and activity as merchants sold their wares, music of drum circles resonated, and smells floated through the air from smoky fires at food stalls. Madam Tonalnan and her sister, Madam Calli, sat on the steps of the Palace of Quetzalcoatl, conversing, as they did every market day at the end of their stroll through the displays. They were both elaborately dressed, laden with jewels and decadent headpieces, as was customary of their matronly station. Andoeni and Tohuenyo's other wives sat around them.

"I wish it would rain," said Madam Calli to her sister, cooling herself with a dessert owl fan.

At midday, when the sun was at its zenith in the sky, a commotion stirred in the market place. The two women could see a throng of people crowding around something, but they knew not who or what it was. Before they had time to speculate, two lascivious sirens broke out of the crowds at the bottom of the stairs.

[370]

The concupiscent nymphs were clad in nothing more than nipple-concealing jewelry and a narrow strip of decorative beads fastened by a golden chain at the waist. Their voluminous black hair crowned them in undulating curls and waves. They were twins.

The noblewomen stared in disdain at the spectacle.

"We've come for our audience with the king," One of them said seductively.

Women throughout the crowd gasped in shock and men grabbed their enlarging loins.

One of the guards at the door to the palace came forward to the top of the stairs.

"Eh-hem," he cleared his throat, and looking straight out to the horizon said stiffly, "The king will not receive you. He is otherwise engaged."

One enchantress insisted, "Yes, he will receive us, sir. Just last night he promised to grant us an audience. Go and ask him." Her impertinence sent a wave of shock through the crowd.

Indignantly, the guard turned and disappeared through the palace archway. A buzz of gossip flew through the crowd like a chain reaction. In a few moments, he returned with one of the king's private guards.

Ce Acatl's private guard studied their faces, and much to his chagrin, had to admit that these were the very same women whom his lord and master had agreed to receive the night before. "The whore speaks the truth," he said. "Stand down."

With that, the twins slithered into the Palace of Quetzalcoatl and stained its purity with their sinful presence in front of scores of shocked, Toltec onlookers. The day was Nine Wind.

Inside the Hall of Judgment, Ce Acatl Topiltzin Quetzalcoatl sat behind a cotton screen at the top of the stairs amidst an array of small candles, casting his silhouette onto the screen. The shadows of the exquisite, long tail feathers of his headdress swayed across the screen as he moved. The women approached the bottom of the stairs and prostrated themselves before the king, touching their foreheads to the stone floor, a gesture that was very hard for the guards behind them to endure.

[371]

"So now it is apparent that you have ensnared your king into receiving you, - *You*, who are not worthy to sit before your king," the gentle voice from behind the mask reprimanded.

The women writhed on hands and knees on the floor, looking up toward Ce Acatl Topiltzin.

"Speak!"

The twins sat erect with their feet folded properly under them. The one who had not spoken yet then addressed her king in a voice of honey that sounded like a morning dove, "Son of Mixcóatl, we bring a message from Tezcatlipoca, Lord of the Here and Now. We are to inform you that a sacred resting place is awaiting you in Tlillan Tlapallan, where you are to die."

Ce Acatl was not alarmed or frightened by this news, as he had already seen this and much more in his visions during penance and meditation.

"The heavens and the stars have told me what they may," he replied. What he did not tell them was that the heavens and the stars had told him that he must leave within four years.

He then commanded the whores to leave his presence, but instead of taking them back outside to the marketplace, his thirsty guards took them to an inner chamber where they eagerly dumped all of their earnings into the whore's purses and all of their *xinachtli* into their vessels.

What the all-seeing Ce Acatl didn't know, however, was that the twin sisters from Zapotlán had received their message from a stranger at the House of Joy. They'd been employed there for quite some time, under the tutelage of the head mistress, Madam Yellow Skirt. At the House of Joy they often entertained the warlord Xolotl and his closest companion, a foreigner named Ichtaca. One night, when the four of them were feasting on delicacies and wine, an ancient sorcerer named Titlacáhuan arrived. He was evil and vile, and did as he pleased, with no one able to stop him, for his black magic was too great and his dark sorcery too powerful. He oftentimes committed abominable acts against men and women, even beasts and children. After sodomizing the succulent twins with the two stupefied men looking on while polishing their maize cobs, he breathed his evil breath upon the courtesans, bewitching them to send Tezcatlipoca's death message to the king.

[372]

"I am the incarnation of the Black Tezcatlipoca!" He screamed victorious. "The Dark Mother, She Who Destroys Men's Souls, Guardian of the Infernal Flames!

Ichtaca had then collapsed at the necromancer's feet and kissed the bottom of his robe.

With an exploding blue light, the evil sorcerer Titlacáhuan vanished into thin air.

Weaving New Designs

The courtyard of the Palace of Previous Kings had long since been taken over by Tonalnan's weaving guild. The back strap looms that she'd used after her marriage were replaced with warp weighted vertical looms that lined the walls under the porticos. There were stations for pulling the fibers through stone rollers to remove the seeds as well as areas for spinning thread with distaffs and spindles.

Through the years she had managed to increase the wealth of her household with the obedient and loyal help of her sister wives. Her husband's taking of more wives had proved fruitful. They were her most intimate companions. They were her clan. They shared feelings, thoughts and ideas. They ate together. They laughed together. They cried together. They nurtured each other in times of pain, quarreled with each other, then reconciled and gave each other gifts and did each other favors. They collaborated to provide nourishment, protection and education for their brood. But as far as Tonalnan was concerned, thank the Mother Goddess that they were also passionately cooperative in her textile production. Yaretzi and Anayel from Teotenanco were especially talented in spinning and weaving, having received a most excellent education as daughters of a king. Through the years they contributed wholeheartedly to Tonalnan's endeavor.

As youngest wife, Xochitl from Jiquipilco oversaw the management of the servants who attended all their children, and a formidable task it was. With the exception of Tonalnan, who only had her one child, the lovely Quetzalpétatl with green eyes, Tohuenyo's other wives had borne between six and twelve children each - a prolific household indeed!

Because of her knowledge of secret herbs and medicines, Tonalnan had managed to force sterility upon herself, an act that had distanced her husband, but freed her to a life of independence and financial enterprise. Emotionally he was in love with her as much as ever, but he could not reason planting his seed where it would not grow. As such, it was his four other beautiful and adoring wives that he brought unto him. Tonalnan, his first wife, was his matriarch, his woman of wisdom and power. She was the one he shared his world with: political conspiracies, courtly intrigues, matters of state, prospects of war. She listened to him with acute understanding of the ways of the world. He paid heed to her intuitive and judicious counsel, as it always brought him favorable outcomes.

Together with her sister wives, Tonalnan had elevated the production of the weaving guild to a fierce, competitive merchant network. They sent their wares to the farthest corners of the realm. Although she did not dominate the textile trade throughout the One World, she controlled a significant part.

The day after the spectacle in the market with the lascivious courtesans, the noble women of Tohuenyo's household stood working at the warp weight vertical looms and sat diligently cleaning, spinning and dying their never ending supply of cotton. No one wanted to be so vulgar as to broach this crude subject, even though they were privately burning up with impatience, so they worked silently, listening only to the soft music of Tlacatl's enchanting flute and the sounds of their many children echoing throughout the palace walls.

"Oh I just can't stand it any more! I've got to say that I think it not proper or right for the king to have received them," said Madam Calli indignantly.

The other women responded with "ohs" and "ahs" and sighs of relief that someone finally put into words what everyone was thinking.

"And to show up naked!" Anayel said. She was sitting down spinning and shifted the weight of her full term belly as she struggled to pull the spindle to and fro while a toddler stood suckling at her breast.

"To think of our beloved king putting his –"

"Hush Andoeni!" Madam Tonalnan interrupted. "There will be no talk like that in this house, lest you blaspheme!"

The women fell silent and Tonalnan noticed that Andoeni was, as usual, far behind the others. While Andoeni supported the work of the guild wholeheartedly, she always struggled to keep up with

[376]

the other expertly skilled women. No matter. Quality prevailed over quantity.

Calli worked swiftly and diligently at a loom, separating the warp threads with a long, flat paddle that would be twisted to open them, allowing passage of the shuttles containing the different colors of thread. The conversation had caused her to go red in the face as though she were burning up with pent up passions. Everyone knew that her husband had long ago forsaken her and left her bed. He spent most of his nights in the House of Joy.

"Well if our priests can have carnal exploits with *whores*, why not with *us*, the most beautiful flowers of his realm?" Andoeni boldly said.

Most of the women gasped at the thought, but Madam Calli slyly caught her eye.

"Do not his actions imply that the priests of this realm are prepared to love their daughters?"

The women all held their tongues, but Andoeni could tell that Madam Calli was lending her attention.

"Our priests are *chaste*, Andoeni, and this makes their hearts free from *sin* and therefore *pure*! Speak of it no further!" Madam Tonalnan commanded.

Andoeni then went over and whispered something in Madam Calli's ear. Madam Calli smiled and nodded her head.

⁂

Not long after, women of higher status began frequenting the temples of their gods and goddesses more often. Their offerings became more and more elaborate. Where traditional offerings had always been sweet confections, baskets of maize cobs, or jars of seeds, the new trend among the *pipiltzin* noblewomen was to leave bolts of brocaded fabrics, gold jewelry encrusted with jewels, obsidian mirrors and *pulque*. The women were engaging in much longer visits, with their personal guards posted at the temple doors. Screams of ecstasy could be heard coming from within, but everyone insisted that the women were dancing in an enlightened trance, communing with the gods. The Toltec noblewomen would never incite their priests to acts of transgression! Or would they? As time went by, the priests' demeanor changed very notably from their usual solemnity to a constant state of euphoria.

The new pretense of religious fervor continued to such an extent that it finally came to a head. It so happened that one of the zealous women frequenting the temples was a virgin of the royal house named Mayel, a very noble princess close to the king. During a celebration of the anniversary of Mazapa, she solicited a beautiful monk named Huitzli and together their passions led them into the fires of forbidden knowledge. Their immorality continued for quite some time. As a consequence of their sin, she became pregnant and gave birth to a disfigured and misshapen creature covered in hair. They named the boy Colotl, and hid him away in a temple in shame.

Despite the nobility's efforts to hide the disgrace, everyone knew, for the scandal of their promiscuity flew between friends and family, across backyard walls and through neighborhoods, until it was known all about town.

Ce Acatl recognized the part he had played in the unfolding of these unholy acts. His heart was heavy and for the first time he began to doubt his ability to effectively rule his empire. He began to turn his duties over to his First Administrator, Lord Tohuenyo, more and more, and retreat to his secluded chambers or his beloved Pyramid of Coral northwest of town. He spent his time in prayer and meditation, and only left his rooms for his nightly penance at the river, or to go to the *ullama* court where he would quietly pray.

Life's great Wheel of Fortune was spinning, taking the Toltecs on its descent. And still, it did not rain.

The Jadestone Prophecy

Tonalnan heard a woman's bloodcurdling scream in the black pitch of night. She was frozen, unable to move, and the scream got louder and louder. Then she noticed it was coming from her own throat, even though in the absolute darkness she still could not move. Just when she felt like the sound was going to suffocate her, she awoke with a start, sitting straight up on her sleeping mat. She hadn't screamed at all, it appeared. She was shaking and covered with sweat. Nervously she recounted the phases of her dream.

"I have to tell the king," she whispered to herself in the dark. "I must tell him. I must away." She swiftly looked around, half crazed, not sure of what to do, grabbed her jadestone pouch, rose to her feet and ran through the sleeping palace in nothing more than her night shift, sandaled feet and disheveled hair.

"Must...tell...the...king," she said to herself as she ran across the Yollotli toward the Palace of Quetzalcoatl. Maybe the king was in his sleeping chambers in town. She wasn't sure. Critters scurried away from her in the shadows and the stars shone brightly on this moonless night.

It seemed like it took forever to cross the desolate Yollotli, but she finally prodded her way up the palace steps. There was no guard. She passed through the central archway and into a great room, and veered down the left toward the king's private chambers. Ah. There was a guard at that door.

"Sister, how is it that thou comest about in such a state in the mid of night? What say thee?" the guard said.

"I must see the king, I implore you!" she demanded pushing up on him, her arms on his chest. "I beseech you good fellow, let me pass!"

"Madam, the king is not here. He is at the Pyramid of Coral northwest of town. If thou wishes I can – "

Before he could finish his sentence, she was off, running again like a madwoman in the dark of night.

She descended the stairs and ran past the Pyramid of Quetzalcoatl, then through the stone streets past the houses of the Toltec nobility.

"Must tell... no... this cannot be," she said to herself as she finally approached a hill at the edge of town. She could see a light in the far distance and reasoned that it was the fire basins at the bottom of the pyramid stairs. She ran, her sandaled feet pounding the dry earth, until she finally reached the circular Pyramid of Coral.

Two priest-guards were asleep at the bottom of the stair. They had been playing a board game with stones and drinking mugs of *pulque*. A pair of giant fire basins at the bottom of the pyramid stair continued to burn brightly, their flames still fluctuating between blue, green and turquoise from the copper chloride that the priests had thrown in.

Tonalnan frantically passed the guards and ascended the stair, but on the fourth step the jadestone pouch dropped and rolled to the bottom of the stair into one of the sleeping priests below.

He woke with a start.

"What say you? Who goes there?" His companion then awoke as well.

Tonalnan had no time for them, much less state of mind to bother with them. She flew down, retrieved her jadestone pouch and scrambled back up the steps before they could shake off their *pulque* and pull themselves to their senses.

"Stop! In the name of the king! There goes a madwoman up to the sacred temple!" they yelled.

The guards at the top were thus alerted.

When Tonalnan reached the top of the pyramid, the two guards crossed their spears before her, blocking her from the entrance.

"Please!" she begged, tears streaming down her pallid face. "I must see the king! I must relay to him the vision of my dream!" She fell in a crumpled heap and started sobbing uncontrollably.

"What is all this chaos outside my temple door?" said the gentlest of voices.

Tonalnan looked up and saw Ce Acatl before her, standing unmasked and in a solid white tunic, holding aside the black curtain door. Inside the room she could see the secrets of his inner sanctuary illuminated by the radiant glow of candle bowls.

[380]

The king came out and the black curtain dropped behind him. She wasn't supposed to witness the secrets of his inner chamber and the guards were prepared to execute her for her transgression.

Ce Acatl motioned for the guards to stand down and they immediately returned to their positions of attention on either side of his temple door.

"Gentle noblewoman, just look at you," he said endearingly. He picked her up and moved her to the top of the pyramid stairs where he sat by her side and smoothed her hair. Despite her years and her present condition, she was still a handsome woman. She sniffled in an attempt to compose herself. The demeanor of the king was such that it had an immense calming effect on all those who came into his presence.

She came to her senses and scurried down several steps to his feet.

"Forgive me, Exalted One, for I have sinned. I have come to thee unannounced in ever such a frantic state." She kissed the bottom of his robe and he put his hand upon her head. It was no secret that the king loved Tonalnan above all others. He sat down on the top stair.

"Gentle Sister," he said, pulling her up to sit on the step just beneath him, "I'm sure you have good reason to risk incurring the wrath of your king." He smiled down at her as she looked up at him through her tears. Then he held her face in his hands and softly kissed the top of her head.

She sighed deeply.

"It was a dream, My Lord," she said. "I had a frightening vision in a dream."

"Tell me, Little Sister, what did you dream?"

"At first there were voices," she began, "voices from an ancestor from another world. It was terrifying, yet at the same time, there was nothing said to cause terror. But still I was so afraid! The ancient one in my dream said,

> 'In the midst of prosperity, the mind is elated, and a man forgets himself. Though in hardship, he is forced to reflect on himself, even though he be unwilling.'

"The voice was of an ancient king, but I know him not." She rubbed her crossed hands up and down her arms.

"Then I became a serpent. As I moved about the earth, writhing and slithering, I saw thy face My Lord, and thy image was that of the god Quetzalcoatl. Then I saw the complete destruction of our beloved city of Tula, of our empire and everything that we cherish and hold dear. It all went up in flames and there was nothing left but ash."

This was most disturbing, and Ce Acatl sat perfectly motionless, still holding Tonalnan's head against him.

"But that's not all, My Lord. I heard another ancient voice just then. It said,

'Men are quick to curse the gods for their pains and agony, but they refuse to relinquish their destructive ways. Behold, the end of the world is near. There will be signs in the sun and the moon and the stars. The people of the One World will be beset by drought, by floods, and by plagues. The earth will come down from the sky. Be on your guard, for total destruction is near.'

"That is the best that I can remember, My Lord. May the Ancient Goddess help us noble king! I fear the end of days is near!"

By this time Ce Acatl was sitting two steps below Tonalnan with his hands clasped around hers. She still clutched the pouch with the jadestone.

"Sweet sister, this is a prophecy, indeed," he said. "Now then, what have we here?"

Tonalnan emptied the pouch into his hands and the egg-shaped jadestone started to glow.

The king looked at her in wonder.

"In the face of calamity and destruction one must hold steadfast to love. I am sure of it, Little Sister. I have heard this in my prayers. Love is the conduit of divinity, which is our connection to the Earth, our Divine Mother, and everything that is good," he said.

[382]

The jadestone burned with brilliant green light, a beacon of hope amidst a sea of dread.

"It's like this jadestone here in the middle of this dark night. It radiates with the bright face of God even though it is surrounded by darkness. This is where Quetzalcoatl dwells. I am sure of it."

He smiled up at her radiantly.

"We must keep that radiance here, in our hearts, for if we step out into the darkness, even for one moment, we may become entangled in its malicious snare."

He continued, "Evil is contagious. It grows and passes from one person to another. If you allow the seed of an evil thought to enter your heart, another can come and nurture it with wickedness and lies. Beware! This is how the Queen of Ignorance cultivates Evil, so that soon it grows like an unstoppable vine and will take over nations."

Tonalnan hung her head, bereft of any happy thoughts at that moment. "How can thou beest so holy at a time like this?" she accused. Then her passions got the better of her. "We are almost four winters without rain! The sun has burned up all the fields! The corn and fruits have withered and died! Ometéotl's wrath is falling upon us and thou speakest of Love! The people are in agony. They spend the night with nothing to eat and when morning arises there is nothing for them except dust. Families are leaving in search of water and food, only to find the rotting carcasses of fallen beasts whose bones whither in the sun!"

On hearing such truths, Ce Acatl sunk his face down into his hands on the stair, and overwhelmed, he wept with sorrow and pain.

"When I was ten, my grandfather, Cipactonal, presented me with the inheritance of my mother's weapons," he said, his voice trembling. "'You are the keeper of good deeds and words, of the path of virtue, and of the tree of sustenance for all life,' he told me."

Ce Acatl composed himself and looked up at Tonalnan.

"He told me of the teachings of the ancient astrologer Hueman, who led our people out of darkness to the place of the seven caves, long before the time of my grandfather's grandfather. Hueman taught his disciples that since the dawn of time, there have always been grave persecutions from the heavens, but that afterwards there always follows a greater good. Great calamity, peril and suffering fall on the eve of all the golden ages of mankind.

He looked at her pleadingly and continued, "I fear your prophesy will come to pass, Little Sister, for in the midst of prosperity I did forget myself. Men will curse the Gods for their suffering and turn away from me."

The king raised his eyes to the stars. "Oh Mother God! He cried. Wrap me in the comfort of your cosmic womb, for this burden is too much to bear! The wise woman brings her prophesy that catastrophe is upon us."

Ce Acatl Topiltzin again faced Tonalnan, "If a man responds to violence and aggression with violence and aggression, he becomes his own antithesis. If I am to be the keeper of good deeds and follow the path of virtue, I must stay the course.

"I am to blame," he sighed. "I have offended the gods due to my own negligence and pride. I brought prosperity and morality to my people. I forgave them of their vices and sins, and brought them good laws and doctrine. But now I have incurred the wrath of Ometéotl, and my house will fall!"

And so it was that there, on the steps of the Pyramid of Coral, the king Ce Acatl Topiltzin sobbed lamentations of inconsolable grief.

Tonalnan let him have his cry. What else could she do? After what seemed like an eternity, the rosy dawn started to peek over the horizon and the king's weeping finally subsided.

"I will pray to the One For Whom We All Live," he stated at dawn.

That very day, Ce Acatl, his face distraught with torment, and clad in nothing more than a priest's black robe, walked to Tlaloc´s temple. There he instructed the priests to prepare the sanctuary for meditation and prayer. They immediately set to work filling the temple with fresh flowers, renewing the candle bowls, and smudging the area with incense and sage.

Inside the small temple the king sat before a stela of Tlaloc and prayed.

"Oh Deity," he said, "god of sustenance and giver of life. Take pity on the poor. Forgive thy children, for thy punishment is weighing heavy upon us. Scatter thy cinders and quench thy fires!

[384]

Oh, Sons of Tlaloc, spirits of the waters, come forth out of hiding from the corners of the world, from the underground caverns and mountains where you dwell!"

In this way Ce Acatl Topiltzin prayed for his people and his realm.

But still it did not rain.

Blood Sustenance

The High Chancellor Lord Tohuenyo had noticed of late that land disputes were increasing dramatically between the outlaying *altépetls* of the different clans. Just in the past month alone he'd had to preside over four territorial disputes. He was beginning to notice a trend. As the catastrophic drought progressed, villagers vied for lands with agave holdings, and recent border wars had emerged. In addition, reports were coming in of irregular thefts of agave and prickly pear cactus from the *axcaitls*, the landed estates of the nobility in the countryside.

One day Lord Tohuenyo decided to walk out to the Valley of Fields. He had to see for himself the extent of the destruction that the gods were inflicting on the people. His own sufferings, and that of his family, had been greatly diminished, due to the fact that his first wife, Tonalnan, was the holder of vast agave estates, a crop that withstood the lethal talons of drought. Their fortunes had all but increased, as agave and prickly pear cactus was just about the only thing left to eat, spiking a huge increase in demand.

Normally, as he weaved through the city's streets of stone, people would come out and look at him, wave, and offer him flowers to show their admiration of their favorite war hero and high administrator of the empire. But this time he walked along amidst languid and listless bodies, their skin stretched tightly across their bones, their irises enlarged with starvation and despair.

At the edge of the agricultural district, he stopped at the temple of Mazapa, the doorway to the Valley of Fields. Inside he left two bundles of nutty confections next to the altar and prayed. When he looked back upon leaving, they were already gone.

Tohuenyo was near his mother's neighborhood. Should he make a diversion and go see her? He had not seen her for many years.

By now, the entire Chichimeca tribe had relocated to the city of Tula. At first they'd lived in huts and lean-tos on the fringes of society. With time, they put together shacks, and eventually some of them built dwellings of stone. They made a productive neighborhood for themselves as weapon makers. They were able to churn out vast quantities of spearheads, swords and knives and other weapons. Though shanty and squalid, their *calpulli* on the outskirts of town became the dominant weapons guild of Tula-Tollan.

Impulsively Tohuenyo took a detour and found himself in the central courtyard of the *calpulli* of his true people, the Chichimeca. People in the surrounding shacks and stone houses stared at him with suspicious eyes. Who was this Toltec noble walking into their corner of the world?

He kicked the dry dirt with his gemmed sandal.

"Where is... ehem... the Omecíhuatl?" He coughed as he spat out the words in his native tongue.

A young boy ran off. Tohuenyo could see snake meat smoking on racks and piles of ant eggs, cactus leaves, and deer dung drying in the sun. He knew his people were not starving. No. They wouldn't. For however difficult the conditions had become, the Chichimeca would survive. They had the fortitude of stone.

A crowd of people started gathering round, men clad in nothing more than loincloths, bare breasted women in skirts. Their tongues wagged with excitement.

"Tohuenyo!" a man yelled from behind. It was Cueyatl, or at least it looked like Cueyatl – an older, fattened version of him. "Tohuenyo, the Omecíhuatl calls for you. Come with me!"

They walked through the alleyway to a stone dwelling behind several crude shacks. His childhood friend followed him with exhausting, excited chatter.

" - And I have a fat wife and seven children, Tohuenyo! How many do you have?" Before Tohuenyo could answer, Ichtaca appeared before him and blocked his entry to the door.

"Well hello cousin," Ichtaca sarcastically said. "Nice of you to show up after all these years."

[388]

Cueyatl hadn't quite finished his absent-minded chattering and the sorcerer's apprentice immediately became annoyed. "Silence!" he commanded, startling the gibbering man into abeyance.

Tohuenyo stared Ichtaca down.

Ichtaca then said sardonically, "Cousin, *you* may enter. Cueyatl, you hop along to your fat wife. I'm sure she has another list of things for you to do."

Inside the dark room Tohuenyo could see his aged mother sitting on a mat at the far corner. Candle bowls provided dim light. She was casting fortune telling bones and rocking back and forth, chanting. Her long, disheveled gray hair was woven with tiny human bones.

Ichtaca watched with burning interest from the door, arms crossed, feet spread apart. His black tunic was tied at the waist with a cord made from twisted human intestine. A cluster of amulets and spiritual weapons hung from the cord.

Tohuenyo quietly went up to her, dropped to his knees and bowed his head. "Mother, I have come. You see I have not forsaken you." He softly said.

Nine Winds looked up at him. It took her ancient eyes a moment to focus on him, and her aging memory even more time to recognize who he was.

She slapped him across the side of the head. "It's Grandmother Crone, you fool!" she said through rotting teeth.

Like the last time he had seen her, Tohuenyo sighed. *She's happy to see me*, he thought.

"My cousin Ichtaca has told me you wish to see me," he said, remembering something Ichtaca had told him once, long ago.

"Humph!" she grunted. She continued rocking back and forth and humming to herself.

Tohuenyo reached into his shoulder bag and took out some chocolate balls sweetened with agave nectar. He'd been saving them for his walk back home. He held them up to her.

"Mother, my dearest mother," he said, softening her.

She grabbed the chocolate balls, shoved them into her mouth, and gobbled them, one after the other.

Tohuenyo's stomach churned with conflicting emotions.

[389]

"Yes, yes," she confessed. "I have a message for you." She slurred her words because half her teeth were gone. "Come closer my son."

Tohuenyo leaned his head closer to hers. Her putrid stench filled his nostrils.

"*'Not a battle will be fought to take down our foe.'* Do you remember those words, my son?"

"Yes, mother," he said in obedience. They were the prophecy of the old Omecíhuatl from long ago.

"*We will be sustained by the plants of the earth only if the gods are properly fed with human blood.*"

The powerful crone exhaled her foul breath on him as she spoke. "Those are the words of my brother Titlacáhuan. The time has come."

Then she added, "You think you have stepped into the reality of others, and you believe they exist in yours. It is but an illusion. My son, the time is approaching when loyalties will pull upon you and confuse you. But in the end you will choose to dream your own dream."

A black dog the size of a fawn jumped through the door curtain, pushing Ichtaca aside. It stood, front paws spread apart and head lowered, and growled at Tohuenyo. Ichtaca stroked its ear and the dog curled up in the far corner next to some baskets, from where it continued to stare at Tohuenyo.

"It is time for you to go," Nine Winds said.

"Remember me as the crone who brought our people out of the caves." She then busied herself with preparing a smoking weed, and beckoned him off with a bony, spotted and veiny hand.

As Lord Tohuenyo left the dark stone dwelling, Ichtaca leaned toward him at the door. "Properly fed with human blood," he parroted.

Tohuenyo abruptly tossed the door curtain aside and left. As soon as he was outside, he heard the dog howl, and then *two* men's voices came from within. He flattened his body against the wall and peered inside through a crack between the curtain and the doorway. Inside he spied Titlacáhuan embracing Ichtaca. The black dog was nowhere to be seen.

Tohuenyo left the Chichimeca *calpulli* confused, torn between two worlds. Tolteca-Chichimeca. He was a part of both but belonged to neither.

He would never see his mother again.

His walk to the Valley of Fields was especially melancholy. On the road he witnessed whole families abandoning their homes and moving to wherever they might find water. In vain they carried all of their belongings with them. The search for water was desperate and relentless. The Valley of Fields was filled with the bones of parched crops, and the carcasses of beasts of the forests littered the dusty ground. The waters of the River Xicocotitlan had receded and the aqueducts were completely dry.

Surely this affliction would end.

Lord Tohuenyo made the journey to the River of Tears, which was now a small stream. Women were gathered there with giant pots collecting water, a journey they now had to make several times a day. He decided to venture upstream to a lonely bend where he might find some comfort in solitude.

Soon he came upon an unexpected pool. Grateful of his lucky fortune, he flattened himself to the ground and drank freely of its sacred waters. The cool, crisp drink invigorated and refreshed him.

"Aarh!" He shook out his head and propped himself up against a boulder. He felt enlivened. He looked at the pool and noticed a few reeds coming up out of one side, but as he reached for them, they disappeared. He pulled his hand back, and the reeds appeared again. A second time he reached for them, but again they vanished from sight.

"Magic pool," he said aloud. "You play and laugh at me."

"Be not alarmed, Toltec," said a deep, baritone voice.

Then a face appeared in the pool, but Tohuenyo's reflection it was not. Rather, the apparition was the black and yellow striped face of an elder, with a bone septum spike, giant turquoise earplugs, and a feathered crown.

Then the green leaves appeared again and the apparition said, "Toltec! Cast your eyes upon these succulent leaves of maize!"

Tohuenyo was mortified, for not only did he behold the maize leaves, but he also recognized the apparition as the one and only Black Tezcatlipoca.

"Yes, My Lord," he respectfully answered.

"Eh, Tohuenyo." The apparition's deep voice resonated. "Reflect and define the desires of your heart, for it is within your power to appease the gods for the hubris of your king."

Tohuenyo had never heard such a deep voice. It vibrated through him, enchanting every extremity of his body.

"Toltec, the Sons of Tlaloc have taken it upon themselves to cease the punishment of your king and his people. In exchange, they demand the heart of your first-born daughter. While the blood of her sacrifice nourishes the gods in the heavens above, bounty will return to your king and his people."

Lord Tohuenyo sat spellbound, frozen with fear, dreading above all other things, to offend the Dark Lord.

"Take this armload of succulent young corn to your king. He will recognize it as a sign from heaven. Tell him what the gods have demanded. Make him understand."

Tohuenyo left at once to tell his king.

Message from the Gods

Ce Acatl sat on a throne before his high council in the Inner Chamber of the Sacred House of Healing where he had been anointed in his washing of the face ceremony many years before. On his head he wore a cone shaped hat made of spotted leopard skin, with yellow tail feathers woven into the chinstrap so that it looked like he had a yellow beard. He used an inlaid turquoise mask on a golden stick to cover his face.

A woven maguey floor mat lay stretched down the length of the hall, lined with fire pots down the middle, but this time, unlike the previous years, the floor mat was laden with moderate samplings of foods, a result of the drought, morsels which no doubt came from private reserves.

The smooth stone walls were painted with brilliant murals depicting the journey of Mixcóatl and his four-hundred warriors. The mural's story began when the great warrior burst forth from darkness into the One World, from the great plains beyond the seven caves of Chicomoztoc. It showed how the great war hero led his four hundred warriors to victory in the battle against Itzpapálotl, the Obsidian Butterfly and goddess of war, and then onto Mixcóatl's subjugation of the peoples of the One World.

Ce Acatl's chieftains sat around him on the mat on the floor. Huemac was seated to his left, then Xolotl with his close ally and friend Ichtaca, Ozomatli and several others. A controversial noble sat to the right of the king, creating quite a stir. This position of highest honor was usually reserved for Lord Tohuenyo, the High Chancellor, but he had left the city unexpectedly that morning and no one knew where he was.

A new High Priest had taken the place of Quetzalpopóca Smoking Feather, a zealous astrologer named Huematzin who was obsessed with painting histories in long books. Zolton and Cuilton were there, as well as many other noble lords whose names are too long to mention here.

They'd been discussing the capture of two Toltec spies that were seized by the Zapotec King and his forces in Mitla far to the South. The spies had been sent to find the Zapotec's secret trade route to the villages around Lake Texcoco, but they were careless with their questioning and were found out by a lowly broom boy who reported their suspicious behavior. The fierce Zapotecs burned the spies' feet with torches until the blistering and popping skin sizzled right down to the bone. Then they gouged out their eyes and left them to bleed to death in the cornfields under the blistering heat of the sun.

Ce Acatl decided not to retaliate, reasoning that the spies got what was justly coming to them for their negligence and dimwitted handling of the broom boy.

The following conversations were heated, consisting mostly of arguments over landholdings and bouts of passing blame for the lack of rain that seemed to never end. As there was no corn flour to throw on the firepots, the men restlessly threw potassium chips, which exploded and turned the flames purple. It gave them a means to burn off their anger and send it to the gods.

Whispered inquiries passed discreetly under breath about the woman sitting in Lord Tohuenyo's place next to the king, followed by a variety of reactions. Some were bitter accusations denouncing the presence of women in the high council, followed by criticisms of women's effective judgment. Other whispers, though, defended Tohuenyo's first wife, for many recognized that their alliance with her strengthened their own positions of wealth and power.

"Silence, chieftains!" Ce Acatl ordered, raising a hand.

Everyone fell silent in strict submission to their king.

"The One For Whom We All Live demands your truthfulness and virtue," he said. "We demand an explanation of the disaster at Papantla."

Huemac fidgeted. He dare not reveal the secrets of his heart. For many years, he had been struggling with an inner turmoil, a surge of conflicting beliefs. One day, he knew, for he felt it with every fiber of his being, the military leaders in the One World would come to rule over the priests – but that time had still not come. The gods themselves were the head of state, more specifically, Quetzalcoatl and his ordained king.

[394]

"The armies have scattered from Papantla, My Lord," Huemac said, amidst squirms of discomfort.

"Toltec supply lines could no longer sustain our warriors, My Lord, and they weakened and fled." Xolotl added. "The deserters that were captured were strangled immediately, My Lord."

"Hmm," the king interjected. "And the supplies? Why were they not delivered? Have we not thousands of slaves who serve our holy empire?"

The council members fell silent, each man reluctant to be the one to reveal the distressing news.

"There were no supplies, beloved *tlatoani*," Madam Tonalnan boldly said. It was the first time she had spoken in the council meeting. A wave of relief flooded over the council members, but it was short-lived.

"Aaaaaaarrrgh!" The king yelled, rising to his feet. He threw the turquoise mask to the floor in exasperation. It shattered to pieces. All the council members immediately prostrated themselves right where they were, foreheads to the floor.

The king started pacing around the council members. "And the supplies?" the king demanded, "What happened to them?"

No one moved.

"Oh for the love of Mother God! Sit up and talk to your king!"

The chieftains of the council sat up with their heads cautiously hung low, determined not to look upon the face of their king.

"There is no cotton for armor, My Lord, for the Sons of Tlaloc have withheld their blessings." Tonalnan said.

"You see gentlemen? This is why we let the Madam into this council. She speaks to her king!" Ce Acatl was still circling.

Not to be bettered, Cuilton added, "There is no corn to feed them, Exalted One. The aqueducts have run completely dry. The fields are nothing but dust and bones."

"We suppose that next you'll tell us there is no stone to make weapons, that the mountains themselves have shriveled up and died!" In a momentary fit of fury, the king reached down to the chieftain below him and grabbed his ramekin of potassium chips and threw the whole lot at a firepot causing a huge purple explosion. The men sitting there felt their eyelashes singe.

"There is stone, My Lord," said Xolotl. "But there is no water for the crafting of weapons. The armies lack armor, food and weapons, and porters are defecting as well, in search of water."

"Our nation is starving to death, My Lord," said Huemac numbly.

Ce Acatl leaned on his throne at the end of the room, placed his hands on the armrests and hung his head low.

"There is one more thing," Huemac added, for he truly was the bravest of all of Ce Acatl's chieftains, and had the courage to inform him. "Because of our weakened condition, we run the risk of invasion from foreign armies."

You have no idea, Ichtaca thought, smiling so discretely that no one could see.

The red tassel at the top of the king's cone-shaped, leopard-skin crown forebodingly fell to the floor. The king sat in his throne and allowed a reverent slave who had been hiding in the shadows to retrieve the tassel, and attach a veil to his cone-shaped crown.

Just then a commotion stirred down the long corridor at the entrance to the inner chamber. The chieftains could hear yelling and running footsteps echoing toward them.

"Exalted One!" A man burst through the stone archway carrying a huge, cloaked bundle in his arms. He was huffing and panting and drenched in rolling sweat and caked-on dust from having run so far and long. "My Lord! My King!" he repeated. He then uncloaked the bundle on the floor before the king and his entire council. A pile of glistening, young succulent corn lay before them. The exhausted man then prostrated himself before his king, forehead to the floor.

It was Tohuenyo.

They gave him maguey water, which he gulped down freely. He then delivered Tezcatlipoca's words to the horror of most of the chieftains and the secret delight of a few.

No one knows whether it was intentional or not, but in his relation of the message, Tohuenyo missed the mark, and instead of saying *his first-born daughter*, he said *the Toltec's first-born daughter*. Everyone knew immediately this meant the virgin Princess Quetzalli, who was barely more than a child, daughter of Calli and Xolotl. Quetzalli was older than his own daughter Quetzalpétatl, and the eldest of the Toltec's highborn virgins.

[396]

Ce Acatl understood that ideas were contagious, and spread from man to man, and then multiplied in waves of thousands, affecting the collective consciousness of entire nations. He knew this momentous belief had started within his kingdom, and that people were morbidly calling for human sacrifice, the most vile and wicked sin he could imagine.

Rulers do not become leaders on their own. They rise to lead because others choose to follow them. Ce Acatl knew this as well, and sought the advice of his council before administering his ruling, which he knew would change the face of his nation.

The new high priest Huematzin had neither the predisposition nor the inclination to carry out such an abomination and refused.

Xolotl said he knew a great and powerful sorcerer, a high priest among his own followers, who could officiate the ritual.

Eventually the king reluctantly acquiesced, saying only, "Oh brothers, if this grave atrocity be what is necessary to appease your sufferings and fill your empty spiritual bellies, then let it be so. But where is the reason in killing ourselves to sustain ourselves?"

Before they adjourned, he ordered his nobles of the high council to secrecy and discretion in fear of what was to come, for they were saying, "Only death can bring us life!"

"My children," the king sighed, 'You misinterpret death. You misinterpret life," but the room was quite noisy with chatter so no one heard him say, "You are alive, yet you are dead."

Birth of the Mexica

Soon a small band of supporters rallied around Ichtaca who proclaimed victory for all those who would pray to Tezcatlipoca. Though skeptical, desperate townspeople went to hear his teachings that the gods would be appeased only through human sacrifice, contrary to Ce Acatl Topiltzin's insistence on virtue and prayer.

"What will prayer get you?" He questioned them. "Will it fill your empty bellies? Will it feed your wives and your hungry children? No! I tell you, we must *fight* for our survival, and endure the hardships of the sacrifices we must make for gods! The gods need our blood, the life force within us, in order to be nourished. Only then will they again churn the clouds in the sky to make rain!"

In this way Ichtaca swayed the people's hearts to begin accepting human sacrifice.

When Xolotl and his guards came for his virgin child they had to rip her out of her mother's arms. The woman Madam Calli went into mad hysterics, incurring severe reprimands from her husband for not sharing his religious zeal. She could not, would not, accept this new belief.

"Madam, you know she will go directly to live among the gods!" he insisted, but Madam Calli would have none of it. After the guards left with little Quetzalli, Xolotl beat his wife within minutes of her life and locked her away in her room. She was never whole again.

The next day Tonalnan found herself alone in the courtyard of the Palace of Previous Kings. What used to be a wealth of botanical beauty was now a graveyard of sticks and dried leaves. Dust swirled around empty pots. The birds were gone. So were the butterflies and bees. There was nothing but the sound of the scorching sun.

She was greatly disturbed by the events that were unfolding before her. Disbelief was her most immediate reaction. She'd tried to reach out to her sovereign, but he had cloistered himself away at the Pyramid of Coral and would receive no one.

Her husband Tohuenyo was indifferent and wouldn't commit to an opinion. Ever since the apparition of Tezcatlipoca he was morose and withdrawn. She found no solace in her sister-wives either, as they were uninformed. They had not been told of Princess Quetzalli's abduction and the approaching sacrificial rite. Tonalnan wasn't about to betray the king's wishes and reveal the cursed atrocity.

In her agony she decided to look for Chac, her devoted slave. She went to the great hall and searched about. It seemed like just yesterday that they'd celebrated their king's victory at the ball court. She couldn't believe it had been four years.

Chac was nowhere to be found. Perhaps he-she was at the temple. She decided to venture out and see. There was no market, but the Yollotli was filled with people strolling, hoping to find remnants of food, and hungry-looking boys kicking a rubber ball around. She wrapped her shawl tight around her face and shoulders to keep the dust at bay.

She looked through the eastern hall where she'd been married, then the western Hall of Judgment where she last held her mother in her arms. Still no Chac. The temple, too, was abandoned. She went back to the Palace of Previous Kings and resigned herself to wait for Chac's return.

※

For four days Tezcatlipoca's priests prepared the child. They washed her with their precious reserves of water sweetened with aromatic fragrances, dressed her in the finest clothing, filled her up with dried candy-fruits from distant lands and her favorite confections, and in every way treated her like a goddess. For they knew in their hearts she was to become a goddess, and they wanted to gain her favor once she reached the celestial world in the heavens above.

※

The days passed and Chac still did not return. On the third night, exasperated, Tonalnan sought the comfort of her husband in

[400]

his sleeping chamber, but he rebuffed her and called Yaretzi and Anayel to his bed.

⚜

On the fourth evening, Tezcatlipoca's priests, with Ichtaca, Xolotl and a handful of followers among them, trekked out of the city and marched up the hill of Xicocotitlan with the Toltec princess. They perfumed her hair and dressed her in a skirt of the finest cotton in the realm. Her budding breasts were left bare, but they decorated her in a collar necklace of the finest gems and beads of gold. Then they fed her a concoction of a bewitching substance containing *ololiuqui*, *tlapatl*, and *nanácatl* and prayed to Tezcatlipoca while musicians wailed out sacred hymns and pounded on drums.

At the fated hour of the setting sun, Titlacáhuan ceremoniously arrived with an air of ferocity and scorn. He instructed the priests to arch her unconscious little body backwards over a sacrificial altar. The Chichimeca sorcerer then made some unintelligible utterances, clasping an obsidian dagger with both hands high over his head.

He looked to the heavens and chanted an incantation in a language nobody understood.

No one saw his sinister smile.

Then with one hand, he slammed the dagger into the soft flesh under her ribs and sliced open her chest. With the long, yellowed fingernails of his other hand he reached into her convulsing, bleeding body, grabbed her beating heart and ripped it out of her, tearing the tissues and threads that held it in.

He held the pulsating organ high in the air.

Then he turned and placed it on a ceremonial altar - It was a stone sculpture of an asexual youth, reclining on his-her elbows with buttocks on the ground, knees bent and feet pulled in. The sculptured youth was looking sideways and wearing a flat-topped cap textured like rows of corn with two giant buns on the sides of his-her head. There was a basin resting in the abdomen of the stone sculpture. This is where Titlacáhuan put Quetzalli's pulsating heart.

He doused the freshly severed organ with a black, flammable liquid and lit it on fire and then went into a series of frenzied chants.

[401]

The only intelligible words were *Huitzilopochtli*, *Mexitl*, *Mexica* and *Chac Mool*.

After the incantation was over, he ordered his priests to burn the body. He instructed his Chichimeca-Toltec companions to pray to Mexitl, the god of war, and from then on refer to themselves as Mexica. He said the maiden Quetzalli had been sacrificed to appease the gods for the sins of the people.

"Her death will bring us life!" he prophesied. He then commanded that they forever honor her as the Virgin Mother of the Mexicans, followers of Mexitl, god of war.

Rain

The next day the Sons of Tlaloc churned the massive clouds and opened the floodgates of heaven. It rained. They threw the crystal spear and lightning struck the hills and horizon. They shook the black, gourd rattle, and thunder boomed across the land.

The people were ecstatic and danced in the alleys, passageways and streets, raising their arms to the sky as the rains showered down upon them. It rained more, and day and night the parched earth drank, for it was dry and thirsty.

The Mother became impregnated and the plant kingdom sprouted forth and began to grow. Soon, the people recovered the blessings of the gods and came to thrive in the bounty of their Mother.

Many people were grateful to Tezcatlipoca, and prayed to the daughter of the Mexica, the princess Quetzalli, for knowledge of her great sacrifice had quickly spread.

Ichtaca and his accomplices went among the people and successfully convinced them to accept the new corporeal ceremonies saying, "You see? The gods are happy! Only in this way, by opening ourselves and giving them that which gives us life, will they stay nourished and bring us rain. If we give them blood sustenance, they will sustain us!"

The people then spoke amongst themselves, neighbor to neighbor, in the streets, and in their temples and homes.

"It must be so," they reasoned.

"Yes, human sacrifice is what brought us rain!"

"Hail to the child Quetzalli, Virgin Mother of the Mexica!"

And so it came to pass that the cult of human sacrifice began in Tula.

✄

Many people sought the priests of Quetzalcoatl and beseeched them for their guidance.

"Tell us what our king professes," they begged.

The priests of Quetzalcoatl responded, "He insists on the need to continually seek the Divine Power in order to attain the highest form of spirituality, Wisdom. Only through Wisdom is it possible to seek the deeper meaning of man and woman in our One World. Wisdom and the Divine Power are what nourish the gods!

"Our world will always be threatened by death and destruction. Listen with your hearts, oh Toltecs! Wisdom and the Divine Power will overcome calamity and devastation. You can reach the dwelling place of Wisdom and Divine Power through fasting and prayer. You have the power to become everything the gods have created you to be! You are well able to fulfill your true destiny!"

Thousands of inhabitants continued to follow and support Ce Acatl, their king and divine representation of Quetzalcoatl in the One World, but others dissented and the cult of human sacrifice spread everywhere so that a chasm of beliefs soon emerged.

The Sway

The rains brought returning prosperity to the Toltecs and their world. Renewed bounty strengthened the infrastructure of the empire, reinforcing the many facets of society. As the aqueducts surged, corn and cotton production resumed. Pottery, weaving, stone masonry, construction, and commerce all soon began to flourish once again. As people returned to the metropolis, the *tianguis* market resumed, more resplendent than before the dry years, as everyone was even more grateful for the renewed bounty. The *ullama* ball court reopened, hosting famous athletes from as far away as Palenque, Acapulco, and Michoacán.

General Huemac was able to reclaim the distant lands and bring them back into the folds of the empire, strengthening his wealth and position. As a result, he decided to host a huge celebration in his home, the First General's Palace. The banquet included duck and wild turkey with strawberry chutney, and a splendid display of fruits including guava, pineapple, papaya, zapote and even fresh cacao. Honey-roasted peanuts, pecans, sunflower and pumpkin seeds were available as well. The squash and corn was stewed with *epazote* and tomatoes, and the bean curd paste was exquisitely spiced and shaped and wrapped into balls. The favorites, though, were the nutty confections made with agave nectar and pecans.

Huemac insisted that his two daughters help him host the grand affair, a task they both did with heavy hearts and long faces – Calli because she'd been left disfigured from the brutal beating of several months before, and Tonalnan because she was never able to recover her adored slave Chac, who also had been her closest friend. Rumors ran rampant that the great sorcerer Titlacáhuan had changed her slave to stone for use in his morbid atrocities. She never knew, but stone sculptures of Chac had started appearing at certain temples in town. Priests were using them as sacrificial altars and calling them Chac Mools.

Tonalnan must be strong: for her sister's sake, if nothing else. She wouldn't give the slightest semblance of her thoughts of defeat. One exceptional thing had happened, though. Her husband had taken it upon himself to indulge her of late. For the past several days, he had called her to his bed and repented for his heart's absence from her since his return from war so many years ago. He cried, purged his guilty conscience and confessed his sins. He begged for her forgiveness and assured her that his love for her was greater than that of any of his other wives. What Tonalnan didn't know, however, was that her husband's beleaguered heart was drowning in conflicting loyalties. She would never suspect that the real reason he sought to be near her was his naïve attempt to immerse himself in the creative forces of the Divine Feminine, that part of the cosmic Primordial Being where the light of the sun radiates from the womb of the First Mother. Comfort. Acceptance. Guidance. Tolerance. Love.

On this day of Huemac's celebration she watched as her husband Tohuenyo was surrounded by his multitude of children. He teased them and taunted them, pulling their noses and finding pecans behind their ears. He even let them ride on his back, pretending to be a great stag.

Everyone was in the same jovial mood. It felt so incredibly good to be in prosperity once again. Dancers were performing in the courtyard. There was a drum circle in the back field. Hot baths were open to anyone who wanted to avail themselves of the steamy jojoba and vanilla experience.

In a secret room, hidden away from sight, the elder Huemac, Xolotl, and Ichtaca, accompanied by their closest friends, were smoking tobacco, drinking *pulque*, and chewing *nanácatl* mushrooms and coca leaves imported from Peru.

They spoke of military conquests and the status of tributes owed to the empire. Xolotl told them tales of days gone by, of his battle at Jocotitlan and the taking of Atlacomulco in the Toluca campaign. They discussed the strategic retaking of Papantla and argued over the reasons it was successful. Ah, war. It provided the way for a man to survive.

"Our followers are increasing everyday," Xolotl said, taking another puff of the tobacco mixture.

[406]

"The gods favor our endeavors," Ichtaca said.

"I see this movement is going to need a leader, *Lord Huemac*," Xolotl said, emphasizing the words Lord Huemac, for he rarely called his father-in-law by his official title in private, tending rather, to refer to him by his honorific, *Father*.

The men passed around a plate of coca leaves and each man took another one.

"Let the gods do with this old warrior what they will," Huemac said, slapping his bare paunch a few times. His graying hair was woven in two braids. He slurped down a mug of *pulque* and wiped his mouth with his arm.

The men had roasted turkey legs smothered in strawberry chutney laden before them, but nobody was hungry.

"Where's my other son?" the First General demanded.

"He's out there with the *other* crowd," Ichtaca answered.

"Somebody go get him. You there!" He pointed to one of Xolotl's companions who was at that moment dropping another mushroom into his mouth with his tongue hanging out and his mouth wide open.

"Go get him!" Huemac ordered.

The man put the *nanácatl* down and begrudgingly complied. He got up and left the secret chamber grumbling something under his breath that nobody heard.

"I think you should take another wife," Huemac said to his son-in-law.

"What for, dear Father? Why I have the most obedient and dutiful wife in the realm. She has so much self control that you can see the femininity in her face." Xolotl replied.

"You need an heir," Huemac informed him.

"I have an heir."

"Ah yes, the flute player." Huemac patted Xolotl's hand. "But my son, you only have one heir. What would we do if your one leaf falls from the tree? You should have more children." Huemac stated mater-of-factly. "I'm going to arrange it. Those whelps of yours born out of wedlock don't count."

Ichtaca laughed.

"You too, young friend. You also need a wife." Huemac pushed.

"Ah, beloved General, you see, I am already married." Ichtaca said. "I keep my wife confined in a pumpkin gourd," he teased. The men laughed heartily.

"Well, young friend, it is just as well, but what about a *position*? You are constantly with my son-in-law here, yet you have no position to speak of." He turned to Xolotl. "Is that not so?"

Xolotl replied, "Ichtaca is a man who knows many positions." All the men laughed at the double entendre and Huemac smacked Xolotl over the head.

"A position of *authority*," Huemac clarified.

"No sir. He does not have a position of authority." Xolotl answered.

"Well then we must give him one." Huemac insisted. "How about commander of forces? We could put him in charge of something local here, since you're so fond of him, somewhere close, like Pachuca. What do you think?" He asked Xolotl.

"Oh my great lord," Ichtaca interrupted. "My gratitude of your trust in me is ever abundant, but I am not a warrior, My Lord. I am a priest."

"A priest!" Huemac barreled. "A fornicating priest who practically *lives* at the House of Joy!" His belly shook he laughed so hard.

"Well not a priest, exactly, Father," Xolotl clarified.

"Well exactly *what*, then?" Huemac and the others were still chuckling.

"Well, exactly... like... a..." He hesitated and looked at Ichtaca.

"A sorcerer," Ichtaca said flatly.

The room fell silent.

A cold wave of fear rushed about the room.

"Which means he knows how to officiate the duties of a priest," Xolotl added, trying to dispel their apprehensions.

"Humph," the elder Huemac said. He reached for a turkey leg and devoured a huge bite, then said with his mouth full, "That could work. We'll make him a priest, but he'll have to restrict his fornicating to his own temple. No more House of Joy. He can offer relief to the noblewomen who come to his temple for meditation and prayer. Yep." He said, smacking his lips. "See to the construction of a new temple to Huitzilopochtli, Xolotl. I like the idea."

Of course Ichtaca had no say in the matter, but he was not opposed. Rather, he was elated at the trust that the First General was instilling in him. A position of authority! This was a nice surprise.

"Yes, My Lord," Xolotl answered. "It is done."

The door opened and Tohuenyo entered, agitated.

"Come my son. Come sit down before your father-in-law and your brothers who love you." Huemac said.

Tohuenyo and Xolotl glared at each other. Tohuenyo then looked at Ichtaca with a penetrating stare. Their eyes locked for an instant, which held a lifetime of memories.

"Brother," Ichtaca said. "Blood brother," he added, but no one knew the truth behind the statement except Tohuenyo and Ichtaca, for they had never revealed their secret identities.

Tohuenyo suddenly remembered his very first hunting day. He touched the scar on his chest where he had made the blood oath with Ichtaca all those years before. He knew Ichtaca's deepest, darkest secret – that he had murdered King Naxac in his youth. He couldn't deny the closeness he felt to Ichtaca, despite their rivalries.

"Son Tohuenyo," Huemac started, finishing his turkey leg. "Our respected Protector of the Palace of Quetzalcoatl. How the people love you.!" He licked his fingers and looked at Tohuenyo earnestly. "How go the affairs with your administration of justice?"

"Well, Father," he said, sitting on the mat, "Men are less apt to quarrel in times of plenty."

"This is true," they all agreed.

Tohuenyo cast a sidelong glance at Ichtaca, his kin. The sorcerer was smoking a fragrant concoction of tobacco and psychoactive herbs. He exhaled directly at Tohuenyo. A wave of smoothness overtook him, a serene calm.

"The nation is divided, brother," said Xolotl, feigning friendly civility.

"Some people don't understand the sacrifices that have to be made." Huemac continued.

"Lord Tohuenyo," said Ichtaca, placing the plate of coca leaves before him, "You have been a very long time away from your true family. Look into your inner nature to who you really are." Ichtaca

[409]

puffed his smoking herbs and exhaled at Tohuenyo again. Then he offered Tohuenyo the pipe.

Tohuenyo took a long draw on the pipe, held it in his lungs and then released it. Tension left his body with the smoke. He then proceeded to chew a coca leaf from the plate.

"There comes a time when a man must choose," Xolotl said, taking the pipe from Tohuenyo.

"The people are shifting their loyalties, brother, and they need strong men to lead them." Ichtaca smoothly added.

"And you want to know where my loyalties lie." Tohuenyo did them the favor of saying it.

"This could be an opportunity for you," Xolotl said, refilling the bowl of the pipe.

Ichtaca leaned toward Tohuenyo and lowered his voice to almost a whisper. "*We will be sustained by the plants of the earth only if the gods are properly fed with human blood*," he said, repeating the teachings of his master, Titlacáhuan. He then threw a pinch of fire sand on the firepot in front of them. The flames burst and crackled, sending orange and red sparks everywhere.

Huemac took the smoking pipe from Xolotl and drew in its magical vapors, inhaling deeply. He exhaled before he spoke.

"Then there is the question of your family," the First General said. "We want to make sure they stay safe, my son," he said. "These are troubled times." He passed the pipe to one of Xolotl's companions.

Tohuenyo knew that of all his children only the princess Quetzalpétatl had the First General's protection. By formally recognizing Tonalnan as his daughter, Huemac accepted the princess as one of his legitimate heirs. He understood quite clearly, though, that his father-in-law meant to coerce him into submission through unspeakable abominations to all his other children. After all, there was not a drop of noble Toltec blood in any of them.

"Abductions have increased, as you well know Lord Chancellor, by fanatics looking to appease the gods," Xolotl said, returning to his feigned friendly civility.

Tohuenyo said nothing.

"Of course if I were sure of your loyalties I could guarantee their protection," Lord Huemac said plainly.

[410]

Ichtaca leaned toward him and whispered, "It's time to choose."

All his life Tohuenyo had managed to stay out of power struggles. In his position as Protector of the Palace of Quetzalcoatl he'd been too busy to involve himself in the political affairs of the ruling class. He'd rested at ease in the soothing waters of neutrality. He was one of the king's closest and most trusted advisors, but his Chichimeca relations had never challenged him – not even after he'd defected and married his enemy. That is, not until now. This was where the road of his life split in two.

"Father, I'll give you my eldest daughter to raise as your own so that she may receive the blessings of your protection," Tohuenyo said, with intuitive foresight.

This act of submission was well received by Lord Huemac and his companions. The first general's face stretched into a wholehearted grin.

"Ah my boy," Lord Huemac said chuckling. He stood and the others all stood with him. He opened his arms, and hugged his son-in-law, then took Tohuenyo's shoulders squarely in front of him. "What fools we were to ever doubt you." He continued smiling and left the dark room.

Xolotl embraced Tohuenyo's forearms with his, confirming their new alliance. "My daughter's death will not have been in vain," he said in a dry, unemotional voice. "You'll see. We must now look to the future and forget our past differences."

Before Tohuenyo left, the sorcerer Ichtaca gave him a small, woven, black and tan box. He opened the lid to find a lock of white hair inside.

Ichtaca hesitated and looked back at his childhood friend. "From Nine Winds," was all he said.

The whole of Tohuenyo's existence turned to dread.

Gift to the Gods

Ideas are more powerful than men. They are like great white clouds, drifting through the collective consciousness, stronger than our ability to quell them. They are like drifting seeds that scatter in the wind. Because of this, more and more Toltecs turned to the cult of human sacrifice.

As the days of Ochpaniztli passed into Teotleco, Tula's deciduous trees turned from dry green to fiery orange and then to a withered brown. Cold winds whisked the last battered leaves off their branches and threw them to the ground. It was during this time that Tohuenyo fell into a morose pool of emotional doom. He took up a copious indulgence of *pulque* that led to continuous inebriation, started to neglect his hygiene, and began to give away his personal belongings in an effort to rid himself of their emotional memories that were too painful for him to bear. He became withdrawn, and preferred to be left alone so he could secretly endure his helplessness and fear. Instead of attending to his duties at the Palace of Quetzalcoatl he walked the alleys and passageways of Tula, doubting his beliefs and not trusting his own judgment. The path of his life had split in two and he was forced to choose which one to follow. He was a tormented soul.

Ce Acatl Topiltzin Quetzalcoatl, or his nemesis Tezcatlipoca? On the one hand, he was Ce Acatl's trusted ally. He would never forget the master's teachings in the Pyramid of Coral when he first heard Quetzalcoatl's words. "*Quetzalcoatl is the divine Spirit that is blown into all of manifestation by the holy breath of* Ehécatl*, the wind,*" the master had said. Ce Acatl taught him that the divine spirit of Quetzalcoatl was forever omnipresent and spoke of the stages of awareness of a spiritual warrior:

> "*When we are naïve we are like the serpent who spends her life forever connected to the earth, looking for nourishment and hiding from*

[413]

predators. She slithers along gracefully, but spends her life only seeing what is immediately in front of her.

"When the seeker of knowledge grows in spiritual awareness and rises above the pyramid of consciousness, he soars, like an eagle in the heavens above. But the spiritual warrior only reaches this great height when he surrenders his attachments to the mundane. This consists of judgments, fear, and lies that have been programmed into his mind by others, confusing him with rules and agreements about who he is and how he should live his life. But the more he eliminates the distorting lies in his mind, the less susceptible he is to their power. He becomes an eagle, a seer. He flies free from old judgments and fears, soaring high on his own currents and living life effortlessly and impeccably."

Now it seemed too hard. "Surrender my attachments to fear," he thought. How was this possible when his fears were so real, his children's lives threatened? Maybe the path of Ce Acatl was just a lot of fancy words and sparkly illusions. Maybe it was just easier to live life as it came to him, in the Here and Now without such lofty aspirations. In an epiphany, he realized that this was the very essence of Tezcatlipoca, Lord of the Here and Now. He began to understand that seeing only what was in front of him was, in essence, the way of living in the Here and Now. Wasn't it easier to just live life than to try and figure it all out? No wonder Tezcatlipoca had so many followers.

He decided to go to the Yollotli and walk amongst the crowds. It was market day. He wanted to enjoy the moment, not think about anything but the present. No past. No future. Just the exact moment he was in – the Here and Now.

At the market he encountered an ancient woman in front of the wall of serpents selling painted flags on *amatl* paper. She was proselytizing the cult of Tezcatlipoca, convincing people to offer themselves in human sacrifice.

It was true. People had started to offer themselves for sacrifice all over Tula, because they were convinced that with this sacred death they were turning into gods - in heaven, in the after life, and beyond.

Tohuenyo stopped to listen to her speak, where a few interested listeners had gathered round.

"Come, my son," the crone said. "Offer thy heart to nourish the gods and go to live among them." She raised a paper flag in front of him. "Choose thy god, noble lord."

Should he offer himself to the gods? Shouldn't he abhor human sacrifice as a devotee of Quetzalcoatl's teachings? He was a Toltec now, but how could he deny that he was also Chichimeca?

It was true what Ichtaca had told him. It *was* time to choose. If he remained loyal to himself and his king, Huemac and his cronies would start abducting his children for their heinous rituals. On the other hand, if he chose to transfer his loyalties to the cult of human sacrifice, it would surely result in the downfall of Ce Acatl Topiltzin, his benevolent protector and guardian of all things divine.

He remembered the last words his mother ever said to him, "You think you have stepped into the reality of others, and you believe they exist in yours. It is but an illusion. My son... in the end you will choose to dream your own dream."

"Here, take one." The crone pushed a flag into Tohuenyo's hand.

It was Xolotl, the canine god of sickness and deformity who accompanies the dead to Mictlán.

"Not that one," he said, pushing it back. "Show me that one, over there."

"Ah," the crone said, "Tonatiuh, god of the sun and heavenly warriors. 'Tis the god of eagles, they say."

Then a destitute, emaciated woman stepped forward. "Old crone, sell me Toci, the heart of the earth and mother of the gods! I will do it," said the feeble skeleton of a woman. "I lost my family in the years of no rain. I withstood my husband's abandonment and watched my children starve to death. I have nothing to live for."

She gave the old hag her strand of coral beads, the last of her worldly possessions, and took the flag.

"Go to the temple of Itzpapálotl and wash your face," the old crone instructed.

The impoverished woman's resolve gave Tohuenyo the impulse he'd been lacking. He emptied the gemstones of his purse into a woven vessel at the crone's feet – a veritable fortune, indeed. She handed him the flag of Tonatiuh, god of the heavenly warriors, and said, "Go to the temple of Itzpapálotl and wash thy face."

Tohuenyo walked away with his flag and did not look back, so he never saw what happened next.

They say that the crone turned into an apparition. Before vanishing, there was a semblance of Titlacáhuan in her physique. She lifted up into the wind and started spinning. She spun faster and faster and swirled into the woven vessel like a tornado dancing in the wind. Then the vessel, too, dissolved from sight.

For four days the noble Lord Tohuenyo was nowhere to be found, and it was only later that people discovered what had happened. He'd been washed and cleansed, robed in fine clothing and adorned with precious jewels. He was fed the finest delectables imaginable, and pampered and doted on by the followers of the cult of Tezcatlipoca and Itzpapálotl. He was kept in an altered state, imbibed with great quantities of intoxicating wine, and gorged with psychotropic plants and herbs. Believing he was soon to become a god, a stream of women came to him hoping to conceive.

On the fated day at dawn, the priests of Tezcatlipoca and Itzpapálotl killed him by cutting off his head. After drilling holes in the sides of his skull, they rammed a pole through it and hung it on a raised altar in the Yollotli where the buzzards pecked it clean and night critters feasted on his brains. The necromancers danced and wailed out sacred songs and initiated their honored skull rack to the cult of the dead. They called it the *Tzompantli*, and soon it started filling up with the severed heads of victims whose souls had turned into gods.

[416]

The Mourning After

Tonalnan and Andoeni laid out their deceased husband's clothing, weapons, and armor on a *petlatl* mat in the courtyard of their home. There was no obsequy for him, as the priests of Itzpapálotl had already cremated his torso and limbs. In this intimate, private ceremony, they were accompanied only by their other sister wives, most of the *nahuallis* who had been his closest companions, and the young priest-astrologer Huematzin, their trusted ally and friend.

The three *iztacs*, who were no longer youths but a generation older, sprinkled his possessions with jojoba and coconut oil, by dipping sacred eagle feathers into the perfumed, viscous liquid and flinging it into the air. The now white-haired *xolome* said a prayer. He sat on a chair the women had brought for him, hunched and cowered over, as his severe kyphosis had progressed with age. Miztli, who was the only *tlatoque* still alive, sat on the ground shaking a gourd rattle and chanting sacred songs.

Tohuenyo's many children filled the courtyard around them.

Tonalnan and Andoeni gathered his belongings and reverently placed them in a woven trunk. His warrior's dorsal disc and gold pectoral butterfly along with all his jewelry were then given to Tonalnan so she could bury them under the stele of Quetzalcoatl near the hearth in their home.

The women mourned quietly, and wiped their tears on fragments of paper, which they then stuck into the folds of the woven trunk. Then, as the trunk burned, the flames carried their tears to the spirit world. Hopefully the gods would hear their cries and relieve them of their pain.

A man of few words, Huematzin then spoke. "The villain who killed your lord and master Tohuenyo is not a monster or a demon, but a human need - the need to sacrifice oneself for the greater good," was all he said.

[417]

Quite possibly, he was the only one who understood what he meant.

Tonalnan showed no outward emotion, but at night she mourned deeply. Her grief caused rivers of tears, as she felt like her soul was being twisted right out of her. She'd had to live all these years without her mother. Now the gods had taken the love of her life as well. Surrounded by her sister-wives, their children, her father, and extended family, she felt completely alone.

The White Child

After Lord Tohuenyo's death, Tonalnan was hurled into the position of Protectress of the Palace of Quetzalcoatl by her king. Ce Acatl came out of seclusion and called an emergency meeting of the high council. In the meeting, the chieftains passionately discussed the recent wave of self-sacrifice that was spreading over the nation, but no one dared agree with the practice in front of the king. Lord Tohuenyo's death had them in a stir.

The king insisted on advancing Tohuenyo's first wife to the position of High Chancellor thereby instating her as Protectress of the Palace of Quetzalcoatl. It wasn't common for a woman to reach such a high status of authority, but it wasn't unheard of, either. Remember, the queen of Teotenanco successfully ruled her realm for many years after her husband Black Snake was defeated and her city-state was incorporated into the Toltec nation. Sadly to say, after Madam Tonalnan's instatement, the king returned to his life of seclusion, penance and prayer, overwhelmed by the horrific events taking place in his realm.

And so, this was how it came to pass that the woman, Madam Tonalnan, Mother of Light, became High Chancellor and Protectress of the Palace of Quetzalcoatl in the empire of Tula-Tollan.

She started her duties immediately. As High Chancellor, she sat in a jewel-encrusted chair at the top of the stairs of the Western Hall and presided over property disputes, thefts and other criminal behavior, drunkenness in public, civic complaints against unruly *pipiltzin* youths, faulty business transactions, accusations by angry fathers at the loss of their daughter's virtue, and other cases such as these.

After two months time, on the day 4 Monkey, it so happened that Madam Tonalnan was presented with a most unsettling tale. She sat on her throne donning a snowy white egret feather stole over a red and white *huipilli* blouse and a black on black brocaded garment that fell all the way to the floor. Her stoic face was painted completely white, with lips as red as ripened *chilli*. On her head she wore a flat, step shaped gold headpiece with golden tassels at the sides that covered her ears. In her hand she held the coral scepter of justice, an addition that she herself had instated. She was accompanied by the *nahuallis*, who sat scattered along the stair. Xolome rested on a buffalo hide that had been brought all the way from the northern corner of the world. Lately she had come to keep the *nahuallis* in her constant company.

"My Lady, most high Lady, Madam Tonalnan," the potter said. "We beg to inform you of the goings on of the *calpullis* in the city. Oh, gracious Madam, pray hear us."

There was a potter, a basket maker and a feather worker kneeling at the bottom of the stair before her. They had come representing their distinctive clans.

"Continue," she allowed.

"Several moons ago some porters found a white child in the forest," the feather worker said. He remained kneeling, and fidgeted with his hands. "The child was tall, taller than a man, and very beautiful with long white hair." He looked nervously at the basket maker for reassurance. "The people of the area were afraid he was a demon, so after several days the clansmen's hunters captured him."

Tonalnan looked at Blue *Iztac* who returned her glance, sharing her intrigue.

"The white child had a *xiquipilli*, made of brocaded cotton with a strap that he wore over his shoulder," the potter continued. "He reached in and offered the villagers mysterious substances which they ate and drank, and they became inebriated and elated with joy."

Then the feather worker spoke. The timbre of his voice trembled, but he managed get the words out clearly. "They brought the white child here to Tula, and he continued to gift his strange edibles to everyone he saw. All who ate his gifts became intoxicated and wanted more. When the people brought the child to the middle of the city, he began to change." The feather worker looked at the basket maker, indicating that he should continue.

[420]

"Well, My Lady, his beauty faded and when he opened his mouth, a sticky black sludge poured out of it with a filthy, rancid odor."

"Take that demon back to where you found him!" Madam Tonalnan ordered.

"That's just it, My Lady, when the people tried to move him, he resisted with a supernatural strength and grew even taller. He continued to give away his peculiar foodstuffs and the people kept taking them," the basket weaver said, "but soon their euphoria turned to confusion and fear."

"Soon after that some guards killed him, My Lady," The potter interrupted. "They cut off his head and opened his body but there was nothing inside. He was empty and meaningless."

"Oh! How horrid!" Madam Tonalnan exclaimed.

"Then the people tried to cast a huge net around the fallen child's body," the feather worker chimed in, "but the white child arose, and grabbed his own head and started walking around the city. In the chaos that resulted, many people who were holding the ropes of the net became entangled and the child trampled them to death!"

"All the while, the white child kept dispensing the harmful substances, which the addicted people continued to consume, intensifying their euphoria," the basket maker said. He added emotionally, "It was easy to bring him into the city, My Lady, but to get him out was not possible!"

Then the potter shifted his weight on his knees. "Then a priest of Huitzilopochtli appeared and started singing to him. He bewitched the child and led him out of the city. The people entangled in the ropes of the net were dragged behind. As the white child walked along, blood oozed out of his severed head, filling the air with a poisonous stench and causing a stream of sickness and death behind him."

Madam Tonalnan listened intently, her eyes fixed on the messengers of this nefarious tale.

"But the priest of Huitzilopochtli led the white child to the Northern Cliffs, and because he was blind from having no head, he fell off the cliffs, taking the many entangled citizens with him," the basket weaver said. "Then an ancient sorcerer appeared, a little old

[421]

man hunched over a twisted cane with a snakehead handle. He was wearing a leopard skin cloak, and his face was dusted white except for a black ash band across his eyes. He laughed sardonically at the people of Tula and told them that they had released this demon themselves."

Madam Tonalnan turned to the *xolome* to hear what he had to say.

"The people of Tula are eating the fruit of forbidden knowledge - the mushroom, peyote, morning glory and jimson weed. These are the magical weapons of sorcerers and *nahuallis* who spend lifetimes learning how to use them. They released the demon by abusing esoteric knowledge," Xolome said.

"Death is their punishment!" proclaimed Madam Tonalnan. "They are fools to use the weapons of sacred magic for simple pleasures! They dishonor the aged Goddess of the Earth, Toci. They will hear her roar when she comes for them. Let the Mother Toci take them!"

She pounded her scepter four times on the floor, sending echoes bouncing off the walls of the Western Hall.

The Tiny Dancing Man

Not long after that another unexplainable incident occurred. Tonalnan, now the matriarch of her clan, was at her home, the Palace of Previous Kings, praying before the stele of Quetzalcoatl when her youngest sister-wife Xochitl appeared at her side.

"Madam, I must speak with thee," the daughter of Jiquipilco whispered after respectfully sitting with her feet properly folded under her.

"Then speak," Tonalnan said, opening her eyes.

"The house slaves are talking amongst themselves, Madam, and there is much discord."

"Go on."

"This morning in the *tianguis* there appeared an old man in the center of the Yollotli where everyone could see him. He wore nothing more than a loincloth and his ancient body was as wrinkled and dry as the face of a cliff." She looked at her sister-wife for confirmation to continue her tale.

"Before all the merchants and buyers to see, the grandfather elder held a little dancing man in the palm of his hands. Everyone surrounded him to get a closer look, but he just kept playing with his little dancing man.

"Then an old woman yelled through the crowd, 'Oh Toltecs! What kind of sorcery is this?' and the horde of onlookers became agitated. The grandmother then said, 'It is a spell of the Dark Lord, look! He is a magician! He communes with Tezcatlipoca and the cult of the dead!' and the people were afraid."

Xochitl looked at Tonalnan with imploring eyes. "Thou must believe me, sister. I saw it with mine own eyes," she affirmed.

"Then a young man spoke out, 'Kill him with stones! Kill the necromancer before he unleashes more demons upon us!' and all the people started stoning the unfortunate old wretch, right there in the marketplace! The flying rocks parted his flesh in two and knocked him down, yet the frenzied mob continued the barrage until

[423]

the poor creature was stone dead. His lifeless cadaver just lay there, mutilated and covered in blood."

Tonalnan sighed heavily.

"Then a man spoke out, 'What have you done? Oh, evil sinners! You have wronged that poor old soul and offended the gods!' As sure as I sit here by thy side Madam I tell thee that just then a great white heron passed above us, flying high in the sky, flapping her massive wings. We all looked up and saw that she was pierced with a flaming arrow. Then she fell down from the sky, down, down she went, toward the River Xicocotitlan. Everyone ran toward the river to try and find her, merchants and buyers alike, leaving the *tianguis* deserted, guarded only by the gods.

"I stood there, dear sister, over the pitiful soul, his body cast away and unwanted. Then I ordered my slaves to carry the body to the caves and hold a humble ritual.

"Here, Madam. I brought thee this."

Tonalnan opened her hand and Xochitl placed a little wooden doll in her palm. It was painted with grotesque features, its face distorted in pain.

It was the tiny dancing man.

Deadly Forces

When Tonalnan told the king of the unfathomable events that were taking place in Tula he put his head in his hands and cried, "Oh! Our golden age is fading and the shadow of darkness is upon us!"

✄

One day Tonalnan found herself at Huemac's palace. Her father had summoned her back to the halls where she grew up. She sat in the outbuilding thinking that the white gauze curtains along the back windows would be more beautiful still if they were a pinkish-orange embedded with fire opals. But alas, no time for textiles anymore. The duties of her new position consumed all her time and energy. In fact, she'd handed off the weaving guild to her sister, Calli. She would have her sister make new curtains for the outbuilding. She made a mental note of it.

It felt oddly different to be sitting in this room as High Chancellor. She sat in a carved, wooden armchair and waited, spreading her blue full-length tunic over her gemmed sandals. Her long hair, just turning white at the temples, was gathered at the middle of her back and folded under, and she donned a simple coronet of black and white woodpecker feathers. What could her father possibly want with her?

"Daughter," the old man said, coming in as though he'd read her mind.

The adolescent Quetzalpétatl was with him. "Mother!" she exclaimed, and went rushing into Tonalnan's arms.

"My beautiful daughter! Let me look at you!" Tonalnan was delighted at this unexpected surprise. Since her father had taken the child away from her, he'd not allowed them to be together.

"She's receiving the best education," her father said grunting as he sat the expanding girth of his old body in an armchair across

[425]

from Tonalnan. "She studies weaving and etiquette with the sisters of the Order of Tonantzin."

Quetzalpétatl was sitting on the floor right beside her mother with her feet properly folded under her, with her arms resting on Tonalnan's lap. She looked up at her mother adoringly with her jade-green eyes. They were made brighter still by her clothing the color of foliage and her jewels of emeralds and gold.

"Where did you get those eyes, my darling, I do not know," Her mother said lovingly.

Her father was up to something. He wanted something. She looked at the old First General and feigned a smile.

"Daughter, let me be frank with you."

"Yes father," she replied, but she thought, *have you ever been anything other?*

"The citizens are much divided. There are wars among the *calpullis*, fighting between neighbors over loyalties to the gods," he said.

So this was it. He was going to call her on her alliances. She'd known for some time that her father had grown apart from the king. He'd distanced himself further and further, the more he'd associated with that brother-in-law of hers, Xolotl. She had no proof, but she was sure that they'd swayed him to accept human sacrifice and worship of Tezcatlipoca and the powerful sorcerer Titlacáhuan.

Tonalnan held steadfast to her beliefs, unwavering in her faith in Quetzalcoatl and all the glory of the holy wind Ehécatl that blew divine breath into all that is.

"Well, my daughter," he continued, "You are expected to honor your father and the gods, always." He petted Quetzalpétatl's head. "Like your obedient daughter here." The burgeoning woman smiled.

Huemac knew that Tonalnan was greatly loved by the Toltec people, and had influence over thousands. Her loyalty to a new regime (and that's what it was coming to) would further his plans considerably and benefit his new allies.

This is it, she thought. *He's going to order me to betray my god and king and swear my loyalties to him and his beloved new god Tezcatlipoca.*

Before she could think of a clever response, a great sonic boom shook the building, reverberating through the stone halls and shaking the stone foundation.

Then a huge explosive smack sounded within the palace.

A woman's bloodcurdling scream came from the servants' courtyard, high-pitched, shrill cries, and then more wails and lamentations.

Tonalnan and her daughter and father got to their feet, but before they could make it to the servants' quarters, they heard another explosive smack, with a resounding thud, a couple of houses away, and then another, and another!

"It's raining stones!" the wailing woman screamed. "The wrath of the gods is upon us!"

When they reached the servants' courtyard, they found a young slave boy on the ground amidst a pool of blood. His head had been split in two and his brains splattered everywhere. A shiny black rock lay next to him.

"A stone, from the sky..." the horrified kitchen slave exclaimed, her eyes protruding with fear. "My Lord – "

Then, *crack*! Another loud crash exploded in the street outside the palace.

"In here!" Huemac said, steering his women along by their arms. He led them to an underground cellar beneath the stairs of the great hall. All the while they could hear the multiple explosive smacks and thuds of rocks falling across the city.

Boom! Crack! Thud!

Then a rumble slammed the earth with unimaginable volume, followed by the continued barrage of lesser, explosive claps.

When the storm was over, the people crept out of their houses to assess the damage.

The frightened cries of children, wails of infants, and lamentations of those who just saw their loved ones killed were too much to bear.

A swarm of stones had fallen from the heavens and were strewn across Tula and the adjacent fields. Some hit houses and knocked out rooftops; others lay scattered in the fields. There were cavities in the streets where stones had fallen, and a huge, waist-high boulder lay in the center of the Yollotli.

[427]

The priests of Titlacáhuan called the giant stone a *téchcatl*, and in two days time they hauled it away to their new temple of Huitzilopochtli and started using it as their most sacred sacrificial stone.

※

The calamities continued as the Black and White Tezcatlipocas battled for supremacy of the One World. Next came torrential rains. Drenching downpours unrelentingly surged out of the heavens and rushed across the earth. Rivers swelled and soon the cornfields were inundated. Nobles, who lived in raised houses, watched from their windows and doors as the *macehuallis* built makeshift shelters on their rooftops and waded through the streets in waist-high, sewage-infested waters. Slaves paddled nobles around in dugout canoes: across the Yollotli, through the alleys and passageways of Tula and beyond.

Madam Tonalnan and her family were forced to ration their stores, and when these ran low, they sent their slaves with *petlacalli* baskets and great earthen vessels on their shoulders, to higher ground for food and fresh water.

The immortal sons of Tlaloc played havoc in the heavens. They crashed their crystal spear sending white-hot bolts to the earth. They shook their black gourd rattle and thunder rumbled. Still it continued to rain, and rain, and rain.

In an effort to escape the waters, vermin entered the houses to breed, so that residents took to killing them and throwing them out their windows, infecting the toxic street water all the more.

Soon, for lack of clean water, diseases set in - chills, fever, fatigue, sweats, and vomiting - sometimes combined with seizures. Desperately, the weakened Toltecs rolled the corpses up in *petlatl* mats and hoisted them into dugouts, in the downpour and through the infested waters to higher ground where they burned the corpses of their loved ones in a cave.

Even more of the Toltecs started to pray to their new gods;

"Eh god, all powerful, thou who gives life to
man, hear our cry! Eh, Titlacáhuan, have mercy

[428]

*upon my wretched soul, nourish me with
sustenance, for I toil and suffer great need in
this world. Have compassion, oh god, for I am
naked and poor. I toil to serve thee; in your
service I sweep and clean and fill my hearth
with tinder in my humble abode filled only with
that which thou hast bestowed upon me.*

*"Eh, Titlacáhuan, thou who hast bestowed
poverty and misery upon our wretched souls.
Thou hast bestowed contagious and incurable
diseases upon us for not performing penance
and for lying with our women and friends in
times of fasting.*

*"Eh, Titlacáhuan, have mercy upon me and
relieve me of this fatal disease, so that I should
look to life and serve you, work for you,
celebrate you with all that I work for, all that I
earn, the words I speak and my very being."*

Some of the wretched, sick people were angry and said,
"Wicked Titlacáhuan, you laugh at me! You gave me this sickness
and can take it away but you laugh at me in scorn and disdain. Why
don't you just kill me instead?"

Some of the diseased Toltecs were healed, but most of those
who contacted the illnesses during the torrential rains and floods
died.

❁

The rains beat down upon the Toltecs for several consecutive
growing seasons, with their deadly floods and pestilence, and then
one day the rain subsided. The rivers returned to their natural
homes. The people of Tula swept away their agony and suffering
together with the debris left behind by the floods.

Grasses and new vegetation sprang up everywhere and it
seemed that a more bountiful harvest was never more promising.
The *tianguis* market resumed, and Tonalnan sat once again in her
chair in the Western Hall to administer justice. The weaving guild

reopened, and the High Council even convened, though Ce Acatl, greatly disturbed by the complexity of devastation, assigned Huematzin as his ambassador priest to relay information, while he stayed hidden in meditation and prayer.

Until the fields were ready to harvest, the long-suffering Toltecs sent envoys far and wide to forage and gather food, but just as they were about to reap their hard earned crops, the gods once again engaged in battle and the casualties were the Toltecs themselves.

They were noticed first by children, hopping and jumping in the fields of corn. Then, flying in the air, they came and descended over Tula. They were the *chachatls*. Soon there were great clouds of them, buzzing and clicking and clacking, landing on everything in sight. The Toltecs thought them horrific creatures only when they arrived in great swarms. Normally, they would catch them and eat them, served roasted or dipped in sweet-hot chilli powder and lightly fried, but *en masse*, this seemingly undisturbing creature was deadly.

The insects formed nests on the ground, which added to the plague. Soon the air was thick with the flying arthropods. They easily became entangled in people's clothing and hair. They entered houses through windows and doors where they landed on tables and walls and beds. They even chewed on people when they were sleeping, and on the babies of negligent mothers. They became a great nuisance inside homes, as people had to spend a great deal of their time swatting, catching, squashing and trapping them.

The *chachatls* consumed all the vegetation in their path: the agricultural fields as well as people's gardens. They even ate the bark off the frames of the market stalls, and chewed holes in the flowing lengths of cotton that covered the scaffoldings. They chewed and chewed, leaving the devastated Toltecs in yet another state of famine. The astrologer Huematzin painted the stories of their sufferings in his *amatl* paper long books;

> *The chachatls left the once-invincible Toltecs with nothing. But now they tremble with hunger. They are the very image of death. They have naught. Merchants sell nothing more than salt and discarded maize cobs, and there is no*

market to sell foods so that the merchants go from door to door trying to sell their wares.

The only sustenance of any magnitude is a great quantity of dried locusts.

The people are sedentary for want of strength. They recline against walls and crouch in corners in the shadows. To stave off their hunger, they chew on rotten wood. They sustain themselves with roasted chachatls, cactus leaves and the dung of the beasts in the forest.

Women walk about lamenting and wailing, their guts sucked back under their ribs. Men, emaciated and destitute, have their skin stretched so tightly over their skeletons that it's possible to count their bones.

There is no greater pain than to see the torment on their faces. Oh brothers! The mighty Toltecs have fallen into an abyss of misery and shame!

Sadly, it was under these conditions that many people again left the previously glorious and magnificent empire of Tula and migrated to more hospitable lands.

Secret Meetings

It came to pass that one morning before dawn, Tonalnan was summoned by her king.

"Quick," she told her chambermaid who was hastily making her presentable. She shimmied into an emerald green tunic and spread her arms out so the maid could fasten the belt. "The white egret coronet," she said, "and the gold beads."

As she left the Palace of Previous Kings with her two personal guards, she noticed a shrouded young washerwoman hovering in the shadows of the porch. The pitiful creature had a mangled foot and was wavering on a crutch made of twisted wood. In the darkness Tonalnan caught her eye, and for a brief moment, it seemed as if the woman's eyes were aglow.

As she crossed the Yollotli, she could see Venus the Morning Star, burning brightly in the velvety black sky. Venus, also known as the god Tlahuizcalpantecuhtli, was believed by the people of Cem Anahuac to be one of the manifestations of Quetzalcoatl. At the beginning of his life, Venus emerged as the Evening Star, ever so faint, and grew in strength and brilliance nightly until, at the middle of his life, he fought the great battle with the sun. For eight days, Tlahuizcalpantecuhtli cast arrows and darts at Tonatiuh, the sun, until he emerged again into the realm of the stars, burning brightly with victory. In the second voyage of his life, Tlahuizcalpantecuhtli emerged as the Morning Star. Alas, night after night his brilliance would fade as he grew into old age and eventually he would again be devoured by the sun and submerged into the underworld for fifty-two days.

On her way to the Palace of Quetzalcoatl, Tonalnan wondered what could be so pressing that the revered Ce Acatl should send for her in the wee hours of the morning.

At Huemac's palace, the high chiefs gathered in the outbuilding for a clandestine nocturnal meeting to discuss the unrelenting destruction of the empire. They sat on the floor around the edges of a huge, square *petlatl* mat and spoke in soft voices and whispers in case there were any spirits hiding in the walls. They called themselves the Council of Tezcatlipoca.

"These calamities are a sign from the gods," someone said.

"The *chachatls* descended upon us because we failed in our penitence and sacrifices!" another man insisted.

"The sons of Tlaloc are angry with us because of the arrogance of our king!" Ozomatli affirmed. "This is why they threw the crystal spear and shook the black gourd rattle that caused the floods!" He was infuriated because he'd lost his young wife in the wave of fatal diseases that followed the inundations.

Just then a shrouded young washerwoman hobbled through the front archway on a crutch of twisted wood. She hunched down and whispered into Huemac's ear.

"Brothers, my second daughter was just seen leaving her palace." There was a stir among the chiefs. "Apparently she consorts with the king under the cover of darkness. Let us be swift, lest her spies shape shift into night creatures and lay their eyes upon us."

There was general agreement, nodding, and grunts of approval.

Then the decrepit miscreant who brought the message turned and faced everyone. Her voice was high-pitched like that of a tiny quetzal.

> *"Lord Huemac's reign will ride upon a wave of death and destruction.*
> *A king is not a king who rules over ashes and dried bones.*
> *But succumb he will to power in all its seduction,*
> *To rule in peril or its twin...*
> *Over Tula and half her sons."*

The washerwoman's black eyes glowed in the soft light of the dimly lit room as black and yellow stripes began to faintly appear across her crooked face. She swung around on her crutch, tossed her frayed shawl over one shoulder, and hobbled out the room.

⁂

Madam Tonalnan was led to the king's residence behind the pyramid, where an elderly monk brought her to the door of his private chamber. Several guards lined the walls of the low-lit hall, standing stone still, spears at the ready. The four walls were richly embellished with precious stone mosaics that reflected the glowing, warm light of several candle bowls. The air smelled like fragrant blue sage and fresh juniper.

The king sat with his back to them before a stone altar at one side of the room, with his knees brought to his chest and his head in his hands. He wore a long, white tunic, and his long gray-white hair hung loose around him.

The monk announced their presence.

"Enter," the king commanded.

The monk led Madam Tonalnan to a mat on the floor an appropriate distance from the king, and then sat down along one wall, to ensure order and propriety. A woman in the presence of the most-chaste king was frowned upon. A woman in his private chambers was unheard of.

Tonalnan prostrated herself before her king, touching her forehead to the floor. "Most high grace, incarnation of the Sacred Spirit, I am nothing in thy presence and live only to honor thee," she said.

"You may rise, Little Sister," the king said, lowering his hands from his face. He turned to look at her. His eyes were moist and sunken, his cheeks hollowed and pale.

Tonalnan caught herself staring aghast at her king. While no one was ever allowed to set eyes on the face of their king Ce Acatl Topiltzin, she had seen him once before, at the Pyramid of Coral when she'd told him of her vision. Now he looked like a different person, almost starved and twig like. She cast her eyes down appropriately before the monk could redress her audacity. She could see that the informal intimacy she'd shared with Ce Acatl at the Pyramid of Coral was not going to be repeated here.

She sat with her head bowed and her feet properly folded under her, her hands clasped together at her waist. Her wispy, white egret coronet picked up the light of the candle bowls, and her gold beads reflected a soft glow.

"Little Sister, I seek your counsel," the king whispered softly, so the monk could not hear. He reclined on one elbow at her side, ever mindful of the monk's watchful eye.

"Of course, My Lord," she replied, keeping her head reverently bowed.

"I have had a disturbing vision," he whispered.

The monk's bitter face showed that he could see, but not hear, the communication between them.

"Yes, My Lord," she said.

"In my vision I was visited by a little old man, wrinkled and hunched over like a *xolome*," he mouthed, the words only intelligible to her. "He came here to my palace and the guard did not want to let him pass. When the guard said that the ancient one insisted on presenting me with a gift, only for mine own eyes, I acquiesced and allowed him to enter."

The king innocently picked up the corner of Tonalnan's emerald-green dress as if to hold something soft between his fingers. The elderly monk slapped a woven paddle against the stone floor. The king dropped the soft cotton and glared at the old monk.

Tonalnan thought it a twisted interplay, that the *king*, the divine and absolute ruler of the realm, should be so controlled by those around him. He could easily order them all to leave, but that would jeopardize his image of chastity.

"In my vision the ancient one told me he was going to show me my bestial self," he continued in whispers, "and he presented me with an obsidian mirror." The king tucked his knees to his chest, wrapping his arms around them. "But when I peered into the looking glass I saw none other than a bloodied rabbit staring back at me!"

Tonalnan shuddered at the thought.

"Then the ancient one laughed at my corporeal attachment to reality, mocking my vision of my animal self, ridiculing me for transgressing from my divine essence." The king sat as still as stone.

Tonalnan looked at him in fright.

[436]

"When I awoke from my vision, the *xolome* was gone, but at my side I found this," he quietly said.

The king secretly passed something behind her so that the old monk and guards could not see. It was round, and wrapped in cloth, no bigger than her hand. He unwrapped it and there at her side, she could see a small obsidian mirror. The image of a bloodied rabbit stared out at her from the black reflection.

"Brothers, let us be swift," Huemac repeated. "We must decide and away whilst darkness still protects us. Dawn is soon upon us."

"The government is perishing," Cuilton asserted.

"He hides from his people and grows old and feeble. It has been many moons. The people are restless without proper direction," Huemac declared.

"The coup d'état must be swift and complete, lest a civil war ensue," Xolotl boldly stated. Ichtaca, who was sitting at his side, gestured in agreement.

"But thousands still love him, My Lord," said Zolton. "He is chaste and pure of heart."

"Perhaps, Brother. There is no doubt that he is a holy man. But does he effectively *lead*? No, I tell you!" Xolotl exclaimed.

"There is always the sorcery of the painted corn," Ichtaca quietly said.

The chieftains stirred. Some flinched at the thought. "Murderous treachery!" someone said aloud.

Corn magic was one of the most powerful spells a sorcerer could employ. First it was necessary to find a small kernel of corn with a streak of red running through it. Then the sorcerer would prepare the kernel in a potion of black lizard tongues mixed with his own blood. All the while, he would chant forceful incantations into the kernel, filling it with the energy of his evil intent. When the kernel was fully charged, he would put it inside the bud of a golden-yellow flower and place it on the road where the victim was sure to walk everyday. As soon as the victim stepped on the kernel, or touched it in any way, the evil contained within it would transfer itself immediately into the victim's body and the sorcery was done. Death by corn magic was painful and slow, arriving only after a person's body was burning in flames from within, accompanied by profuse bleeding from the victim's every orifice.

"I caution you to think well upon it, My Lords, for we look not to make him a martyr. Also, such severity would cause massive unrest and lead to the ruin of the Toltecs," Huematzin asserted.

"We must find a way to discredit him in the eyes of his people," a younger lord opined.

To this everyone agreed.

And so it was that together they devised a secret plan.

In the darkness of the early morning they secretly dispersed, seen by none, except for one. Tlahuizcalpantecuhtli, the Morning Star, was silently watching. He set his arrows to flight, piercing the hearts of but a few of the conspirators, inoculating them with misgivings of their betrayal of their king. In this way, three of the chieftains of the secret meeting were inwardly unable to renounce their loyalty to Ce Acatl Topiltzin.

⁂

"Madam, I seek your counsel," the king reiterated, whispering, He covered the mirror and calmly tucked it under the *petlatl* mat.

"The Toltecs are starting to demand thy presence, My Lord," she replied. "Thou seest the bloodied rabbit in the obsidian mirror, but it is only a reflection of how thou seest thyself," she wisely interpreted.

"I am old and weak," he confessed to her, looking sidelong at the elderly monk who still could not hear them. "My hideous aspect is more than I can bear."

"Then thou art attached to the bestial and the mundane, and thou hast digressed from thy spiritual being," she whispered.

"Wash thy face, My Lord," she counseled, "and in so doing, thou wilt cast off old appearances and don an image new."

The Pilgrims of Actopán

Not long after these occurrences, it came to pass that two well-dressed travelers appeared before the guards at the Palace of Quetzalcoatl. Their fresh cotton tunics were elaborately brocaded, and they donned a multitude of feathered streamers in their hair displaying an array of hues - browns, beiges, burnt orange, black and sage. They wore ankle cuffs of tiny, golden bells that jingled at every step, and their leather sandals were adorned with turquoise and jade.

"We come from Actopán," they announced, "to pay homage to the king."

The guards were reluctant to admit them. "The king is in seclusion," they said, "and will receive no one."

"We come bearing gifts of food and wine," they insisted, "from the fields of Actopán." They turned and revealed several woven trunks filled with fine foods. Tired slaves set the litters carrying the gastronomical cargo on the ground.

"The king is unwell and refuses all audiences," the guards repeated.

"Oh but you must admit us, for we bring strong medicine to cure the king of his ills. When he learns that you denied him this healing power, he will have your heads!" the pilgrims demanded.

On hearing this, the guards went immediately to inform their king.

"There are two pilgrims at the portal who request to see thee, My Lord, and offer homage to their king," the guards said, after prostrating themselves on the stone floor.

"I am in seclusion," the king replied, "and will receive no one."

"They come bearing great gifts of fine food," they added.

"Tell them to go away. I am old and feeble and wish to see no one."

"My Lord," the braver of the two insisted, "they claim to bring with them a powerful remedy to cure thy ills."

[439]

"Oh, very well then, let them enter!" the fatigued Ce Acatl said.

When the pilgrims of Actopán came softly jingling before the king, they had their slaves lay out a great feast, light a multitude of candle bowls, and burn fragrant and relaxing incenses. They even brought with them caged mourning doves that calmed the room with their soft cries of *coo-oo, coo-oo, coo-oo.*

"Oh great and wise king," they said, bowing on bended knee, their feathered streamers falling to the floor. "We come to honor thee with the finest harvest of our lands, that thou be blessed by the Gods on High."

"The gods do not bless me in the autumn of my life, for my journey is much extended and my bones are long tired," the weary king said from behind a screen.

The king had grown suspicious in his old age because of the civil unrest in his kingdom and the perilous wrongdoings that had been going on. His people were still just recovering from the plague of *chachatls*, and there were many quarrels between the neighborhoods. Caution was his sharpest weapon. He commanded that a slave taste a morsel of each exquisite delicacy spread out before them.

"Who are you? And why do you come?" Ce Acatl demanded.

"We are pilgrims from Actopán, great lord," they said. "Word has reached our lands that the king of Quetzalcoatl is unwell. We bring an elixir of the ethers to thee, oh Great One, to relieve thee of thy sufferings."

The king, being a great penitent, was chaste in all ways, and did not consume intoxicating beverages. Thus, he declined, "Brethren, I must refuse, for I am an abstinent priest and do not partake of intoxicating nectars."

"Oh, but lord, this is good medicine. It will heal thy ills, renew thy strength, rekindle thy stamina, and much improve thy mood," they insisted. "Many days traveling we have spent to bring thee this powerful medicine, great lord, and our wives labored with great love over its preparation."

The mourning doves cooed. Their soft, melodic voices gently brushed the gem-embedded walls of Ce Acatl's inner chamber.

Ce Acatl had been alone for so long. A life of solitude and self-sacrifice had strained him beyond all his capabilities. Were self-

[440]

discipline, isolation, meditation and penitence greater than compassion or the comfort of human companionship? Was it right for him to lock himself away, wither and fade away? As the son of a king, he had been kept apart from others his whole life, made to devote himself to arduous learning and vehement prayer. Self sacrifice and denial had ruled his life as sure as Tonatiuh ruled the daytime sky. A shroud of loneliness consumed him. It was eating away at his soul. It pierced his heart as a worm bores a hole in *tlaqualli*, the red fruit of the *nopalli* cactus.

Ce Acatl sat in numbness behind his screen, frightened to show his shriveled face to those around him. Frightened to accept how weak he had become. His eyes welled up with tears, and one spilled over and rolled down his cheek. He looked at his hands. They were trembling.

He had no doubt that he had brought the wrath of the gods upon his kingdom.

Was he not a man? And in so being, was he not tainted with mortal flaws? Oh, how he had strived a lifetime for perfection!

Now he was presented with this nectar, this powerful medicine that would relieve his suffering. If only he could just end this pain that he was living. The white nectar... end the pain... drink the elixir... end the suffering...

With a heavy heart, the king donned a black veil, lifted himself from the mat behind his screen, and joined the pilgrims of Actopán. He partook of the feast and was happy.

"Brothers," he rejoiced, "Let us eat and drink to the glory of the gods!" Ce Acatl raised his mug. "I command that we eat and drink and be joyful, for the great pleasure of feasting comforts us in our sufferings in all the days of our lives!"

"Yes, My Lord!" the pilgrims agreed.

They ate and drank the splendid bounty before them.

The king much enjoyed the drink his visitors had brought to him, for it was sweet and delicious, and its powerful medicine soon began to work great magic.

"More of this white nectar!" the king raised his mug and demanded.

So it was that the pilgrims of Actopán filled and refilled the king's mug.

"Oh, but I do feel fine!" the king exclaimed, overjoyed. "The light of the candles, it is so colorful! And the gems in the walls! Just look at how they reflect a thousand rainbows! My whole body feels fuzzy! Why, I feel so invigorated!"

The king started dancing around the hall. He summoned his monks and bade them drink the rejuvenating white nectar with him, and dance to the continued cooing of the mourning doves. He sent for his court musicians. They danced and ate and drank, so that there, in the king's private chamber, Ce Acatl broke his vow of abstinence for the first time in his life and reveled in the mysteries of the *nanácatl* and *ololiqui* wine.

After some time of enlivened merriment, the king said to his monks and visitors, "Go and find my Little Sister, that we may sing and drink together, and rejoice in gratitude for all the blessings bestowed upon us by our god."

Forbidden Knowledge

When the princess came before the king she said unto him, "Oh lord, I come to thee from the darkness of dreams, where death walks among the living, from the house of the smoking mirror and the land of the nine winds. Fill me with thy truth, My Lord, that thy sacred light fill the vessel of my being."

"Oh fair goddess of water," the king returned her greeting, "be of good cheer. Let us not reside in the cave of torments, but in its stead immerse ourselves in the perfume of magnolias, as does the butterfly, and cleanse ourselves with the essence of golden honey. Drink with me! Sing with me!"

Ce Acatl was then left alone with the woman that he loved.

He filled her mug and raised it to her responsive lips. She drank eagerly, and soon they forgot themselves in the *nanácatl* and *ololiqui* wine.

The earth trembled as the gold and silver sunshine reflecting off her face aroused the sleeping volcano of his passions.

He sang to her.

> *Night turned itself over to Day,*
>
> *Where Being was crowned by Her warming sun.*
>
> *Quoth the songbirds of four-hundred voices, 'Let thy beauty grace the human one.'*
>
> *The essence of a thousand flowers perfumed the air of Her realm.*
>
> *Blossoms sparkled down from the heavens,*
>
> *And enraptured the heart of man.*

[443]

So lost was he in the light of Her beauty,

That navigate he could not,

Neither sea nor land

So that Day, full of grace and compassion,

Consumed the yearnings of man.

The sun and the stars and the moon filled the cosmos with their laughter,

For the hearts of mortal men were enslaved to Day thereafter.

Ce Acatl took her face into his hands and said unto her, "I am the son of god, Ometéotl, the one for whom we all live. But am I not a *man*? Shall I live forever and deny the virility that makes me mortal? I have always loved you."

Red-hot passions churned and pressurized beneath his steadfast virtue.

"I yearn for you, woman!" he whispered. "You are the breeze that refreshes my heart, the sweet star of my flesh, the bud that blooms upon the dawn. No longer can I deny this hunger, my flesh burns for you so!"

And so it was that the king of Tula took the ardent Toltec princess unto him and learned the secrets of her womanhood, for in that moment, his flesh was stronger than his spirit. As the Spider of Destiny wove her inescapable web of fate, Ce Acatl Topiltzin became ensnared and planted his seed deep inside the virgin with green eyes.

✄

Outside the king's private chambers, the pilgrims of Actopán were satisfied. They left the palace of Quetzalcoatl in triumph, for they were none other than Ichtaca and Titlacáhuan in disguise.

[444]

In the morning, Quetzalpétatl woke up disoriented, surrounded by gem-encrusted mosaics that she didn't recognize. Caressing her nude body, she rolled over to find that a shriveled grandfather elder lay in nakedness by her side.

The princess with green eyes was horrified to discover that her womanhood had been opened.

"What have we done!" she whispered.

The king woke with a start. "Woman!" he shouted. "Cover your nakedness and look away from your king, lest your eyes burn from the sin!"

Quetzalpétatl shrunk in fear.

Ce Acatl's manservant, the elderly monk, came into the chamber and clad the king in a full-length, black tunic.

"My Lord," she said with her head lowered beneath a mass of black hair, "my elders sent me here only to sing with thee. I am but a maiden, a little bird, and yet thou hast indulged in my femininity so." Quetzalpétatl began to softly weep as a new and grim future unfolded before her.

The elderly monk helped her into her red cotton dress. Composed, she said, "My heart grieves, My Lord, for thou hast taken my maidenhead and my virtue."

"Oh Sister!" the king moaned, "Daughter of the Jades, I have sinned and I cannot wash away the stain of that which I have done! The pilgrims deceived me with their evil trickery, for I drank their potion and fell into temptation!" Ce Acatl grabbed her by her shoulders and looked squarely at her.

"The purity of my sacred body has been ever defiled by your... your... mortal flesh!" he yelled. He pushed her away and turned to hide his shame. Then he said to himself under his breath, "Her crime is her celestial beauty, which gives great pleasure and entices mortal men. "Take her from my presence!" he demanded.

As his monks were escorting her out, he yelled angrily, "This woman carries my divine fluid within her, the seed of mine own person and lineage of the gods! She has no right to be in the presence of mortal men! I forbid it! Take her to her mother and cloister her away!"

After that, Ce Acatl washed himself four times, but he could not wash away his transgression.

✿

Madam Tonalnan was in the courtyard with her sister-wives weaving the first harvest since the destruction of the *chachatls* when she received the news. A commotion arose as they heard house slaves bustling and footsteps slapping the flagstone floor toward them.

"Mother!" Quetzalpétatl cried as she slumped into a disheveled heap at Tonalnan's feet.

"What is the meaning of this!" the madam demanded, turning from her weaving and towering over the crumpled girl.

"Mother I have been deceived! I come from the chamber of gems where my grandfather Huemac sent me to sing with the king," she said, her head down and sobbing.

Madam Tonalnan could feel her heart pounding in her throat as she struggled to maintain her composure.

"The gods have forsaken me, oh Mother!" she sobbed. "Whilst in the midst of hallowed levity I committed the most grievous carnal sin!" She grabbed her mother's skirts and clung to them. Looking up at her mother with pleading tears she added, "My virtue vanished..."

Tonalnan could hear no more. The implications of such a tragedy immediately overwhelmed her. She raised her hand and with all her force brought it down broadside against her daughter's crying face, knocking the fallen woman to the floor.

"Enough!" Tonalnan shouted, her black eyes flashing. Her sister-wives and the house slaves looked on, as still as statues, in astonishment. "My heart sickens to think how you shame this house! You have behaved no better than a woman for sale!" Madam Tonalnan was now walking around the courtyard, ranting. "How am I to punish such abomination? For it will be *my* affair to judge in the end! Am I to *put to death* mine own child? Oh but were I not the hand of justice in this kingdom!" She turned to face her defeated

[446]

daughter. "Leave me! I banish you from this house! Return to your grandfather Huemac and never again come before me, lest I cast upon you the punishment of death that you deserve!"

Loyalties

The leaders of the Council of Tezcatlipoca sat in the inner chamber of the Sacred House of Healing where Ce Acatl had had his washing of the face ceremony so many years before. It was mid-day.

The white haired elder Lord Huemac sat in the king's throne at the end. To his right sat his most capable daughter, High Chancellor Madam Tonalnan. Next to her sat Xolotl, Huemac's minister of war. On the other side of the floor mat in the place of highest regard sat the ancient sorcerer Titlacáhuan, Lord Huemac's newly appointed high priest. Ozomatli, chief *Pochteca* of the Cintéotl clan, by far the wealthiest clan leader in the empire, was by the high priest's side. Ichtaca and Xolotl's son Tlacatl were also there, along with numerous elders from the loyal factions that had been springing up throughout the city.

They'd all been listening to Madam Tonalnan.

"Yes, Father. These are my words and my exact meaning. I tell thee with unwavering intent." As a gesture of good will, she took out a special blend of smoking herbs from her rabbit skin bag and prepared a long pipe for the ancient sorcerer. He'd been sitting directly across from her glaring at her with suspicion since the council meeting had begun.

Tonalnan drew heavily on the pipe as Xolotl held a flame to the herbs in the bowl. The smoking blend burned bright orange as it ignited in the bowl.

Lord Huemac nodded at Titlacáhuan in affirmation. "My daughter prepares the finest smoking blend in the court of Tollan," he said. The ancient sorcerer's amulets and bracelets shook as he took the pipe from Tonalnan.

"Unwavering intent," Lord Huemac repeated Tonalnan's words. "What say you then, daughter? You agree to hold the scepter of justice and preside over this ruined king?"

[449]

Madam Tonalnan paused and then exhaled the thick cloud of smoke she'd been holding within. It was almost the same color as her gray egret feather coronet. "Father," she said calmly, "my life is thine to command. My duty is to obey."

Lord Huemac and his allies had everything to gain with this alliance; Thousands of Toltecs would readily give their lives for this unique woman whom they adored.

Tonalnan then did something that had never been done before in the council chamber. She leaned up and kissed the ring on her father's hand. The chieftains watched in awe. True this bold gesture had never been played, but neither had a council member ever been a woman, nor the daughter of the man sitting on the throne.

"Lord Huemac," Ichtaca boldly spoke out, "what shall the sentence be?"

Unsettled murmurs and comments resounded throughout the long room as the painted ancient heroes of the murals on the walls listened on. The words *burning peppers*, *death by stoning* and *strangulation* were heard.

"Silence!" Huemac threw fire sand on a flaming urn causing an ear-piercing pop and a barrage of crackling sparks. The room fell silent.

"Lord Huemac," the elder Titlacáhuan hissed, "We must offer his heart to the gods. Tescatlipoca shall consume the blood of Quetzalcoatl. It is only in this way that the Lord of the Here and Now will defeat his nemesis."

"So it shall be!" Lord Huemac proclaimed, pounding the arm of the throne to magnify his authority. "Madam, do you understand your obligation?"

All eyes turned upon Tonalnan. "Yes My Lord," she decisively agreed. "In this way we shall avenge ourselves of the stolen maidenhead and the shame he brought upon our house," she added.

"Excellent!" the First General confirmed. "Xolotl, you know where to find him. Take your men and retrieve this fallen king. Let us away and make ready for the trial!"

As the chieftains adjourned, Lord Huemac discretely detained his daughter. "Madam," he whispered, "I am providing you with a personal escort." She looked at him perplexed. "For your safety," he added. "The streets are filled with marauders. These are treacherous times."

"Yes, Father," she answered curtly.

Outside, the streets were barren, with an occasional desperate neighbor running to and fro. For the most part, the citizens of Tula had locked themselves behind closed doors, frightened of abductions by their enemies.

As the high chieftains left the inner chamber and made their way into the Yollotli, a rock flew down and hit one of them in the shoulder.

"Make haste!" one of the men said, and they quickly dispersed.

Tonalnan, followed by her two *escorts*, made her way directly to the Sacred House of Healing instead of returning home. When one of her father's guards objected to this diversion, she slapped him across the face and spat on the ground, crushing the man's resolve.

"Imbecile! I come to retrieve a calming tincture for my father," she snarled, climbing the portal stairs. The two guards were forced to wait at the threshold of the Sacred House lest they taint the virginal purity of the temple priestesses and women physicians within.

Tonalnan's sandals slapped the flagstone floors and echoed off the plastered walls as she rushed through the corridors toward the apothecary closet at the end of the south hall. Some women stopped their chores and stared at her as she stormed through the portals and courtyards, while others, curious about the commotion, followed. The apothecary closet was a small, well-ventilated room adjacent to the south courtyard. Tonalnan pushed back the black door curtain and went in alone.

"Call for the Madam," she heard one of the novitiates whisper after the curtain fell closed.

A plethora of dehydrated plants hung from the rafters, while floor to ceiling shelves held an abundance of vials, urns, jars, boxes and baskets, containing a wealth of medicinal tinctures and dried herbs. Tonalnan slowly passed over the lethal tinctures of water hemlock and snakeroot, contemplating possible outcomes, but instead reached for the healing properties of lizard's tail and mullein, and a thick paste of damiana to fight fatigue and lift the spirits.

"I see you've taken what you came for."

Tonalnan felt her heart jump. A tall, well-groomed crone, the Madam of the Sacred House of Healing, was standing in front of the door curtain. Her hair was neatly tucked into a headdress similar to the headpiece of the Goddess Mazapa. Her floor-length black tunic was dotted with tiny gold rings and she wore a heavy length of coral beads. Tonalnan was flooded with memories from a lifetime ago –

> *Donned in simple white tunics and armed with sacred amulets and their most treasured magical weapons, a stolid group of middle-aged women had approached her in the Sacred House of Healing. They were the other women physicians with whom Tonalnan had spent her whole life, working, laboring, and studying together to strengthen the body of knowledge of medicinal herbs and healing powers.*
>
> *"We've brought you a gift," one of them had said, masking grief and envy in her tone. She'd held up a strand of coral beads. Tonalnan leaned forward and the woman placed them upon her, pulling her long black hair through the lengthy, blood red strands. "We bestow upon you the office of matron,"*

But she had broken her vows of chastity and had married instead. She'd had to swallow her pride as she handed over the strand of blood-red coral to the new matron, who had beamed with pride and smirked with an *"I'm the head matron now"* gleam in her eye.

Tonalnan now turned around to face the aging head matron who had displaced her all those years before.

"Yes," she said. She handed her once rival the medicines. "You are the only one who can reach him now. He will be under heavy guard."

The grandmother elder Ayotlcíhuatl took the remedies and tucked them into her medicine bag.

"Here, give the king this." Tonalnan handed the crone a small, glowing jadestone. "He will know it comes from me. Tell him they've decreed execution," she added, "sacrifice to their flesh-eating god."

Strong emotions welled up in the head matron's eyes.

Madam Tonalnan answered her pleading expression, "He will tell us what to do."

It was mid-afternoon.

Flames of Transformation

By late evening Madam Tonalnan, Mother of Light, High Chancellor and Protectress of the Palace of Quetzalcoatl in the realm of Tula-Tollan, found herself once again upon the throne of judgment. She sat in the jewel-encrusted chair at the top of the stairs in the Western Hall and gazed in disbelief at the disorderly crowd of nobles pressed together throughout the great, pillared room.

Once again she donned the garments commensurate with her station; the snowy white egret feather stole over a red and white *huipilli* blouse and the black on black brocaded garment that fell all the way to the floor. Her stoic face was painted completely white, with lips as red as ripened *chilli*. On her head she wore the flat, step-shaped gold headpiece with golden tassels at the sides that covered her ears. She cradled the coral scepter of justice.

Her arrival to the palace had been alarming at the very least. She'd been conveyed in a shaded litter upon the shoulders of porters together with her father's entourage. Surrounded by elite warriors armed with obsidian swords, they were able to press through the disorderly rabble that filled the streets and the Yollotli under the rolling gray clouds of an impending storm.

Tonalnan turned and looked at her father, First General Lord Huemac, who sat at some length to her right. He did not face the crowd of Toltec nobility, however. His gem-encrusted chair was turned inward, so that he was directly facing Xolotl, ceremoniously situated at the far side. It was *she*, Tonalnan who would have to face the nation and deliver the fateful sentence. *Well played, Father*, she thought, for who better than the devoted chancellor of Ce Acatl to deliver his final judgment? He would save his honor. She would not.

Tonalnan faced the crowd of anxious nobles. All eyes were upon her. Could they see her trembling? Did they perceive her difficulty breathing? Was the fear on her face apparent through her painted mask? Even the gods and ancient heroes of the murals around the room were watching her, waiting... waiting for her pronouncement.

Ce Acatl entered the room humbly, pushed on by Huemac's guards. The crowd parted so that she could see him. He was barefoot and wearing nothing more than a long white cotton tunic belted at the waist. His long, gray-white hair fell in wisps, and was plain and unadorned. He stood morose, his hands grasped together before him and his head hung low.

"Stop priest, and come no farther!" Tonalnan shouted. "Are you not ashamed of the dishonor you have brought upon your people? You have pressed your seed into the most beloved princess of the Toltecs, but in all truth you have raped an entire nation!" But even in the midst of her violent accusation, her love for him was stronger than her anger.

She clutched the coral scepter of justice, desperately hoping for some inkling of comfort. Up until this moment she'd been able to engage her enemies as well as her allies, avoid offending others, and adroitly attain her own ends without opposition. Now, however, a critical moment had arrived - she must publicly choose. Should she remain steadfast and support this fallen king? In his lifetime he had achieved unheard of accomplishments. He had led great armies to victory from Xochicalco to Tulantzinco all the way to Tula. He had made their nation into a great empire with monumental architecture and far-reaching economic ties. He'd brought art, astronomy, medicine and counting - why he'd even developed a calendar and established schools where scribes were writing down their histories. And as a spiritual master, he'd transformed faith beyond belief toward the experiential awareness of one, true god.

"What say you, priest?" Madam Tonalnan demanded.

Ce Acatl Topiltzin said nothing, but lifted his head and stared forward.

Xolotl could no longer contain his impatience. He stood and pointed at the accused man, "You are the owner of two faces!" he yelled. "It is with a mask that you profess chastity and purity, yet the face behind the mask indulges in wickedness!" He turned to his brethren and added, "Remember too, brothers, that it was his god that brought deadly forces upon us! Good men died painful and

[456]

untimely deaths just as easily as those who were evil. His god does not discriminate, my brothers!"

Having spoken his passion, Xolotl sat down. There were nods of approval all around.

Ce Acatl lifted his head and stood firm as he addressed the crowd. "I drank the white nectar of *ololiqui* and *nanácatl* wine and my heart is alone in the middle of the Underworld," he confessed. "My kingdom has suffered. What was once a glorious crown of marigolds now lies in barren waste."

"Have heart, beloved king!" somebody in the crowd yelled, "Thou still hast many friends! We will give our lives for thee, priest. Thou art our hallowed teacher and king!"

"Yes, yes!" several others shouted.

There was a great commotion in the hall as the divided nobles began to quarrel aggressively. From where she sat, she could see the glow of the magical jadestone that the king held in the palm of his hand. Tonalnan raised the coral scepter and stood. Silence blanketed the room. "Ce Acatl Topiltzin, son of Mixcóatl," she began, "your reign over Tula is ended."

The jadestone slipped from Topiltzin's hands as he flinched, fell to the flagstone floor with a *crack* and split in two.

Lord Huemac held his tongue. Execution had been his greatest desire. Waiting for its deliverance would solidify his long-awaited victory.

Tonalnan looked at her father and again considered the reasons to ally herself with him – wealth and power. Betraying her father would mean her own execution, this she knew. She could give him Topiltzin, execution by strangulation, and save herself in return.

She glanced at the severed jadestone that lay there, mocking her loyalties, and then addressed the overthrown priest and the assembled nobles in the hall, "Go out once-king and take your false gods away from this place! Leave us now, I say!"

The men of the Council of Tezcatlipoca booed and heckled the banishment, for their greatest desire had been a sentence of death on the sacrificial stone.

"Go quietly and do not refuse," she yelled, "for if you resist, you know what will become of you!"

[457]

This unexpected judgment caused such an uproar in the Great Hall that what happened next was unclear. For generations afterward stories told that violence broke out between the followers of Quetzalcoatl and his foe Tezcatlipoca. A great wind swirled within the hall, so much so, that the gods and ancient heroes lifted themselves out of the murals along the walls and restraining the Toltecs, prevented them from killing each other.

Ce Acatl Topiltzin was heard to say, "Children, brothers and sisters, we will away to the East, to the ethereal waters of Tlillan Tlapallan, the dwelling place of Knowledge and the Land of Light. Search deep inside yourselves, my friends, and always follow the wisdom of the Sacred Spirit. Quetzalcoatl is ever present, and will not forsake us."

In the panic, his followers hesitated, "But our homes, dear lord! What is to become of our homes?"

The king stood tall. "Burn them!" he is said to have commanded. "Burn it all! Bring only what you can carry on your backs or on your travois. Bury your treasures and hide your works of art. Pluck the gems from the murals in the walls, and scratch out the remains. Leave nothing of grace for these heathens who cut out the hearts of the children of The Mother! Go now, I tell you. Burn it all, for we shall leave our memories behind!"

It is said that at that moment a lightning bolt struck the palace, and a huge *crack* was heard - a crossbeam came crashing down, ripping out part of the ceiling as it fell. The nobles of the assembly ran for their lives amidst screams and yells. The gods and ancient heroes of the murals ascended through the gaping hole in the ceiling toward the starry nighttime sky, and Ce Acatl Topiltzin was nowhere to be found.

In the streets and alleys and passageways throughout Tula the news spread quickly of the king's banishment, for, feigning sadness, Titlacáhuan and his minions went out immediately and spread the great humiliation.

Quarrels broke out among the people at all levels, brother against brother, neighbor against neighbor, and then soon whole groups against each other, in attack or defense of Quetzalcoatl, their god and king.

"How dare you blaspheme against our king! He is a God! Look at all he has done for our people. Why, when he first came to this city it was nothing! He brought our city to the glory of an empire! Think, man! Our king needs our loyalty in his darkest hour!" some men cried.

Still others said, "It is the fault of that king of Quetzalcoatl that we suffer so! The priest Ce Acatl Topiltzin is a hypocrite! Look at him Brothers, pretending chastity whilst ravaging our daughters! Who can follow such a man? Tezcatlipoca rules us now!"

Shouts and screams escalated as those unwilling to hold the hot coals of blame in their hands quickly deflected any condemnation, tossing it to others.

When words would not suffice, desperate men turned to sticks and stones. The districts of the city were turned inside out, as like-minded people banded together in their houses, arming themselves and protecting themselves with weapons.

Gangs started marauding the streets, and leaders of different factions of the city fought for power and control. They went about bullying and intimidating one another, and burned each other's stores of maize and other supplies. Acts of vengeance stacked one upon the other so severely that the clashing factions of the city destroyed each other's provisions and decimated the very means of their survival.

And so it was that the fires that consumed the city of Tula were so mighty that they reached the other dimension of the Great Beyond, where all I could do was watch the spider of time weave her silver thread into an ever more intricate web of events that my progeny endured.

Houses that had once smiled with potted flowers and hummed with singing birds were set to flame. Walls that had once enclosed garden parties were knocked down. Furnishings where philosophers had gathered to talk about the planets and stars were shattered, and great works of art were smashed with cudgels and swords. Broad sheets of fire blared into the night, as storehouses exploded in flames. Women's shrieks and the wailing of infants echoed through the streets. Chaos prevailed, as men and women ran about calling for their loved ones, lost children cried, and still others stood bewildered and confused. The whole while the fighting continued

[459]

between the Toltec brethren as gangs of armed men and women sliced away the life of their foes to defend their favored god. Some prayed for death, while others lay bleeding and dying. Some added to the perils by screaming out that this was the end of days, for surely the magnitude of such suffering comes only from divine retribution.

Tezcatlipoca looked down from the heavens and smiled.

The Promise

The final day of fighting brought smoking cinders and ash, with moans and lamentations from survivors too exhausted to continue to fight. Huemac stood at the top of the stairs of the Palace of Quetzalcoatl; its roofs caved in and turned to charcoal as the palace was now destroyed by the hungry flames. Titlacáhuan and Xolotl stood by Huemac's side. They donned the vestments of their respective offices, Xolotl his military attire, the priest his black tunic and blood-matted hair, and Huemac a scepter and feathered crown. They looked down upon the aging priest and his followers.

"What say you, priest?" demanded Huemac loudly for all to hear, for the Yollotli was filled with the exhausted citizens of Tula that had endured the storm of violence throughout the ordeal.

Ce Acatl Topiltzin Quetzalcoatl stood humbly, clad in nothing more than simple sandals and a full-length white tunic belted at the waist. His long gray-white hair hung freely, and blew amidst the breezes, contrasting with the smoking cinders of the city and the azure sky. He possessed nothing more than his sacred staff, his knowledge, and his immeasurable wisdom. Hundreds of faithful followers stood behind him.

"What a terrible revelation, priest," Xolotl chided, "to strive for a lifetime only to realize that you have failed!"

"I have been devoured by the fangs and talons of men," Ce Acatl said, "trampled down and scourged by mine enemies with the arrows and swords of trickery and deceit."

The Toltec priest continued, "Slaves of Tezcatlipoca! You have dug a black pit of doom in the hopes of entrapping me, but it is you who have fallen into the dark abyss. In your effort to destroy me and for your greed, you have shattered the very pearl of your envy.

"Behold your kingdom of rubble and ash!

"Beware, O followers of the Here and Now! As serpents you move through life focused only on that, which is immediately before you.

"I now away, to the land of the rising sun," he added, "to the Goddess Xipe Totec in Tlillan Tlapallan! I will be reborn! While my soul wears this body of flesh and bones, I am burdened by the yearnings and failings of mortal men, but I tell you now, for all of Cem Anahuac to hear, I am the son of the sun! I am He Who Brings Light Into The World, messenger of The One For Whom We All Live! My house is not within the heavens, but resides upon the gentle winds in the hearts of men."

He raised his staff to the heavens. "Be ever vigilant, I tell you, for out of the darkest depths of destruction Quetzalcoatl will return on a golden throne! Watch for me at the awakening of the Sixth Sun. My kingdom of glory will return!"

With that, the last Toltec king turned east toward the land of rebirth and renewal, and left Tula-Tollan.

"I have something for you," the king was heard saying to Madam Tonalnan as they set out on their journey. He then wrapped her fingers around half a jadestone and kept the other half for himself. "You chose well."

Countless Toltec worshipers followed Ce Acatl Topiltzin to the land of the rising sun, men and women whose hearts were convinced that the enlightenment of Quetzcoatl will one day prevail over the Queen of Ignorance, destruction, and the entrapments of the Here and Now.

The End

Nahuatl Glossary

Acapulco (äh-käh-**pool**-kōh), A tribal nation in the great jungles of the farthest realms of Cem-Anahuac; south of Tula-Tollan.

Actopán (äc- tōh-**pän**), A landed estate near Tula-Tollan.

Ahuahuete (äh-wä-**wĕh**-tĕh), A giant cypress of the river valleys and highlands of Cem Anahuac.

Ajusco (äh-**hoos**-kōh), The snowy, white-capped mountain peak between the Valley of Texcoco and the Vally of Toluca; resembles and eagle in flight.

Altépetl (äl-**tay**-petl), A region or district in which a number of villages and/or clans are bound by socio-economic, cultural and familial ties; Has similarities to a feudal barony.

Amatl (**äh**-mätl), Paper.

Anahuac (äh-**näh**-wäk), The world we live in; the universe.

Anayel (äh-nä-**yĕl**), Sister of Madam Butterfly, twin of Yaretzi.

Andoeni (än-dō-**ĕn**-ee), The beautiful Otomí virgin, daughter of legendary warrior Anyeh, betrothed to Blue Hummingbird of Jocotitlan.

Anyeh (**än**-yay), Otomí warrior, father of Andoeni.

Atlacomulco (äh-tläh-kōh-**mūl**-kōh), Tribal nation just north of Jocotitlan.

Atlatl (**ät**-läh-təl), A powerful dart thrower with a long, flexible shaft.

Atolli (äh-**tōh**-lee), A sweet, hot beverage made with corn powder.

Axcaitl (äsh-**käy**-ee-təl, or äx-**käy**-ee-təl), A rural estate.

Axochitl (äh-**shō**-chee-təl, or aks-**ōh**-chee-təl), a peasant child.

Ayotlcíhuatl (**äh**-yōh-təl – **see**-wa-təl), Matron of the Sacred House of Healing.

Azcatl (**ahs**-cäh-təl), Ant.

Aztlán (äz-**tlän**), The place of the first tribal nation of people from the north.

Blue Hummingbird (n.a.), Governor of the tribal nation of Jocotitlan.

Blue Iztac (Blū Ees-**täk**), A nahualli Spirit Walker who accompanied Tohuenyo on his journey through the Jilotepec Mountains and beyond.

Cacamilhuacan (kä-kä-meel-**wä**-kän or kä-kä-meel-wä-**kän**), Obsidian mines in the Toluca Mountains controlled by the Teotenancas.

Calli (**käh**-lee), House.

Calli (**käh**-lee) Eldest daughter of Huemac and sister to Tonalnan.

Calmecac (Käl-meh-**käk**), a school for noble youths that offered religious training.

Calpulli (cäl-**pool**-lee), Village.

Caltzalantli (kält-zä-**länt**-lee), Avenue, road, thoroughfare.

Camotli (käh-**mōt**-lee), Sweet potato, yam.

Ce Acatl Topiltzin Quetzalcoatl (Say **Ah**-cäh-təl Tōh – peelt-**zeen** Ket-säl-**kōh**-wä-təl), Son and Prince of Mixcóatl the first warrior and heir to the Nonoalca dynasty.

Cem Anauac (Sĕm – Äh-**näh**-wäk), The One World.

Cenzontli (sĕn-**zōnt**-lee), Mockingbird.

Chac (chäk) Hermaphrodite slave who belongs to Tonalnan.

Chachatl (**chä**-chä-təl), Locust.

Chalchihuitl (chäl-**chee**-wee-təl), Emeralds.

Chantico (chän-**tee**-kōh), Goddess of fire.

Chantli (**chant**-lee), Abode, dwelling, house.

Chichimeca (chee-chee-**mə**-kä), Name given to a variety of nomadic tribes who came into the One World from the north.

Chicomotzoc (chee-coh-mōt-**sōk**), Place of the seven caves.

Chilli (**chee**-lee), Chile peppers.

Chimalli (chee-**mäh**-lee), A warrior's round shield made of animal skin.

Chimalman (chee-mäl-**män**), Princess of Tepoztlán, and mother of Ce Acatl Topiltzin.

Chocolatl (chō-**kōh**-läh-təl) Chocolate.

Chupícuaro (chū-**pee**-kwä-ro), Distant place in the region of the setting sun.

Cihuacoatl (see-hua-**kōh**-wäh-təl), Snake Woman; see also Coatlicue.

Cihuacoatl (see-wä-**coh**-ah-təl), Snake Woman, the crone who raised Ce Acatl Topiltzin when he was but a child.

Cihuanacayo (see-wah-nah-**cay**-yo), Vagina.

Cintéotl (seen- **těh**-oh-təl), Dried maize still on the cob.

Cipactli (see-**päk**-tlee), The dragon-serpent whose monster body sustains the world.

Cipactonal (see-päk-tōh-**näl**), Grandfather of Ce Acatl Topiltzin.

Citlali (seet-**lah**-lee), Daughter of Quiáhuitl; trained in the arts of herbal healing and lore by her grandfather Ollin Ehecatl.

Coatepantli (kōh-äh-těh-**pänt**-lee), A sculptured wall with a long-running frieze of majestical animals believed to contain spiritual powers.

Coatepec (kōh-äh-těh-**pec**), A tribal nation southeast of Tula-Tollan on the road to the ethereal waters.

Coatl (**kōh**-wä-təl), Snake, serpent.

Coatlicue (kōh-aht-**lee**-kway), She who gives birth to all that is, Woman of the Serpent Skirt, Mother of all the Gods, Goddess of the Earth, Goddess of Life and Death. Also known as Toci, Quilaztli and Cihuacoatl.

Colotl (**kōh**-lōh-təl), Disfigured offspring of Mayel and Huiztli, born out of sin.

Comal (kōh-**mäl**), Griddle.

Coyotl (**kōh**-yotl), Coyote

Coyotlatelco (Coy-yōt-lah-**tel**-kōh), A style of pottery characteristic of the Toltec dynasty; recognizable by its yellow and red coloring.

Cozcacuautli (kōs-kä-**kwout**-lee) A vulture who informed Ce Acatl Topiltzin that his father had been slain by his own treasonous uncles.

Cozcacuautli Miquiztli (Kōs-kä-**kwout**-lee Mee-**keets**-lee), Lesser noble of Tollan whose name means vulture's death.

Cuauhtémoc (kwow-**těh**-mōc), A war party leader and commander in Xolotl's army.

[467]

Cuauhtli Océlotl (**Kwout**-lee Oh-**say**-loh-təl), The youth who captured Citlali's heart.

Cuayatl (**kwāy**-yah-təl), A Chichimeca warrior whose name means frog.

Cuilton (**kweel**-tən), Toltec chief of agriculture; a noble on the high council.

Ehécatl (eh-**heh**-cah-təl), God of Wind; Sometimes encountered a variant name for Quetzalcoatl.

Elotl (**eh**-loh-təl), Corn

Epazote (ĕh-päh-**zoh**-tĕh), A green, leafy plant similar to mint used as a spice or medicinal tea.

Grey Iztac (Grey Ees-**täk**), A nahualli Spirit Walker who accompanied Tohuenyo on his journey through the Jilotepec Mountains and beyond.

Huapalcalco (huä-päl-**käl**-kōh), Tribe and ceremonial center north of Tulantzinco.

Huehuetl (**way**-way-təl), a large drum.

Huemac (**way**-mäk), Counselor of War and First General, father to Tonalnan; A noble on the high council.

Hueman (**way**-män), Ancient astrologer and wiseman who lived in the time before time; led the first people out of darkness and into the world of Cem-Anahuac.

Huematzin (way-mät-**seen**), Toltec astrologer and scribe who succeeded Quetzalpopoca Smoking Feather and recorded the history of Tula-Tollan.

Huetzin (wait-**seen**), An ancient king.

Huipilli (wee-**pee**-lee), Blouse.

Huitlacoche (weet-lah-**kōh**-chay), corn fungus.

Huitzilopochtli   (weet-see-lōh-**pōch**-tlee),   The Hummingbird God; twin of the Black Tezcatlipoca known as Mictlantecuhtli. While The Black Tezcatlipoca is He Who Causes Death, Huitzilopochtli demands death in order to be sustained.

Huitzli (**weets**-tlee), A young Toltec monk in Tula-Tollan.

Ichcahuipilli (**eech**-kä-wee-**pee**-lee), Thickly padded, quilted cotton body armor.

Ichtaca (eech-**täh**-käh) Chichimeca war party leader of the Red Ant Clan.

Itzacíhuatl (eat-sah-**see**-wa-təl), Little sister of Citlali's friend Miyáhuatl.

Itzali (**eets**-äh-lee), Madam of the house of Huemac; noblewoman and wife of First General Huemac, mother of Calli and Tonalnan.

Itzcuintli (eats-**skweent**-lee), Dog.

Itzcuintli Coyotl (Eats-**skweent**-lee – **Kōh**-yoh-təl), a peasant of the altépetl.

Itzpapálotl (eats-pah-**pah**-loh-təl), The warrior goddess whose name means Obsidian Butterfly. Known for her ruthless attack on Mixcóatl and his four hundred warriors that ended in her defeat.

Ixmitl (**eesh**-mee-təl or **eeks**-mee-təl), a slave.

Ixtlahuaca (**eeks**-läh-wäh-käh), A tribal nation located in the marshy central valley of Toluca.

Iztac (ees-**täk**), White.

Iztaccihuatl (ees-täk- **see**-wäh-təl) The Sleeping Woman; snowy white capped mountain range south of the Valley of Texcoco.

Iztacs (ees-**täks**), People with white hair, light skin and eyes the color of gems; worshipped as divine beings; revered as nahuallis.

Iztatl (**ees**-täh-təl), Salt.

Jilotepec (hee-loh- tĕh-**pec**) Mountains, The high country mountain range between Tula-Tollan and the Valley of Toluca.

Jiquipilco (hee-kee-**peel**-kōh), A tribal nation at the foothills of the Jilotepec Mountains.

Jiquipillis (hee-kee-**pee**-lees), People of Jiquipilco.

Joco (**hōh**-kōh), Short for Jocotitlan.

Jocotitlan (hō-kōh-teet-**län**) A nation whose people lived at the northern rim of the Valley of Toluca, at the base of the Xocotitlan Hill.

Macehualli (mä-say-**huä**-lee), A peasant.

Macehuatl (mä-**say**-huätl), Of the peasant class.

Manah (mä-**nah**), Aslave girl at the axcaitl.

Maquáhuitl (mäh-**kwä**-wee-təl), a deadly wooden sword embedded with obsidian blades.

Matlacueyatl (mat-lah-**kwey**-yah-təl), Mother in the legend of the water genies.

Matlal (**mät**-läl), Governor and overseer of the tianguis market.

Maxatlatl (mäx-**äh**-tlä-təl), Apron-like garment worn by a Toltec warrior.

Mayel (mäh-**yĕl**), A young woman of the Toltec nobility.

Mazapa (mä-**zä**-pä), Goddess of fertility and maize.

Mazatl (**mah**-zah-təl), A Chichimeca warrior whose name means goat.

Metlatl (**mĕh**-tlä-təl) an ancient grinding stone similar to mortar and pestle but flat.

Mexica (mĕh-**shee**-käh), A great warrior nation devoted to human sacrifice that would appear in many generations to come.

Mexitl (**mĕh**-shee-təl), God of war.

Meztli (**mĕs**-tlee), One of the names given to the moon.

Michoacán (mee-chwä-**kän**), An empire far to the west of Tula-Tollan that extended all the way to the ethereal waters, place of the the Tarascan king and ceremonial center of Tzintzuntzan.

Mictlán (meek-**tlän**), The Underworld; frozen region of the north; place to which we go after we die; Hell.

Mictlancíhuatl (mĭk-tlän-**see**-wäh-təl), Lady of the Underworld.

Mictlantecútli (mĭk-tlän-tĕh-**coot**-lee), Lord of the Underworld; one of the four children of Ometéotl; god of death and the realm of the dead; also referred to as the Black Tezcatlipoca.

Miquiztli (mee-**keets**-lee), See Cozcacuautli Miquiztli

Mitla (**meet**-läh), Ceremonial center of the Zapotec people, located far south of Tula-Tollan in the land of Tonatiuh, god of the sun.

Mixcóatl (miks-**kōh**-wä-təl), Father of Ce Acatl Topiltzin; The great warrior who led the first men from the hills in the north and defeated the warrior goddess Itzpapalotl, the Obsidian Butterfly.

Mixquiahuala (**Meeks**-kee-ah-**wah**-lah), Lord Miquiztli's rural land holdings.

Miya (**mee**-yä), Shortened name for Citlali's closest friend.

Miyáhuatl (mee-**äh**-wa-təl), Citlali's closest friend.

Miztli (**meest**-lee), A tlatoque of the Toltec nahuallis.

Moyotl (**mō**-yō-təl), A Chichimeca warrior whose name means mosquito.

Nahualli (näh-**wäh**-lee) A person's physical body in the Here and Now; human or animal form a spirit can take.

Nahuallis (näh-**wäh**-lees), A group of the king's spiritual sages that included rare individuals with albinism, dwarfism, or kyphosis; seen as personifications of Nanahuatzin and worshipped as gods. Also called the Spirit Walkers.

Nahui Tecpatl (**näh**-wee **těk**-päh-təl), calendrical assignation; tecpatl means flint.

Nanacatl (nä-**nä**-cäh-təl), wild, hallucinogenic mushrooms.

Nanahuatzin (nä-nä-wät-**seen**), A crippled and deformed god who was chosen to illuminate the world in the creation of the world at Teotihuacan.

Nauhyotl (**now**-yōh-təl), Brother to Cozcacuautli Miquiztli; a respected Toltec noble.

Naxac (näh-**shäk**), King of Tollan.

Nine Winds (n.a.) A matriarch of the Chichimeca tribe; Sister to Titlacáhuan; mother of Tohuenyo.

Nochtli (**nōch**-tlee) fruit of the prickly pear cactus.

Nohueltiuh (nōh-wail-**tyoo**), My older brother.

Nopalli (nōh-**pah**-lee), Prickly pear cactus.

Oaxaca (wä-**hä**-kä), Kingdom far to the south in the land of Tonatiuh, the sun, at the edge of the ethereal waters.

Ocelotl (ōh-**say**-lotl), Jaguar.

Ococintli (ōh-kōh-**seen**-tlee), pine nuts; pine seeds.

Ocoyoacac (ōh-kōh-yō-äh-**käk**), A tribal nation at the foothills of the Jilotepec Mountains.

Ocoyoas (ōh-**kōh**-yō-ähs), People of Ocoyoacac.

Ohtli (**ōt**-lee), Road.

Ollin (**ōh**-lin), Movement; God of Movement; The Fifth Sun, the age we live in today.

Ollin Ehécatl (**Ōh**-lin Eh-**hey**-cah-təl), Grandfather of Citlali; healer of his clan.

Ololiuqui (ōh-lōh-**lee**-kwee), Morning glory.

Omecíhuatl (ōh-meh-**see**-wäh-təl), Honorific given to the eldest matriarch of the clan.

Ometéotl (ōh-meh-**těh**-oh-təl), The oldest and first of all the gods, both masculine and feminine; Father and Mother to the four Tezcatlipocas, The One for Whom We All Live;

Omeyocan (ōh-meh-yōh-**kän**), The highest heaven; the place of duality where the oldest of old gods, Ometéotl, resides.

Otumba (ōh-**tūm**-bäh), A tribal nation southeast of Tula-Tollan and halfway between Tulantzinco and the waters of Texcoco.

Oxochitl (ōx-**oh**-chee-təl), A peasant child.

Ozomatli (oh-zo-**mät**-lee), Chief merchant of the Toltecs, a noble on the high council.

P'urépecha (pū-**rěh**-pěh-chǔh), Language of the Tarascans of Michoacán.

Pachuca (päh-**chū**-käh), Place of mines east of Tula-Tollan, subject to the Toltecs.

Palenque (päh-**lěn**-kay), A tribal nation in the great jungles of the farthest realms of Cem-Anahuac; south-east of Tula-Tollan.

Panuco (päh-**nū**-kōh), A tribal nation northeast of Tula-Tollan at the edge of the ethereal waters.

Papantla (päh-**pän**-tlä), Tribal nation located far to the east of the Toltecs, in the land of rebirth and renewal, realm of the goddess Xipe-Totec, place of the rising sun.

Patlachi (päh-**läh**-chee) The people of Pachuca, subject to the Toltecs.

Petlacalli (pet-lä-**cäl**-lee), Alarge cargo basket carried on the back and held in place by a thick strap across the forehead.

Petlatl (**pet**-lä-təl) A woven mat.

Peyotl (**pay**-yotl), Peyote.

Pipiltzin (peep-peel-**tzin**), Of the noble class

Pixahua (peeks-**ah**-wah), A slave at the axcaitl.

Pochotl (**poh**-cho-təl), Lord Mizquitli's steward.

Pochteca (pōch- **těh**-kä) Merchant; esp. travelling merchant.

Popocatépetl (pōh-pōh-käh-**těh**-pəh-təl), Snowy, white capped volcano south of the Valley of Texcoco.

Pulque (**pool**-keh), An inebriating beverage made of fermented cactus juice.

Quetzal (**kĕt**-zäl), An iridescent bird prized for its blue-green feathers; feather; plummed.

Quetzalcoatl (ket-säl-**kōh**-wä-təl), One of the four children of Ometéotl; God of creation and fertility who resides in the land of the setting sun; also referred to as the White Tezcatlipoca.

Quetzalli (kĕt-**zäh**-lee), Daughter of Xolotl and Calli, first cousin to Quetzalpétatl through her mother Calli, and eldest of the Toltec princesses.

Quetzalpétatl (kĕt-zäl-**pĕh**-täh-təl), Daughter of Tohuenyo and Tonalnan whose name means feathered mat; first cousin to Quetzalli through her mother Tonalnan.

Quetzalpopoca (kĕt-zäl-poh-**poh**-kah), A Toltec priest and noble on the high council.

Quetzpalin (kets-**pah** -leen), A peasant.

Quiáhuitl (kwee-**ä**-wee-təl), Citlali's father, leader of his clan.

Quilaztli (kee-**läts**-tlee), See Coatlicue.

Tamalli (tah-**mah**-lee), A morsel wrapped in a cornhusk made of corn meal dough with various sweet or savory fillings.

Tamoanchan (täh-moh-ähn-**chän**, or täh-moh-**ähn**-chän) Place to which the god Quetzalcoatl took the bones of the first man and the first woman, where the crone Quilaztli ground them into dust.

Tarascans (tär-**äs**-cäns), The people of the kingdom of Michoacán.

Taximaya (täsh-shee-**may**-yäh), Tribes subject to Tula that lived along the eastern foothills of the Jilotepec Mountains.

Techcatl (**tĕch**-käh-təl), A sacrificial stone over which the victim is extended in a backwards arch, to facilitate cutting out the heart.

Techuchulco (tĕh-chū- **chūl**-kōh), A forested, tribal nation located in the eastern foothills of the Jilotepec Mountains.

Teciztécatl (tĕh-sees-**tay**-kä-təl), One of the names given to the moon god.

Tecoyotl (tĕh-**kōh**-yoh-təl), a peasant

Tecucistécatl (tĕh-sus-sees-**tĕh**-kä-təl), A proud god who offered to take charge of illuminating the world in the creation of the world at Teotihuacan.

Temoaya (tĕh-mōh-**äy**-äh), A tribal nation in the eastern foothills of the Jilotepec Mountains.

Teotenanca (tĕh-oh- tĕh-**nän**-kä), A person from the tribal nation of Teotenanco.

Teotenanco (tĕh-ōh-tĕh-**nän**-kōh), Great ceremonial center and powerful tribal nation at the southern edge of the Valley of Toluca, near the snow-capped Mountain that Roars.

Teotihuacan (tey-oh-tee-**hua**-cän, also tey-oh-tee-hua-**cän**), City of the Gods, ancient civilization and place where the world as we know it was created.

Tepeapulco (tĕh-peh-äh-**pul**-kōh), A tribal nation southwest of Tulantzinco.

Tepehí (tĕh-peh-**hee**) of the River, A tribal nation south of Tula-Tollan situated downstream along the Xicocotitlán River.

Teponzantli (tĕh-pōn-**zänt**-lee), woodblock.

Tepoztlan (tĕh-pōs-**tlän**), One of the regions conquered by Mixcoatl, in the land to the left of the setting sun.

Tetépetl (tĕh- **tĕh**-peh-təl) Hill; Name of the hill upon which the ceremonial center of Teotenanco was built overlooking the Valley of Toluca to the north.

Texcoco (tĕsh-**kōh**-kōh), Sacred lake south of Tula-Tollan; domed by the blue celestial heavens where the god Popocatépetl was turned into a volcano for all eternity because of his love for the sleeping woman.

Tezcacuitlapilli (tĕs-kä-kweet-lä-**pee**-lee), A great dorsal disc, the highest recognition of a Toltec warrior.

Tezcatlipoca (tes-kät-lee-**pōh**-kuh), One of the four children of Ometéotl, the oldest and first god; Lord of the Here and Now; The Smoking Mirror.

Tianguis (tee-**än**-geese), Open –air market.

Ticitl (**tee**-see-təl), Tonalnan's nursemaid.

Titlacáhuan (tee-tlä-**cäh**-wän), Chichimeca shaman, brother to Nine Winds, necromancer and sorcerer of Tezcatlipoca.

Tlacatl (**tläh**-käh-təl), Son of Xolotl and Calli whose name means man or noble lord.

Tlahuicole (tlä-wee-**kōl** or tlä-wee-kōh-lay), He who brings water to the corn.

Tlahuizcalpantecuhtli (Tlah-wees-cäl-pän-tĕh-**coot**-tlee), Venus the Morning Star, Venus the Evening Star, Lord of the Earth, Devourer of Men.

Tlaloc (tlä-**lōk**), God of rain; impregnates the earth and gives live to corn.

Tlaltecuhtli (tläl-tĕh-**coot**-lee), The night creature, god and devourer of beasts and men.

Tlapatl (**tlä**-päh-təl), Jimson weed.

Tlaqualli (tlä-**kwä**-lee), The juicy, red fruit of the prickly pear cactus.

Tlaquatzin (Tlah-kwä-**tseen**), Opossum.

Tlatoani (tlä- tōh-**ä**-nee), King of a tribal nation.

Tlatoque (tlä-**tōh**-kay), An individual with dwarfism, revered as a nahualli.

Tlaxcalli (Tläsh-**cah**-lee), Tortillas, a flat bread made of corn.

Tlillan Tlapallan (**tlee**-län – Tlä-**päh**-län), Realm of Xipe Totec; place of rebirth and renewal, located beyond the ethereal waters in the place of the rising sun.

Toci (**tōh** -see), Our Grandmother; The Earth Mother; another name for Coatlicue. Also called Quilaztli.

Tohuenyo (tō-**wayn**-yō) Son of Nine Winds of the Chichimeca tribe.

Tollan (tōh-**lähn**), The ancient name for the city center of the Toltec people. Also known as Tollan Xicoctitlan or Tula or Tula-Tollan; place of the cattail reeds.

Toltec (**toll**-teck), A Toltec person.

Tolteca (toll-**tĕh**-kah), The Toltec people; also used as an adjective.

Toltecoyotl (toll-tĕh-**koy**-yōh-təl), All that which is Toltec.

Toluca (tōh-**lū**-käh) Mountains; another name for the Xinantécatl Mountains west of Teotenanco; place of the Cacamilhuacan obsidian mines; place of the snow covered Mountain that Roars.

Tomatl (**tōh**-mä-təl), Servant in the house of Citlali and her father, Quiahuitl.

Tonalli (tōh-**nah**-lee), Light body, spirit, soul.

Tonantzin (tōh-nän-**tzeen**), Our Grandmother; The Earth Mother; another name for Coatlicue, Toci and Quilaztli. Name given to the order of priestesses who taught the daughters of Toltec nobility.

Tonatiuh (tōh-nä-**tyoo**), God of the Sun; the sun; one of the four children of Ometéotl; also referred to as the Blue Tezcatlipoca. Also known as the god of the heavenly warriors, of eagles.

Tula (**tū**-lah) Also known as Tula-Tollan; see Tollan.

Tulantzinco (tū-länt-**sing**-kōh), Place behind the reeds, east of Tula-Tollan where Ce Acatl spent four years in meditation and prayer.

Tuxpan (tūks-**pän** or tūsh-**pän**), A tribal nation east of Tula-Tollan at the edge of the ethereal waters.

Tzintzuntzan (tzĭn-tzŭn-**tzăn**), Ceremonial center of the Tarascan kingdom of Michoacán.)

Tzompantli (tzōm-**pänt**-lee), A rack of human skulls, thought to contain magical powers of the dead.

Uitcnáuac (weets-**näh**-wäk), One of the regions conquered by Mixcoatl, also known as The Place Next to the Thorn.

Ullama (u-**lä**-mä), a ball game played with the hips or buttocks.

White Iztac (Wīt Ees-**täk**), A nahualli Spirit Walker who accompanied Tohuenyo on his journey through the Jilotepec Mountains and beyond.

Xaltitlan (shäl-teet-**län**), One of the conquered regions in the dynasty of the Mixcoa warriors.

Xicocotitlan (shee-kōh-kōh-teet-**län**) River west of Tula. See also Tollan.

Xinachtli (see-**näch**-tlee), Sperm.

Xinantécatl (zee-nän-**těh**-kä-təl) Mountains; another name for the Toluca Mountains west of Teotenanco; place of the Cacamilhuacan obsidian mines; place of the snow covered Mountain that Roars.

Xipe Totec (**Shee**-pĕh – **Tōh**-tĕk), One of the four children of Ometéotl; The flayed god; God of rebirth, renewal and seasons; also referred to as the Red Tezcatlipoca.

Xiquipilli (shee-kee-**pee**-lee), a woven shoulder bag.

Xiuacan (shyoo-ah-**cän**), The place of hunting, one of the conquered regions in the dynasty of the Mixcoa warriors.

Xochicalco (sōh-chee-**käl**-kōh), Great kingdom of the southern realms; cosmopolitan and spiritual center.

Xochitl (**sōh**-chee-təl), Maiden of Jiquipilco whose name means flower.

Xochitonatl (sōh-chee- **tōh**-näh-təl), Realm of Cipactli, the great serpent-crocodile in the afterlife.

Xocotitlan (shō-kōhh-teet-**län**) Hill; The place where the people of Jocotitlan lived at the northern rim of the Valley of Toluca.

Xolome (**shō**-lōh-mĕh) The oldest of the nahuallis, a wise man revered as a manifestation of the gods.

xolome (**shō**-lōh-mĕh), An individual with kyphosis; revered as a nahualli.

Xolotl (**shō**-lōh-təl), Canine god of sickness and deformity who accompanies the dead to the realms of Mictlán.

Xolotl (**shō**-lōh-təl), Son of Lord Nauhyotl and nephew to Lord Cozcacuautli Miquiztli. Joined in marriage to Calli of the house of Huemac; War-party leader distinguished for his fighting skills in battle.

Xonacas (shō-**näh**-käs), People of Xonacatlan.

Xonacatlan (shō-näh-kät-**län**), A tribal nation at the foothills of the Jilotepec Mountains.

Yaretzi (yar-**ĕt**-see), Sister of Madam Butterfly, twin of Anayel.

Yauhtli (**yowt**-lee), A fierce warrior in Xolotl's army.

Yayauhqui (yäh-**yow**-kwee), Name associated with the Black Tezcatlipoca.

Yellow Skirt (n.a.), A young woman of the Chichimeca tribe.

Yollotli (yōh-**lōt**-lee), Heart.

Zacualtipán (zä-kwäl-tee-**pän**), A tribal nation northeast of Tula-Tollan.

[477]

Zapote (zäh-**pōh**-těh), A tropical fruit similar to a peach.

Zapotec (zäh-pōh-**těk**), A person from Zapotlan.

Zapotlán (zä-pōh-**tlän**), A tribal nation far to the south of Tula-Tollan located in the lands of Oaxaca, Place of Tonatiuh, god of the sun.

Zinapécuaro (zee-näh-**pěh**-kwä-ro), A tribal nation many days travel to the west of Tula-Tollan, place of the Mountains of Obsidian.

Zolton (**zōl**-tōn), Toltec chief architect and builder; a noble on the high council.

Sources

Alva Ixtlilxóchitl, Fernando de, *Obras Históricas*

Anguiano Valadez, Adolfo,
    -El Corazón de Quetzalcóatl
    - Cumbre y Ocaso de Quetzalcóatl

Bierhorst, John, *History and Mythology of the Aztecs: The Codex Chimalpopoca*

Boehm de Lameiras, Brigitte, *Formación del Estado en el México Prehispánico*

Castañeda, Carlos, *The Teachings of Don Juan: A Yaqui Way of Knowledge*

Clavijero, Francisco Xavier, *Reglas de la Lengua Mexicana con un Vocabulario*

Clendinnen, Inga, *Aztecs*

Davies, Nigel,
    -The Ancient Kingdoms of Mexico: A magnificent re-creation of their art and life
    -The Toltecs: Until the Fall of Tula

De la Torre Villar, Ernesto y Navarro de Anda, Ramiro, *Historia de México I: Época Prehispánica y Colonial*

Díaz, Frank, *The Gospel of the Toltecs: The Life and Teachings of Quetzalcoatl*

Fernández, Adela, *Dioses Prehispánicos de México*

Florescano, Enrique, *The Myth of Quetzalcoatl*

Gibson, Charles, *The Aztecs Under Spanish Rule: A History of the Indians of the Valley of Mexico, 1519-1810*

Hardman, Allan, *The Everything Toltec Wisdom Book: A complete guide to the ancient wisdoms*

León-Portilla, Miguel,
    -"Introducción al período posclásico" encontrado en *Historia de México*; Salvat Mexicana
    - *Los antiguos mexicanos: a través de sus crónicas y cantares*
    - *Quetzalcóatl*

[479]

- *Lecturas Universitarias No. 11, Antología; De Teotihuacán al los Aztecas*

Madsen, William and Claudia, *A Guide to Mexican Witchcraft*

Manzanilla, Linda and López Luján, Leonardo, *Historia Antigua de México, Vol. III: El horizonte Posclásico y algunos aspectos intelectuales de las culturas mesoamericanas*

Nicholson, H.B., *Topiltzin Quetzalcoatl: The Once and Future Lord of the Toltecs*

Ramírez, Jose Fernando, *Anales De Cuauhtitlan (1885)*

Ruíz de Alarcón, Hernando, *Tratado de las supersticiones y costumbres gentílicas que hoy viven entre los indio naturales desta Nueva España*

Sahagún, Fr. Bernardino de, *Historia General de las Cosas de Nueva España*

Salvat Mexicana, *Historia de México, Tomo III*

Scheffler, Lilian, *Cuentos y Leyendas de México*

Sullivan, Thelma D., *Compendio de la Gramática Náhuatl*

Tau Malachi
- Living Gnosis: A Practical Guide to Gnostic Christianity
- Gnosis of the Cosmic Christ: A Gnostic Christian Kabbalah

Von Hagen, Victor W., *The Ancient Sun Kingdoms of the Americas*

Zambrano, José Antonio, *La Zona Arqueológica de Tula*

About the Author

Julie M. Black (b. 1963 -) has a degree in History of Latin America from the University of California at Davis. She also studied at the Mexican National Autonomous University (UNAM) in Mexico City, after which time she spent more than a decade teaching English and History in Morelia, Michoacan and San Miguel de Allende, Guanajuato. Ms. Black currently teaches Texas History at Webb Middle School in Austin, Texas, where she resides with her son.